I0593302

OUT OF THE ASHES

SAMANTHA GROSSER

SAM GROSSER
BOOKS

OUT OF THE ASHES

Cover Design by ArtMishel

For David
who showed me the beauty in broken china

Chapter One

The telegram came on a perfect summer's day. The storms that had battered the last few days had retreated to leave clear, washed skies of flawless blue, and Clare was in the kitchen garden behind the farmhouse, pulling weeds from between the strawberry plants and enjoying the caress of the sun on her arms. The day was glorious and the sun was a gift. Lifting her face towards its light, she closed her eyes, suffused by the heat. She would bring out a chair, she decided, so she could doze in the warmth a while before Eric came back from fishing – wet and excited and wanting his tea.

Wiping her hands on her apron, she got up from the strawberry beds and walked through the garden towards the house. Inside the kitchen she blinked, blinded briefly in the sudden gloom after the brightness outside. The cool enfolded her, the summer warmth held at bay by the thick wattle walls and decaying thatched roof. Slowly her eyes adjusted and the room that was the heart of the house settled into focus. A great oak table with mismatched chairs took up half the floor. A dresser against the wall was stacked with willow-pattern plates and on the opposite side the empty fireplace was neatly set and ready to be kindled. Beside it was the paraffin stove that left a vague but permanent taint of fuel in the air.

She was just about to pick up a chair to take outside when there was a rap at the door. Her mind ticked off the possibilities in quick succession, but no one in the village ever waited for the door to be answered; people knocked and opened the door themselves. It had been one of the hardest things to get used to when she first came to live at the farm, accustomed as she had been to her privacy.

The knock sounded again, harder this time, and a thread of presentiment wound around her heart, a tightness in her chest. She let go of the chairback she was holding and wiped her hands on her apron, then tucked a loose strand of hair behind her ear.

'Just a moment,' she called out, and the words came out as a croak. 'I'm coming,' she added more clearly, forcing her voice to obedience. She swallowed, her mouth dry, and stepped around the chair to go to the door.

The telegram boy stood on the doorstep with the slip of paper in his hand.

'Mrs Chapman?'

She nodded.

'I'm sorry, missus,' he mumbled, head down so that she could not see his face. He was not much more than a child, she thought, and far too young for such sad work. 'Telegram for you.'

She lifted an automatic hand to take the proffered note.

'Thank you,' she managed to whisper, closing her fingers around the sheet of paper. The boy waited a moment longer in case she wanted to send a reply, but she simply stared past his shoulder into the yard outside and after a moment he nodded, replaced the cap on his head and walked away.

Clare closed the door and leaned her back against it. The wood was cool through the thin cotton of her summer dress and she shivered – all the warmth of the summer seemed to have faded away. She gripped the telegram in both her hands, willing it to be something other than it was. Then, pushing herself away from the door with sudden determination, she strode across the kitchen and once more into the garden. She needed air and light, her breath hard to find.

In the sunlight she stopped, blinking again in the brightness. The telegram was still grasped tightly in her fingers, knuckles white beneath the dirt from the garden that had remained on her hands. Walter would have laughed at the state of her fingernails, and instinctively she smiled at the thought of it before she forced herself to lower her eyes to the telegram, and commanded her fingers as they fumbled to open it.

Deeply regret to inform you ..., she read, then raised her head to the sky, her breathing quick and uneven as she searched for the courage to read the rest of it. The moment hung in the air, the precious seconds before the news became a fact, undeniable. A wood pigeon began to coo from the branches of a tree beyond the fence and somewhere further off a dog started barking. Life going on, untouched, unchanged. She dragged her reluctant gaze towards the words at last. *... your husband was killed 6 August 1944 ... letter to follow.*

Clare stopped reading and scrunched up the piece of paper in her fist. A hard ball of some emotion she could not even name burned inside her and she simply stood frozen, incapable of thought or feeling. The minutes passed uncounted, and afterwards she could not have said how long she stood there in the sunshine on that perfect afternoon before the rattle of a lorry in the lane outside tugged her attention back to the present.

Walter was dead and she would never see his smile again.

Lifting the telegram once more she straightened out the creases where she had crushed it in her hand. Tears half prickled at the backs of her eyes and she swallowed them down, setting her jaw against them. Letting her gaze drift across the little garden, so bright and full of life, she felt a savage urge to destroy it all. How dare it grow so abundantly, when Walter's life was over? But instead, she clutched the hateful telegram to her chest, wiped from her cheek the single tear that had fallen, and went back in to the cool gloom of the kitchen.

She sat at the table, numb. She should have sweet tea, she thought, remembering it was supposed to be good for shock, but she was unable to bring herself to make the effort and the stove remained blank and unlit. She waited, expecting the numbness to pass and the pain of the grief to take over, but there was nothing. Her body felt as though it belonged to someone else, and her thoughts drifted, hazy and unformed. What was wrong with her? She had heard of other women collapsing with such news, weeping and hysterical. Why did she feel so empty?

She laid the telegram on the table and straightened it out against the tablecloth, letting her eyes wander over the brief impersonal notice again, Walter's death contained within it. How could so few words hold such momentous news? A letter would follow, it said. But really, what more was there to say? She would never hear her husband's voice again, nor hold him in her arms. Their son no longer had a father.

She let out a breath, unaware she had been holding it, and feeling began at last to creep through her veins, a hollow in her guts. She placed her hand on top of the telegram, covering the words. She had always known, she thought. Right from the beginning when he told her he was going she had known, and she had spent all her tears and anger then in bitter fights and cruel words she had regretted ever since. Now she would never have a chance to make up for saying them.

The memory of the last time she saw him flickered through her thoughts – the sadness in his eyes as he turned to walk away from her along the platform with the kitbag on his shoulder, a stranger in his uniform. She had watched him mount the carriage steps, squeezed his hand a final time, until with a hiss of steam and a whistle he was gone. She had known even then they would not meet again.

A dog's bark outside in the yard roused her from her thoughts and she lifted her head towards the noise. The clock on the mantelpiece struck the half-hour. Soon Eric would be home and she would have to tell him that his father was dead. She shuddered at the thought of it and sighed, tracing the words on the telegram with her fingertips as though she might feel Walter's presence within them – his warmth, his kindness, his laughter. The hollow inside her began to fill with pain, and her vision blurred with sudden tears. She pressed her hand against the sheet of paper under her palm. She would have to tell Walter's mother too, she remembered then, and his sister and her husband, everyone else in the village. She would have to say it aloud.

Walter is dead.

She wrapped her thoughts around the words and tried to roll them on her tongue, but her mouth refused to form the sounds. Her breath began to catch in her chest and as she wiped at her face where the tears had started to fall, she cast a glance towards the door. She wasn't sure if she could face it. It was the thought that she must say the words to others that finally broke her defences. Lowering her face into her hands, she began to weep at last.

Eric came home red-faced from the summer sun and ravenous. She heard the patter of his sandals in the yard before the door burst open. She had busied herself with preparing tea – the remains of a pigeon pie, bread and butter, potatoes and radishes from the garden: the table was neatly laid and ready. She sat facing the door with an undarned sock lying lifeless in her hand and when her son ran in she looked down at the wool in surprise; she had no memory of even picking it up. Setting it aside, she watched Eric lean the fishing rod against the wall.

He was so like his father with his dark hair and pale eyes that were too serious for a ten-year-old boy. She saw glimpses of Walter in him every day, and now she had to turn her face away to hide the gathering tears.

'Did you catch anything?'

He shook his head. 'Michael caught a grayling but it wasn't big enough to eat so he threw it back.'

'But you had fun?'

'I did. And now I'm starving.' His gaze passed across the table with interest in the moment before he sensed something was amiss. He looked up at his mother.

'Am I in trouble for something? Did I do something wrong?' He flicked a glance to the clock. 'I'm not late.'

'No,' Clare agreed. 'You're not late. And you're not in trouble, only ...' She stopped. The words she had rehearsed in her head seemed utterly inadequate now that she was faced with the physical presence of her son. But she wanted to tell him first, before Walter's mother returned and claimed all the grief as hers.

'What is it, Mum?' he asked, edging forwards and sliding into his usual seat at the table. He was still eyeing the food and now she had assured him he was not in trouble he was only half interested in hearing what she had to say.

She swallowed. He was so young, so innocent, and it seemed so cruel to tell him. He had idolised his father, thought him a hero for choosing to go to war. For half a heartbeat she considered not telling him at all, but it was only the most fleeting thought and she let it go as soon as it arose. To hide the truth would be more cruel.

'There was a telegram today,' she began.

'Dad?' He looked up sharply, tea forgotten. She saw the fear in his eyes. Walter's eyes, and her heart broke again.

She nodded. 'He was killed. I don't know where.' In the end, she simply blurted out the truth because there was no easy way to say it – there were no words that could soften the blow.

For a moment he was silent, staring blindly at the table before him. Then, with an abruptness that made Clare jump, he sprang up from his chair and raced up the stairs to his room. She heard the door slam and the slight scrape of the bed on the floorboards as he threw himself across it. A few more seconds and she heard the sobs begin. Rising from her own chair, and taking long, deep breaths for strength, she followed him up the stairs to try and comfort him.

She stayed with Eric for a long time. They sat close but not touching on his bed in the attic room of the farmhouse that had been their home since Walter went away, and together they watched the twilight turn the sky pink and orange through the little latticed window. They hardly spoke, each alone with their sorrow. The sunset was almost absurdly beautiful. Walter would have claimed it was God's work in all His glory, and she would have smiled and said nothing, unconvinced that God even existed. How could He, when such terrible things happened in the world? How could He allow it?

As the colours of the sunset flared and faded at last, Clare could hear the clatter and chatter of the family downstairs. Walter's family – his sharp-tongued mother, his sister and her husband, their two children, whose company Eric found a trial despite their similarity in age. She sympathised with him: she too missed the privacy and peace of the vicarage they had left behind when Walter went away. Finally, when the dark had settled across the room and the night had grown cool, she turned to Eric beside her.

'We should go and tell Grandma,' she said, 'and the others. Will you come with me? I could do with some help.' She gave him a small smile, drawing him in as a co-conspirator.

Getting up from the bed, her limbs were stiff and awkward. Like an old woman, Clare thought, as she rolled her shoulders in futile hope of softening the tension in her muscles. Her head pounded with the movement and her eyes were sore with unspent tears. Eric propelled himself to the floor and landed on the rug with a thud that vibrated through every part of her. She flinched. Then, to distract herself, she checked her reflection in the little mirror on the dresser, but the face that looked back at her seemed barely to resemble her own at all. Red swollen eyes peered from a pale and haggard face, and stray strands of hair had stuck to the tears. Appalled, she slid her gaze away and went to the door.

'Shall we?'

Eric nodded, and followed her down the stairs.

In the vast kitchen Mrs Chapman was at the table, folding the last of the laundry. Her features were sharp in profile, her hair caught up in a scarf. She turned when she heard Clare's step on the stairs.

'Oh, hello.' She nodded to the washing basket. 'I wondered where you'd got to. You didn't want supper?'

Now that she had made it this far Clare felt her courage returning. She turned to her son. 'Go and find the others.' His cousins, she meant, Henry and Lizzie, who would be playing last-minute games before bedtime somewhere in the warren of the rambling house.

'Don't want to,' Eric answered, without lifting his head. He kicked at the step with the toe of one sandal, hands in his pockets.

Clare said nothing, only drew in a deep breath instead before she stepped forward towards her mother-in-law. 'Let me give you a hand.'

The two women worked side by side in silence to finish folding the washing. It had been a good day for laundry, warm and breezy, and the clothes were still warm to the touch, scenting the room with a clean soap smell. They emptied the basket. Eric was still standing at the base of the stairs, still digging at the ground with his foot, and for the first time Mrs Chapman actually looked at her daughter-in-law.

'What's the matter with Eric?' she asked, with a flick of her head towards her grandson.

'Nothing,' Clare answered. 'Can we sit down and have some tea?'

'I've still got things to do – I can't just sit and drink tea.'

Clare tightened her lips and lifted her eyes briefly skyward in search of patience. She said, 'Please?'

The older woman must have heard the heaviness in Clare's tone because she hesitated, observing her daughter-in-law more closely. Clare looked away from the scrutiny and cast her gaze across the kitchen towards the back door where Walter's sister had just come in, an empty bucket in her hand. Mrs Chapman followed the look and after a moment called out, 'Bridget! I'm making some tea.'

Bridget nodded her understanding and went to the sink to wash her hands. Clare sat at the table. She had long since stopped offering to help – even after all this time living at the farm she was still considered an outsider. Bridget took a seat across from her and smiled again. Clare raised a small, tired smile in return.

'Is everything all right?' The concern in Bridget's voice was genuine.

Clare shook her head and bit at her lip. Don't cry, she told herself. Don't you dare cry. She blinked and looked around for Eric. He had moved to the window to stand with his back to the room, gazing out into the dark. She wondered what was in his mind. Poor child.

'What's happened?'

Clare could barely hear Bridget's whisper above the hiss of the kettle on the stove and Mrs Chapman's clatter as she set out cups and saucers, and plates for biscuits.

Clare blinked and pressed her lips together, hands balled into fists. Her vision blurred. She closed her eyes and breathed deeply.

Bridget reached out across the table and put a hand on one of Clare's. Her fingers were cold from where she had washed them and the skin was chapped and rough. A countrywoman's hands, Clare thought, though the fingers were elegant and long, the same as her brother's. She lifted her head to meet Bridget's gaze, and Walter's pale eyes looked back at her.

'Is it Walter?'

Though the words were only whispered, a mother's instinct made Mrs Chapman freeze. She stood immobile with the warmed teapot in her hands. Very slowly, she turned her eyes to Clare. The two women waited, but Clare could not bring herself to say the words, looking instead from one scared face to the other. In the end it was Eric who told them, wheeling from his place at the window and shouting with all the force in his body.

'He's dead! The Germans killed him and I hate them!' Then he ran from the room out of the back door into the fading twilight, and the three women watched him go in silence.

'Should you go after him?' Bridget asked after a moment, gently.

'He'll be all right,' Clare replied, with a small shake of her head. 'He just needs some time.' She guessed he would find a secluded spot somewhere to hide himself, or perhaps he would go to the stables and find solace in the company of one of the draught horses.

Mrs Chapman set down the teapot with deliberate care and lowered herself onto a chair. She was scarcely breathing. Clare fumbled in her bag for the telegram and slid it across the table to Bridget, who picked it up with reluctance and scanned it. Then she passed it to her mother, who glanced at it briefly and let out a wail of grief before turning her eyes towards Clare.

'This is your doing!' she hissed.

'Mum!' Bridget touched her mother's arm, as if to restrain her, but the older woman snatched her hand away.

'He didn't have to go! You should have stopped him.'

The injustice of the accusation lit a spark that ignited Clare's anger.

'How dare you accuse me?' she hissed back, and though she knew she would regret it later she could not stop the torrent of words that fell from her lips. 'Do you think I didn't try? That I wanted him to go? Do you think it was my choice to leave my whole life behind to live here with you in the middle of nowhere? I loved our life at the vicarage. It was our home and I was happy. I begged and pleaded, but he refused to listen. I didn't want him to go.'

'You should have tried harder.' His mother was intractable.

Clare shook her head, silent now, and the rage dissipated as fast as it had risen. She could have fought with Walter until the end of time and it would have made no difference. He had seen the war as a sacred duty and he was stubborn as a mule.

'He did what he thought was right, Mum,' Bridget said. 'You know how he was – he wanted to save the world.'

Mrs Chapman made no answer. After a moment Clare got up from the table, picked up the teapot and stepped across to the range to finish making the tea. No one tried to stop her. When the tea was poured she sat down again. Mrs Chapman lifted her cup and a small splash of tea spilled over the rim from the tremble of her hand. Bridget reached and took away the cup, setting it with care on the table as her mother seemed to shrink into herself, breaking into sobs that gradually swelled into great howls of grief. Clare watched with a detachment that surprised her as Bridget wrapped her arms around her mother and held her like a crying child, her own face wet with tears.

Getting up, Clare followed her son outside, breathing deep in the fresh summer night. She could hear the shifting of the animals in their stalls and the trudge of wellington boots. Simon, she guessed, Bridget's husband, doing a last round before turning in for the night.

Walter had grown up in this house, a farmer's son. He had

played in this yard as a boy and gone to the village primary school where Clare was now a teacher. She tried to imagine it but the images eluded her – she could only think of him as he was the day he boarded the train that took him away from her in the ill-fitting uniform, his face drawn and sad. She raised her head to the stars above. Venus shimmered against the velvet black – it was the only star she could recognise. As a child, her father had sometimes pointed out the constellations but she had never paid much attention – she regretted it now.

'Are you up there now, Walter, watching me? Watching us?' she whispered. 'Was it worth it? Did you find your purpose in the battle with evil, brief though it was? I hope so.'

Behind her she could hear his mother still wailing and though she knew it was unreasonable the noise irked her, stirring her own grief into irritation. She flicked a glance over her shoulder and saw she had left the door open, light falling into the garden. They would have the air-raid warden on their backs for that, she thought, though the old man rarely troubled to leave his own fireside these days. It was not like it used to be when the bombs rained down on the cities, and everyone was terrified of showing a light that might guide the German planes. At least those days were over.

The scuff of boots grew louder and the flicker of a torch beam crossed the yard.

'All right?' The scruffy figure of Simon emerged from the gloom and he switched off the torch when he got to her. She said nothing, unable to summon words to her mouth.

Stopping beside her, he turned to survey the farm. 'You should've closed the door,' he said, but she knew from his tone the words were automatic, and he didn't much care. Mrs Chapman's cries filled the silence.

'What's wrong?' He jerked his head towards the house. There was little concern in his voice, more an idle curiosity.

'Walter's dead.' The words left her lips as a monotone, devoid of feeling, and she wondered how many more times she would have to say it and if she would ever get used to the feel of them on her tongue.

Simon turned sharply towards her. His face was in shadow, barely lit with the glow from the door, but she could see the darkness of his stubble and the mess of uncombed hair. He was standing very close to her and instinctively she took a step back. He had an uncanny knack of making her uncomfortable and she had never quite understood it.

'Killed in France?'

She shrugged and he said nothing but merely turned his attention once more to the yard before them. No words of condolence, no offer of sympathy. They stood in silence for a while, and Clare watched the stars peep and brighten, until at last Simon turned towards the house.

'Better go and see about Bridget,' he mumbled. Then he was gone and she was alone once more, a speck beneath the vastness of the sky.

She should find Eric, she thought then, and in the half-dark of the starlight she set off across the yard towards the stables.

Chapter Two

I n her dream Clare is in a graveyard she has never seen in her waking life. A harsh wind blows in gusts that whip her hair across her face and the sky is heavy and bruised with clouds that promise rain. The spire of an old Gothic church stands out black against the grey, and beside the church a hawthorn tree reaches bare winter branches over row upon row of untended graves.

A small group of mourners is gathered around an open grave, their coats flapping in the wind. The vicar stands at their head with a bible in his hand and Clare smiles when she recognises Walter. Now and then the wind delivers snatches of his words towards her.

Man that is born of a woman hath but a short time to live, and is full of misery. He cometh up, and is cut down, like a flower; he fleeth as it were a shadow, and never continueth in one stay.

His voice is deep, honeyed, mesmerising. She could listen to him talk all day.

Lord, have mercy upon us.

She wonders who is being buried, and picks her way through the weeds to go closer. Thistles catch at the hem of her coat and the long grass blows sharp against her legs, leaving painful nicks in the skin.

Walter lifts his head as she approaches and she waves, but he does not seem to see her. He is still talking, mouthing the words of the service, but the wind has shifted and snatches the sound away to blow unheard across the churchyard.

No one seems to notice her as she takes her place among the mourners, not even Walter. A woman is crying softly, her sobs competing with the wind. Clare steps forward to stand at the edge of the grave and as she does so all eyes turn as one towards her. Suddenly self-conscious, she feels like an intruder, but when she casts her eyes down into the pit at her feet she sees Walter, broken and bloodied, pale eyes staring lifeless into the sky.

She woke from the nightmare sweating and in tears, sitting bolt upright with a gasp of confusion to find herself in her bed at the farm. Her heart was pounding – she could feel its knock in every part of her body, and her breath was ragged and uneven. Hugging her knees into her chest she laid her cheek against them, curling into herself as though she might contain the horror that way, but the memory of the dream refused to fade.

Beside her Eric lay curled and sleeping, warm and sweet with his dark hair mussed against the white of the pillowcase, a boyish scent of earth and soap. The sight of him steadied her, and she reached a hand to smooth back a tendril of hair that had fallen across his forehead. He stirred slightly at her touch so she let her hand fall away.

Slowly, her breathing began to settle and the thud of her heartbeat abated so that she could hear the quiet of the outside world, and the regular whisper of Eric's sleeping breath. She watched him for a while; the serious face was peaceful in his sleep. Had Walter looked the same at that age?

Restless, she slipped out of bed and put on her dressing gown.

From the window she could see the lane and the fields on the other side of it lit silver by a bright low moon that was shrouded in mist. Almost full, she noticed – a bomber's moon, though the night was almost done. A lone scarecrow stood out against the barley with its white face and shirt, leaning at a drunken angle that made her almost smile.

The image from her dream played across her thoughts, vivid and horrible. The staring eyes and smashed limbs, the gaping wound across his chest. She shook her head in an effort to shift it but it refused to fade: it was all she could see. Where was Walter's body now? Or what was left of it. Was there an unmarked grave in France somewhere? A wooden cross above a rough-dug mound of dirt? She had not thought to wonder until now. They would have a funeral without him, she supposed. She realised she had no idea how these things worked, though as a vicar's wife she probably should. Walter must have held services at the church for men killed overseas and she trawled through her mind to remember the wives and mothers in Walter's parish who had lost their men but her memory failed her. Then she thought of the village vicar here in Ashenden, as different from her husband as apples from snow. She must speak to him, she thought, and make the arrangements. She would go first thing and get it over with.

In spite of the season it was still cold inside the farmhouse with its thick walls and tiny windows, and an image of the sunlit vicarage flickered through her mind – Walter in his shirt sleeves at the great oak desk in the study, his face bright in the morning warmth. She gave herself a small smile at the sight of it, so familiar, before her thoughts slid back to the image of her dream. Turning from the window with a shudder, she went down the steep narrow stairs and set about lighting the stove to make herself some tea.

. . .

The dawn brought a change in the weather and by the time Clare stepped outside, a fine cold drizzle hung in the air, the clouds bulging overhead and threatening heavier rain to come. From across the yard she could hear Simon's low croon from the milking parlour, and the old sheepdog briefly pricked up his ears as she passed him. Buttoning up her coat, she thrust her ungloved hands deep into her pockets and set off along the lane towards the vicarage, a half-hour's walk away at the far end of the village.

The high street was already coming to life when she got there: the sweet smell of fresh bread drifted from the bakery, and a dray with two shire horses stood outside the pub, the cellar doors open to the street. One of the horses tossed its head as she passed it, the drizzle glistening on its coat, and she could hear the rumble of the landlord's voice from underground.

When she reached the yard that surrounded the church Clare kept her head averted but even so, she could not help but glimpse the mossy gravestones from the edge of her vision, and she saw again in her mind's eye the funeral of her dream. Tensing against the onslaught of emotion, she hurried on to the vicarage next to the church, pushed open the white wooden gate, crunched up the gravel path to the door, and knocked.

A dog began to bark inside with quick, short yaps, and she stepped back to wait, observing the profusion of flowers in the well-tended garden. She recognised lupins and asters, and the sweet smell of honeysuckle drifted from a trellis by the wall. It was pretty, she thought, but the vicar should have been growing food the same as everyone else, though no one ever dared to challenge him about it. Finally, she heard footsteps on the tiles inside the house and the door swung open at last. Reverend Keane filled the space, looking down at her as the dog slid past his legs and into the garden.

'Ah,' the vicar said. 'Mrs Chapman.'

She gave him a small smile.

'I was very sorry to hear about your husband. Do come in.'

She followed him through the hallway and into the reception room where met his parishioners. She had never been inside the vicarage before and her first impression was one of neatness – everything perfectly in its place.

'Please, take a seat.'

She perched on the edge of the sofa, reluctant to disturb the careful arrangement of cushions, and undid the buttons of her coat. Reverend Keane made no move to take it. Walter would have hung it on a hook for her, she thought, and offered a cup of tea. The vicar eased his bulk into an armchair across the expanse of the rug from her. He was large and silver-haired, and not the sort of man who invited confidence. She wondered why he became a vicar.

There was a silence. On the mantelpiece the clock marked the passing seconds with a loud and regular tick. Somewhere else in the house a radio was playing and Clare could just hear the strains of a piece of classical music that might have been Mozart.

'I don't know how this works,' Clare said. 'Do we have some kind of service for him?'

'A memorial service would be appropriate,' he replied.

'A funeral without a body,' she murmured.

'A memorial service,' he corrected.

'I see.' Then, turning her gaze from the blackened iron of the unlit fire to meet his eyes, she said, 'Did you know my husband?'

The vicar let out a sigh. 'Barely,' he admitted after a moment. 'He had already left for Oxford when I took up the living here. We met briefly, once or twice, on his rare visits home. The previous incumbent died, you know. Mr Frenchman. It was all very sad, very sudden. Apparently he was hit by a lorry out in the street one night. He had gone to look for his cat, by all accounts. Killed instantly, which was a mercy.'

'Mr Frenchman,' she murmured. The name was familiar. Walter must have mentioned him to her at some time but she could recall no other details. 'Poor man.'

'Yes.' He seemed to recollect the purpose of her visit and cleared his throat, perhaps regretting his insensitivity, but it was hard to tell – his fleshy features gave very little away. 'What kind of service would you like, Mrs Chapman?'

She hesitated. What would Walter have wanted? She couldn't think. Her mind was weary and sluggish from the sleepless nights and she could already sense the vicar's slight impatience with her. It occurred to her that he was in the wrong job – she could imagine him better as the manager of a bank.

'Something simple,' she said. 'He would have wanted no fuss. He was a humble man.'

'Favourite hymns? Favourite pieces of scripture? He was a clergyman, after all – he must have had some preferences.'

'Yes. Yes, of course.' She tried to remember, but nothing came to mind, nothing at all. 'I'll have to think about it.'

'And will you speak? Your son, perhaps?'

'Me? I … I … don't think I could …' Her voice faltered and she trailed off, trying to picture herself at the lectern in the little church, speaking of Walter before the whole village. The thought of it was terrifying. 'No. I don't want to speak.'

He waited, regarding her with a look she could not quite read. Impatience, perhaps, or irritation. When she said nothing else, he drew in another deep breath before reaching for a diary that was on the side table next to his chair. He set it on his lap and opened it up to peruse the pages, turning them softly.

'When were you thinking?'

'As soon as possible,' she replied. It was the first definite answer she had been able to give him.

'Of course. Shall we say at the beginning of next month? How does that sound?' He looked up at her with an encouraging smile. It was the first sign of kindness he had shown, and an unexpected wave of gratitude flushed inside her. 'That will give you a little bit of time to think about hymns and readings, and put a notice in the paper, organise flowers and refreshments and the like. Mrs Jarvis usually sees to all that. You should speak to her.'

She said nothing. The vicar's small kindness had threatened her composure – she dared not even speak for fear of crying. He must have understood her mute distress, because he kept on talking, filling the silence.

'Shall we say the second Saturday of the month? In the afternoon – perhaps three o'clock? Then the refreshments will do for people's tea.'

Clare smiled at that and gave him a nod – Walter would have approved of the practical approach. 'That would be fine,' she managed to say.

He noted it down in his diary, and another silence fell. The distant music had ceased, and she heard the rattle of a bicycle in the lane. After a moment or two she realised the interview was over, and she got up.

'Thank you, Reverend,' she said.

'You're very welcome,' he said, showing her to the door. 'You have my deepest sympathy. If there's anything else I can do, you know where to find me.'

Clare looked up at him then, trying to read his expression and failing. It had been easier when she disliked him – his kindness threatened to unravel her defences, and she could feel the tears beginning to gather behind her eyes.

Outside, on the gravel path, she buttoned up her coat and shivered. The drizzle had thickened – she hoped the rain would not destroy the harvest. Then, with a lift of her chin and a deep breath, she blinked back the threat of tears and stepped out into the lane.

The main street of the village was quieter now, few people about in the morning rain, and Clare kept her head down, watching her step on the rutted path where the potholes had remained unmended since the war began. Outside the pub, the dray with the shire horses had moved on but she caught the lingering sour taint of old beer and cigarettes in the air as she passed. Her stomach heaved, empty and churning, and she remembered she had not eaten. She hurried on, and just beyond the reach of the smell she looked across the road towards the little row of shops on the other side. The saddler's shop with its dusty window display of harnesses and saddles hadn't opened yet, but the bakery was open and, with a sudden hunger, she crossed the road and went inside. She bought iced buns – one for herself and one each for Eric and his cousins. She ate hers as she wandered home, careless of the drizzle.

The hedgerows either side of the lane glistened with the rain, and she walked with care across the muddy ground, thinking of nothing. When she had almost reached the gate of the farm, the postman pulled up on his bicycle alongside her, startling her from her abstraction. She had not heard him approach.

'Mornin', Mrs Chapman.'

She swallowed the last mouthful of the bun and wished she had bought more. 'Good morning, Mr Stokes. Not much of a day for delivering the post.' She gave an upward tilt of her head towards the lowering clouds.

'I've had worse,' he laughed. 'And summer's half over already.'

'Yes, I suppose it is.'

'I got a letter for you.' He rummaged in his bag and drew out a slim white envelope. Clare's breath seemed to stop in her chest, limbs heavy with a sudden ache. 'You're Mrs W. Chapman, aren't you? Walter's wife? And his mum would be Mrs A?'

'That's right. His father's name was Alfred.'

'Just wanted to be sure I got the right Mrs Chapman – I could get in a lot of trouble if I give it to the wrong person, you know.'

'Well, we don't want that,' she replied. The evenness of her tone surprised her, the way she could still act as though every-thing was normal. She held out her hand for the letter and he passed it quickly across so that it would not be out long in the rain. Clare took it and slid it into her bag without so much as a glance. 'I'll read it at home in the dry,' she said.

'Good idea.' With a touch of his hand to his cap, he swung his leg over the seat of his bike and turned back along the road the way he had come. She turned to watch him go, the bike weaving dangerously around the potholes. Then, with one hand clutching her bag with its precious letter inside it to her side, she set her feet once more towards the farm.

The farmhouse kitchen was empty when she got there. Everyone was outside, working in spite of the rain. Lighting the stove, she set the kettle on to boil. Then, standing close to it for the warmth, she drew out the letter from her bag, and ran her eyes across it.

Mrs W. Chapman
c/- Rowan Farm
Ashenden, SOMERSET

The name and address were transcribed in a neat and regular hand she did not recognise and there was no return address, but she knew at once what it was. She held it between her fingers for a moment before she put it aside, slipping it into her cardigan pocket for later, unequal to the emotion she knew it would evoke.

The back door swung open with a creak and Clare swung abruptly towards it, a flash of guilty heat across her body as though she had been caught in the middle of some forbidden act. But it was only Bridget and the rush of panic subsided. The two women gave each other an instinctive smile. Not for the first time Clare wished she knew Walter's sister better, but there never seemed to be the chance: the farm, the children, Simon, her mother – Bridget rarely had a moment to herself.

'You were out early.'

'I went to see the vicar. There's going to be a memorial …' Clare shrugged.

'Mum will like that.'

'How is she?' In the hollow of her own grief in the days since the news she had barely spared the other woman a thought.

It was Bridget's turn to shrug. 'She's still refusing to leave her bed.'

The kettle started to hiss and Clare moved to warm the pot. When she turned back Bridget had sat down at the table, head resting on one hand. Her eyes were shadowed and dark, and Clare saw traces of the same sadness she had often glimpsed in Walter. She looked exhausted.

'And how are you?' She moved behind Bridget's chair and touched the other woman's shoulder. Bridget shifted her hand to catch at Clare's fingers and gave them a squeeze.

'I'll be all right,' she said, though her tone belied her words. 'I'm just worried about Mum.' She let go of Clare's hand and made to get up to see to the tea, but Clare stopped her with a gentle press of her fingers.

'I got some buns for the children,' she said. 'But you could have one if you like? I ate mine walking home.'

Bridget smiled and nodded and a companionable silence fell as Clare made the tea and Bridget took out a bun from the bag.

'Poor Mum,' Bridget said at last. 'I think after losing Dad as well last year, it's all just too much. Walter was her baby boy. She always loved him best, in spite of how she treated him.'

Clare gave a small smile of agreement. 'He wasn't meant for war,' she said, and her fingers instinctively sought out the letter in her pocket, touching the cool sharp edges of the envelope. She wanted to read it now with an almost fierce desperation to know the truth. But she wanted to read it alone, so she brought her hand back once more to the table, and took another mouthful of tea.

'He was a good big brother,' Bridget went on, filling the silence. 'He was never mean to me. Not once. He teased me, of course, but it was always good-natured, never unkindly meant.'

Clare smiled. 'He was always kind. It was his gift. Even when I provoked him.'

'He was a saint with Mum,' Bridget said. 'I don't know how he did it – she was awful to him at times. Especially when he decided to join the church.'

Clare looked up from her tea with interest. Walter had only told her a little of this story – it had not been his way to talk ill of anyone, no matter how deserved.

'What happened?'

Bridget set down her cup and fingered the handle as she spoke. 'Mum and Dad always just assumed he'd take over the farm eventually, even though it was obvious to anyone with eyes that he wasn't cut out for it. He had no interest, no aptitude. Even as a boy he always had his head in a book and though he did his chores and helped out when he was asked, it was always only out of duty. I always knew he'd never take it on, right from the start, but I suppose they simply saw what they wanted to see.'

Bridget took a mouthful of her tea and shifted her gaze to look out of the window towards the farm, remembering.

'I think they started to worry when he refused to leave school at fourteen like the other boys hereabouts. There were awful rows that went on for days – it was like living in a battlefield at times, but he got his way in the end. Under all that sweetness, there beat a heart of steel – once he decided on something, nothing could sway him from his purpose.' She turned back to Clare with a smile. 'I'm sure you know that as well as anyone. The same as joining up, I'm guessing.'

Clare nodded. 'A will of iron.'

'He finished school and won a scholarship to university. That was the end of it really – Mum and Dad had no say after that – he didn't need their support and though he asked for their blessing, he would have gone regardless.'

She said nothing, waiting for her sister-in-law to continue. They had never talked so openly before, and for the first time Clare saw the possibility that they might become proper friends. Walter would have been pleased to see it – he was very fond of his sister, and in a rare moment of regret he had once told Clare that his own freedom from the farm had cost Bridget hers.

'After he left Mum and Dad blamed each other, and the rows went on. So when Simon proposed I was only too eager to accept, to escape. Too eager, it turned out …' She trailed off, thoughts apparently turning briefly down a different track before she remembered the story she was supposed to be telling. But Clare stored that moment away in her memory, another tale to be told at a future time that might bring them closer.

'You lived in the village?' she prompted.

'Yes. Simon's parents ran the post office back then and we lived with them there. Like all the local boys he'd done farmwork from childhood, so when Dad couldn't manage any more, it was only natural we'd move back and he'd take over the running of things.' She looked up with a small shrug of resignation. 'You know the rest.'

She did. She could remember in perfect detail the conversation at the farmhouse table, the final appeal for Walter to return to his roots. They had borrowed a car to drive down from Bristol not long after they were married, and she was heavy with Eric, her time nearly due. Walter had still been a curate then but he had not wavered even for a heartbeat, in spite of his mother's tears and his father's gruff appeals to make an old man happy.

'I'm sorry you got saddled with it,' Clare said. 'Walter was too.'

Bridget shook her head with a smile. 'I don't mind being on the farm. It's what I know. I love the land and I've no desire to do anything else. It's just ...' She stopped mid-sentence and lowered her head to look at her hands where they were clasped on the table in front of her.

'Living with your mother?' Clare supplied.

Bridget raised her eyes, and her fingers twisted against each other on the table, as though she were suddenly nervous. She opened her mouth as if to speak, hesitated, then closed it again. Clare waited, but then the other woman unclasped her hands and sat back, and the moment passed.

On the mantelpiece the clock struck ten with soft quick chimes and they turned their heads towards it. Clare remembered the letter and took it out of her pocket.

'This came today,' she said, holding it out to show her sister-in-law. 'I couldn't bring myself to open it straight away.'

She laid it on the table and Bridget shifted round so that they were sitting side by side. Clare lifted her head to the door in the brief fear they would be interrupted but there was no one close by, and the noises they could hear were of people working further off – the distant hum of the tractor, voices catching now and then on the breeze. The letter lay unopened on the tablecloth in front of them and Clare let out a rush of breath, heartbeat quick and a tingling in her limbs. Then she reached out and as she picked it up it trembled in her hands. She cast a quick glance to Bridget, who gave her an encouraging nod. Slowly, Clare slid the butter knife along the fold of the envelope, took out the single sheet of paper and opened it out to lay it on the table so they could read it together.

Caen, France,
10 August 1944,

Dear Mrs Chapman,
It is my unhappy task to write to you with the details of your
husband's death.

Clare lifted her eyes from the page. Her breath seemed to stop
in her chest at the word. So brazen there in black and white. Neat
bold letters that spelled it out. She still couldn't frame it in her
mouth. She looked sideways to Bridget, who had stopped reading
too, waiting so that they could continue together. With reluctance, she lowered her eyes again to the page.

I had the great privilege to know your husband for some months before
he died in the battle for Caen. He was a brave and conscientious man,
whose presence among us brought much comfort and hope to us all. He
was not only a wonderful chaplain but also a generous and big-hearted
man, whose spirit and good humour will be very much missed by all of
us who served with him. I am sure I'm not telling you anything you
don't already know, but please be assured that we appreciated every-
thing that Walter Chapman had to give to the world, and I am very
grateful to have had the pleasure of knowing him. He will not easily be
forgotten.

You will be relieved to hear that his death was quick, and that he
died surrounded by his comrades, who were able to ease his passing with
kind words of comfort.

I hope this brief letter helps you in this most difficult time. Please
accept my sincere condolences,
Yours sincerely,
CAPT. Roger Allan.

. . .

Clare leaned back in her chair, eyes blurred with tears, and the two women sat in silence. Outside in the yard they heard the clop of hoofbeats and the rumble of wheels on stone. The old sheepdog gave a half-hearted bark in its wake before lapsing again into silence.

'I wonder if it's true,' Bridget said. 'That he died quickly, I mean. Dad told me once that in the last war the officers always used to write stuff like that, whatever really happened.'

Clare nodded. She had wondered the same thing. 'I choose to believe it,' she said. It was easier to bear than the visions of her dreams.

'Yes,' Bridget agreed. 'Perhaps that's best.' She drank some of her tea, and glanced at the clock. 'I should get back,' she said. 'Always lots to do. A woman's work and all that …'

They smiled at each other. 'I'll get started on lunch. I was going to make some pasties. If you see the children, send them in for their buns.'

At the back door to the cottage, Bridget turned back. 'Are you going to show Mum the letter?'

She hesitated, ashamed to realise she had not even thought of it. 'What do you think?'

'Not yet. I'd wait a while. It'll only upset her more.'

Clare nodded, unaccountably relieved. She could put off talking to Mrs Chapman a little while longer.

Halfway through making the pasties the children clattered in, wet and flushed and arguing. Eric came in last and she saw at once he had been crying. She wiped the pastry from her hands on a towel.

'What's all this?' she demanded.

The children fell silent – Clare was rarely sharp, but years in a classroom had left its mark. They stood in a little group, fidgeting as she looked them over. Henry was only eleven but he already had his father's roughness, dark hair tousled and wet with drizzle. He stared resolutely at a spot on the flagstones just before his feet. Beside him, Eric rubbed at his eyes with the back of his hand, and Lizzie, the youngest, was still trying to catch her breath.

'What have you been up to?'

'Just playing, Auntie Clare.' Lizzie was a natural peacemaker. Clare imagined Bridget had been just the same at that age; they shared a sweetness.

She looked towards Eric, who had lowered his head to stare at the floor so his face was hidden.

'Eric?'

'Just playing,' he confirmed, without raising his head.

She hesitated. She was concerned for her son, but she had no wish to embarrass him in front of the others. She would talk to him later, she decided; perhaps he would tell her more when they were alone, though she suspected he probably would keep his secrets – recently he had stopped confiding in her as he once used to do.

'Go and get cleaned up,' she ordered. 'There are buns for morning tea, but you'll have to share them out. No arguing.'

Their faces lit up and they turned as one to run to the stairs, a thunder on the floorboards. She could hear them overhead, footfalls and excited chatter as she turned her attention back to the half-made pastry, working it without care or attention so that it was difficult to roll out, and would not hold together.

Walter's mother finally left her bed at suppertime and the kitchen subsided into an awkward silence when she took her place at the table. She said nothing, her head bowed, and Clare exchanged a look with Bridget.

'How're you feeling?' Simon asked, and his voice was rough and loud in the hush.

Mrs Chapman raised her head and fixed him with eyes that were bloodshot and puffy. 'How do you think I'm feeling?'

He shrugged, and Clare liked him better for his refusal to be bullied. 'Just asking,' he replied, and dragged out a chair from the table to sit down. The legs screeched on the stone floor and Mrs Chapman flinched at the sound. Clare drew in a deep breath. Be kind, she reminded herself. Walter would want you to be kind. She has lost her only son, after all.

Sensing the tension, the children put aside their card game in uncharacteristic silence and took their places. Bridget began to ladle out the stew.

'Rabbit?' Mrs Chapman sniffed at her bowl.

'Yes,' Bridget said. 'Fred Wakeman brought them this morning.'

'What did you give him in return?'

'Some potatoes and a loaf of bread. It's all he'd take.'

'I don't like that man,' Walter's mother muttered as she picked up her fork. 'I don't trust him.'

No one replied. Fred Wakeman lived in an all-but-derelict cottage on the edge of the village and got by as best he could foraging and hunting, and growing what vegetables would survive in the poor patch of ground beside his house. The children loved him, and Walter had told her of happy hours spent in the old man's company. Now and then, if she thought Mrs Chapman wouldn't notice, Clare took him a pasty or a jar of jam. She promised herself to do it more often.

'Walter liked him,' she heard herself say. She couldn't help it, even though she knew it was unkind.

Mrs Chapman's fork froze on its way to her mouth. The table held its collective breath as she turned her head towards her daughter-in-law.

'My son thought the best about everyone he met. He was not always right.'

Clare said nothing. It was true that Walter always saw the

good in people – it was one of his gifts, and she had often envied him for it. She tried to see the good in his mother now and find a connection in the grief they shared but she could see no chink in Mrs Chapman's armour, no place to reach out to. Try, she told herself. Walter would want you to try.

'I went to see the vicar this morning,' she said.

'Did you now?'

There was an awkward pause.

'And why was that then?' Simon prompted, helpful for once. She flashed him a grateful glance.

'To ask about a memorial service. For Walter.'

'I don't want a memorial service,' Mrs Chapman snapped. 'Either it's a funeral or nothing.'

'I want a memorial service,' Clare said, though until that moment she had barely cared one way or the other. 'It's the proper thing to do. Walter would have wanted one, to lay him to rest.'

'I'm his mother and I'll decide.' She put down her fork and shoved the bowl with the remains of the uneaten stew away from her, like a child who has refused to eat her dinner. She folded her arms.

Bridget shot a look towards Clare that was full of sorrow and fear. For all the older woman's bitterness she was still Bridget's mother, and worthy of her daughter's love.

'Walter was a grown man,' Clare said gently, and with effort, 'with a wife and a son. He was a Royal Army Chaplain, and a service in his memory is the right thing to do.'

She was aware of Eric staring at her across the table. He had never seen his mother challenge his grandma before – she wondered what he would make of it. For a moment Mrs Chapman hesitated. Then, with all the dignity she could muster, she patted her mouth with a napkin, rose from her chair and crossed the room to the stairs. With one hand on the newel post she turned back to look at them.

'You come here to eat at my table, live under my roof, and you think you know it all. All of you, parasites.' The last word she spat between tautened lips, and she was ugly with hatred. Then she mounted the stairs with slow and regular steps and everyone at the table watched her go, silent with surprise. When they heard the click of the latch on her bedroom door fall into place at last they turned to each other. Bridget's cheeks were wet with tears, her breath uneven, and Clare caught at her hand and squeezed. One of the children let out a nervous giggle.

'You're excused,' Clare said. 'All of you. Take the dishes to the sink.'

There was a commotion as the children got down from their places and carried out the plates.

'The old bitch,' Simon murmured. 'Parasites, indeed. She'd have lost the farm years ago without us.'

'She's grieving,' Bridget offered. 'Give her some time.'

'We're all grieving.' Clare bristled, pain sliding into anger. 'All of us.'

The children drifted back from the sink where they had stacked the dishes and loitered, unsure if they were welcome or not.

'Go to your rooms,' Bridget told them, her voice weary. 'You can play upstairs for a while. But no running about or shouting. The grown-ups need to talk.'

They turned away, and Eric cast his mother a questioning look, as if to ask if he was included in the order. She gave him a small nod, and with a sigh he followed his cousins up the stairs. She watched his narrow back and the skinny knees, the sweater that was almost too small and would not last him another winter. Not for the first time she wondered if she could learn to knit. Then she looked at Bridget across the table.

Her sister-in-law was observing her, and there was little kindness in her eyes. 'Why did you provoke her about Fred? You must have known it would set her off.'

'I'm sorry,' Clare replied. 'I just couldn't help it. She's always so mean to Fred and he's such a nice old fellow ...' She trailed off with a half-shrug of one shoulder.

'It wasn't Clare's fault,' Simon said. 'Your mother wanted a fight – she would have picked up on anything.'

Bridget sighed and briefly lowered her face into her hands. Then, gathering all her resources, she rubbed her palms across her hair and stood up abruptly.

'I'm going to wash up. Clare?'

Clare followed her sister-in-law to the sink, and Simon slammed out of the back door to do a final round outside. The women worked together in silence but there was no awkwardness between them – there was simply nothing more to say. When they had finished and all the plates were back in their places on the dresser, Clare made more tea and turned on the radio. The news was just finishing – another thousand Germans had been taken prisoner after weeks of bitter fighting at Falaise, and Clare refused to think about the cost to the Allies, how many men had died for the victory.

After the news there was the light relief of *It's That Man Again*, and though she was tempted to turn it off, hardly in the mood for comedy, at a word from Bridget she left it on. One by one the children wandered back, drawn by the familiar voices and the laughter, and by the end of the show even Clare had raised a smile.

But later, in the night, when she lay sleepless and alone, she could no longer hold back the tears she had kept at bay in the daylight.

Chapter Three

With the start of autumn the school term began and though a part of her rebelled at this demand on her time and attention when all she wanted was to be left alone to grieve, Clare knew she had no choice. She was needed, and she supposed the work would be a good distraction from her sorrow.

On the first day back she left home early, leaving Eric to make his own way to school with his cousins later on. The rain that had fallen overnight had eased off by the time she left the house, and the puddles in the road were almost blinding with the morning sun that shimmered through the gaping clouds. Walking fast, the movement helped to steady her nerves, but a sense of longing rippled through her as a physical ache for their old life before the war, for Walter. Despite all her fears and premonitions, she had still hoped, she realised, that one day when the war was over they would return to that life and she had not allowed herself to ponder the alternatives.

But now...

Clare took in a deep breath and let her eyes scan the scene around her. The late summer fields were still vivid with life, and blackberries beckoned from the hedgerows. She could see Simon, already hard at work in his shirt sleeves, digging at something she could not make out in the distance, hat tilted on the back of his head. Was this to be her life now? Here on this farm, forever dependent on Walter's family? She could see too clearly the years stretching out in front of her, growing old as a teacher in a village school far from all she had loved before, an unwelcome guest of the Chapmans. Shaking her head against the thought of it she quickened her pace, skipping over a rut in the road. Overhead, a lone Spitfire droned across the sky and a startled pair of crows took flight in a flurry of wings. They wheeled away and the sun caught their feathers, making them glisten. She wished she could fly away as easily.

The school stood at the edge of the village like an afterthought. A Victorian red-brick box, it housed two cramped classrooms that served all the local children, their numbers swollen with evacuees since the start of the war. In heavy rain the roof leaked here and there and they had to put out buckets to catch the drips.

In the staffroom Clare shrugged off her coat and hung it on the hook by the door before setting the kettle on the hob for tea. Surprisingly, it felt as though she had never been away and the familiarity was comforting: for the first time since she had opened her eyes that morning she thought she might actually make it through the day. A moment later and Susan breezed in, stopping mid-stride at the sight of Clare.

'Oh, darling!' she exclaimed. 'I'm so sorry.'

She held out her arms and Clare stepped into them. The two women embraced, and Clare was aware of her friend's warmth and vitality, the sweet scent of the soap in her hair. She held her tightly, grateful for the touch of another person. She hadn't realised how much she had needed to be held. When they stepped back from each other Clare turned her head away, reluctant to be so closely observed, self-conscious of the redness of her eyes and the pallor of her cheeks.

'You look awful,' Susan observed with her usual candour, and Clare couldn't help but smile. 'You shouldn't have come to work – we'd have managed somehow. I thought when you didn't come in yesterday to prepare that you wouldn't be back for a while.'

'I wanted the distraction,' she replied. And to get out from under her mother-in-law's feet, she thought, but didn't say so. The two women had been skirting around each other at the farm with care, walking on eggshells for the last month. 'I'd just have been moping at home.'

Susan nodded and went to make the tea, and Clare leaned her hips against the counter as she waited.

'How are you?' Susan asked, turning briefly from her task. 'How's Eric?'

Clare shrugged. 'I don't know about Eric. He doesn't tell me anything any more. He's just been very quiet ...' She trailed off.

'Did they tell you what happened?'

'I had a nice letter from a captain that Walter served with but it didn't really tell me much. Only that he was killed in a place called Caen.' She shrugged again. The name of the place meant nothing to her: she wasn't even sure how to pronounce it. She had stopped listening to the news, unable to bear the thought of the deaths that she knew were the price for each victory, each patch of ground the Allies won.

Susan said nothing. Through the window, they could hear the rising hubbub of the children's voices, and the start of the rhythmic slap of a skipping rope. Clare took a mouthful of tea. The door opened and the tweed-clad figure of Miss Finch appeared. The two younger women exchanged a glance and moved away from the hob towards their respective desks.

'Good morning.' The headmistress gave a curt nod to them both. 'Ah, Mrs Chapman. I'm so glad you felt able to come to work today. We should have missed you otherwise. We certainly missed you at the planning meeting yesterday.' Then, remembering her manners, she added, 'I was very sorry to hear the news about your husband. Very sorry indeed.'

'Thank you,' Clare mumbled.

Miss Finch backed out of the staffroom and closed the door. They heard her heels briefly on the floorboards of the corridor, and the click and clunk of the door to her office as it opened and closed.

'So kind,' Susan said, with a smirk, and Clare almost laughed. She was glad she had come.

Even so, the day dragged, weariness in her bones and her usual patience hard to maintain. The children began the day quietly, circumspect, unsure what to expect from their grieving teacher. They would have been warned by their parents, she supposed. But as the day wore on they forgot about her sorrow, as children do, caught up in their own small dramas and concerns and she let them be, allowing them their chatter. When Miss Finch finally rang the bell for home time, Clare sighed with relief, and as the children bolted from the door she understood their eagerness to be gone – it was tempting to run out with them. Then she remembered the farmhouse and the welcome that awaited her, and depression settled itself once again on her shoulders.

When Clare finally got home from school, the kitchen was warm, and the aroma of some kind of stew or soup hung in the air. She could smell rosemary and sage, and she observed that she was actually hungry for the first time in weeks. Her mother-in-law was at the stove and Clare cast a brief glance around in the hope of seeing Bridget, but they were alone. Mrs Chapman replaced the lid on the saucepan, wiped her hands on the chequered threadbare apron she always wore, and turned to look at her son's widow.

'Oh, it's you,' she said, and hauled open the drawer of the dresser with a savage jerk. The cutlery rattled inside it.

'Yes,' Clare agreed. 'It's me. Home from work.' She hesitated. She had still not shown the letter to Walter's mother and the longer she left it the harder it became. Guilt suffused her. Mrs Chapman had lost a son after all and she deserved better, but in the days since the letter had come Clare had simply been unable to face the other woman's grief and bitterness. Drawing on the last of her reserves for the day, she said, 'I received a letter from an officer Walter served with. I thought you'd like to see it.'

Her mother-in-law raised her head and fixed Clare with tired eyes, dark rings beneath them. She had taken off her headscarf and the greying hair was dragged back from her face too severely – it made her look far older than she really was. A rattle at the back door drew the attention of both of them, and Bridget appeared. Her face was glowing with the warmth of the afternoon sun, and wisps of blonde hair had worked free of their grips, soft and shiny. The contrast with her mother was stark.

'Clare!' She smiled. 'How was work?'

'The same as always.' Clare returned the smile, a growing bond of warmth between them. It would have made Walter happy to see, she thought again; he had loved his sister dearly. Then she turned and saw her mother-in-law glaring at them both, jealous, she supposed, of her daughter's affection.

'I've had a letter,' she repeated, and Bridget feigned surprise.

She sat down at the table and, after a moment's hesitation, her mother-in-law did the same, clearing a space in front of her. Clare fumbled in her bag and handed across the precious envelope, although she was reluctant to set it into the other woman's hand, half expecting to have it snatched away from her, never to be returned. Mrs Chapman held it before her between the fingers of both hands, studying the writing, and searching for the courage to open it just as Clare had done.

Be kind, she reminded herself. Be forgiving. She heard

Walter's voice in her head, the soft deep tone that was like a caress. It was his voice that had first beguiled her when she heard him reading scripture at the church near her father's house, and she prayed she would keep the memory of it always.

Her mother-in-law gave a little tilt of her shoulders, and coaxed the sheet of paper from the envelope, opening it gently with reverent fingers. She cast her eyes across the words, then handed it in silence to her daughter. Bridget read through it once then gave it back to Clare, who folded it and put it on the table, fingers just touching its edge.

'When did it come?' Mrs Chapman's voice was little more than a whisper.

'A few days ago,' Clare lied.

'Why didn't you show it to me before?'

Clare lifted one shoulder in a half-shrug. 'I ... thought it might upset you,' she offered, though she felt no need now to explain herself. The letter had come to her, Walter's wife, and it was her choice whether or not to share it.

'How could you?' The other woman demanded.

'Mum!' Bridget's voice was a soft reprimand that her mother ignored.

'How dare you keep this from me? It's *my* son who is dead, my loss.'

Anger flared as heat across Clare's skin. 'He was my *husband!*' she breathed. 'Do you think you are the only one grieving?'

'I've lost a husband. I've lost a son. And I'll tell you this for nothing, the pain doesn't begin to compare.'

'Mum, please.' Bridget tried again to rein her mother in. 'It's not Clare's fault.' She slid Clare a desperate glance of apology and embarrassment, and Clare reached a hand to touch Bridget's wrist on the table beside her in a gesture of reassurance.

'It's all right,' she said. The cold detachment that settled inside surprised her – she had always hated conflict before. But her voice was strong and even and her heartbeat knocked with a steady beat in her chest. 'Your mother's always hated me because she knows that Walter loved me,' she said. 'I made him happy, because I understood him in a way she never could. She barely knew him at all.'

Mrs Chapman stared as though Clare had slapped her.

'I know you're hurting,' Clare said, lifting her eyes to meet the other woman's. 'But you are not the only one.'

'You're young,' her mother-in-law spat through lips drawn tight with bitterness. 'You'll get over it. Husbands are ten-a-penny. I warrant by the end of the war, you'll have found someone else to hold your hand and keep you warm at night. But losing a child is a different thing – nothing can ever replace the hole it leaves. No one can ever fill that gap.'

Clare said nothing. Outside, she could hear the voices of the children playing: Henry issuing orders and Eric complaining. From further away, there was the muffled thud of a hammer. Simon, she guessed, who was always mending something. After a moment she reached across the table for the envelope and slipped the letter back inside.

'I'm not your enemy,' she said. Her self-possession was starting to wane and Clare could feel the tears beginning to gather behind her eyes. Her throat was dry. 'It was the war that killed him. The Germans. You should save your hatred for them. I never did anything but love him.'

Mrs Chapman was silent then, gaze lowered to where her hands were twisting together on the table. Bridget got up to stir the stew. Outside, the hammering stopped and the only sound was the hiss of the stove and the distant voices of the children.

Chapter Four

On the day of the memorial service the air was cool and damp with drizzle and the clouds hung low and oppressive overhead. Summer seemed well and truly over. The little church was filled to overflowing. Clare had put a notice in *The Times* but still, she had not expected so many would come and she stood just inside the porch to welcome them as they filed inside. Villagers who remembered Walter as a boy, his old parishioners from Bristol who had made the long trip by train and bus; friends, colleagues, teachers. There would have been more, she realised, if there had not been so many fighting overseas, and she was humbled by the number of lives he had touched.

'So sorry for your loss ...' she heard over and over.

'He was a wonderful man ...'

'He's with God now ...'

The last of the mourners trickled inside as the vicar emerged from the vestry and strode to the lectern, heels clicking on the flagstones. The murmur of the congregation dwindled to a restless hush, broken by a cough here and there and the shuffling of feet.

'We are gathered here to remember before God the life of

Walter Chapman,' the vicar began, 'to give thanks for his life, to commend him to God our merciful redeemer and judge, and to comfort one another in our grief. Let us pray ...'

The congregation shuffled again and bowed their heads, and Eric fidgeted beside her. She laid a reassuring hand on his shoulder and smiled down at him when he looked up in surprise.

'After graduating from Oxford with an honours degree in Divinity ...'

She stopped listening. The vicar had barely known Walter, and there was nothing he could possibly say that would comfort her. Her Walter, reduced to a list of the schools he had gone to and exams he had passed. No mention of his kindness or the ready, lopsided smile, his clever wit, the sad, pale eyes. A memory of the last look they had shared on the station platform curled around her thoughts, and she had to blink back the tears that prickled behind her eyes. It seemed such a long time ago.

Hauling her mind back to the present, she tried to recall telling the vicar the facts he was delivering with such apparent lack of interest, but the memory eluded her and she lost interest in the thought almost as soon as it arose. She turned again to look at Eric, sitting bolt upright beside her, tense and alert, eyes fixed on the vicar. She had tried to talk to him about the service to prepare him in advance but he had shown no interest at all, as if it were nothing to do with him, simply listening to what she had to say with bored compliance until she released him to go back to his games.

'Bravely, he volunteered as an army chaplain ...'

On the other side of Eric, Walter's mother sat with her head bowed and a mourning veil lowered to hide her face. She had spoken to no one that morning, not even Bridget, who bore her mother's moods with dogged resignation. Clare could never understand how she managed it. She could still recall how she had wanted to rail in Bridget's defence from the moment she sat down at the farmhouse kitchen table for the very first time all those years ago, but Walter had counselled her against it. *They love each other*, he had told her. *It's just their way.* But even then it had been many years since he had lived alongside them as Clare did now: he hadn't seen the day-to-day toll on his sister.

'All rise for hymn 402, He who would valiant be.'

They got to their feet and fumbled with the hymn books. The untrained voices struggled with the high notes and the discordant chorus filled the small church. Clare had struggled to choose most of the hymns and readings, but this one had been a favourite of them both. Her voice caught in her throat, remembering the sound of the song in Walter's clear, deep tone.

The eulogy was given by an old friend of Walter's from his university days, when they had studied Divinity together at Oxford. James had become a teacher after graduation, discovering in the course of his degree that he was not called to the church after all, but the two men had remained friends: James had stood as godfather to Eric, and had visited them now and then. Clare liked him. He had a kind, open way about him, and a wry, shy sense of humour.

But today the words he uttered in praise of his friend blurred into a meaningless jumble of sound in Clare's head, and unreasonably she hated him for being alive when Walter was dead. Glancing around the church, she realised she hated them all; she would have sacrificed every single one of them but Eric to have Walter at her side again, and the feeling surged with such savage ferocity she had to place a hand upon the back of the bench in front of her to steady herself. Next to her, Bridget laid a hand on her arm and turned towards her with concern in her eyes.

'Are you all right?' she whispered.

Clare nodded. But she was not all right. Not at all. She wondered if she would ever be all right again. She heard nothing more of the service and when the people around her began to file out of the pews, she lifted her head in surprise.

Afterwards there were tea and sandwiches and some kind of

cake Clare could not quite identify in the church hall alongside the church. The mourners traipsed through the drizzle in the churchyard to stand in small awkward groups, and she watched the vicar moving deftly among them, a word here and there, a smile. She remembered Walter doing the same at other people's funerals, while she was the one serving the tea and sandwiches.

The villagers offered the widow their condolences but their first concern was Walter's mother, who had collapsed into a chair, overcome. Eric hovered by the cake and Susan appeared, smart in a tailored black coat, hair sleek with rain. Clare hadn't seen her in the church.

'Sorry I'm late,' she said. 'How did it go?'

Clare shook her head – there was nothing she could think of to say about it except that she had hated every moment.

'Oh dear.' Susan reached to squeeze Clare's fingers. She was a good friend and Clare was glad that she had come.

On the far side of the hall she saw James withdraw from the little group that was clustered around Mrs Chapman and come towards her. Without formality he opened his arms and took her inside them, holding her tight. His jacket was rough against her cheek and reeked of damp wool, but it was a good smell that reminded her of happier times.

'How are you, Clare?'

'Oh, you know ...' She didn't dare to tell him the truth, not here in front of everyone – his kindness would undo her. She turned to Susan.

'This is my friend and colleague – Susan Minter. We teach together at the school here. Her father's at the War Office. Susan, this is James, one of Walter's dearest friends and Eric's godfather.'

He shook Susan's proffered hand with a smile. 'Ah, lovely to see you,' he said, and then they stood together in a silent huddle, no one quite sure what to say. They were saved by the arrival of Eric, who had vague memories of his godfather, though it had been a while since they had seen each other last.

'Uncle James.'

'Eric, my boy! How are you? Are you doing a good job looking after Mum? I hope so.'

Eric looked down and shuffled from one foot to the other. His jacket was too small for him, Clare noticed, and the cuffs of his shirt poked out beneath the sleeves. After a moment he lifted his head as if to answer the question but instead he asked, 'Why aren't you fighting?'

'Eric!' Clare's embarrassment made her sharp.

'It's a reasonable question,' James replied, 'and the answer is very simple. The army wouldn't take me. I have asthma, you see, and if I so much as break into a run I can barely breathe. So I don't think I'd be much use on a battlefield, do you? Something of a hindrance, really.'

Eric considered this for a moment before he shook his head.

'I'm far more useful teaching boys like you how to grow up to be good men like your father.' He looked up at Clare. 'You should send him to us.'

She stared. 'I … I … can't.' Without Walter that kind of education was out of the question – she could never afford it on her own small salary. Besides, she wasn't sure she wanted to let him go.

'Would you like to go away to school, Eric?' James apparently was taking no notice. 'The school term's not long begun – you've turned eleven now haven't you? I'm sure we could fit you in somehow. Eh? Or perhaps next term might be better. After Christmas, perhaps? Give you some time to prepare.'

He raised his head to Clare as though the timing was all that needed to be decided. 'I can't,' she murmured.

'Don't worry,' James reassured her. 'I'm his godfather and I live at the school, and God knows I've done little enough in his life so far. I've been very remiss. I'll take care of it.'

She said nothing, shock and grief tumbling in equal measure inside her. Eric looked up at her, and her heart turned when she saw the hope in his eyes. How could she refuse? It was his chance to escape the farm as Walter had done. His chance to make something of himself.

'Can I go, Mum? Can I really?'

'I'll have to think about it.' His face was so bright with eagerness and hope that she had to swallow down the tears she could feel rising behind her eyes. She turned away for a moment to master her feelings.

'Thank you, James,' she managed to say after a moment. 'I'll let you know.' Then, 'Where are you staying?'

'At the pub. I was going to ask if you'd like to have an early dinner, though I understand it might be difficult.' He glanced around the hall. The villagers were beginning to drift away towards the door now that the tea and sandwiches were finished. Few of them could meet her eye as they took their leave, awkward and ill at ease, uncertain how to be with her. She didn't blame them – even in the middle of a war death was still the great taboo.

Susan bent down to speak to Eric. 'Would you like to stay with me tonight, Eric?' she asked. 'Up at the big house? We could have hot chocolate and play chess or cards if you like?'

Clare gave her friend a grateful smile.

Fred Wakeman came over to take his leave, turning his threadbare cap between his fingers, nervous. 'He was a good man, Mrs Chapman,' he said. 'One of the best.'

'Thank you,' she whispered.

He stepped in closer. 'I got a bit of French brandy come my way the last few days, if you'd like?'

She smiled. 'I would like that very much. Thank you.'

James lifted his eyebrows in mock shock as the old man shuffled to the door, but she had long since given up her moral outrage about the black market. People survived how they could, and in the country there was plenty enough to go round – a few illicit pleasures did no one any harm.

At last they were the only ones left, and she realised she hadn't noticed Mrs Chapman leave. She assumed Bridget and Simon had taken her home, but she wondered that they had not said goodbye. From the little kitchen she could hear the clatter of Mrs Jarvis clearing up the plates and cups. The vicar was nowhere to be seen.

'Shall we?' James asked.

They trooped out into the last light of the afternoon, where the long autumn shadows fell across the graves. She averted her eyes from the scattered headstones and watched Susan and Eric head off towards the big house at the end of the village, sure he would have a marvellous time. It was really very kind of Susan to take him.

At the pub they ate fish and chips and Clare allowed herself two bottles of beer, which helped to take the edge off her sorrow. Keeping her head averted from the pity she saw in the landlady's eyes, she gave James her full attention. She was comfortable in his company, a reminder of better times, and for the first time in weeks she felt a little of the tension seep from her muscles.

'It's good of you about Eric,' she said. 'I'm very grateful.'

'Walter hated the farm and he'd want something better for his son. It's the least I can do.' He hesitated. 'I take it you accept?'

She nodded, reeling slightly from the enormity of the decision she had just made. But how could she refuse?

'And what about you?' James continued.

'What about me?'

'Can we get you out of there too somehow?'

She laughed, warm and a little light-headed from the beer. 'That would be wonderful. But I don't see how.'

'Perhaps a teaching job in Wellington? So you can be close to Eric.'

For a moment she tried to picture herself in a town she had never been to, living in a down-at-heel rented room that was all she could afford, and nowhere for her son to return to in the holidays. She said, 'You do know how much female teachers earn, don't you?'

He sighed. 'Yes, I'm afraid I do. But perhaps in time ...' He let the thought trail off and took a mouthful from his pint, the froth catching on his upper lip until he wiped it gently away with the tip of his tongue. 'I really can't imagine what Walter was thinking when he sent you here to live. He must have known you'd be miserable.'

She said nothing and took a sip of her beer, recalling the arguments. Fear for Walter had been only one of the reasons she had not wanted him to go.

'He thought he could make a difference,' she said, with a half-shrug, 'and that it was worth the sacrifice. He wrestled with his conscience for years before he finally went.'

'It was damn selfish of him,' James retorted, with uncharacteristic vehemence.

She lowered her face away and brushed lightly at her eyes so that he wouldn't see the tears his words provoked, though she could not have said whether it was relief, grief or anger that prompted them. When she thought she could control her voice she turned her head towards him. He was watching her with such concern in his eyes she had to slide her eyes away once more.

'I know everyone thinks he was a saint,' he said, 'and to some extent he was – his faith certainly burned brightly. But those of us that live close to the fire get singed from the heat from time to time. In your shoes, I'd be furious with him.'

She gave a half-laugh that was almost a sob. It was such a relief that someone understood, and that she didn't have to carry the burden of her anger alone, heavy with guilt and unacknowledged. He laid a reassuring hand on her wrist, warm and heavy, and after a moment she shifted her hand away, its weight suddenly uncomfortable. They sat in silence for a while.

Idly, she looked around her. Cheap reproductions of hunting scenes and horse brasses hung on tobacco-stained walls, but the place had a homely, comfortable air. At the bar, Mrs Jarvis was having a sherry with Fred Wakeman. They were talking quietly and laughing, but their words didn't carry to where Clare was sitting. The old man's ancient labrador lay on the floor between the bar stools, watching everything with sad brown eyes.

A sudden memory cut across her mind, vivid and painful. Walter had brought her here on her very first visit to the farm before they were married, when they had needed to escape from the house for an hour. He had made her laugh at something she had forgotten now, and promised she would never have to spend much time with his mother.

'I should go,' Clare said. She wanted now to be alone.

'Back to the farm.' James lifted a sardonic eyebrow. 'The dutiful daughter-in-law.'

She gave him a tired half-smile. 'It's been a long day,' she answered, and got up, sliding her arms into the sleeves of her coat as she moved. By the time he had stood up to help her she had already fastened the buttons.

At the door to the pub he said, 'I'll walk you back.'

'No,' Clare answered firmly. 'Thank you, but I'd rather be alone.'

She saw him hesitate, wanting to press the point but knowing it was unfair.

'It was lovely to see you,' she said. 'Thank you so much for coming.'

'I wasn't going to miss Walter's funeral.' He tilted his head, the glimmer of a smile in his eyes, but she was weary now and the cheeriness struck a sour note.

She stepped out into the lingering twilight where the clouds above the village were edged with burnished orange. The windows across the road blinked blankly, the blackout blinds hiding the light and life she knew was behind them. She hated the blackout and the sense of solitude it fostered. She was a city girl at heart, who loved lights and people, the press of close humanity, and she wondered if she would ever get back to it again.

Patting her pocket to make sure of the little torch, she lifted her head to James. He was looking awkward now as though embarrassed by this farewell. 'I'll write to you about Eric,' he said. 'And we can make the arrangements.'

'Thank you,' she replied. She wanted to be gone, aware of the falling night. 'Have a safe trip home tomorrow.'

They stepped in close to embrace again but this time it was brief and perfunctory and she didn't understand what had changed during the evening they had spent together – she only knew she no longer wanted his company. Then she set off along the main road of the village towards the farm that was her home, and she knew without turning that he watched her until she was out of his sight.

It had been almost two years since Walter decided he could no longer stand by while other men risked their lives in the fight against evil. She still remembered with perfect clarity the moment he had told her. There had been a beam of sunlight across the breakfast table, and they were eating toast with marmalade that Mrs Ellis who did the church flowers had made for them. Clare had never dared to ask where the oranges had come from.

His parishioners could live without him, he had said; the army's need was greater. He had a duty to go and help, and the knowledge was a burden on his conscience. He needed to do his bit. Clare had been horrified – the thought of Walter at war was beyond her capacity to imagine.

'You're not exactly soldier material,' she had told him, and regretted the words as soon as they were out of her mouth in spite of the truth they contained. He had recoiled at the unexpected cruelty – their marriage had always been polite, respectful, and they had never tried to hurt each other before. 'You're a man of God,' she went on, almost tripping on the words in her haste to say them. 'It's not in your nature to go to war.'

'You think I'm incapable? That I can't do what is needed to fight off evil?' Hurt had transmuted to anger.

'That's not what I meant.' She looked at him across the table. 'You're not a soldier.'

Walter's mouth tightened. 'Neither are most of the men out there fighting the Nazis. They're milkmen and office workers, teachers and shopkeepers. What makes me different that I should be excused from the danger?' He set down the piece of toast that was in his hand, and dragged a napkin across the stickiness of his fingers.

'There are other ways to serve that are just as important,' she said. 'You're needed here, at home. There's suffering here too, people need the comfort of the church, a priest who can give them succour in their hour of need. And God knows,' she added, to make up for the cliché, 'our need has never been greater.'

'Their need will be greater still if the Germans win, and it isn't the power of prayer that's going to stop them.'

He unfolded his long limbs from under the table and went to the fireplace to poke at the logs, though the fire was already burning well. She observed him, trying to imagine him on a battlefield tending to the dying as bullets and bombs wreaked their carnage all around him, but she could not see it. He would die if he went to war, she was sure of it.

'You can't go.' She got up and went to stand beside him at the fire and when the heat began to scorch her legs, she lowered herself into the one of the armchairs beside it. Walter remained at the fire, staring into the flames, and Clare could see the light sheen of sweat across his forehead and the muscle that was working in his jaw against the anger. 'Please don't go.' She reached a hand towards him, catching his fingers lightly, but he flinched at her touch as though she had burned him. She let her hand drop away. They had never fought like this in all their years together, and she could feel the rising sense of desperation that threatened to overwhelm her. She was barely breathing.

At last he turned his head towards her. 'I have to go. I cannot stand by while other men give their lives in the fight for freedom. I'm not a coward ...' He trailed off and returned his gaze to the flames, stabbing pointlessly at the logs with the tip of the poker.

'Of course you're not a coward,' she said. 'It's not about cowardice ...'

'Isn't it?' He dropped the poker back onto its hook and stood with his hands braced against the mantelpiece, tapping at the edge of the hearthstone with the toe of one shoe.

She said nothing.

'Isn't it?' he repeated, and wheeled towards her. 'I think it's exactly about cowardice. I have an excuse not to go and you want me to take it, because you are afraid. And that's all it is, an excuse. You can argue all you like about the need for me here but we both know that's not the real reason you don't want me to go.'

'Why now?' she asked. 'Why after all this time? What's changed?'

For a moment he said nothing, gaze still fixed on the flames. Then, apparently finding the words he needed at last, he said, 'I have wrestled with my conscience for every hour of every day since the war began, and I'm weary of the struggle. It is the right thing to do and I'm ashamed to say that I've known it all along, no matter all the lies I've told myself. I have no choice.'

Clare felt the tears begin to burn behind her eyes and she blinked and took a deep breath to steady herself. 'I want to grow old with you,' she pleaded. 'I want Eric to grow up with a father.'

Walter closed his eyes in a moment of pity, then dropped to his knees on the rug in front of her chair to take her hands between his. His fingers were warm and soft and strong, and her hands were very small against them. He had always made her feel so safe before and now she felt as though she had come unmoored.

'I want those things too,' he whispered. 'But I want us to grow old in a world that is free of Nazis, where Eric can live unafraid.' He lifted his eyes to hers. 'Surely you understand that?'

Her eyes misted and his face blurred before her. She swallowed, unable to form words, the tears too close to the surface to talk without crying. Walter cupped her face between his hands and she thought for a moment he would kiss her but instead he wiped at the tears with the tip of his thumb.

'I simply can't see you in the army,' she managed to whisper.

'Because you don't want to,' he replied.

'What woman wants her husband to go to war?' she asked, finding her voice again. 'And if that makes me a coward then, yes, I'm a coward.'

He gave her a small smile and touched a finger to her lips. Then he had lowered his mouth to hers, and kissed her.

The growing chug-chug of the Fordson tractor in the field beside the lane shattered the memory and brought her back to the evening in front of her, and she realised she was standing in the lane with a smile on her face at the memory of the kiss, and the love that had come afterwards. So naughty, on the hearthrug of the breakfast room before the fire, so unlike their usual quiet and gentle intimacy. A warmth spread across her belly as she remembered, a desire that could never now be met kindling in her blood. Her vision filmed over at the thought of it. Then, with a savage wipe of one hand across her eyes, she turned on the torch to light the darkening lane, and continued on her way.

Chapter Five

The first German prisoners of war arrived late in the autumn when the chill of the coming winter was just beginning to bite. The villagers had been expecting them, warned that the old American camp on its outskirts would soon be put to new use, but still, the distant roar of the trucks as they trundled through the village wrenched Clare from her dreams to startled wakefulness.

The enemy, she thought. Men who had fired guns at Englishmen, men who had killed. Was the man who had made her a widow among them?

In spite of the warmth of the bed she shivered, listening to the dwindling rumble as the convoy headed for the camp. After the Americans had left it on their way towards the invasion of France, the local boys had made it their playground, enacting elaborate invasions of their own. But in the last few weeks, a handful of British soldiers had taken up residence and as the distant racket of hammers and saws and trucks disturbed the usual peace, the children had been forced to find other places to play. The whole village was on edge, nervous about this new and unwelcome influx of Germans into their midst.

The enemy, she thought again.

Then slowly, eyelids heavy, she fell back into a broken sleep of dying men and battle.

The transport trucks were open to the elements; whatever canvas had once covered them had long since rotted away. The night was cool, and overhead a narrow moon peeped now and then through the shifting cloud. How many trucks had Max Peterson ridden in like this to an unknown destination through the past five years of war? Too many to count.

The truck lurched across the potholes. There was little to see in the semi-dark beyond the shapes of the hedgerows either side: Max sensed more than saw the fields that stretched out beyond them. Every so often the bright glow of a cigarette punctured the gloom, smoke blowing across the prisoners' faces as they passed the cigarette between them, sharing. Before the war he had rarely smoked, but on the long trek into Russia the warmth of the smoke in his lungs had offered brief moments of comfort against the murderous chill of the winter. Even now just the thought of it still made him shiver, teeth gritting with the memory.

The men were mostly silent, weary from the long weeks of their journey as prisoners of war from the battlefields of Normandy. Max had lost track of the days since he was captured, the endless marching from place to place with little food and less shelter against the oncoming winter. Not one of the camps so far had been prepared for the vast numbers of captured men, and he wondered if the Allies had been taken by surprise by their success. Surely they might have predicted there would be prisoners?

Above them, the moon broke free of the veil of cloud for a moment and lit up the countryside. Fields, trees and a church spire were briefly outlined against the sky in the distance as the truck lurched in and out of a rut, throwing one of the men from his seat. The man swore as he picked himself up and someone laughed. Max took the cigarette from his neighbour and drew back deeply, tasting the heat in his chest. When, finally, the war was over and he got back to Berlin he promised himself he would quit – Lotte wouldn't like him smoking. He could hear her already, complaining about the smell.

The convoy slowed on its way through yet another village and Max lifted his head to look about him. A row of small stone houses with a couple of shops lined one side of the road and on the other he could make out a post office and a pub with a sign that swung gently and creaked in the breeze. It was much the same as any number of villages all across Europe, but he had noticed that even after all these years of war there was a neatness and prosperity in England that was lacking elsewhere. So much for all the German propaganda that Britain was on its knees – he had seen few signs of it so far. Even on his brief journey through London on his way to be processed and questioned, he saw a city that was still proudly standing, and lively with the hustle and bustle of normal life.

This isn't London, one of the other men had claimed.

The route was chosen specially, said another.

Max had known all along they had been lied to – how could he not after living through the carnage in Russia? But the apparent normality of life in Britain still surprised him and he shook his head at his naivety.

A sudden movement at a window of one of the houses caught his eye as they passed it, but the glass was too dark to see anything more. A watching villager, he supposed, woken by the roar of the lorries. It must be strange for the English to have the enemy in their midst when they had kept them from their shores for so long. How would it feel to meet them face to face at last? Taking a final drag on the butt of the cigarette, he stubbed the end of it on the side of the truck and tucked the remains into the pocket of his tunic. Saving scraps had become second nature.

Not far past the village the convoy ground to a halt. Max leaned out to look along the line of trucks. Up ahead he could see the outlines of a camp of some kind with rows of squat dark huts. Solid buildings boded well – in Belgium they had been housed under canvas, if they had been housed at all.

The others began to shift in their seats, waking from the apathy of their journey and looking about with idle curiosity. It didn't pay to care too much – for all they knew they could be moving on to another place tomorrow, but Max had got used to the not-knowing. The British never told the prisoners anything beyond immediate day-to-day orders, as if it made no difference to the men where they were headed, or where they would end up. In the end, he supposed they were probably right. If he had known the name of the village they had just passed through, or its exact location on a map of England, it would have changed nothing. He was a prisoner of war, at the mercy of the British, and there was nothing he could do about it.

The men waited with the patience of the powerless as the trucks progressed one by one through the gate. Inside the camp, a pair of Tommies were rattling off orders in English, which most of the prisoners couldn't understand, and though Max understood every word he feigned the same incomprehension. He had no wish to be singled out from the others, no desire to draw attention to himself. He had learned the hard way to keep his head down, knew only too well the price of enthusiasm.

Gradually the men were sorted and led to their huts and Max looked around his new home with relief. The bunks stood in neat rows along the walls with the mattresses folded and topped by two army-issue blankets and for all the world it could have been an army barracks back at home in Germany. Except of course for the large American flag that someone had pinned to the wall at one end. The camp must have housed American troops not so long ago, before they shipped out to France. They all noticed it but not one of them cared enough to take it down.

Picking out a top bunk near the flag at the far end from the door, he made up the bed and climbed onto it. All around him was the murmur and rustling of other men as they settled themselves, but within moments of lying down he was swept into a soft and dreamless sleep in spite of the bare light bulbs that still burned overhead. It had been a long time since he last slept in a bed and it was bliss.

In the morning the village was abuzz with the news, though it had yet to be mentioned at the farm. Mrs Chapman had come to breakfast tight-lipped and stiff, as though a soft word or a smile would break the wall she had erected around herself. She barely spoke to anyone any more beyond the necessities, inhabiting the world of pain that had come to define her – she appeared to have lost all interest in anything beyond it. Clare saw the toll it took on Bridget to realise her mother simply didn't care about her any more: Mrs Chapman had lost her boy, and the love of her other child seemed to mean nothing.

At the breakfast table no one spoke. The children fidgeted as they ate and bolted from the room at the first opportunity. Simon had long since left the house and the three women cleared the table in silence. Then, with a brief word of farewell, Clare buttoned up her coat, retrieved her bicycle and set off after the children towards school.

Autumn seemed to have given up the ghost overnight and the first wintery wind gusted cold and damp along the lane, collecting the last of the leaves from the trees. Clare took off her hat before the wind snatched it too, and her hair blew across her face. Dragging it clear with a gloved hand, she wondered if the school roof would have lost any more tiles. She hoped not – the leaks were bad enough already. Alongside the lane they were sowing the winter wheat, though the soil, like the men, was exhausted. The roar of the tractor's engine ebbed and flowed towards her with the wind, and now and then she caught the drift of men's voices, though the words were lost before they reached her. Beyond the field where the hedgerow marked the ridge was the road that led down to the camp.

The enemy.

She straightened her shoulders and pedalled harder. There was nothing to fear, she told herself. They were prisoners of war, after all. Defeated. No danger to anyone. But Walter was dead because of them and their presence rekindled the heat of her grief, wounds gaping and open once more.

Arriving at school, she parked the bike and paused briefly to search for her son among the playing children. She found him easily – kicking a ball back and forth to a friend – and she stopped to watch him for a moment. He was so like his father that at times it hurt to look at him. Peas from a pod, Mrs Chapman had once said, and she was right – there was no mistaking whose son he was. But Eric laughed a lot less than his father used to, and he was too young to be so solemn. Walter had possessed a keen sense of the ridiculous – it had been one of the things she loved most about him, and she gave herself a small smile at the thought of it. Perhaps Eric would develop the same sense in time, she consoled herself, when he realised he could no longer resist the world's absurdity.

'Did you hear the lorries?'

In the little staffroom Susan's eyes were wide when Clare walked in. 'Did you see them?'

Clare hung her coat on the hook. 'I heard them,' she replied.

'I watched them go past from the window. There must have been at least a dozen. I didn't think to start counting until it was too late.'

The trucks would have driven right past the big house at the top of the village. Clare tried to picture it. A dozen, she thought.

How many men was that? But she said nothing and Susan turned from the tea she was making with a look that Clare found hard to bear.

'I don't want your pity,' she snapped. 'I just don't want to think about them being there, so close.'

Susan flushed and tightened her lips before she turned back to pour the tea. The pot trembled in her hand. Clare sighed.

'I'm sorry,' she said, crossing the small room towards her friend. 'I didn't mean to bite. It's just ... well, it isn't long since Walter ...' She stopped. She still couldn't bring herself to say the word out loud. 'It could have been one of those men.'

'I know,' Susan answered, quick to forgive. 'I should have thought. I'm sorry.'

Clare forced a smile. Why did the prisoners have to come here? Soon they would start work on the farms roundabout as the Italian prisoners had done before them, and she would have to see them every time she left the house, each one a reminder of the grief that was lodged inside her, a tight ball of pain she rarely allowed herself to visit. She could not even begin to imagine how she would face the Germans day to day. She took a deep breath and a mouthful of tea. She had not expected to be so rattled, her emotions roiling close to the surface – she had thought of herself as stoic, taking Walter's death in the spirit of the time: keeping calm and carrying on, as the posters so cheerily exhorted. She blinked, twice, to quell the prickle of tears and drank more of the tasteless tea, the last of the week's ration eked out. Then she lifted her glance towards the clock on the wall. It was time.

'I'll do it,' Susan offered, and picked up the bell from the desk.

'No, I will.' Clare held out her hand and took the bell. Then, with a deep breath, she strode out along the corridor and towards the door. But when she stepped outside, the usual play-ground chatter had already subsided and the children were standing as though frozen, staring out towards the street where a column of half a dozen German prisoners had halted just beyond the gate to the school. A British corporal was talking to one of them, using arm gestures to get his message across. A couple of the older boys moved towards the gate. Clare didn't see who threw the first stone but it became a hail of missiles in moments and the Germans broke ranks in startlement to move out of range while the young corporal who was their guard shouted orders they ignored. Then a stone caught the British soldier on the shoulder and he wheeled towards the school in anger.

Clare found her voice. 'Stop it!' She raced down the steps towards the gathered children. 'Stop it at once!'

All but one of the children dropped their pebbles to the ground at their feet and shuffled slightly away, but a single final stone took flight to catch one of the prisoners hard on his cheek.

'Eric!'

For a long moment her son made no move, staring down the soldier he had hit. Then, abruptly, he turned and, pushing his way through the other children, he broke into a run, careening around the side of the school towards the open fields behind it. Clare watched him go, torn between the mother's need to comfort her own child, and the duty she owed to the other children in her care. Keep calm and carry on, she remembered, and almost laughed. By the time she had made her decision, Eric was out of sight behind the school. She would never have caught up with him anyway.

She stepped forwards and the children parted to let her through, eyes lowered but still sliding often towards the enemy at their gate. The corporal, flustered, moved nearer to speak to her, and the Germans stood in a huddle at his back, strange in their repurposed British fatigues with the great red patch sewn on the back like a target. The man Eric had hit stood a little apart from the others and she was aware that he was watching her intently. Her skin prickled with self-consciousness under his attention, a flare of heat spreading over her neck, until she reminded herself he was the enemy that had killed Walter. Then she had to quell the urge to find a stone to fling at him herself.

'Perhaps next time you stop, Corporal,' she said, and her voice was louder and more clipped than she intended, perhaps to cover the tremble in her limbs, 'you could choose somewhere other than outside the school. Some of these children have lost fathers.'

The corporal looked chastened. He was clearly out of his depth.

'Sorry, miss,' he replied. 'It won't happen again.'

She nodded her acceptance of his apology and as she began to turn away to usher the children inside, she caught again the gaze of the soldier Eric had hit. A thin trickle of blood had begun to ooze on his cheek but he didn't lift a hand to wipe it away as she would have expected. They locked eyes for the briefest of moments and the same rush of self-consciousness swept over her again. She felt exposed, her nerves raw and open, and she dipped her head away, confused. He was a German, a prisoner of war, and he had no right to make her feel that way.

She turned towards the children. They were already assembled in neat lines by the steps, mute and watchful under the gaze of Miss Finch. Clare hadn't noticed her arrive. She wondered if the headmistress had seen Eric throw that final stone, and if her vigilant gaze had noticed yet that he had run away. He would be in trouble when she did, and instinctively Clare curled her hands at the thought of his punishment. She remembered too well the pain of a beating to the hand from her own days at school, and she had never beaten a child herself in her life.

The children filed inside on Miss Finch's command, and Clare followed them up the steps. At the door she turned back instinctively to look out over the empty playground. The little party of prisoners had resumed their file and moved on along the road, but she could still pick out the figure of the man who had made her so uncomfortable as they marched away. She watched them until they were out of sight. Then, with a slight shake of her shoulders and a deep breath, she went inside to begin the day at school.

She found Eric at playtime, sitting alone with his back against the wall of the school, hidden from the general gaze of the playground. He was crying. Clare settled herself on the ground beside him, the rough brick digging into her back.

'Did she beat you?'

He nodded. His hands were tucked tight beneath his armpits.

'Show me.'

With reluctance he drew out his hands from their hiding place and held them out to her. The palms were striped with raised red welts where the ruler had landed. She swallowed, and her heart turned in pity. He lifted his tear-stained face towards her and dragged a sleeve across his nose.

'It isn't fair,' he whispered. 'If I'd been a grown-up man with a gun and I'd shot him, I'd have been a hero. But throw a stone and I get beaten.'

'It isn't fair,' she agreed. She remembered the brief surge of desire towards violence in her own blood, the lust for revenge. 'But those men are our prisoners now. They surrendered to us in good faith so now we have a duty to protect them and keep them safe, whatever they've done and whatever we might think of them.'

'I hate them,' Eric breathed. 'They killed Dad.'

'I know,' she murmured, and shifted closer along the wall to put her arm around him. 'I hate them too.'

They sat for a while, holding each other in a way they had not done for far too long, and Clare let her gaze wash across the corner of the playground that was in her line of sight. The usual games of football and skipping and hopscotch had been abandoned and the children had returned to the war games of a few months before – storming the beaches at Normandy. She could hear the beginnings of a disagreement taking place out of sight, voices getting louder, tempers roused. Soon they would start to shove at each other and a fight would break out. She should get up, she thought, and intervene before things got to that stage, but her son was snuggled warm against her and for once she left them to it. One of the others could sort it out – this time her place was with Eric.

Chapter Six

'What's wrong with you?' Simon was chiding Eric over dinner. 'You haven't said a word.'

Eric slanted a glance towards his mother and for the first time she realised he was afraid of his uncle. All this time and she had not known. She opened her mouth to speak but was cut off by Henry.

'He got beaten at school by Miss Finch. She's brutal.'

'What did you do?'

There was a silence, and even Mrs Chapman raised her eyes to look at her grandson. Eric shot another look towards Clare, who gave him a small nod of encouragement. *Tell the truth*, it said. *It will be all right.*

Henry began to speak into the hush but his father cut him off. 'Let Eric speak for himself.'

'I threw a stone at a German.'

'We all did!' Henry chimed in. 'It's just you were the one Finch saw.'

'*Miss* Finch,' Bridget corrected her son.

'Did you hit him?'

Eric nodded.

'He got him good, right on the cheek. Here.' Henry pointed to his own cheekbone. 'Drew blood and everything. Then Auntie Clare told the British corporal off for stopping outside the school.'

'You should have let them do it,' Mrs Chapman murmured, looking at Clare. 'You should have joined in and helped.'

Clare exchanged a glance with Bridget.

'Mum,' Bridget coaxed. 'They're prisoners ...'

'I don't care. The only good German is a dead one and if one of them dares to cross my path, I'll scratch his eyes out.'

'Good for you, Grandma!' Henry looked around the table for more approval, but the smile faded when he met only worried faces. Eric was staring at his plate – he hated to be the centre of attention.

Simon looked at his wife, who nodded, and with a lurch of weight in her gut Clare realised what he was about to say. Her limbs went light and she closed her eyes against the sudden sense of dizziness.

'About that,' Simon began.

She had never heard him sound so tentative.

Mrs Chapman swivelled her eyes to him and raised her chin in challenge. 'Yes?'

'I've arranged for a couple of them to come and work on the farm to help with the sugar beet and potatoes.'

Walter's mother tensed. Laying down her knife and fork, she placed them neatly next to each other with extravagant care as though she were in a fancy London restaurant. A muscle in her cheek began to twitch and she dabbed at her lips with a napkin before she looked at him again.

'Then you'll need to unarrange it.'

Simon ran the tip of his tongue across his lips.

'Germans coming here?' Henry shouted. 'No! They killed Uncle Walter ...'

'We're not having them here for tea.' Simon's answer was

testy. 'They'll be working in the fields. The land girls have gone elsewhere and we need all the help we can get.'

'No.' Mrs Chapman fixed him with a gaze he could not hold.

He lowered his eyes away but he stuck to his guns. 'We can't bring in the potatoes and beet without them.'

'I'd rather die than let a single German set foot on this land. How dare you go behind my back?'

'It was the War Ag, Mum,' Bridget said.

The War Agricultural Executive Committee, she meant, who had controlled every acre of every farm in England since the war began. Clare wondered if Bridget was telling the truth or if it was merely a lie to placate Mrs Chapman.

'They could take the farm away from us if we don't comply.'

'Then let them take it.'

Simon shook his head with a new sense of resolution. Clare saw the shift in the change of his posture, the set of his jaw.

'I run this farm now,' he said. 'And I decide who works on it. I'm not going to let them take it away because you're too stubborn to take help when it's offered.' He sat back in his chair and folded his arms across the stained woollen waistcoat he always wore.

The kitchen held its breath. Every gaze was intent upon Mrs Chapman except for Eric, who was still studying his plate. Clare laid an automatic hand on his arm and he looked up at her in surprise before he shifted his head to follow the line of his mother's sight.

'No Germans, Grandma,' he said into the hush. 'Isn't that right? No Germans.' Then he got up with such haste that the chair tipped behind him with a crash onto the flagstones. His shoes pattered on the stone as he ran for the stairs and took them two at a time, thundering overhead, the bedroom door shutting with a slam.

Clare closed her eyes for a moment of indecision.

'Even the boy understands. He loved his father.' Mrs Chapman swung an accusing gaze towards her daughter-in-law. 'More than you, evidently. What's your opinion? Should we let the enemy farm our land for us?'

Clare shook her head, words catching in her throat, tears too close to the surface to risk a single word of speech. The bitter taste of vomit rose in her throat. It was not her decision to make. Not her farm. Reassured that her opinion of Clare was correct, Mrs Chapman brought her gaze back to Simon, now as much her enemy as any German.

'The farm is still in my name,' she said. 'I still make the decisions.'

'The War Ag makes the decisions, Mum,' Bridget countered, and Simon nodded his agreement. 'It's not up to us.'

'They won't be allowed to talk to us or to do anything but work. They won't be coming near the house, Ma,' Simon tried to reassure her, but she rounded on him with a venom in her look that Clare had never seen before.

'I'm not your ma,' she hissed, 'and I never have been.'

She got up from the table with surprising dignity and followed her grandson up the narrow flight of stairs towards the bedrooms overhead. They heard her pacing to and fro, the floorboards creaking and the sounds carrying easily through the plasterwork. No one spoke until Bridget told Henry and Lizzie they were excused. They scrambled down and took their plates to the kitchen before disappearing into other parts of the house, eager to escape the tension.

Bridget began to clear up the remaining detritus, and lit the stove for more tea. Simon let out a sigh. 'We've got no choice,' he said, in the end. 'It makes no odds what any of us thinks about it.'

Clare watched her sister-in-law as she collected plates and dishes, hands deft with quick, sure movements. Long, elegant fingers like her brother, Clare observed again. The image of her dream flickered through her thoughts, and she forced her mind to close against it. She didn't want German soldiers on the farm any more than Walter's mother did.

'If we've got no choice then there's nothing more we can do,' she said. 'She'll have to come round.'

Bridget flicked a glance upwards to the ceiling. The pacing had stopped.

'When are they are coming?'

'Tomorrow morning.'

'So soon?' She drew in a deep breath to steady herself against the rush of dread that rippled through her, and the raw nerve that the prisoner had touched that morning began to burn again. Bridget passed her a cup of tea and she took it with a smile of thanks, letting her fingers play against the warm porcelain, something to focus on.

'Sounds like Eric's got a good arm on him,' Simon said finally. 'Does he like cricket?'

'Walter was a good batsman,' Bridget said. 'He got a blue at Oxford.'

'Chip off the old block, eh?'

Clare gave him a weary smile of agreement. She should be marking the children's books, she thought, and preparing for tomorrow's lessons, but there was an inertia at work inside her that she couldn't shake off. Tomorrow morning the enemy would be at the farm and she was uncertain how she would face it, so she stayed at the table doing nothing for the rest of the evening.

Clare woke abruptly, startled into wakefulness by some unknown force. Beyond the window the day was just beginning, grey light filtering across the sky, but she could already hear the trudge of Simon's boots across the yard and the clank of the milk bucket. She had slept badly, but with the first light of the morning the dreams that had disturbed her night faded mercifully out of memory. Rolling out of bed, she dressed hurriedly in the chill and went downstairs where the warmth of the kitchen was welcome. It was empty, but the kettle was hissing on the stove, and the table was laid with bread and butter and a jar of last year's strawberry jam. She poured some tea, ate a slice of bread, and kept her eyes averted from the window: if the Germans were there she would prefer not to see them.

She went early to work to prepare for the day, cycling along the lane between the hedgerows. The morning was damp and cool, and lit by a pale sun that glimmered behind a patchy screen of cloud. A low mist hovered across the fields, just starting to lift with the first warmth of the day. She had hoped that movement would help to ease the sense of dread that dragged at her limbs but she still found herself peering over the hedges to search for signs of the prisoners already at work.

She had almost reached the first houses of the village when she saw the little party walking towards her in the lane. She stopped and looked about her for an escape, but there was nowhere at all to hide – she would have to pass them on the narrow road. Her heartbeat quickened and her breath came short as the distance between them lessened. Getting off the bike, she shifted to the edge of the verge where the ground was rough and uneven underfoot.

The figures of the men settled into clearer focus. Four of them were walking two abreast with a British army guard in front, a different man from the callow corporal of the day before. They walked casually, not marching, which surprised her – they were still soldiers of the German army after all. But they walked in silence and though she wanted more than anything to turn her head away, her gaze was drawn against her will towards them – curiosity and loathing in equal measure.

'Morning, miss.' The guard slowed his pace as he approached. He held his rifle at the ready and for an instant she saw herself taking it from him and mowing down the prisoners right here in the lane, before she squashed the image flat, shocked at herself. Perhaps she was not so unlike Walter's mother after all.

'Morning,' she managed to reply, though her throat was parched and the word came out as little more than a croak. She wondered if he even heard it.

'Rowan Farm this way, is it? Got some workers for them.'

She nodded and let her eyes drift towards the little group of prisoners. The same man as yesterday met her gaze. Green eyes, she noticed this time, that looked at her with unnerving intensity. Fine blond hair framed a face with features that were regular and neat except for the cut on his cheekbone and the dark bruise that was spreading underneath it. He didn't look like a monster. None of them did, she realised. They were just regular men caught on the wrong side of the argument. But still, their actions had brought the world to its knees and taken Walter away from her, and she was not ready to forgive them for that.

She lowered her eyes to the rough ground at her feet and walked on without another word. The tread of the prisoners dwindled quickly into silence behind her, but she could not shake her thoughts free of the image of that man and the way he seemed to look right into her, exposing every nerve. Angry with him for the way he made her feel and with herself for allowing it to happen, she got back on the bike and pedalled hard for the last little bit of the journey through the village; by the time she arrived at the school, she was sweating.

Chapter Seven

The men trudged on along the lane and Max cast a single glance behind him at the retreating figure of the woman – the teacher who had stopped the children throwing stones the day before. It was almost laughable to be wounded by an English child so long after he'd been captured. Then he recalled the hatred in the boy's face and the teacher's words – *some of these children have lost fathers* – and the wry smile he had allowed himself died on his lips.

He let his thoughts return to the image of the woman: her look had been harder to read than the boy's. A studied coldness to mask the feelings underneath, he guessed. He had unsettled her, he was sure, though he couldn't say for certain why. He only knew he wanted to see her again with a ferocity that was visceral, his insides burning with need. It had been a long time since he had desired a woman, longer still since he last saw his wife on the platform at *Anhalter-Bahnhof*, the final farewell. The memory of it flickered through his thoughts, but the images were so broken and incomplete that it was hard to recall the details of her face to mind. He could only remember the tears in her eyes and the determined tilt of her chin as she struggled not to let them fall.

Not long afterwards her letters had stopped and there had been no more news of her since. Nothing about his daughter, Hanna. Nothing from anyone. It was as if his whole life before the war had been simply wiped away.

The work party turned off the road and down a lane between two fields that were lined with winter-clad hedgerows. He knew nothing about farming – he had lived his whole life in the city until the army swept him away from it, but the crop either side looked like potatoes to him and he suspected a back-breaking day ahead. Inwardly, he sighed.

Beside him, his friend Theo turned and rolled his eyes. 'Well, at least no one's shooting at us,' he murmured, and Max smiled in answer.

'At least there's that.'

The corporal called them to a halt and they waited while he went ahead through the gate that led into the farmyard. Max looked around him. A grey stone farmhouse occupied one side of a large cobbled yard, and sheds and barns and outhouses of various size and age made up a rough square around it. A carthorse with a white stripe on its nose leaned out of a loose box to watch the newcomers with interest, ears flicking, and an old sheepdog lifted its head, tail thumping on the ground.

The corporal spoke to the farmer, who looked over the workers with a cursory glance, and did not introduce himself. Later, they would learn his name was Woodman. He was a rough-looking man in his early forties, Max judged, unkempt, with dirt-stained clothes and a chin that was dark with stubble. He touched his own freshly-shaved face with his fingertips. He was clean for the first time in months. There had been hot water at the camp that morning; the shower and shave after so long without had felt like heaven, and though the repurposed British uniform was scratchy and ill-fitting it had been freshly laundered before it was given to him: he could still smell the perfume of the soap they had used.

The men waited by the gate – patience became second nature in the army and nothing much had changed in that regard except the orders came from the enemy now. But though Max gazed across the farmyard as though the words meant nothing to him, he listened intently. Only Theo knew of his fluency in English.

'*Kartoffeln?*' Theo asked. Potatoes?

'*Kartoffeln,*' Max replied.

Exchanging a rueful glance with his friend, he followed the corporal into the muddy field and the men bent to begin their work.

'I had a letter from Bertie!' Susan's eyes were alight when she rushed into the staffroom just as Clare was going to ring the bell. 'Three, actually! Three came at once. Can you believe it?'

'That's wonderful.' Susan's delight was infectious, and Clare found herself grinning at her friend, the bell silent and forgotten in her hand.

'How is he? Where is he?'

'Somewhere in France,' Susan shrugged. 'He's a bit vague about the details.'

'Of course.' She remembered Walter's early letters with whole sentences blacked out by the censor. When she told him about it in her replies he had become more careful, leaving hints instead like a treasure trail for her to follow. He had always written marvellous letters, perceptive and wry, and she had kept every one of them. They lived in a wooden box her father had given her as a child for her precious things, and she kept it on the top shelf of her wardrobe along with the little sketchbook and sticks of charcoal that she had not used for far too long. Through the months of his absence those letters had kept her world together but since the telegram she had not been able to bring herself to open it except to place inside the single unopened letter that came after his death.

'But he's in good spirits,' Susan went on. 'I don't know how they do it, really. Face such horrors and not fall to pieces. I'm not sure I'd be joking in my letters home if I were in his shoes.'

'Walter wrote once that it's the camaraderie that makes it possible, the desire not to let down your friends.'

Susan looked doubtful. 'Hmm, perhaps. But even still – I'm not sure not wanting to let you down would make me laugh in the face of danger.'

Clare laughed. 'Then it's lucky it's Bertie over there and not you.'

'Yes,' Susan agreed, with a smile. 'Isn't it just.' Then, 'Speaking of danger, hadn't you better ring that bell before the old bat notices the time?'

Clare gave another little laugh, tightened her grip around the handle of the bell and, with a nod, she headed out into the playground to start the day.

The hours dragged. She was weary from the sleepless night and her patience with the children teetered on a knife edge. By the afternoon she could feel the edges of her temper fraying, her thoughts returning again and again to the party of prisoners at the farm, treading on Chapman land with their German boots, unwelcome. Would they still be there when she got home?

When the day finished at last, she lingered in the staffroom longer than she needed. Reluctant to make the journey home, she hoped that by being late she might avoid seeing the prisoners again. Then she was afraid that if she left it too late she might meet them on the road, so she gathered up her things in a rush and hastened out into the gathering darkness.

Late October, and the nights were drawing in. In the city she had loved this time of year – the lights in the houses, the mist, cups of cocoa before the fire, and Walter's body warm next to hers in the soft double bed. But in the relentless grind of the farm the change of season merely brought darker mornings, and a house too cold to stray far from the kitchen fireplace so that the whole family was trapped together in the one room that was warm.

Eric had long since gone home from school in the company of his cousins. When they first arrived to live at the farm he had waited for her to walk home together so they could spend time just the two of them as they were used to. But he was no longer afraid of the village children: he had found his place among them and his mother's company held no more attraction. She supposed she should be proud that he was growing up and becoming independent, but she missed his rambling tales and the big questions about the workings of the world he used to ask of her, questions that could sometimes shift her own perspective on the way of things. Why do we dream? Does God plan out our life in advance or can we make choices for ourselves? They were the kind of questions that she had talked about with Walter in the early days of their courtship, before the day-to-day matters of a life together began to take precedence – family, work, the house. Did Eric's mind still travel down those paths, unspoken? Or had he abandoned such musings altogether? She couldn't say.

She glanced up to the darkening sky, and hoped she would make it home before the last light left it. The fields either side were growing dim in the gloom beyond the hedgerows, and the sudden caw of a rook taking flight from a tree overhead made her jump. Her heart hammered, nerves on edge.

She was not far from the farm when she heard the approaching trudge of boots in the lane. The prisoners, she realised. She had come just too late to miss them altogether, but in the soft-falling dark perhaps she could pass by them all but unnoticed. She hopped off the bike and moved to walk on the verge again, her gaze lowered to the ground just in front of her feet. In another moment she saw them, their forms large and misshapen in the gloom, and she gave an involuntary shiver of anticipation. But this time they did not slow at her approach and she hurried past them without even so much as a word of greeting to the corporal, though she heard him call out a *'good evening'* as he went by. Afterwards she felt guilty for her rudeness – it was not his fault, after all.

When she reached the farm she struggled with the gate, the latch sticking and immovable however hard she tried until she was almost crying with frustration. It was Bridget who came to her rescue, crossing the yard on her way back from feeding scraps to the chickens, the empty bucket swinging from one hand.

'Thank you,' Clare breathed, as the gate swung open to let her through with the bike. 'It just wouldn't open.'

'I know. It does that sometimes. It needs fixing.' She sighed, and cast a look around the yard. 'Like most other things ...'

They stood together in the almost-dark for a moment.

'How's it been today?' asked Clare. There was no need for her to clarify her meaning.

Bridget shook her head with a shrug and the now familiar ripple of depression filtered through Clare's insides.

I just want to go home, she thought. Back to the vicarage. Back to how things were in my old life with Walter.

Simon's voice at the farmhouse door cut through the gloom. 'Bridget? Where are you?' There was an edge of impatience in his voice. 'Hurry up, would you!'

'Coming!' Bridget called back, and the two women hurried across the yard towards the warmth of the house.

Chapter Eight

The kitchen was warm after the chilly evening outside and filled with the inviting aroma of some kind of stew. Rabbit again, she suspected. It was the meat they ate most these days – she couldn't remember ever having eaten it at all before the war. She hung her coat on the hook by the door. The children were sitting at the table with their school books spread across it and briefly she thought that she should ask them if they needed any help, but she couldn't summon the energy and let the thought drop away as she went to the sink to wash her hands. Eric barely lifted his head to acknowledge her presence as she passed him, just touching his shoulder as she went. He was starting to get sullen, she had noticed – she supposed he was missing his father's guiding hand. Mrs Chapman was at the stove, stirring the stew. If she heard Clare arrive she showed no sign of it, her attention never shifting from the pot in front of her.

'Time to lay the table,' Bridget announced, joining Clare at the sink.

There was a clatter behind them as the children closed their books and scrambled from their chairs. The two women exchanged a smile.

A few minutes later and Mrs Chapman was serving dinner. Everyone began to eat as soon as their plate was in front of them and it still felt wrong to Clare not to wait for grace to be said; in her mind she still always murmured a brief prayer of thanks. It was no more than habit really, but it brought Walter's voice to her thoughts, so she could imagine for that moment he was with her still. Eric had stopped hesitating long ago – like most children of his generation, he had learned that the first to finish was the most likely to get seconds. She watched him as he wolfed his food, one eye on the progress of the others. He had put on weight since they moved from the city, their diet in the country less constrained by rationing – eggs and milk and rabbit were plentiful here. He looked healthy and strong, and for that at least she was glad.

'How did everything go today?' she asked no one in particular, and she felt the tension tighten around the room.

'They're good workers, I'll say that for 'em,' Simon replied, without looking up from his food. 'They work hard. If they keep it up, we'll have the potatoes in by the weekend.'

'That's good news.'

'Your father must be turning in his grave.' Mrs Chapman raised her head to look at her daughter, chin lifted as if daring Bridget to disagree.

Bridget said nothing and Clare observed the effort it took in the almost imperceptible flicker in Bridget's eyes and the deliberation of her movements as the fork paused briefly in its journey to her lips.

'He'd want the potatoes in one way or another,' Simon replied. 'That much is for sure.'

'What do you know about what he would want?'

'He was a farmer through and through. The land was everything. It would have killed him to see a crop rotting in the ground when there were hands available to harvest it. He wouldn't have hesitated to use those men.'

'It's for the war effort, Grandma.' It was Lizzie, the peace-maker. 'If we don't have enough food we can never win the war. Isn't that right, Mummy?' She turned to Bridget, who nodded.

'That's right, Lizzie.'

'Even the little girl can see the sense in it, Ma.'

Clare flinched. Simon was enjoying himself, deliberately provoking Mrs Chapman now, and she wished that he wouldn't. Things were bad enough already.

Walter's mother turned her gaze to Clare across the table. 'What do you think, Clare? Are you happy to have the men here that murdered your husband?'

All eyes turned to her, even the children, and she flushed beneath the sudden attention, skin flaring with heat, heart quickening.

'I don't like it,' she managed to say. 'Of course I don't. But it can't be helped. We're at war.'

Mrs Chapman turned away, her nose wrinkling in disgust. 'If only Walter were running the farm …'

'And I was the one who got killed instead?' Simon's tone was harsh. 'Or Bridget? Is that what you're saying?'

Mrs Chapman's eyes widened briefly and she drew in an audible breath. Clare felt an unexpected wash of pity. She remembered her own surge of hatred at the memorial service, visceral and almost overwhelming, and she knew how tempting it was to get caught in the weeds of *if only*: she had found herself there far too many times not to feel a flutter of sympathy.

'That's not what she meant,' she heard herself saying, and it was Walter's voice in her head.

Mrs Chapman turned to her in surprise.

'She just wishes Walter were here, that's all. The same as the rest of us.'

'I don't think that *is* what she meant,' Simon replied. 'But have it your way. No point in arguing with a woman…'

Clare and Bridget exchanged a glance and in the pause that followed Clare told the children to take their plates to the sink.

'What about seconds?'

'Plates,' Mrs Chapman said in a voice that brooked no dissent, and, still grumbling, the children did as they were told.

'Stupid bloody woman!' Simon's hiss carried through the door of the bedroom as Clare made her way along the landing from the bathroom in the dark. She halted, listening against her will. 'And you're no better.'

There was a thud. Then silence. Clare waited a moment more but hearing nothing else, she hurried to the safety of her bedroom and closed the door. Throwing her dressing gown across the end of the bed, she slipped under the covers, the sheets icy against her toes. At the vicarage she would have made herself a hot-water bottle for a night like this, but at Rowan Farm only invalids and old folk were entitled to such comforts, as if suffering for its own sake were a virtue. Walter would have scoffed and boiled the water for her himself, saying God had no need of such pointless sacrifices. The thought made her smile as she huddled, shivering, under the quilt that had once covered them both. Then she listened for voices, straining to hear Simon's whispering from along the landing, but the house was quiet and she was aware again of its loneliness. She still missed the constant hum of the city she had grown up with, the liveliness of so many people in close proximity. The knowledge of the nearness of others had always reassured her, a reminder she was part of something greater than herself. But at the farm the silence was almost eerie and she wondered again if she would ever get used to it, or if she even wanted to. She still hankered to return to the city, had not yet given up hope that in time she would, but as she drifted off finally to sleep her last thought was to wonder how.

. . .

In the morning Bridget came into the kitchen from the yard as Clare was about to leave for work. The children had gone to brush their teeth and for a moment they were alone.

'Is everything all right?' Clare asked, her voice low.

'Yes,' Bridget answered too quickly. 'Everything's fine. Why do you ask?'

'I just ...' She trailed off with a shrug. Now that it came to it her suspicions seemed absurd. She had probably imagined it. She said, 'What Simon said yesterday about arguing ... I just thought perhaps there was more to it.'

Bridget ran the tip of her tongue across her lower lip and her gaze tracked something in the yard beyond the window. Clare saw the hesitation.

'Bridget?' she said gently. 'Is everything all right?'

The other woman drew in a deep breath and lifted her face to her friend.

'Yes,' she replied, 'everything is fine. Thank you.'

Clare didn't answer but she knew from the evasive way Bridget's eyes slid away that everything was anything but fine. Perhaps she would confide in her another time. Perhaps she was not ready yet.

'I've got to go to work,' she said.

'I'll see you later.'

Clare picked up the heavy bag with the children's exercise books and put it over her shoulder. The strap dug uncomfortably into her flesh as she went across the yard to fetch her bike. Heaving it into the basket on the front, she walked the bicycle through the gate and into the lane.

The prisoners were already bent to the earth at work in the fields as she cycled past, marked out by the great red diamonds on their uniforms. Clare kept her head bowed so as not to have to look at them, and the low pale sun glinted off the dampness of the road, almost blinding her.

. . .

Max's back ached from the work and he straightened up for a moment to stretch the soreness of his muscles, looking out across the rolling fields. It was a soft autumn morning, damp and cool with a watery sun that hung above the treetops. The other prisoners were spread out across the field of potatoes and he observed them briefly, these new companions who would be his world now for God knew how long. So far, they were all right. A mixed bag in age and experience but no one yet that set alarm bells ringing. He flicked a glance to the corporal who was guarding them as he lounged against the gate with his rifle propped on the bars, gazing into the sky. It was cushy work for a soldier, Max thought, when his comrades were fighting and dying in France.

It would be easy to escape. The hedgerows offered good cover, their branches thickly knotted even in their leafless state. He would be long gone on his way before the sleepy corporal noticed he was missing. But where would he go? Even if he could find a boat to France he would only meet more Allied soldiers when he got there. The war was going badly for the Germans. Aachen had fallen and the Allies were on German soil now – it was only a matter of time until it was over. All that hubris. All that national pride. For what? How many more would have to die before Hitler surrendered? It was madness – Germany was done for. Hitler had gambled and lost, and millions had paid with their lives.

Max rubbed at the sore point in his lower back with his fingertips but it made no difference to the ache. He was getting soft, he thought, and old before his time. He allowed himself a wry smile – it was almost impossible to remember the man he had been before all of this.

A sudden bright flicker of colour beyond the gate drew his eyes towards the lane that bordered the field. The corporal had awoken from his reverie and turned to look too; Max saw him nod his head as the woman cycled past. She was wearing a deep-red coat and a wool hat that covered her hair. It was the teacher, and warmth flared inside him. He waited, hoping she would turn towards them, that he might get another glimpse of her face, but she kept her head resolutely forward and cycled quickly past.

Some of these children have lost fathers, she had said, and he wondered if her own child had been one of them.

Then, with a last look along the lane towards the woman's disappearing back, he sighed, and bent once more to the soil.

Chapter Nine

By December, two of the prisoners had become a more or less permanent fixture on the farm, and the flash of the red diamonds on their backs was a familiar sight as Clare made her way to and from the village. She still turned her head away whenever she passed them but the flutter of dread at seeing them had begun to wane, and she no longer felt the rush of emotion that they had first evoked.

Simon began to refer to them by name, so that they were no longer simply the prisoners or the Germans, but Max from Berlin and Theo from Hamburg. Now and then, she knew, he gave them a few potatoes or an egg or two to supplement their meagre rations at the camp, despite the laws against it. You could be heavily fined for as little as a conversation beyond the needs of the job, and the papers had recently reported on a couple of nurses who had lost their jobs for a single moment of kindness. At all times the prisoners remained the enemy.

They were just men after all, Clare tried to remind herself. Men caught on the wrong side of history. Walter would have forgiven them in a moment yet, though she strove to find it in her own heart to absolve them, she could find no way past the grief and the rage that were lodged there. Walter had been a saint, she decided, and she in all her human frailty could never hope to match his capacity for love – she hated every single German in existence for all that they had done. Not just for making her a widow but for all the death and destruction, for every single life that had been lost to the war.

But for all that she hated them, their presence settled into a part of her everyday life. The little work parties walking through the village at the start and end of each day. The lorries that took them to the farms further afield, lurching over the potholes. The flash of the patches on their uniforms against the dark winter earth as they toiled in the fields. She had to admit they were quiet and respectful, far more so in fact than the Americans who had roared into their lives a few months before with their cocky confidence and jeeps, handing out gum and chocolate for the children and stockings for the girls. The kids had loved them, of course: they had brought glamour and excitement to the sleepy village, and when they finally left to ship out to France the sudden return to peace had been surprisingly hard to get used to.

With the prisoners it was a different kind of invasion. The Germans existed at the very edges of the villagers' lives, always there as a constant reminder of their losses and their grief, and though the children soon lost interest once they understood the Germans were not the monsters they had imagined them to be but merely men like any other men, a residual hostility still lingered, a sense of us and them, and Clare was glad of the restrictions that kept them apart.

The men had been ditching all day and Max's feet were numb with cold. The wheelbarrow at the ditch's edge was full to the brim with choking weeds and, with a final shovelful of dirt, the water began to flow more freely at last. Max clambered out and stood at the edge of the field looking out across the countryside, shielding his eyes against the pale sun that glinted behind the clouds, low above the treetops.

In the quiet of the afternoon he could hear the high-pitched voices of the farm children playing beyond the hedge by the river. Instinctively he touched the little scar on his cheek from the stone the boy had thrown. They had met face to face once or twice since then, crossing paths in the lane, but they had looked away from each other, eyes averted. He didn't blame the boy – he guessed he would have done the same at that age – but the recollection of the hatred in the boy's eyes that day still cut him to the core.

A pair of crows landed on the fresh-ploughed earth close by and the sun lit their feathers so that they shone a metallic blue-green. He watched them for a moment and one of them turned towards him, head tilted, assessing. He gave the bird a smile and it stalked away, as if reassured. For that moment Max was alone – the guarding corporal had disappeared to check on his other charges in other fields – and he lifted his head to the gleaming sky, drinking in the peace, the war a far-off, half-forgotten impossibility. The silence was beguiling.

The silence.

He realised with a start that caught in his gut that he could no longer hear the voices of the children, and he spun towards the gap in the hedge he knew they used as their gateway to the riverbank. He hadn't seen them come back that way. An instinctive thread of fear quickened his pulse, and as he dropped the spade atop the wheelbarrow and took a step towards the hedge, a sudden shout rang out, high with panic.

'Help! Somebody help!'

His instincts had been right. Max broke into a run and forced his way through the narrow opening, oblivious to the scratch of the branches against his hands and face as pushed them out of his way. On the other side of the hedge he paused for a breath to take in the scene.

A grassy bank sloped away to meet the slow-moving river that was frozen at its edge. The boys were kneeling close to the water, too close, and trying to reach out across the strip of ice. The little girl was nowhere to be seen. He ran down the slope and the two boys turned in startlement. If they hated him now they didn't show it, too relieved, he supposed, by the presence of a grown-up.

'What's happened?'

'Lizzie fell in – she can't swim.'

Max stripped off his jacket and boots. Then, tensing against the cold, he waded into the water and the shock of it took his breath away. It was surprisingly deep, and he had to tense against the current that pressed against his legs, threatening to take his balance. Behind him he could hear the boys shouting but he had already seen the slight ripples on the surface of the water and the bubbles coming up. With a deep breath, he dropped under the surface. In the murk he could barely see more than a few inches in front of him, but he struck out in the direction of the ripples he had seen. For a moment he saw nothing but the grey-green water and deeper darkness beyond. He blinked, trying to clear his vision as he peered harder into the gloom. Nothing. He swam forward again. Stopped, wheeled slowly, still searching. His lungs began to burn with the need for air. One more turn, and then he saw her – a pale flash of hair. With two strokes he reached her – her arms flailing, her eyes wide with terror. And in one more, he caught her in his arm. A moment later they broke the surface with a gasp, spluttering in the air. The cold closed vice-like against his head, the air painful in his chest, and by the time he had dragged them both clear of the river and on to the safety of the bank he was wracked with shivers. The girl vomited up a burst of water and began to cry. Max almost laughed with relief – she was going to be all right. But he had to get her into the warm.

'We need to take her home,' he said to the boys, shoving his feet back into his boots before he bent to scoop the girl into his arms. She clung to him, wrapping her legs about his waist and her arms around his neck. He could feel the cold wet of her face against his neck, and a sudden memory of carrying his own daughter the same way almost felled him. Hanna. His beautiful girl. He shook his head to clear it.

The boys sprinted along the riverbank towards the farm's back gate. One of them swung it open to let them through while the other raced on ahead towards the house. It was hard going on the uneven ground and though the girl was not heavy, Max's arms began to ache, the air cold in his lungs.

At the door of the farmhouse he hesitated. He knew he was not welcome here. He wanted to give the child to someone else and slink away unnoticed but the boy who had thrown the stone looked back at him over his shoulder.

'It's all right,' he said. 'You can come in. You saved Lizzie's life.'

Max gave the boy a nod and followed him through the door into a large low-ceilinged kitchen that was warm from a good fire in the hearth and steamy from the pots that were cooking on a paraffin stove. There was a welcoming aroma of meat and herbs, and Max remembered he was hungry. But he was always hungry, the camp rations only just enough to keep the men going.

'Mum! Dad!' The older boy was shouting for his parents.

A door opened. Woodman strode across the kitchen and took the girl from Max without a word. The farmer was the only person at the farm that Max had ever spoken to, the only contact he was allowed. He watched from the doorway as two women, one older, one younger, laid the child on an armchair drawn close to the hearth and fussed over her, and though his whole body shuddered with cold, he dared not move closer to the fire.

Then the teacher appeared. He didn't see where she came from and she too stood for a moment on the outside of the group by the hearth, watching. She looked different today, in a thread-bare apron and her hair tied up in a scarf, but she still looked as though she did not belong on a farm.

'Is she going to be all right?' the boy who had thrown the stone asked no one in particular. 'Should we get Dr Lewis?'

'She's going to be fine,' the teacher said. Then, with visible effort, she turned towards Max. 'Come to the fire, get warm. You must be frozen.'

He hesitated. The older woman left off her fussing over the girl and got to her feet.

'Get him out of here!' She did not even turn towards him.

'He saved Lizzie's life!' The teacher lifted her chin, defiant, and he tried to work out the relationships – who belonged to whom.

'I don't care. I'm not having a German at my hearth.'

There was a silence. The farmer and the other woman were too absorbed in the care of the little girl to pay any attention. The child's parents, he assumed, and the older woman must be the grandmother. So who was the teacher? Where did she fit in?

'I'll find you some dry clothes,' she said, and made for the stairs.

He was uncertain if she meant for him to follow her but he wanted to be out from under the older woman's rage, and so he went up the stairs behind her, his arms folded around himself, trying vainly to control the shivering. When she turned off the passage through a doorway he followed her, and once inside the room she swung round in surprise that he was behind her. He heard the sharp intake of her breath and saw her sudden awkwardness at being alone with him, the tension in her movements. He hovered by the door and she threw him a towel that smelled sweetly of soap as he rubbed at his head and his arms until a burning warmth of feeling began to return. He cast a glance around the room. They were in her bedroom, he realised; no wonder she was awkward – she had led him to her bedroom. It was an old-fashioned room with dark and heavy furniture, faded reproductions on the walls, and he understood by instinct that it was not a room she had chosen for herself.

He watched as she knelt at a wooden trunk that was set below the window, and sorted through the carefully folded clothes, neatly wrapped in linen. A faint scent of lavender touched the air.

He towelled roughly at his hair. Eventually she got up and turned towards him with a shirt and pair of trousers in her hands.

'Do you speak English?' she asked.

'A little.' The lie was instinctive and he regretted it immediately.

'These were my husband's.' She held out the clothes. 'You may as well have them.'

'What happened to him?'

'He was killed at Caen.' He heard the effort in the words, her tone devoid of emotion. 'Do you know it?'

He nodded. 'I was there.'

The possibility hung in the room between them, unspoken but acknowledged by them both. Max stepped forward and took the clothes from her, feeling the quality of the linen in his fingers. He refused to allow himself to think of the dead man who had owned them as he began to peel off his uniform, eager for the dry warmth of fresh clothes.

The woman stared, disconcerted, and he saw her observe his pale wet body, her gaze sliding over the vivid scar at his shoulder before she turned away abruptly and went back to the window to stare out at the fields behind the house. He dressed as quickly as he could then stood, feeling awkward as he waited for her to turn to him again, his wet clothes held in a ball in his hands.

Finally, she must have judged she had given him long enough because she turned from the window to face back into the room. The light was growing dim in the fast-falling evening, and he wanted to close the door behind him, so that it could be just the two of them alone in the half-dark.

'We should go down,' she said, as if she had read his thoughts.

'You'll be in trouble with your guard.' Then she held out her hands for his uniform. 'I'll take those. I can dry them for you.'

He paused, knowing he should keep them. He could just as easily dry them on the stove at the camp, but he wanted her to take them so that he could have a reason to see her again, to talk to her. He handed them over. 'Thank you.'

She nodded towards the door and they went out together into the gloom of the passage. At the top of the stairs he turned back towards her and she stopped mid-step, surprised.

'What's your name?'

She looked away as though considering whether or not to tell him. Even asking for it was against the rules, but he had already broken so many rules today he no longer cared.

'Clare Chapman.' Her voice was a whisper, aware of the family in the room just below.

'Max Peterson.'

They stood close together for a moment at the head of the stairs in the reflected flicker of the light from downstairs. Then she held out her hand, the English habit of courtesy hard to break even with a man who might have killed her husband. He took it gently, her fingers small and cold against his palm, and bowed his head. To his immense pleasure she blushed, heat flaring over the pale skin.

'Danke schön,' he murmured, and was surprised when she gave the German response.

'Bitte.'

He let her hand go and turned and went downstairs.

Clare did not follow him, but remained at the top of the stairs with the sopping clothes in her arms and listened to the commotion at his reappearance: the British corporal shouting and gruff, Eric's staunch defence of the man who had saved Lizzie's life, and

Simon arguing with Mrs Chapman whose voice grew shrill with fury when she realised the German was still in the house.

She found herself smiling at her son's innate sense of justice, and thought how proud his father would have been. Slowly the arguments faded to a stop and when she heard the sound of the men's boots finally dwindling into silence across the yard and the squeak and scrape of the gate, she set her foot on the stairs and went down to the kitchen.

'What did you do?' Walter's mother almost launched herself across the kitchen.

'I gave him some dry clothes.' Clare's voice was surprisingly calm and she held the older woman's gaze with a steadfast look in spite of the dryness of her mouth and the rapid tapping of her heart.

'You gave him Walter's clothes?'

'They're no more use to Walter,' she snapped, and though she knew the whole kitchen was staring at her with shock, she gripped the little bundle of wet uniform tightly in her hands, marched through to the door at the back of the kitchen, and did not stop until she reached the ramshackle laundry building with its old stone basin and the rusting mangle beside it. Only then did she realise she was standing in the dark and had not thought to bring a lamp.

Letting the wet clothes slide into the basin, she leaned on its edge and stared down into it, head light from the confrontation, unfamiliar emotions roiling inside her. Max Peterson. Her thoughts lingered on the name. It was impossible that she could like him, but she could not rid her mind of the image of his half-naked body in the bedroom, his skin sleek with damp, and the vivid scar, muscles taut and strong. His green eyes had held hers with an intensity she realised now was hunger, and a rush of guilt washed over her for taking pleasure in the knowledge.

A footstep behind her made her spin round from the basin, on edge and easily startled. It was Bridget with an oil lamp in her hand, and her face was ghostly in the flickering glow.

'How's Lizzie?' Clare said.

'She'll be fine. I think she's enjoying the attention to be honest.' She gave a tired smile. 'It was lucky he was there.'

Clare nodded, still not quite sure of Bridget's loyalties. Her sister-in-law gave little of her own thoughts away, a defence, Clare supposed, against the clash between her mother and her husband. It must be a hard place to occupy and Clare did not envy her.

'How's your mum?'

Bridget let out a long low breath and shrugged. 'You know how she is. She's not happy you gave him Walter's things.'

'He saved Lizzie's life and he was frozen to the bone.'

'Yes, but still …'

So Bridget agreed with her mother. Clare said nothing.

'They would have been better given to Simon if you were giving them away.'

The two women stood in silence for a moment, and Clare shivered. The night was cold and she had no coat. Bridget cast a glance to the basin.

'Are you going to wash his uniform?' Her tone was incredulous.

'Yes,' Clare replied. 'I thought it was the least I could do.'

'But he's a German!'

'He saved Lizzie's life,' Clare repeated, 'And Walter would have given him the shirt from his own back without a second thought.'

Walter's sister stared, though Clare had only spoken the truth. Then, without another word, Bridget spun in the doorway and half walked, half ran across the small yard towards the house. Clare watched her go, saw the back door open and close with a glimpse of the light and warmth inside. Then, with another shiver, she turned on the tap to fill the basin and began to wash out the sodden uniform.

. . .

For three days Clare vacillated. She hung the prisoner's clothes away from the house where her mother-in-law would not see and they dried hard and stiff in the crisp cold air, so she ironed them to softness when no one was around to notice. She wanted to give them back to him herself and feel the warmth of his gaze on her again, the touch of his hand, but guilt for her feelings and the sense of duty that had always made her live her life within the rules until now, weighed against it. And she was afraid of getting caught. Conversation with prisoners of war carried heavy fines and public shame. She was already in trouble enough for the small kindness she had shown him – her mother-in-law hadn't spoken a single word to her since. So she swung between what she wanted to do and what she should, and in the end the latter won out. She would deliver the uniform to the surly guard and make herself forget all about Max Peterson.

It was a cold hard morning when she set out after breakfast, the uniform neatly folded and tied in a bundle, wrapped in a towel under her arm. A watery sun lit the clouds and the mud in the lane had frozen overnight. It would be cold work ditching today.

On one side of the lane the fields sloped away into a shallow valley where the river ran and she stood at the first gate she came to, sweeping her gaze across the countryside, searching. Far off to the south she could just make out figures working against the dark ploughed earth, but she could see neither the corporal nor the prisoners. She climbed up on the bars to see further, and at last she caught a tell-tale glimpse of red near the hedge at the far corner of the field. She scanned the landscape for a sign of the guard, standing up higher on the gate to see across the hedges into the neighbouring fields, but the only person she could see anywhere near was the solitary prisoner in the ditch.

She took a deep breath, hoping to quieten her racing heart.

It might not even be him, she told herself as she clambered down from the bars of the gate and began to make her way across the field. It might be one of the others.

It might.

Twice on the way she stopped and glanced back to the safety of the gate. He had not seen her yet. There was still time to go back. Still time to be good. But some other force was at work inside her and both times she resumed her journey across the furrowed earth. She had come quite close before he noticed her, and he clambered out of the ditch straight away, wiping his hands on his trousers. He was sweating in the cold from the work, and the sun caught the sheen across his forehead. She stopped a small distance away, and he cast a glance towards the gate, checking for the guard.

'I brought back your clothes,' she said, stepping closer. 'I was going to leave them with the guard but I couldn't find him.'

'I'm glad,' he said, and smiled. He seemed younger when he smiled, and the sad intensity left his eyes. She found herself returning the smile.

'Me too,' she admitted.

He moved closer and wiped his hands once more on his trousers before reaching out to take the bundle. Briefly their fingers touched, and it was a moment before Clare dropped her hands away and stepped back.

'How is the little girl?' He had barely a trace of an accent – his English was flawless. She wondered why he had lied until now.

'Lizzie? She's fine, thanks to you. Were you in trouble? I heard the guard shouting.'

He shook his head, but she was uncertain if he was telling the truth. 'The boy,' he said instead. 'The one who threw the stone. Is he your son?'

'Yes.'

There was an awkward silence and both of them glanced towards the gate. They were still alone.

'You should go,' he murmured. 'I would hate for you to be in trouble because of me.'

She nodded in agreement but she did not move, held in place by the same unaccountable force that had propelled her across the field towards him. For five long breaths they stood together in silence in the cold quiet morning until the sudden roar of a tractor in a neighbouring field shattered the silence and the spell was broken.

She stepped back, suddenly self-conscious and suffused with guilt.

For fraternising with the enemy. For breaking the law. For betraying Walter.

'I'll see you again, Mrs Chapman,' he said.

'Perhaps,' she managed to reply, before she turned away and began what seemed like an endless trek across the hard furrowed ground. She guessed that he was watching her and it took all her willpower not to turn back to see. Only when she finally reached the gate and had hauled herself up and over it did she allow herself to look. He was still there, still watching, and he lifted an arm to wave farewell. In spite of everything she returned the wave. Then, angry with herself for giving in to feelings she was not allowed to have, she jumped down from the gate and hurried on her way into the village.

Chapter Ten

Christmas morning dawned white with fog. Grief for Walter hung over them all, and the frostiness that existed between his wife and his mother thawed a little as the two women trod carefully around each other, maintaining a fragile peace that Clare was grateful for. Seeing the pain that was permanently etched in the older woman's eyes as a reflection of her own sorrow, she made great efforts to be kind. Mrs Chapman was Walter's mother after all, she reminded herself, and she had not always been such difficult company. In a photograph on the mantelpiece she was smiling and pretty, with dark hooded eyes and a fashionable bob, the world spread out before her full of possibility. Clare had heard how Walter's father swept her off her feet at a dance, and how she found herself as a farmer's wife before she had time to think twice. The hardness of the life must have been a rude shock to a girl who had grown up the daughter of a prosperous hotelier, and Clare sometimes wondered if she ever regretted her choice, if she would do it differently if she had her time again.

After breakfast the family walked together to church, and in the lane the children were quickly swallowed from sight in the fog as they ran ahead.

'Stay together!' Bridget shouted after them. There was no reply.

The church was full – even the village unbelievers worshipped at Christmas, and Clare had to brace herself against the onslaught of memories of all the other Christmas mornings when Walter had led the service. Then, in the soft low voice she had loved so well, the story of that very first Christmas had been beguiling, but it seemed a different tale altogether coming from Reverend Keane, and she paid little attention, allowing her thoughts to wander. She was glad when it was over and they could retrace their steps homeward through the fog.

Back at the farm they gathered round the little tree that the children had decorated to give each other small home-made gifts. A knitted scarf. A sewn purse. Sweets made from long-hoarded sugar rations. Clare gave everyone small sketches she had made, and for Mrs Chapman she had done a portrait of Walter from the photograph of him she kept by her bed. She had found an old frame to mount it and though she thought it was beautiful she gave it with a sense of trepidation, uncertain how Mrs Chapman would react. She need not have worried. Walter's mother was delighted and her face widened with a genuine smile of pleasure for the first time in months. She was still attractive when she smiled, Clare thought, a remnant of the girl she used to be, the woman in the photograph. She gave her daughter-in-law a rare hug, and as they held each other Clare noticed how thin the older woman was, not much more than skin and bone in Clare's embrace.

Only Eric received shop-bought presents: a stationery set and satchel ordered especially from London to take to his new school, and Henry watched with ill-concealed resentment, impatient to start secondary school himself. Clare had asked James for his advice about what to get, and Eric's pleasure and excitement when he ripped the paper open took the breath from her body. She had to turn her head away to hide her tears.

In the new year Eric went away to school. It seemed to be a long road to Wellington – a tortuous bus trip that led them through a myriad of villages Clare had never even heard of and two changes where they had to wait at the roadside in the bitter cold. Eric was quiet and thoughtful, gazing out of the window at the passing countryside and answering her efforts at conversation with a polite lack of interest. She could almost feel him moving away from her as the distance from Rowan Farm increased, and she knew that by the time they reached the end of their journey he would no longer be her little boy.

The winter afternoon was almost done when they arrived in the neat market town, and the sky glowed yellow with a final flare of the sun before the darkness fell. Clare shivered as they stepped down into the road, and drew her coat closer about her. Eric seemed oblivious of the cold but he put on his new school cap and buttoned his blazer, straightening his shoulders before he picked up the suitcase. He looked very small as he strained against its weight and her heart turned over again.

'Are you ready?'

He gave her a nod, tight-lipped and curt, and she saw the effort he was making to be brave. James had promised to meet the bus, and she looked up and down the high street in hope. The town was quiet – it was late on a Sunday afternoon and most people were at home in the warm. Two young soldiers jogged across the road and climbed aboard just before the bus pulled out with a belch of fuel. She held her breath, but even so, she could still taste the petrol fumes. Eric gave a theatrical splutter and they exchanged a small smile.

Clare wondered if they should make their own way to the school. It wasn't far, James had said, only a few minutes' walk, and it was too cold to stand and wait. She had just decided to start walking when James's tall frame emerged from the growing gloom. She watched him approach. Apart from his height there was nothing in his looks that was similar to Walter. A hank of straight blond hair half covered a face that remained stubbornly boyish with plump rosy cheeks. He smiled when he saw them and quickened his pace, and she was pleased when he greeted Eric first.

'Welcome to Wellington, Mr Chapman. I hope the journey wasn't too arduous?'

'It was fine, thank you, Mr Clough, though a little long.'

Clare smiled. He had remembered that James was no longer Uncle James, but a schoolmaster to be addressed by his formal name.

'Let's get you to the school and settled in. I've partnered you up with a boy I think you'll get along with – he'll show you the ropes. His name's Martin and he's from Taunton …'

James took Eric's suitcase with an easy motion and they fell into step beside each other, still talking. Clare followed on behind with her little overnight bag dragging at her arm. She already felt redundant: Eric's attention was fully engrossed by his godfather, his mother all but forgotten.

James had been right – it was no distance at all, and far too soon they were at the school gate.

'You need to say goodbye to your mother now,' James said, and to her surprise Eric threw his arms around her for a hug so tight it almost knocked her breathless. She blinked back the tears and when he let her go, she bent so that their faces were level.

'Enjoy it,' she said softly, though James had stepped tactfully away, 'and work hard. Write when you can and I'll see you soon. I'm very proud of you. You're so grown up now.'

'Thanks, Mum,' Eric said, and she heard the small tremor in his voice.

'Shall we?' James moved closer again, and this time he spoke directly to Clare. 'Your hotel is on the high street – the Traveller's Inn. It's easy to find and they're expecting you. I'll meet you in the dining room at about seven o'clock, once I'm free to get away.'

She nodded, holding in the tears. Eric gave her a final uncertain wave then followed his godfather through the gate and into the school. Clare watched his small back disappear into the half-light. The next time she saw him he would be a different boy, full of thoughts and experiences she would never know. Taking a deep breath, she forced herself to turn away and retrace her steps back towards the high street.

When she arrived at the hotel Clare ordered tea and sandwiches to have in her room and she was delighted by the electric lights and the hot running water in the bathroom along the corridor. After two years on the farm without either it felt quite luxurious. Promising herself that she would never take such things for granted again, she filled the bath with far more than the wartime regulation five inches (since she had gone so long without) and lay in the heat until her skin began to wrinkle, spoiling herself. But it was the unaccustomed privacy she relished the most, no one watching her or judging, and no need to have an explanation for every move she made.

At seven o'clock she wandered down to the dining room. She paused in the doorway and looked around. An ancient couple were sitting at the bar and by the window a young man in a cheap and shiny suit was flirting with a girl with a ribbon in her hair. After a moment she spotted James, waving a hand in the air to catch her attention, and she crossed the room to join him at a table not far from the roaring hearth. He had ordered himself a pint of beer, and though she would have liked a gin and tonic she didn't want to embarrass anyone by asking for something they might not have, so she contented herself with a glass of sherry. The landlady served them, looking on with an approving smile, and the mistaken assumption about her relationship with James lit a slight unease in Clare. To cover it, she sipped at her sherry and felt her head begin to go light. She was unused to drinking.

'Did he settle in all right?' Her first concern was for Eric.

James nodded. 'Absolutely. He'll be fine. Boys are generally much tougher than their mothers realise.'

She said nothing, unreassured. Vaguely, she wondered if she had made a mistake entrusting Eric into James's care.

'And how are you managing, Clare?' he asked. 'You seem …' He tilted his head to consider her and she looked away, resenting the appraisal. 'You seem … very tired,' he went on. 'Are you all right?'

'I'm all right.'

The landlady made her away across the carpet towards them. 'Would you like to order some food?'

Clare looked up, appetite sharpened by the sherry.

'We've got steak and kidney pudding, leek and potato soup, or sausage and mash.'

'Steak and kidney pudding, please,' she answered. Leek and potato soup had been Walter's favourite and she hoped James would not order it. But he did, and they watched the landlady make her way back behind the bar to the kitchen to shout out the order to the cook.

For a moment then they sat in silence and she could think of nothing to say. They had written often in the months since they had seen each other last, mostly about the practical arrangements for Eric's schooling, but they had exchanged little snippets of news as well. She combed through her memory, searching for inspiration.

'How is your mother?' she remembered. 'You said in your last letter she'd been unwell.'

'She's coming along nicely. It was influenza apparently but she's on the mend now, thank heavens. My sister has been staying to look after her.'

'That must be a great relief.'

He nodded and took another mouthful of beer. Another silence fell, and she realised she barely knew him at all. Without Walter as the link between them they struggled to find any common ground.

'You're still at the school?' he asked.

'Yes. Of course, our term has already started. I had to beg the headmistress for the day off to bring Eric here. She wasn't happy about it but she could hardly refuse.' She smiled and he gave a small laugh, relieved to have found a topic they could talk about.

'She's a stickler then?'

'She's a bit of a tyrant, actually. Rules the roost with a rod of iron.' She wondered if he would judge her for the mixed metaphor – she was speaking quickly in the awkwardness. 'All the children are terrified of her.'

'And the teachers too?'

She gave a genuine laugh. 'Yes. And the teachers too.'

The food arrived and gave them something to do. She tried not to look at the soup but the scent of it still woke memories of other pub dinners, evenings with Walter on the trips they had made in the early days of their marriage before Eric came along and they began to travel less. She smiled to herself at the recollection – they had been happy days, full of hope.

The conversation moved in fits and starts but despite the silences in between and the awkwardness it was wonderful to be away from the oppressive atmosphere of the farm, where Walter's death hung in the air like a physical presence, and every word Mrs Chapman spoke to her felt like a reproach. She remembered James's suggestion of finding a job in Wellington. At the time it had been beyond her even to consider but now that she was here it seemed to be more of a possibility. Perhaps she could live on a teacher's wage, if she could find a job. *If.* It would be a frugal life, for sure, but it would be her own. The prospect was tempting.

They finished their food and the landlady came and took their plates.

'I haven't forgotten about your idea of moving here,' Clare said. 'I'm still thinking about it. But I'd need to find a job ...' She let the sentence hang and he picked it up as she had hoped.

'I'll keep my ears open and let you know. Another sherry?'

'Goodness, no.' She held her hand over the glass and laughed. She could still feel the effects of the first one, a pleasant wooziness in her head that blurred the sharp edges of the world. 'But perhaps a cup of tea?'

James stayed later than she had expected on the night before the first day of term, and though the conversation continued to limp and halt, the silences had become less awkward by the time he finally got up to go. Clare walked with him to the door and they stood close together on the step in the dark. The high street was lit by a narrow moon that peered through a gap in the clouds, and his face was pale in its light, his hair almost white.

'Thank you,' she said. 'For everything.'

'It's my pleasure, Clare,' he answered. 'It's what Walter would have wanted and it's the least I can do.'

'We always planned for him to go the grammar school but when Walter joined up it just sort of got forgotten. Wellington is a good school – I'm sure Walter would be very happy with it.'

He leaned in to kiss her cheek as he had always done when Walter was alive, but to Clare it felt awkward now and wrong, and though she tensed he didn't seem to notice.

'I'll write,' he said. 'Boys never tell their mothers the truth in their letters home.'

She smiled. 'Thank you. I'll look forward to it.'

'Have a safe trip home tomorrow.' Then he was gone, swallowed into the dark of the high street, his footsteps quickly fading into silence.

She turned with a shiver, rubbed her arms with her hands, and went back inside the welcoming warmth of the hotel.

Chapter Eleven

I n the morning the clear cold had given way to an icy drizzle and Clare left the warmth of the hotel after breakfast with reluctance. Shifting from foot to foot as she waited for the bus on the high street, she wrapped her arms around herself – she hadn't thought to bring an umbrella and her hair was dripping by the time the bus finally arrived. It was not much warmer inside it and she sat huddled in her coat, staring out at the damp and grey fields beyond the window as the bus swayed and lurched along the endless country lanes. The warm comfort of the hotel already seemed not much more than a distant memory and to take her mind away from the cold she let her thoughts wander over the conversation of the evening before.

She had always considered James as much her friend as Walter's, though Walter had known him longer, but she realised now she had never once met him alone until these last few months, and it seemed that Walter had been the glue of the friendship. Last night she had felt awkward in James's presence, something uncomfortable between them. Perhaps it was only the fact of Walter's death and in time they would readjust – she hoped that was the case. But a deeper sense of worry nagged

inside her: they had been like strangers, the evening full of difficult pauses when neither could find the right thing to say. Or
anything to say at all for that matter. She marvelled at the easy
conversation they used to have across the table at the vicarage
when they had talked of everything and anything. What, in fact,
had they talked about? However hard she racked her memory,
she couldn't remember a single conversation they had shared.

The return journey took less time and it was still early afternoon when she stepped off the bus in the village. She could hear
the children playing at the school, and the postman was deep in
conversation with the landlord on the doorstep of the pub. Both
men gave her a desultory wave of greeting without interrupting
their discussion. The drizzle had cleared but there were dark
clouds overhead that promised more to come. Clare buttoned her
coat and set off on her way back to the farm, thinking of nothing.

She had not long left the village outskirts when an unexpected
flash of red against the dark earth just up ahead startled her
attention towards it. One of the prisoners was fixing a fence close
to the lane. A flare of heat lit across her – hope and shame in
equal measure. She had barely allowed herself to think of Max
Peterson again, distracting herself with preparations for
Christmas and Eric's departure to school. Grief for Walter, too,
had helped to restrain illicit thoughts, guilt suffusing her every
time the German entered her mind. But the unwelcome truth
was that she *wanted* to think about him. In spite of the shame and
the sense of disloyalty her feelings awoke, the excitement of it
gave her pleasure: it was a reminder that she was still alive and
capable of feeling something other than anger and sorrow.

Caught in the apparently never-ending cycle of guilt and
excitement, the image of the German's half-naked body in her
bedroom flickered again into focus behind her eyes. She shook
her head to chase it away but the memory lingered in her mind,
vivid and immovable. Feeling the flush of colour rise across her
neck and cheeks, she lowered her gaze once more to the lane.

It might not even be him, she told herself. Keep walking. Keep your head down. You're not allowed to speak to him. But as she approached, she still saw from the edge of her eye that he straightened up and turned towards her, and though she dared not lift her head, she knew without a shadow of a doubt that it was him. In spite of herself she slowed her pace, and when she drew level she halted. Instinctively she looked about her for the guard but he was at the far end of the field with one of the other men, too far away to see much. She took a step back to stand behind the shelter of the hedge.

'Hello.' Max's voice was low. 'Happy New Year.'

She smiled. 'Happy New Year.'

They stood in awkward silence, and she cast a glance both ways along the lane but there was no one to see them. Max turned briefly towards the guard before he brought his attention back to her.

'You finished work early?' He gestured with his head towards the village.

'I … I didn't work today – I took my son to his new school. It's in Wellington, a town not far from here …' She trailed off, unsure of herself and self-conscious under his gaze. She wondered if he had noticed the blush or if the redness of her cheeks from the walk would cover it.

He said nothing. In the pause she lifted her eyes to meet his and saw a slight smile behind the sadness in their depths, a mirror of her own pleasure in his company.

'You should go,' he said then, with another glance behind him. 'Before someone sees you.'

She nodded but it was hard to find the will to move away. She wanted to stay and talk longer, in spite of the cold.

'Go.'

She smiled and stepped away with a lightness in her step that had not been there before, and even the prospect of Mrs

Chapman and life at the farmhouse without so much as her son for company could not darken her mood.

Max watched her walk away, committing every detail of her to his memory to revisit in his head until the next time he could see her and reassure himself she felt the same. A gust of wind caught at her hat and when she raised a hand to steady it he smiled at the movement. She had delicate hands, fine wrists, and he recalled with a shiver the way their fingers had brushed as she gave him back his uniform. When he had opened up the bundle back at the camp he realised she had taken the time to iron it so it would be soft for him to wear, and the towel she had wrapped it in had been a gift.

He had told himself then it was a simple kindness, gratitude for saving the little girl. It could be nothing more, after all – she was a war widow. He was the enemy. But that simple kindness had almost undone him, breaching the wall he had erected to defend himself against the brutality of a life at war. Lying sleepless in his bunk that night he had attempted to rebuild it, trying to put the blocks back in place, afraid of what it meant to be so exposed, his emotions bared for the first time in years.

After that, he had promised himself to set thoughts of her aside, supposing that in time she would fade from his thoughts. The war would end, he would go back to what was left of Germany to find his family, and Clare Chapman would be no more than a memory he would visit now and then to wonder what became of her.

But today they had met again by chance in the lane and, in spite of all the reasons she had to keep on walking, she had chosen to stop and talk to him, and he had chosen to reply. At the sight of her all his resolution had failed him, melting away like dew in the morning sun.

He watched her retreat along the lane until she passed out of his sight. In the hedgerow beside him a red-breasted robin began to chirrup and he turned to look, observing it distractedly while the rest of him ached with thoughts of Clare. Then, with only half his mind on the job, he hefted the weight of the hammer in his hand and went back to fixing the fence.

At the camp there was a noticeboard with a list of the names of men who had mail to collect from the office. Every day every man studied the board, sometimes more than once. For most of them there had been no news from home for months, a silence heightened by the news reports about the Allied bombings. All of them were desperate for any kind of word, so the men who were lucky enough to get letters read them out loud to the others – it was a link to home, however small.

'No news is good news, right?' Theo nudged at Max's arm as they stood at the board that night.

Max turned to his friend. Their paths had crossed often in the years of the war as they had moved from unit to unit, frontline to frontline. It had been good to meet a familiar face at the camp, and they had arranged a swap with another man so that now they shared a bunk.

'*Veilleicht.*' Max shrugged. Maybe.

'If they were bombed out Lotte wouldn't have got your letters, so she doesn't know you're here. For sure, that's all it is.'

Theo's natural optimism never waned, even on the retreat from Russia when Max had long since given up all hope of surviving. *You're already dead,* the old hands had told him, right at the beginning. *Accept it and it's easier.*

'You've got to have hope, Max, otherwise what's the point of it all?'

'I don't know,' Max answered. 'I've got no idea what the point of it is, or if there even is one.'

His friend placed a reassuring hand on Max's shoulder. '*Die*

Hoffnung stirbt zuletzt.' The last thing to die in a person is hope. 'Don't give up. You'll find each other. You'll see.'

He said nothing. He had no hope at all that anything from his old life had survived. He had heard the news of the raids and seen the bombed streets of Berlin in his dreams. He envied Theo's faith – he had lost his own a long time ago.

They walked back to their hut side by side.

'Have you seen the English woman again?'

He shook his head. When he had told the story of rescuing the child, he had briefly mentioned the woman who gave him the clothes he wore back to camp, but he regretted it straight away. With little else to occupy the prisoners' minds, the woman had become a topic for endless discussion.

'Was she pretty?'

'Was she young?'

'Blonde hair or dark?'

'Plump or skinny?'

He had answered all their questions with an uninterested shrug and told them nothing more, but afterwards the men who worked near Rowan Farm looked out for her often, and nodded with satisfaction when they caught a glimpse of her in the lane. It was as if her kindness had touched them all, a small spark of hope for the future. Though he feigned indifference, their sense of shared ownership lit a flare of jealousy inside him he knew was absurd.

But then he reminded himself that everything he felt for her was absurd.

It simply could not be.

Chapter Twelve

The cold dark of winter gave way at last to spring, and the countryside bristled with new life, the skeleton branches clothed once more in lush and verdant green, full of promise. Soon Eric would be back from his first term at school for the Easter holidays, and it was hard to remember that not so far away the war was still raging, soldiers fighting and dying, civilians cowering under enemy raids. Clare could remember the taste of her own fear as she took shelter in the vicarage cellar against the German bombs early in the war, but it seemed like a memory from another world: she had been a different person then. How much longer could the enemy hold out? The Allies had crossed the Rhine and the Russians were almost at Vienna. Surely it must be over soon.

Breathing out with hope, Clare set her foot to the pedal of her bike and rattled across the muddy ruts of the lane between the brilliant hedgerows on her way to work for the last week of school.

. . .

Just before Easter the tractor broke down, and no amount of Simon's tinkering with its innards could bring it back to life: it simply would not start. It was a disaster for the farm. Even with the war's end in sight, the War Ag was still demanding increased production. Without the Fordson to help them sow and fertilise, dependent solely on the pair of draught horses, they would struggle to meet their quotas.

'You should ask Max to have a look at it,' Lizzie said in a lull in her father's grumbling over Sunday lunch.

The table fell silent and everyone looked at her, the tension taut enough to cut with a knife. Clare felt the familiar rush of guilty heat at the mention of Max's name and took in a deep silent breath to slow the sudden quickness of her heart.

'He was a motor mechanic before the war,' Lizzie explained, and her tone was touchy, as though it should be obvious. 'Didn't you know?'

'You shouldn't be talking to him,' Bridget scolded. 'You know that. The prisoners are out of bounds.'

'But he saved my life,' Lizzie replied.

Simon threw his fork onto his plate and sent a splatter of peas and gravy across the tablecloth. Mrs Chapman drew in a sharp hiss of breath and got up to get a towel to wipe it.

'So he speaks English, does he?'

Lizzie nodded, starting to become aware of the effect of her words. She looked from her father to her mother with eyes that betrayed her nervousness. She was not used to being in trouble and tears were not far off. She put down her knife and fork, placing them neatly side by side across the plate.

'Bloody lying German!'

'Simon!' Mrs Chapman paused in her cleaning up to turn to him. 'Mind your language. The children.'

'Never a word to me. Never a hint he understood a single thing I've ever said to him. Lying bastard!' There was almost a hint of admiration in his tone.

Bridget stretched out a gentle hand towards his wrist but he jerked his arm away from her with a snarl. She turned instead to the children.

'Take your plates out, then go outside to play.'

'But Mum ...' Henry wanted to stay, too old now to be fobbed off with half-truths and evasions. Clare wondered if he too had spent time with Max and a shiver of jealousy rippled through her at the thought of it.

'Outside!' Mrs Chapman echoed their mother in a tone the children knew not to talk back to. They got down from the table and shuffled towards the sink, still listening, but the silence persisted around the table until the back door finally swung shut behind them.

'We need the tractor,' Bridget said. Her voice was tentative, unsure. 'One way or another.'

Simon sat back in his chair and folded his arms with a sigh. Mrs Chapman took the cloth she had used to wipe down the table to the sink then slid back into her place at the table. Her eyes were still lively above the hollowed cheeks and it seemed her tongue had lost none of its sharpness.

'That means he'll have to be in the yard.'

'It does,' Simon agreed.

'I don't want him in the yard.'

Simon looked across to his wife, who gave a small shrug in answer. 'We need the tractor,' she repeated.

He nodded. 'I'll have to ask the guard.'

Walter's mother got up and started clearing the plates in silence, but there was no need for her to say a word; her fury was clear in the tremble of the dishes in her hands and the set of her jaw. Clare left the table to help.

'Leave it!' Mrs Chapman hissed. 'I'll do it.'

Clare hesitated, dish in hand, and exchanged a look with Bridget, who nodded. She replaced the dish on the table and followed the children out of the back door and into the soft spring damp beyond it.

Clare liked the yard behind the house. A neat, south-facing courtyard with a little row of outbuildings along one side led through a gate to the kitchen garden and orchard beyond. A profusion of herbs and flowers in pots were arranged along the walls, making the most of the southern sun – geraniums and lavender, rosemary and chamomile, chervil, dill and rocket – come summer it would be a riot of colour. Now, in spring, it was ripe with the promise of the spectacle yet to come, and the air was sweetly tainted with their scent.

Dragging the heavy wooden bench from its place against the wall she placed it in the sun, facing towards the orchard and out of sight of the kitchen window. Then she sat and lifted her face to the warmth, watching the shapes of the clouds as they dissolved and reformed. It had been a game she had sometimes played with Walter – making pictures in the sky. Now she could see a dolphin with a warship close behind it and she smiled, allowing herself to be comforted by the simple pleasure, thoughts drifting until the rattle of the kitchen door behind her startled her from her reverie.

Max, she remembered abruptly.

Bridget appeared at the edge of her vision, and Clare moved along to one end of the bench to make room for her to sit down. Bridget took the proffered seat but she remained on the edge of it, tensed and ready to rise at a moment's notice as if waiting for a summons. Perhaps she was.

'Is everything all right?' Clare asked.

Bridget sighed. 'He just always handles her so badly,' she said, and Clare knew exactly what she meant. 'Of course we need the tractor. And of course we should ask the German if he can fix it. But ...' She trailed off, raising her head towards the sky as if the effort of explaining was all too much. Then she turned towards Clare beside her on the bench. 'Fancy not letting on he speaks English. After all this time.'

Walter had told Clare once that secrets are the only power a prisoner has, a way of keeping a piece of himself from his captors. Even the smallest scrap can represent a rebellion, a fragment of his life that is free.

'It's an army thing, I expect,' she said. 'Keep your head down, don't volunteer.'

Bridget smiled, and they sat for a moment in silence. Despite the goodwill between them, they still hadn't managed to breach the small awkwardnesses that seemed to stop them becoming close, their lives drifting on in close but parallel lines. And each time they were alone together Clare regretted it.

Bridget said, 'Did you give him back the uniform?'

Clare turned in surprise. 'Yes,' she answered. 'I gave it to the guard as soon as it was dry.' The lie was instinctive – her own prison secrets, she thought with a rueful sigh. But she had seen him only once since then, exchanging a few brief words at the side of the lane before she had decided once and for all that she must put him out of her mind. She was a war widow and he was the enemy. In an earlier age she would still have been wearing her widow's weeds, and every time her mind strayed to thoughts of him, it felt like a betrayal. What was wrong with her that another man could make her heart race so soon? But for all her resolution, even the mention of his name still brought a flush across her skin, and her helplessness in the face of those feelings appalled her.

From the orchard, the voices of the children playing reached them on the breeze. The sounds almost made her smile until she remembered her son was not with them, and the hurt of his absence sidled through her, insidious. She had never felt so alone.

'Are you going to punish Lizzie?' Clare asked.

Bridget shook her head. 'What's the point? He did save her life. Of course she wants to talk to him.'

They sat for a few moments more before Bridget, too restless to sit still for long, got to her feet. 'Back to it, then,' she said, raising her eyebrows.

Clare laughed. 'Back to it.'

But even after she heard the door click shut she lingered in the yard a while longer, letting the pale warmth of the day suffuse her. Only when the clouds began to gather in front of the sun, and the afternoon turned cool without it, did she get up from the bench, drag it back to its place against the wall, and make her way back to the house to help with tea.

Inside the house the argument was still going.

'It's bad enough they're on the land at all. God knows what your father would have thought. He fought them too, you remember? He was never the same after that. Never.' Mrs Chapman threw the ball of pastry she was kneading back into the bowl, and Clare could already taste the toughness of it in her mouth. The older woman looked up sharply when she heard Clare come in.

'How can you live with yourself?' she demanded. 'Giving him Walter's clothes.' She gave a theatrical shudder. 'I can hardly bear to think of it.'

'Then don't,' Clare heard herself reply.

For months she had tiptoed around Walter's mother on eggshells, trying to keep the peace, reminding herself of the other woman's grief and sorrow, the need to be kind. Walter's voice had whispered at her shoulder. But this time she refused to listen to him.

Mrs Chapman stared, hands resting on the sides of the pastry bowl. There was a streak of flour across her forehead and Clare had to quell an urge to lean across and wipe it off, as she would have with one of the children.

'The prisoners are here, a fact of life, and wishing it were otherwise won't change anything. So we might as well make use of them.'

From the corner of her eye she saw the colour leaving Bridget's face. Simon, who might have been her ally, was nowhere to be seen. The two women faced each other across the table, silent, and Clare could see the muscle working in the older woman's cheek, the skin flushed with fury and shock. After a moment, Mrs Chapman lowered her eyes away, bringing them to rest once more on the unlucky ball of pastry. Clare swallowed, waiting, light-headed from the confrontation, but Mrs Chapman said nothing else, merely taking up the dough in her hands and kneading it with indifferent attention.

All the fight flooded out of Clare in a wash that almost made her stumble. She turned away and, half-blind with tears, she picked up her coat and bag. At the door she looked back towards Bridget, who was still staring in shock.

'I can't do this any more,' she said. Then she yanked open the door and headed out into the late afternoon cool.

She walked briskly, growing warm with the movement. The lane was bright with the spring, the new green leaves almost iridescent amid the frothy white flowers of the hawthorn. She counted the magpies that crossed her path, the nursery rhyme keeping rhythm in her head.

One for sorrow, two for joy, three for a girl, four for a boy.

There were no prisoners in the fields today and she remembered it was Sunday. What did the men do to keep themselves busy at the camp on their days off? It would not be so different to the army, she supposed, though there would be no training. Perhaps they played sports instead, or read to pass the time. She found it hard to imagine.

She reached the village before she had even had time to decide where she was headed. She had been thinking only of escape from the farm, from Mrs Chapman, but now that she was in the village she slowed her steps. Nothing was open and the street was deserted. The ginger tabby at the post office watched her from its spot in the window with green judgemental eyes. She stuck out her tongue at him in a fit of childishness, and walked on. Past the church. Past the school. The road began to climb and wind its way out of the village, and on the bend the big house that belonged to Susan's parents loomed into view behind the tall iron gates that guarded it. The wide drive swept away from the road and, on an impulse, Clare pushed open the gate and crunched across the gravel to the house.

She cast her eyes across the front of the building. It was a beautiful house, late mediaeval and dark with age beneath an ivy vine that was beginning to encroach across the mullioned windows. A part of Clare envied her friend, but she guessed it would be a lonely place to live alone with only the servants for company. There were no cars parked on the drive – Susan's parents must still be in London. They came home more rarely than they used to, Mr Minter keeping busy at whatever it was he did at the War Office.

The doorbell chimed inside when she pulled it, and a dog barked. She could hear its claws scrabbling on the floorboards. Then Susan's voice. 'Get down, Pepper!'

The door opened and there was a fraction of a second of hesitation before Susan's face brightened into a smile.

'Clare! Come in, won't you? What a lovely surprise.'

It was the first time Clare had been to the house. In spite of their friendliness at work they had seldom met outside of it; though they had talked of it often they had never quite managed to make the time.

'Come through to the kitchen – I was just making myself some cheese on toast. Would you like some?'

Clare smiled and nodded. Cheese on toast had been a favourite with Walter for Sunday tea. She followed Susan through to a vast kitchen with two large two ranges and fireplace big enough to roast a hog. A great table stood in the middle.

'Not quite Hampton Court,' Susan said, looking around, seeing it with Clare's eyes. 'But almost! Have a pew.'

Drawing up a stool to the table, she settled herself as her friend made tea and toasted the cheese on the fire with practised ease. When it was ready Susan slid into place and looked Clare full in the face with a questioning tilt of her head.

'What's happened?' she asked. 'What's going on?'

Clare sighed. Her complaints seemed ridiculous now that she was here. She felt ungrateful, and weak for being so miserable. She should be more stoic, she thought. Mrs Chapman was not really so bad and compared to many others she had much to be thankful for. She had a place to live, a job, a family. But however often she told herself so, the feeling of trapped depression remained.

'Life at the farm ...' she began. 'I just needed to get away.'

'Mrs C getting you down?'

Clare gave a half-laugh at her friend's blunt appraisal and nodded.

'She's always been difficult,' Susan said, 'but when Walter's father was alive I think he kept her in check.'

She nodded her agreement. She remembered their early visits – brief dutiful overnight stays that Walter always dreaded, though he never said as much. But she had known from the tension in his muscles and the shortness of his usually even temper that faded the moment they boarded the bus to take them home.

'I've been walking on eggshells for months,' she said, taking a mouthful of tea. It was stronger than she was used to and more flavourful. She guessed Mr Minter's role at the War Office served him well in a multitude of ways. 'But I just snapped today.'

'Anything in particular?'

'The prisoners on the farm.'

'The enemy.'

'Precisely.'

Susan drew in a deep breath, and contemplated her plate of toasted cheese. 'You can kind of see her point, though, can't you?'

Clare swallowed. She had come for sympathy, she realised, and she was not prepared to be challenged. She had assumed Susan would take her side.

'I mean, they did kill Walter.'

'I know how my husband died, thank you.'

Susan looked up sharply. 'Yes, of course. I didn't mean ...' She trailed off, apparently embarrassed.

There was an awkward silence and Clare regretted she had come. For something to do, she took a mouthful of the toasted cheese.

'You could move out,' Susan said after a while.

'I've been looking for a job in Wellington,' she replied, 'to be near Eric.'

'I'd miss you,' Susan said, 'but it sounds like a fine idea. There's not much to keep you here any more.'

Clare ate more of the cheese on toast. It was really very good, tastier than the cheese they had at Rowan Farm. She let her mind run over the possibility of having her own place, however humble. She would be her own master. No one judging her, no need to walk softly all the time, minding her manners and her tongue – the prospect was very appealing.

'If I can find somewhere,' she said, 'what with the housing shortages and everything.'

'Come on,' Susan chided. 'Think positive.' She lifted her tea in salute. 'Here's to independence.'

'Independence.' They clinked their cups together and laughed.

The conversation flowed more easily after that. She had let herself forget that Susan knew Walter as a child – they had grown up together, and it was a joy to hear new tales that her friend recounted with a tentative sensitivity Clare found touching.

'You don't mind me talking about him?'

'Not at all,' she replied. 'It's lovely to hear these stories. He never talked much about his childhood.'

'I don't think he was very happy,' Susan said. 'Not until he went away to school anyway – I think he was always afraid of getting stuck here, being saddled with the farm.'

Ironic, Clare thought, that he had escaped and she was the one who was trapped. Only unlike Walter, she was unwanted and unwelcome here, an interloper. Mrs Chapman would not miss her a whit.

They finished their tea and Susan opened a bottle of wine from her father's cellar. The age and expense of it was wasted on Clare, who only rarely drank more than a sherry at Christmas, but its warmth rounded the edges of the evening, thoughts becoming softer and more pliable.

'You should stay the night,' Susan said when they counted the chimes from the clock in the hall and realised it was ten o'clock already.

'Is there room?' Clare asked, and giggled.

'There is most definitely room. Come on, I'll give you a tour.

They wandered through the house until they reached a pretty bedroom with matching flowered curtains and bedspread, and a blue carpet that was soft underfoot. Susan clicked on the bedside lamp, and Clare remembered how much she missed having electricity.

'Will this do?' Susan asked.

'It's lovely.'

'I'll find you some pyjamas and a toothbrush.'

A few minutes later and Clare was settled under the covers, warm and comfortable. Just as she was drifting off to sleep, her last thought was to wonder if they had missed her at the farm yet, and whether or not they cared.

. . .

In the morning they got up early and ate ham and eggs in the sunny breakfast room that looked out over the gardens at the back of the house, where the daffodils were blooming in ranks of vivid yellow.

'The garden is lovely,' Clare said.

'Actually, it's a mess.' Susan flicked a glance to the window with a sigh. 'With the war we've had no gardeners – just Fred Wakeman now and then to have a go at the weeds.'

'What about the prisoners?' she suggested, and immediately wished that she hadn't.

Susan's mouth tightened almost imperceptibly. She said, 'I don't think so,' and though the tone was light Clare knew she had offended.

'It was just a suggestion,' she offered, and Susan smiled in answer, apparently quick to forgive.

They finished their tea and wandered out to the terrace to look over the garden. It was a soft spring morning, a dust of cloud in the sky after the rain in the night and a pale sun that promised more warmth later on. Closer to, Clare could see the weeds and uncut lawns, the trees that needed pruning. But the daffodils dazzled the attention away from the imperfections, and she drank in the loveliness. It was beauty for its own sake, which made it all the sweeter. Everything that grew at the farm had a purpose – not a single stalk was ever wasted in the constant battle for food, the demands of the War Ag ever in their thoughts. The flowers there belonged to herbs and fruits and vegetables. The grass was for grazing. Even the nettles could be eaten. A brief memory of the pretty lilac tree in the garden at the vicarage tugged at her thoughts and she shrugged it away, not wanting to spoil the moment.

The two women gazed out from the terrace.

'Before the war we used to have parties. They would put up a marquee on the lawn and for my twenty-first birthday we had a jazz band from Paris. Lord, what a night that was!' She chuckled to herself. 'And for Teddy's wedding, we had over five hundred guests. Can you imagine? We booked out every hotel room in the district.'

Teddy was her younger brother, in the army now and serving somewhere in France. 'His wife has taken the children and gone back to live with her mother somewhere in the middle of nowhere. I think she's happy.' She turned a bright hard smile towards Clare as if to say she really didn't care.

'How's Bertie?' Clare asked, pleased she had remembered his name. Susan's beaux changed rather often and it was sometimes hard to keep track.

'Bertie?' Susan shook her head. 'I'm not with Bertie any more.' She offered no explanation and Clare didn't like to ask.

'Is there anyone else?' There was always someone, Clare thought, though it puzzled her why there was never anyone who lasted. Susan was a catch by any standards – vivacious, pretty, clever, rich. It was a mystery to Clare that no one had snapped her up yet – time was getting on.

'No. Not at the moment,' Susan answered, and laughed at Clare's look of surprise. 'I'm having a rest from men for a while. I've been finding them rather demanding recently.'

'That's because you haven't found the right one yet,' Clare said.

The light of laughter faded out of Susan's eyes, and Clare realised she had stepped on thorny ground.

'I found the right one a long time ago,' her friend said in a brittle voice. 'But ... it wasn't to be.' She gave Clare a tight smile that closed the subject, then turned abruptly and went back inside the house. Clare swept a last glance around the garden, drew her cardigan tighter around her in the sudden breeze, and followed her friend inside to get ready for the day at work.

. . .

The day at school passed slowly, and a slight headache from too much wine lingered into the afternoon, a dull throb behind her temples. At the end of the day she took her time walking home, enjoying the solitude of the place in-between. Not work. Not the farm. A no-man's land where she could put aside both the teacher and the daughter-in-law and be simply Clare, lost in her thoughts and careless of the face she presented to the world.

The threat of rain had cleared and the clouds rode high and pale above the fields. A kestrel hovered over the freshly drilled sugar beet, looking for prey, and from somewhere in the distance a dog's bark carried on the breeze. The sunlight glimmered on the puddles that had remained in the ruts on the road, the world new-washed.

She reached the farm too soon, and shoved open the gate with a shoulder. The old collie got up to greet her, tail swinging with hope. She bent to fondle his ears, an excuse to stay out of the house a little bit longer. Then the splutter of an engine across the yard cut across her thoughts and she straightened up abruptly – she had thought she was alone. The engine coughed and died and in the silence the dog nudged at her hand with his nose. She touched the top of his head with her fingertips and hesitated.

The Fordson, she thought. Someone was trying to fix the Fordson. She must have walked right past them at the gate where the tractor was kept at the side of the barn. She wheeled on the spot, suffused with the familiar wash of guilt, and saw Max. He was standing by the front wheel, wiping his hands with a rag, watching her. Her breath caught somewhere in her chest and instinctively she cast a look towards the house. No one had seen her yet – no one was about. She should turn away, she thought, go into the house, and for a moment she vacillated, trying to summon Walter to her side to lend her strength against temptation. But when she couldn't even raise the image of his face to her mind she found herself retracing her steps towards the gate, towards the enemy.

She stopped a little distance away from him but she was careful to move out of sight of the house. He smiled.

'Hello, Clare.'

'Hello, Herr Peterson,' she replied, keeping up her guard with the more formal use of his name. But she liked the sound of her own name on his lips, the slight accent he gave it.

'Do you think you can repair it?' She gestured with her head towards the tractor.

'Of course.'

'It's very temperamental.'

He nodded his agreement. She knew nothing about engines and her ignorance irritated her. She would have liked to ask more questions so they would have something to talk about and he would admire her for her unexpected knowledge. The memory of his half-dressed body in her bedroom flickered through her thoughts and she looked away, flustered.

'I didn't thank you for ironing the uniform,' he said. 'It was kind of you.'

'It was the least I could do.'

There was a silence, the conversation constrained by the situation. In another world she would have offered him tea.

'Was this your husband's farm?'

She raised her head to meet his gaze. In the afternoon light his eyes were olive-green, and they were watching her now with an intensity she found uncomfortable. She was uncertain if she liked him more or less for asking about Walter.

'No,' she answered. 'It belonged to his parents and he couldn't wait to leave. He was a vicar before the war, and then a chaplain.'

Max said nothing but his eyes never left her face. He took a step towards her and Clare held her breath. The slam of the kitchen door broke the moment and she slid around the corner of the wall and into the barn, flattening herself against the cool stone, listening. Simon's boots scuffed across the yard as Max turned the starter handle on the Fordson, eliciting the same sick cough as before. Her heart was pounding in her chest so hard she was sure the men must hear it.

'What do you reckon?' Simon asked. There was no hint of dislike in his tone – he could have been talking to anyone.

'The spark's too weak. I need a button.'

'What kind of button?' She could hear the scepticism in Simon's voice.

'You know, like a button from a shirt or a jacket. You cut the wire, and thread the ends through to make the spark jump across the gap. It should work.'

Their voices dropped to a murmur as they inspected the machine, and after a minute or two that felt like a lifetime, she heard Simon's boots trudge back towards the house. But she waited longer, too afraid to emerge, just in case. She had always been a good girl, too afraid of being in trouble ever to risk it before, but this time the danger was exhilarating.

Max appeared in the open doorway.

'He's gone.'

Clare nodded, unable to find any words, and he stepped closer. They stood for a moment in the lea of the wall, close enough to touch, and she barely dared to breathe. She was aware of his warmth and the scent of an unfamiliar soap beneath the taint of the engine oil that clung to his hands. Raising her head towards him, she wondered if he was going to kiss her and her whole body flared with hope. He reached out a hand to tuck back a tendril of her hair that had fallen over her face, and let his fingertips trail across her temple, behind her ear. She dipped her head towards his touch and as his hand slid away the backs of his fingers brushed her cheek. They stood together in silence then, as if surprised by each other. Finally, Max spoke.

'I should get back to work.'

Clare nodded but she did not move to go, and her hand reached of its own accord to wrap her fingers around his. For one breath, he hesitated. Then he raised his hand to her face again, and cupped her cheek in his palm, the other hand against her shoulder.

'Are you sure?' he breathed.

'Yes,' she replied, and before the word was fully out of her mouth his lips were on hers for one brief moment of gentle intensity that seemed to light every nerve she possessed. They stepped apart and stared at each other.

'I should go,' she whispered.

In answer he stepped back to let her through, but as she moved to duck past him, he grabbed at her hand and drew her to him again. The kiss was longer this time, more urgent, and her hands felt the strong muscles of his shoulders through the wool of his tunic, conscious of the pale smooth skin underneath, their bodies touching.

In the yard the dog barked and they froze. They heard boots on the cobbles and, with a quick exhale, Max stepped out through the doorway to tend to the tractor once again. Clare waited, listening as the footsteps retreated towards the far side of the yard.

'Coast is clear.' Max's voice was low.

She pushed herself away from the wall.

'I'll see you again soon,' he whispered, close to her ear as she slid past him.

She turned back. 'Promise?'

'I promise.'

She smiled. Then, running her fingers through her rumpled hair to smooth it, she replaced the mask of the daughter-in-law, headed across the yard, and went into the house to face the questioning she was sure awaited her.

Chapter Thirteen

'Where have you been?' Mrs Chapman looked up from the ironing. Her face was flushed from the heat and the effort.

'Work,' Clare replied, and hung her coat on the hook by the door.

'You know very well what I mean.'

'Oh. Last night.' She crossed the kitchen to the stove and lit it. The kettle was already full. 'I stayed with Susan. Tea?'

Mrs Chapman gave a quick curt nod and resumed her ironing. Monday was wash day, and at this time of year the sheets were never quite dry from the line in spite of the breeze.

'Let me do that,' she offered, but the other woman shook her head and thumped the iron down onto the sheet. Clare watched for a moment, liking the scent of freshly ironed laundry, before she turned back to the range. 'Is Bridget around?'

'In the yard. She'll be back in a minute.'

Clare slid an automatic glance towards the window. Was Max still there, she wondered, still working on the temperamental Fordson? She hoped so, enjoying the thought of his proximity so that she knew that if she wanted to she could slip outside and go to him again. She could still taste him on her lips and she had to suppress a smile in spite of the guilt that followed the pleasure like a shadow.

She was a war widow, she reminded herself. He was the enemy and his company was forbidden. And yet …

The war was almost over. A few more weeks to go at most, the papers were saying. The Allies had already crossed both the Oder and the Rhine, and in the East, the British had entered Mandalay. What was left for the Germans to fight for? Surely they would surrender now?

She warmed the pot, letting it swirl in her hands and watching the water lap round and round. What would happen to the prisoners once the war ended? Would they send them back straight away? It seemed unlikely. She tipped out the water and spooned in the tea. The caddy was full – Mrs Chapman must have gone to the shop today – so she made it strong the way all of them preferred. Did Germans drink tea? she found herself wondering. Could she take him a cup unnoticed?

She had just poured when Bridget returned from the yard, stepping out of her wellingtons at the door.

'Clare! You're home.'

The two women smiled at each other. 'I've just made some tea.'

'She stayed with Susan,' Mrs Chapman said.

'I'm going to take mine outside,' she said. 'It's such a lovely afternoon.'

No one answered her, and as she opened the door she heard the murmur of the beginning of their conversation, though she could not hear the words. She knew she upset the balance – her presence brought a tension to the house, a slight hostility. They would be glad to see her go.

The yard was empty. The collie lifted his head from his paws with bored curiosity but lowered it again when she paid him no attention. She cast a look around, checking all the doors to all the buildings, listening for movement. One of the horses stamped its foot in its stable with a muffled thud on the straw, and somewhere out of sight a blackbird was singing in pure clear tones. She swallowed, heart racing, and wandered towards the gate for all the world as if she were simply enjoying the last of the afternoon sun.

She reached the gate and leaned against it before she allowed herself to look past the barn towards the tractor. The tractor was still there, but Max had gone. Disappointment and relief twisted in her stomach in equal parts and she gave herself a rueful smile. So much for her little rebellion. For all she knew, they might not meet again.

The sudden chug-chug of an engine beyond the gate made her turn her head towards the noise. She hadn't noticed it until now but the lorry that sometimes took the men back to the camp was in the road outside, and when she looked she saw that Max was watching her from the back of it. In the moment before the truck lurched away she held his gaze across the width of the lane, and thought she saw a glint of mischief in his eyes. Feeling the little lift inside her, and the catch in her breath, she wheeled smartly away and headed once more towards the house.

From the open back of the lorry Max watched her go, her slight form neat in the crisp cotton shirt and dark wool skirt as she walked away, the empty teacup dangling carelessly from the fingers of one hand. Dainty hands, he had noticed, that were small and cold against his fingers when he held them.

What was he thinking?

He drew in a deep breath and leaned forward, forearms resting on his thighs, head in his hands.

'So schlimm?' Theo shouted over the roar from the other end of the truck. That bad?

Max lifted his head with a weary smile and shook it.

He should stop it now, he thought, and break his promise to see her again before he broke both their hearts: too many obstacles stood in their way. Theo traded places with the man sitting next to him and their shoulders bumped and rubbed as the vehicle lurched across the ruts.

'Did you fix it?'

'Not yet.'

'But you can, right? You can fix anything.'

'*Klar*,' Max agreed. Easy. He could have had the thing working today if he had applied himself a little harder, but his thoughts had been taken up with Clare – waiting for her to come home, hoping for a moment alone with her. Then, afterwards, he had given up all semblance of even trying to work, letting his mind wander instead across every second of the brief time they had spent together – the touch of her hand, her lips, her body warm and soft against him.

He should stop it now, he thought again, before either of them fell any deeper. But he knew he lacked the will to do it, drawn to her like a starving man to a feast. He recognised the sadness in her eyes as a mirror of his own, a detachment from the world around them that worked to keep the sorrow at bay. There had been a moment of connection between them the very first time he saw her – brief and unexpected, but nonetheless an unmistakable spark of an understanding he could not have put a name to. That one brief exchange had relit a flicker of life within him: perhaps there was a hope for the future after all, a world to live in beyond the brutality of war.

'You saw her again, didn't you?' Theo was nudging at his arm with his shoulder. 'You've got that smile.'

Max laughed. He never could hide much from Theo. '*Ja*.'

'And ...?'

He hesitated, reluctant to give up the secret of her to his friend, wanting to hold it close to himself, a private treasure.

'Come on. You know you can trust me. I won't tell anyone else.'

Max swung his head away and looked out over the back of the lorry towards Rowan Farm, towards Clare. The fields were beautiful in the fading light, the hedgerows vivid with spring colour, the leaves a luminescent green.

'We kissed,' he said, turning back to Theo. 'I think I'm in love with her.'

Theo laughed. *'Scheisse!'* Then, growing serious, 'What about Lotte? Your wife.'

'I know who Lotte is,' he snapped, guilt making him defensive. 'But I don't even know if she's still alive – I haven't heard from her in more than two years.'

'And the heart wants what the heart wants.' Theo gave a theatrical shrug.

He shook his head in frustration. 'I wish it wasn't so. I wish I could just walk away and forget her but I can't.'

Had he ever wanted Lotte so much? He couldn't remember. He knew that he had loved her – friend, wife, partner, mother to his beautiful daughter, but he had no memory of this all-consuming need. And he could no longer recall Lotte's face to mind in any detail. When he was captured, the British had taken the photograph of her he used to carry along with everything else he owned, and when he tried to think of Lotte now her features were a blur. He was afraid he might not even recognise Hanna any more.

The lorry bounced across a pothole and the men had to grip on to keep their seats. Someone swore.

'Worse than bloody Russia.'

'Nothing could be worse than Russia,' another man replied. 'Russia was hell on earth.'

Max lifted an instinctive hand to rub at the scar across his shoulder, and shivered. The men fell silent and for the rest of the way the driver managed to avoid the worst of the potholes.

Chapter Fourteen

Clare caught the bus to Wellington again to fetch Eric home for the Easter holidays. She was looking forward to seeing him and having him home, though she suspected he would have outgrown the desire for his mother's company. She was half-expecting to find him a young man already instead of the frightened and excited schoolboy she had left at the gate almost three months before. He had written, of course, but in the way of boys his letters had been filled with details of everything except for his feelings about them. Football matches, the best and worst of the food, a boy whose father was an admiral, a good score in his English and Latin exams. Trying to read between the lines, she had sensed he was happy enough, and James's letters had been full of reassurances that he had settled in nicely.

So on the endless journey through the rainswept countryside she let her mind wander away from thoughts of her son until, inevitably, it settled on thoughts of Max and the guilty pleasure of that stolen kiss, his warm, strong fingers against her cheek. She gave a small shake of her head to dislodge the image, but the memory remained behind her eyes, obstinate and vivid.

What was she thinking? she asked herself for the thousandth time.

He had fought at Caen. It could have been a bullet from his gun that took Walter's life, or a grenade that he threw. Her imagination more than made up for her scant knowledge of battle and in the night her dreams were filled with savage detail – the two men engaged in a fight to the death that Walter could never hope to win. How could he? Chaplains went to war armed only with the word of God for protection – they were there to offer solace and support to the men who did the fighting.

Oh, Walter.

At times she still struggled to believe he had really gone, that their life together was truly over. That she would never see his smile again nor hear his quick and ready laugh, that there would be no more glances of shared understanding, no more nights with his body close to hers. All these things and more she grieved for. His company at breakfast and at the fireside in the evenings. The perfect way he made her tea. His help with the crossword and his easy way with his parishioners who loved him.

At the thought of it her eyes began to swim with tears, and the passing countryside blurred, indistinct outside the dirty window. Dragging a handkerchief from her bag she wiped at her face, furious with herself for the sudden loss of control. She thought she had mastered these feelings and locked them safe away. But it seemed Max had turned the key, stirring up emotions she had forbidden herself to feel, and now she felt as though she had no defence against them.

Guilt tapped at her heart for allowing it to happen. She had let him kiss her. She had wanted him to, hoped for it. She must be wicked, she thought, as Mrs Chapman suspected. A host of other adjectives suggested themselves.

Disloyal, easy, shameless, unfaithful, selfish, brazen, sinful ...

The list was endless. It was interesting how many words

existed in the English language for a woman such as her – it would have made for a lively discussion with Walter over dinner one night. She almost smiled at the thought of it.

But she was a widow now, after all, her husband dead and gone these last eight months. He would want her to be happy. The image of Max stepped across her thoughts again, and the pale green eyes spoke of the untold horrors they had witnessed. She remembered the scar, distinct and angry red. Did it still give him pain? She tried not to think of the getting of the wound.

When the bus finally pulled into Wellington, the sudden lurch and silence of the engine jerked her out of a doze. Her neck was sore where her head had fallen to one side against the window, and she blinked hard to bring herself to wakefulness.

'Wellington!' The driver shouted helpfully. 'Change here for Bristol, Taunton and Exeter.'

Clare dragged her overnight bag down from the overhead rack and got off the bus. In the street, a squall of rain whipped at her coat and hair and she raised her free hand to clear it from her face. Then, squinting through the rain, she picked out the hotel from among the line of buildings and was inside the dry warm foyer in moments.

She met James for dinner in the hotel dining room as they had arranged in their letters. She had mentioned her hope that Eric would join them, but when she got to the same table they had used the last time James was alone. She did her best to hide her disappointment.

'Clare! How lovely to see you – you look well.'

'Thank you.' She gave him a smile as she slid into her chair.

'Filthy weather,' he said. His own hair was damp with the rain. 'I couldn't keep my umbrella up on the way here – it turned inside out.' He made a face and she laughed.

He ordered their drinks (another sherry for her) and they sat in comfortable silence for a moment. The dining room was snug against the night, and now and then they heard the spatter of rain as the wind gusted it against the window. In the hearth a low fire glowed and smouldered, warming the room. She sipped at her sherry when it arrived.

'So how are you?' James asked. 'How are you managing?'

'I'm all right,' she lied, 'considering.'

'Have they turned you into a farmer yet? Done to you what they couldn't quite do to Walter?'

'Hardly. And besides, they don't want me to be a farmer. They don't want me there at all. I just serve to remind them that Walter went away to live a different life – I'm sure they can't wait to get rid of me. Well, Walter's mother, anyway,' she qualified. She was still not sure about Bridget.

'Oh dear.' He took a mouthful of his beer. '*No "spangles in the sunshine while the fish glide swiftly by"?*'

The quote was familiar but she couldn't place it. James must have seen the confusion in her face.

'John Clare,' he clarified. '*On a Lane in Spring.*'

She nodded, remembering. Walter too had liked John Clare. Somewhere in the boxes still in storage in Bristol there was a book of his poetry she had given him as a birthday gift years ago.

'I like the farm just as much as Walter did,' she said.

He smiled. 'I've asked around, but no jobs as yet. Perhaps for the new school year, if you can wait that long.'

'I don't have much choice,' she replied. 'And I suppose I should be grateful for a roof over my head when so many families have nothing.'

'I'm sure you are grateful. It doesn't mean you can't want something better. And hopefully,' he looked over the rim of his pint, 'things will improve very soon. It can't be long now until it's all over.'

'Here's to peace.' She lifted her glass and they clinked. It was almost impossible to imagine a peaceful world – they had been at war for so long. Then she thought of Max and wondered what the peace would mean to him, if he would soon be going home. Selfishly, she hoped that he would stay.

'You could come to Wellington more often. For a weekend perhaps? Just for a break.'

She opened her mouth to protest, but he cut her off.

'I'd be happy to stand you the hotel room. It would be lovely to see you more. And you could take Eric out for an afternoon. There are some lovely walks hereabouts. You could get to know the place a bit before you move here.'

She gave a noncommittal shake of her head. She was already far more indebted to James than she wanted to be, and despite all his kindness, she hated the feeling that she owed him.

'Weekends are often busy,' she said, which was another lie. Before Walter went away her life had been full to the brim with the duties of the parish, and at the outbreak of the war she had joined the Women's Voluntary Service. The roles had often dove-tailed neatly – helping with evacuations, food and shelter for bombed-out families, sandwiches and tea for the firemen and the air-raid wardens. She had felt useful then beyond the hours she spent as a teacher, a purpose to her life. But at Rowan Farm she was a spare part with no meaningful role to play, in spite of all her efforts to help.

'I'm sure Ashenden could spare you for one weekend a term,' he persisted, 'especially now the war is almost over.'

She forced herself to smile. 'Perhaps.'

James reached a hand across the table and placed it on hers. 'I intend to keep an eye on you as well as Eric,' he said, 'and see that you're all right too. For Walter, you understand.'

He gave her a reassuring smile that was not quite convincing and after a moment she withdrew her hand.

'Thank you,' she said. 'You're very kind.'

'It's the least I can do.'

The landlady came and they ordered fish and chips. There was no leek and potato soup this time and Clare was glad.

'Eric has settled in admirably this term.' James looked up from his meal. They spoke now and then as they ate, little titbits of chit-chat about the war, the growing hope for peace. They seemed to have refound their ease with each other and Clare was comfortable again in his company. It reminded her that there was a world outside of Ashenden and of old times, good times, before the war; every so often she half expected Walter to chip in to the conversation. 'He is so very like his father.'

She smiled. 'Yes, he is. Except I think Walter used to laugh more often. Eric is such a serious child.'

'A deep thinker, certainly. A budding philosopher perhaps?'

'Walter would have liked that.'

'It's hard for all the boys without their fathers, even those with fathers who will return – they've been gone for such a long time. A child needs a father.'

'In a perfect world,' she agreed.

'Even in the world we have.' He finished his last mouthful of fish and raised his eyes to hers. She held them briefly then looked away, disconcerted.

'What do you mean?' she asked. She laid her knife and fork across the plate.

James reached across the table to take her hand again where it lay on the table. Clare's skin prickled in sudden apprehension, and instinctively she drew her hand away.

'I know it's very soon,' James began. His voice was low and she sensed his nervousness. He cleared his throat. 'I know it's not long since Walter passed away, but I could be a father to Eric. I would be a good father, not as Walter was, of course, but I would do my best to guide him as Walter would have wanted …' He trailed off.

Clare stared, struggling to wrap her mind around what

exactly he was saying. Was he asking her to marry him? Was this a convoluted attempt at a proposal?

'I'm sure you would be a good father,' she managed to say. 'But it's far too soon to think of such things.'

Her eyes flitted to his just long enough to glimpse the disappointment.

'Of course,' he said, with a forced brightness that must have cost him dearly. 'I understand. I shouldn't have asked. Forgive me.'

She gave him her kindest smile, and though his lips twitched in response she could see that he was crushed. Inwardly she sighed. She had thought of him as a sorely needed friend, but now she understood it was not only friendship he had hoped for. How long? she wondered. How long had he nurtured that hope? Had he offered to pay Eric's schooling purely in order to win her? Her mind spun back across all the years she had known him, remembering all the glances they had shared, his little kindnesses. Had he loved her always?

'Please, forget I ever asked – it was foolish of me.' She heard the desperation in his words, the realisation he had given up his secret and blown his chance, and she could feel only sorry for him.

Putting her hand on his where it had remained on the table, she said, 'It's fine. It was kind of you to ask, and Eric is lucky to have such a thoughtful godfather.' She sought his gaze again, trying to reassure him.

The landlady came to the table to take away the plates, and Clare sat back in her chair, grateful for the chance to sit back and put some distance between them.

'Any dessert?' the landlady asked. 'Cup of tea?'

'A cup of tea,' Clare replied, and James nodded his agreement. 'For both of us, please.'

They watched the landlady's solid hips sway back towards the kitchen, and avoided each other's eyes.

'What time should I come to pick up Eric tomorrow?' she asked, adopting a business-like tone.

'Any time after nine o'clock would be fine,' he replied, every bit the teacher with a parent.

They sat in silence then, waiting for the tea, and it seemed to take a long time to come. By the time it finally arrived she wished she hadn't ordered it so that they could have parted sooner and gone their separate ways.

'How's Susan?' James asked, as they took their first sips. It was weak and tasteless and definitely not worth the wait.

Clare looked up in surprise, then remembered they had met at the memorial service. 'She's fine, looking forward to the holidays, like us all.' She smiled. 'She's going to London – she has a lot of friends there.'

'I'm sure she does. She's a very vivacious girl.'

'Yes,' Clare agreed, though it seemed like an odd thing to say. Perhaps he was still rattled from before.

They drank their tea without speaking until finally, finally, he got up to go.

'It was lovely to see you, Clare,' he said, and hesitated. The easy kiss to the cheek that was their usual greeting and farewell seemed unbearably intimate now, and neither of them was willing to risk it. Clare held out her hand and he shook it.

'Thank you for dinner,' she said. 'I'll see you at school tomorrow.'

He nodded. Then, hurriedly, as if he couldn't quite get away quickly enough, he strode across the dining room to the door and was gone.

Exhausted, Clare sank back into her chair and poured out the last dregs from the teapot. The landlady came over. 'Everything all right, love?'

'Yes, thank you. Everything is fine.'

'Only, and forgive me saying so, but you didn't seem as friendly with each other as last time.'

Clare let out a half-laugh. 'You're very observant, Mrs Wallis. That's exactly how it was.'

'As long as you're all right.'

Clare nodded in confirmation that she was indeed all right, drained the last of the tasteless tea then traipsed back up the stairs to her room.

Chapter Fifteen

In May the war in Europe was finally over. Hitler was dead and Germany had unconditionally surrendered.

'At last,' someone said.

The hut was filled with chatter. The prisoners had heard the news in various ways throughout the afternoon – from the farmers, the radio, their guards. Excitement and uncertainty rilled around the camp. The war had ended but what would happen to them now?

'We can go home.' Theo smiled at Max. 'You can go find Lotte and Hanna.'

Max tilted his head, considering. 'Perhaps,' he replied, but he doubted it would be so simple. Germany was defeated, and the Allies could do what they liked with them now. It could be months before they were free to go, and there was still no word from home in spite of all the letters he had sent. He had written to everyone he could think of. To Lotte. To his sister. To Lotte's parents. To the offices in neutral Switzerland that handled all the mail that passed between the warring nations. Even to the baker where they used to buy their bread. But he had heard nothing back from any of them. He wondered what was still left of Germany to return to.

For once Theo said nothing more. They had all dreamed of this day for so long but now it had come at last, the joy was tinged with apprehension.

'The whole of England is having a party tomorrow,' Albert said. He was an older man who slept in the neighbouring bunk, and on sleepless nights Max sometimes heard him crying softly to himself, trying vainly to muffle the sounds in his pillow. He had received plenty of letters from home in the months at the camp and Max did not envy him a single one of them. Perhaps no news was better after all.

'We should have a party too,' another man replied. 'We lost, sure. But it's over and that's something to celebrate, isn't it?'

'Why not?' Max gave a half-shrug, and looked towards Theo. Parties were his speciality.

'Consider it done.' His friend dipped into an elaborate bow, which elicited a laugh from some of the others. Then he was gone to organise God knows what, the hut door swinging shut behind him with a slam.

Later, lying in the dark and listening to the rustle and coughs and breathing of the men all around him, Max thought about what might wait for him at home. Now and then, a distant shout from some impromptu celebration at a nearby farm carried across the countryside, and every so often the night lit up with fireworks.

Max knew from other men's post that Berlin was all but destroyed. He let his thoughts wander back in time and saw in his mind's eye the street where he lived with his wife and daughter – the tobacconist's shop on the corner and the bakery across the road, the café where they sometimes went for coffee and cake. How much of it was still standing now? He had seen enough destroyed cities to easily imagine it all in rubble, its people home-less, hungry, desperate. And he had witnessed too the savagery of soldiers (on both sides) towards civilians. If he had believed in a god, he would have prayed for his family's safety, but frustration at his helplessness burned in his fingertips and he balled his fists against it. He was Hanna's father, Lotte's husband. He should have protected them, should have kept them safe, and however much he tried to rationalise that it was not his fault that he hadn't, it still felt like failure.

As if to reassure him Lotte trod across his thoughts, clear in his head for the first time in months. He smiled to see her, trying to burn the image in his brain to keep and remember always. Hanna followed, her face still young as she had been when he saw her last. She would be almost twelve now, her birthday in just a few days. His daughter. His beautiful daughter. For such a long time Hanna had been his whole world, but the war had swept that life away and he could hardly believe any more that it had ever existed at all.

The bunk shuddered and creaked as Theo turned in his sleep in the bed below. Of course Theo was asleep; he could sleep through anything. He had slept when the rest of them had been huddled and shivering, half frozen to death under Russian artillery, and again when the bombardment in Normandy had made the whole world shake. It was an enviable skill – Max doubted he would ever know sound and dreamless sleep again.

At the other end of the hut someone broke into a fit of coughing, gasps for air rasping through the quiet. Max reached for his cigarettes and lit one. The match flared in the dark and the heat of the first draw back felt good in his lungs. Filthy habit, Lotte would have scolded, and she was right. But in Russia any source of warmth, however scant, had been welcome, and it helped to keep the hunger pangs at bay. The men had shared the precious cigarettes between them, passing the stubs hand to hand with numbed fingers that shook with cold. He gave an involuntary shiver at the memory, and let the smoke trickle through his lips into the dark above him. He was still surprised he had survived, that any of them had made it through the war. *Always the lucky one,* Theo once said when they were still in training and he had got away with some infraction he could barely remember now. He hadn't believed it then, but perhaps his friend had been right – he was still here, after all. He wondered if he would be so lucky in a peacetime world.

Chapter Sixteen

For weeks Clare hadn't caught so much as a glimpse of Max Peterson and she was half afraid that with the end of the war he might have been moved to a different camp. Though she had heard no news of it yet she supposed the prisoners would soon be going home. Disappointment was tempered with relief at the possibility – no decisions to be made, no temptation to be resisted. But even so she thought of him often, and each time, the remembered kiss lit the now-familiar heat across her skin. Had Walter ever disconcerted her in quite the same way? She didn't think so – her memories of the early days with Walter were replete with a sense of the rightness of being with him; a friendship, a love and respect, the prospect of a life to live together. She had loved him and she had been happy – that much she knew.

But what she felt for Max threatened to dismantle her. Forbidden, ill-advised, dangerous – she knew next to nothing about him. What shocked her most was that she simply didn't care about any of those things. His presence haunted all her waking hours, guilt and shame and want and joy all tangled up inside her: the danger of it was delicious, each moment to be treasured, and though at times her saner self counselled caution she knew she had no will to resist.

Saturday morning a few weeks into peacetime, and Clare slipped out from the farmhouse after breakfast, unnoticed. When she had first moved to the farm she had spent a lot of her free time following Bridget or Mrs Chapman around, offering to help until they gave her odd jobs to keep her busy. But she quickly came to understand that for the most part they neither needed nor wanted her help, and she guessed they regarded her as useless, a city girl who wouldn't want to get her soft hands dirty. Now and then she collected the eggs from the henhouse (which was actually the children's job) or worked alongside Bridget in the kitchen garden picking beans or weeding, but mostly she found jobs to do inside the house instead – cooking lunch, cleaning up, sweeping, making the beds. Even so, she still felt like an intruder, a guest whose efforts were politely tolerated. So this morning she abandoned all pretence at being part of the family, took the bicycle from the barn and set out towards the village.

The day was fine, with the kind of breezy warmth that puts a spring in your step. An azure sky was dotted with puffs of clouds like a child might draw, and she lifted her face to the meet the heat of the sun as she rode. She would probably have freckles by the end of the day but for once the thought of it didn't bother her: the war in Europe was over and she was glad to be alive. Above the hedgerow beside her, a pair of speckled butterflies danced into view, and from beyond it she could hear the steady throb of the Fordson. It had been working fine since Max repaired it, and the knowledge imbued her with an absurd sense of pride. Clare allowed herself a smile, acknowledging this carefree, reckless woman she hardly recognised.

She reached a stretch of road where the bike began to rattle over the sun-hardened ruts, becoming hard to steer, and she didn't hear the lorry approaching from behind until it was almost level. Turning in surprise, she almost lost control of the bike, just managing to keep her balance and keep going as the truck came alongside. It was travelling slowly to navigate the furrowed road, and briefly she kept pace with it. Then, as it pulled a little ahead, she realised it was the lorry from the camp that ferried the prisoners to the further farms, and she lifted her head to search the faces of the men in the back of it, eager.

All of them were watching her but she picked out Max at once, sitting at the tailgate.

'Clare!'

She sped up to keep pace with it, and he leaned out towards her.

'Meet me,' he called.

'How?' Clare struggled to keep the bike straight and though she wanted only to look at Max, she needed to watch the road beneath the wheels.

'At the church,' he said. The gap between them was widening, the lorry picking up speed on a patch where the road was less rutted. 'Tonight. After dark.'

The lorry roared as the driver changed gear and put his foot down. Black smoke spewed into the lane and she stopped pedalling, holding her breath as she came to a halt and watched the men disappear behind the fug. When they had rounded the bend out of sight and the last echoes of the engine were fading into the morning, she started pedalling once again, and went on her way towards the village.

After dark? Clare thought. It was almost midsummer – it would be close to midnight by the time darkness fully fell. But she went even so, cycling through the twilight with her headlamp on, unable to resist. No one at the farm saw her leave.

It felt strange to be out so late. When she had lived in the city they had gone out often in the evening – to visit friends, the theatre, a concert – and a neighbour had come to keep an eye on Eric. But life in the country was different. Bridget's eyes had widened with shock when Clare suggested early on that they go to the pub together one Friday night, and she had not dared to ask again. Now and then there was a concert or a dance at the village hall, but they were few and far between. Perhaps now that the war was coming to an end there might be more but somehow she doubted it: people here seemed to like a quiet life.

The light had not yet quite left the sky when she leaned her bike against the churchyard wall out of sight of the road. A dull glimmer across the horizon marked the day's last gasp as the stars began to light up one by one across the heavens. In the warmth she could feel the dampness of the sweat on her skin at the back of her neck. She hoped her face wasn't red from the effort of cycling.

The hinges on the church gate squealed when she pushed it open and she winced, but there was no one about to hear. Inside the churchyard the gravestones leaned at drunken angles and her eyes were drawn instinctively to the headstone they had erected for Walter, though his body would never lie beneath it. It gleamed in the last of the twilight, still bright with newness and freshly engraved. Without thinking she went towards it.

Walter George Chapman.
   Beloved son, husband, father. Taken too soon.
   1909–1944. RIP.

Walter's mother had chosen the inscription, and afterwards Eric had observed the order should have read, *husband, father, son.* She had agreed with him, then explained that some battles were simply not worth the fight. She thought of Eric now, almost at the end of his first year at secondary school, so grown up and independent. He would be home soon for the long summer holidays and she smiled at the prospect – she had missed him.

'You'd be proud of him,' she said to the grave that didn't hold Walter's body, then gave herself a wry smile: it was hard to break the habit of talking to a gravestone.

A movement at the edge of her eye made her turn abruptly away, heartbeat quickening. For a moment she could see nothing but the dark mass of trees and shrubs that marked the border of the churchyard, eyes straining into the gloom. Then a figure emerged from the dark and she froze, uncertain, wondering what on earth she had been thinking to come here like this to meet a man she barely knew alone in the middle of the night. Taking an automatic step back behind the headstone, she held her breath, barely daring to breathe.

'Clare?' His tone betrayed his own uncertainty and she was a little reassured.

'Yes,' she replied, and her voice sounded loud in the silent churchyard, even though she had spoken in barely more than a whisper.

He moved closer until she could see his features more clearly in the starlit dark. A half-moon hung above the treetops.

'I wasn't sure if you would come,' he said.

'Neither was I.'

He smiled. 'I thought I might have frightened you away, last time.'

Clare shook her head. Then, 'How …?' She made a vague gesture towards him with her hand and he seemed to understand.

'We're not so closely guarded now, and it's a simple wire fence around the camp. It's easy to get out.'

'The bolt cutters.' She remembered Simon cursing when he couldn't find them a few weeks before.

'I borrowed them,' he said, and she smiled.

They stood in awkward silence. Then he said, 'Shall we go inside?'

They both looked towards the old stone church that loomed out of the dark. 'It would be safer.'

She nodded her agreement and they walked side by side along the path and into the church. In the sudden cool of the nave Clare shivered. She wondered what the Reverend Keane would think of her, using his church for a secret tryst with a German – he had been preaching a hard and unforgiving line for years.

Max turned on the little torch he was carrying and went towards the altar. Taking a box of matches from his pocket, he lit one of the candles. She followed him along the aisle and when the flame had flickered into brightness they sat side by side in the choir stalls. Neither spoke for a while but she was glad she had come and the fear that had washed across her in the graveyard had all but ebbed away.

'I suppose I should congratulate you,' Max said at last, turning his head to look at her. His face was almost golden in the candle-light, eyes gleaming like a cat's.

'What for?'

'Winning the war.'

She laughed, liking his ability to surprise her, to say the unexpected.

'You're very beautiful when you laugh,' he said. 'You should do it more.'

She looked away to hide the flush of pleasure that crept across her cheek, though in the half light she doubted he would even notice.

'Will they let you go home now?' she asked, raising her head again to look at him.

'I don't think so. Not for a while yet. It's too hard. There are too many of us, and they need us to work.'

'I'm glad,' she heard herself say. 'I'm sorry, I know it's very selfish of me, but I'm glad.'

He reached out his hand to take hers where it lay resting on her thigh. She turned her wrist so that they could entwine their fingers. Strong hands, she remembered, the skin warm and dry. Her own hand felt very small against it.

'You're taking a big risk to meet me,' he said. 'So I think perhaps you like me a little.'

She gave him a wry smile, self-conscious and unsure how to answer. She wasn't used to being teased.

'I like you a lot,' she said, deciding in the end that the truth was the best reply, 'far more than I should.'

'Because I'm German?'

She nodded. 'That was my husband's headstone in the church-yard. It's not even a year since he died.'

'Was he a good man?'

'Yes,' she said quickly. 'He was a wonderful man.'

'Then he'd want you to be happy.'

'Yes, but ...' It was the same argument she had used against herself when the guilt for her feelings sometimes threatened to overwhelm her. She had trouble believing it then too.

'Life is very short, Clare.' He shifted on the bench so that his whole body was facing her, their knees brushing, and when she dropped her head away from the question in his eyes he tucked his fingers under her chin and lifted it gently.

'If the war should have taught us anything, it's to live every day as though it's our last. Because it might be.'

'*Carpe diem*,' she said. 'Seize the day. My father used to tell me that all the time.'

'Your father was right.'

She said nothing. His fingers were still holding her chin and their faces were close enough that she could feel the warmth of his breath and make out the green in his eyes. She had never before been so aware of a man as a physical being – the animal heart that beat in his chest, the pumping blood that gave him life, bone, muscle, flesh. An image of Walter from her dream touched the corner of her thoughts – broken limbs and a heart that beat no more. It was all so fragile, life stripped away in a moment.

With a tilt of her head she let it come to rest against his cheek, and she sensed the change in his breathing before he moved his hand from her chin and trailed fingers gently across her cheek. Walter used to do the same.

She lifted her head away from him and shifted back along the bench. 'What do you want from me?'

His forehead creased in a furrow, confusion in his eyes. 'What does any man want from a woman he likes? I want to be with you.'

'Is that all?'

'Of course not,' he replied, 'but what do you want me to say?'

Caught off guard by his honesty, she looked at him for a moment in the flickering light, observing the high, wide cheekbones and square-cut jaw. He was really very handsome, and she liked him very much.

'It's impossible,' she answered, shaking her head.

'What happened to *carpe diem?*'

In spite of herself she laughed. Then he laughed too and the stern lines softened in his face, the mischief returning to his eyes. Briefly, she looked away from him, trying to calm the riot of her emotions.

'Clare?'

She turned once more towards him. She liked the sound of her name on his tongue, the slight inflection of his accent.

'How did you learn to speak such good English?' she asked.

'I had an English nanny when I was a boy. We had money then when my father was still alive …' He trailed off with a shrug as though he were reluctant to tell the rest.

'What happened?' she persisted, and he looked at her in surprise.

'You want to know about my family?'

'I want to know about you. It seems as good a place to start as any.'

Max tilted his head in acknowledgement. 'My father was an

engineer,' he told her, 'and we lived in a nice part of Berlin – a couple of servants, a nanny for the children. I wanted to be an engineer too but when I was ten my father died. My mother was no good with money and what Papa left us ran out very fast. So we moved to a smaller place in a rougher neighbourhood, and I left school and got work in a garage to support us. It wasn't much but it kept a roof over our heads and we didn't starve.' He turned to look at her then. 'Your turn.'

She smiled. 'There's really not much to tell. My father was a doctor and my mother died when I was very young. I went to teacher training college after school, met Walter, got married ...'

'Were you happy?'

'Yes,' she replied firmly. 'Very.'

'And now?'

She hesitated, unwilling to admit to the feelings he evoked. 'Perhaps,' she offered at last, biting her lip and lowering her head away from the intensity of those flecked green eyes, self-conscious again. 'A little.'

When she looked up he was still watching her, the furrow deep between his eyes. She gave him a half-smile, uncertain, and after a moment he lifted his hand to touch her face again, lightly brushing her cheek with the backs of his fingers. She shivered, her body rebelling against the dictates of her mind, heartbeat quick, breath coming short. She had never thought she could want any other man but Walter.

'It's late,' she managed to whisper. 'I should go.'

He smiled. 'I'll walk with you.'

'I rode my bike.'

'Even better.'

He got up abruptly and blew out the altar candle, plunging the church into darkness. Clare blinked, gazing blindly towards the altar where the light had been. Then Max was beside her, reaching for her hand as he turned on the little torch and led her along the nave towards the door.

Outside, the last of the twilight had long since faded, and the patches of sky between the scattered clouds glimmered with stars. The moon had risen higher, an almost perfect golden half. Max dragged the bike from the hedge where she had left it and she reached for the handlebars to take it from him, but he didn't let it go.

'Get on the back,' he said.

She looked doubtfully at the little rack above the back wheel. Long ago Eric had ridden there as a small child. Max turned on the headlamp, swung his leg across the seat and settled himself on the saddle, one foot on the pedal.

'Come on,' he coaxed. *'Carpe diem.'*

She let out a laugh that was half nerves, half excitement, and settled herself obediently on the rack behind him. Then, because there was nothing else to hold on to, she put her hands either side of his waist and gripped hard as the bike wobbled forward a few yards until it found its balance and picked up speed on the road. The rungs of the rack dug into the backs of her thighs, but the night air was cool against her face and Max's body was warm beneath her hands. She could feel the strength of his muscles as his legs worked the pedals.

'Are you all right?' he asked, when they had rattled past the cluster of buildings that marked the centre of the village.

'I'm fine,' she replied, and realised she was laughing.

Too soon, they came to the corner of the lane that led to Rowan Farm, and Clare slid from the back with regret. Max dismounted too and handed her the bike. They stood close with just the bike between them and she waited, wondering if he would kiss her, half hopeful, half afraid.

He said, 'Can I see you again?'

She lowered her head to watch her hands as they twisted on the handlebars where the leather was still warm from his grip. She could feel the flush in her cheeks from the pleasure of the evening and a lightness in herself from his company she had long ago forgotten. Though a voice in her head commanded 'no', she decided to ignore it.

'Yes,' she replied. 'I'd like that.'

She was rewarded with a smile that lit his whole face. 'Next Friday? At the church again?'

She nodded. Then they stood for a moment, suddenly awkward with each other once more, until at last Max began to back away.

'Friday,' he said, lifting a hand in farewell before he turned away and retraced his steps along the lane.

She watched him go until his back was swallowed by the dark and she could no longer hear his boots on the road. Then, with a deep breath and a smile to herself, she walked the bike the rest of the way back to the farm, thinking only that next Friday seemed like a long time to wait.

Chapter Seventeen

The week passed slowly. The children at school were restless in the summer warmth, impatient for the holidays, and Clare understood their desire for freedom. She felt it herself within the walls of the school and confines of the farmhouse – the sense that life was happening elsewhere and passing her by.

On Friday night, Clare cycled again to the churchyard in the dying light of the day. There was a bench against the wall of the church with a little brass plate on the back of it, and she shone her torch to see the name. *In memory of Charlotte Lewis,* the engraving said. There were no dates but it was an old bench, the wooden slats smooth and worn.

'Thank you, Charlotte Lewis,' she murmured, making herself comfortable. 'Whoever you were.'

The evening was warm, and as the twilight finally dwindled into night, the clouds were high and light enough for the waxing moon to shed her light across the graveyard. Mostly, Clare managed to keep her eyes averted from Walter's headstone. She waited. When the slats of the bench grew hard and uncomfortable under her legs, she got up to wander between the graves, eyes sliding often to the gap in the hedge where he had come from the last time. It was too dark to see the time on the face of her watch, but the minutes seemed to pass by slowly and still he did not come.

How long should she wait? she wondered. How long should she give him? She imagined it might not always be easy for him to break out, no matter what he told her last time. He was still a prisoner, after all. In the early hours she decided at last that he would not come, and when she cycled back to the farm alone, it seemed like a long way home without him.

At the farm Clare wheeled the bike to its place in the shed behind the tractor, and from the yard she could see a light in the window of the farmhouse kitchen. Someone was still up, and she wondered who. Letting out a long breath to steady her racing heart, she crossed the yard and pushed open the kitchen door.

Simon was at the table with a bottle of beer in his hand. Empties were strewn across the surface in front of him and when he lifted his head at the sound of the door she could see straight away that he was drunk – clouded eyes and mottled cheeks, and a belligerent set to his mouth. Instinct kept her near the door, close to the stairs.

For a moment he said nothing, watching her. Then, 'Where have you been?'

'I couldn't sleep,' she said. 'I went out for some air.'

'Where did you go? You've been gone a while.'

Had he been waiting for her? 'I went to the church ...' she trailed off, letting him draw his own conclusions.

'Ah, yes.' He lifted the bottle towards her in a half-salute. 'The vicar's wife. Very devout.'

'I went to his gravestone,' she said.

He turned in his seat to face her. 'Come and sit down. Have a beer.' He gestured to the pair of remaining bottles he had set up in readiness.

She shook her head. 'I'm going to bed.'

'Because you're too good to drink with me?'

'Because I'm tired.'

'Too good for the farm altogether. You and Walter both. Only he got out and now you're stuck here. Ironic really.'

'It worked out all right for you though, didn't it?' she said, one foot on the bottom step, her hand already on the banister. 'You got the farm.'

'You think this is what I wanted out of life?' He gestured to the kitchen with the bottle in his hand. 'To be a farmer? I could have been a soldier, done my bit, same as Walter. Better that than this endless drudgery.'

Clare's hand tightened on the banister.

'But farming's *a reserved occupation*.' His tone dripped with scorn. 'And they wouldn't let me go. So here we are.' He opened his arms wide to signify the whole farm around them. 'You and me both, Clare. Trapped like rabbits in a snare – no escape but death.'

'The war's all but over,' she said, irritated by the melodrama. 'Then you can leave if you want to.'

'And do what?' He turned towards her, his gaze finding its focus on her face with difficulty. She flinched at the fury in his eyes. 'I've missed my chance now. I'm too old to start again, too old to begin something new. And I got no money – it's all in the farm. This is all there is for me now.' Simon lowered his head down and away, anger waning, and she let out the breath she hadn't realised she was holding. He took another slug of his beer, slumped and miserable.

'I'm going to bed,' she told him, but he didn't answer her, nor even raise his head as she climbed the stairs away from him towards the safety of her room.

At the end of the summer term Eric got a lift home from school with another boy whose father had offered, and Clare was greatly relieved not to have to make the journey to Wellington.

James still wrote to her but the letters came less often than they used to, and the tone had become more formal as though he were keeping her at a distance while he nursed the hurt of her rejection. She agonised over the letters she wrote to him in return, struggling for the words, the right mood. She was mortified to think she might have inadvertently encouraged him, and several times she trawled her memory, searching for moments he might have misunderstood. Every smile, every glance they had ever exchanged now seemed to be freighted with a different meaning, and she wondered how she could have been so blind. Then she wondered if Walter had ever realised.

For two days Eric was glad to be back – his own room and a mother and grandmother who doted on him – but he was quickly bored, used to the company of other boys and constant occupation. The term at the village school had yet to finish so Eric spent the days wandering the countryside or reading in the barn, where he had made himself a comfortable spot among the hay.

Clare saw the change in him with dismay – her thoughtful, gentle boy had been replaced by some other child who bossed his cousins and had little time for his mother. Perhaps the long holidays would soften him again, she thought, and he would remember he had no need to prove himself at home.

'What did you expect?' Mrs Chapman said, when Clare mentioned in passing how Eric had changed. 'Of course he has. That kind of school demands it more than most.'

'I didn't mean …' Clare didn't really know what she meant. She only knew she was sad that she no longer seemed to know the boy who was her son: she hoped she hadn't made a mistake sending him away to school.

'I know.' Mrs Chapman softened. 'It's hard when they grow away from you. Walter did the same even though he was only at the grammar school, a day boy. But at that age they just want to be men and they think men have to be hard ...' She trailed off and folded the last ironed shirt with a sigh.

'I'll put the laundry away,' Clare said, getting up from the table and picking up the basket. For once, Mrs Chapman let her take it without a word of protest.

The last week of term at the village school seemed endless, and Clare cycled home from a day that had dragged. The children were eager to break up, the long summer days beckoning beyond the windows, and they were restless and inattentive. At times, she had found her own attention wandering away, towards thoughts of Walter, thoughts of Max. It had been a long day.

Now she cycled slowly along the lane thinking more or less of nothing until she saw the little group of prisoners clustered at a gate. They were smoking and talking and by the time she had picked out Max from among them he had already seen her. With a quick glance across his shoulder he stepped away from the group. Clare slowed the bike, slid from the saddle and walked to meet him. He leaned on the top bar of the gate, his forearms bare and sunburned and his hair golden in the afternoon sun. Clare ran her fingers automatically through her own hair, and wished she was wearing something less dowdy than the plain blouse and skirt she always wore for work.

For a moment neither of them spoke, savouring the surprise of the unexpected meeting. Then Max said, 'I'm sorry for the other night. I couldn't get out. One of the other men got caught and they found the hole in the fence.'

She smiled. 'Have you made another?' It seemed absurd to her that the men were still kept as prisoners despite the German surrender. Already in Berlin, the leaders of the Allies were in conference, deciding Germany's fate.

'Of course.'

The lane was empty and Clare leaned the bike against the

hedge and moved closer. She was aware of the tactfully turned-away other men, and the nearness of Max on the other side of the gate.

'Max!' A warning hiss from one of the Germans broke the moment.

They both turned to look. Someone was approaching across the field, but they were too far away to see who.

'Friday,' he said, and reached out to brush her cheek with the backs of his fingers. Clare's eyes half closed with the pleasure of his touch. 'At the church.'

She nodded and moved reluctantly away, picked up the bicycle and dragged it back on to the road. Placing her foot on the pedal she was aware of Max still watching her and the quick-ness of her heartbeat. Then she turned again to give him a final smile and saw the sudden flicker of alarm in his eyes. Following his gaze with her own, she realised with horror what he had seen in the lane. Eric was standing in the centre of the road, watching her, and in the moment that she met his eyes he wheeled away and ran, sprinting towards the farm.

Briefly, she looked towards Max, who shook his head in baffled disbelief, before she swung herself onto the saddle of the bike and set off after her son.

By the time she threw her bike against the wall of the barn Eric had long since disappeared inside the house. He had cut across the fields – when she stood up on the pedals she had been able to see his small form retreating as he sprinted homeward, away from her. She ran into the house and cast a hurried glance across the kitchen. Mrs Chapman was at the sink, her back to the room. Bridget was at the stove, stirring some kind of stew that gave off a meaty aroma with a hint of bay and rosemary, and she spun round in alarm as Clare clattered in.

'What's wrong?'

'Where's Eric?'

'He went upstairs.'

Clare took the stairs two at a time. Behind her she could hear Bridget calling out after her, asking what was wrong, but she didn't answer. At the door to Eric's room she stopped. She could feel the rapid patter of her heart, the sweat along the runnel of her spine, and she still had no idea what she could say to defend herself. Taking a deep breath that did nothing to steady her nerves, she lifted her hand to the door and knocked.

'Eric? Eric? Are you in there?'

'Go away!' His voice was close on the other side of the door.

'Eric, let me in. We need to talk.'

'I've got nothing to say to you.'

'Please?' She waited, and when there was no answer she pressed down the handle of the door and tried to push it open, but it would not move. He must be sitting on the floor with his back against it.

'Go away!' he said. 'I hate you.'

'You don't mean that.'

'You let that Nazi touch you. You're a slut. A dirty, collaborating slut!'

She took in a sharp breath, shocked by such language in her son's mouth. He must have learned it from the other boys at school; the price of a good education, she supposed. That kind of language at her own school would lead to a thorough beating from Miss Finch. Letting go of the handle, she stepped back, staring at the door, frozen. From the edge of her eye she caught a glimpse of Bridget on the stairs but she paid her no attention, ransacking her mind for words she could say, something, anything, she could do to stop her son from hating her.

'Go away! I never want to see you again.'

She could hear the tears he was trying to hold back and her heart turned in pity. Of course he hated her. What son wouldn't?

'We'll talk later, when you're ready,' she managed to say, then turned and walked along the hall to her own room to stand at the window and gaze out across the yard, seeing nothing through the film of tears until a tentative knock at the door made her turn. Dragging the back of her hand across her eyes, she sniffed and tried to compose herself.

'Come in.'

Bridget appeared in the doorway, sidling around the door and shutting it behind her. 'Are you all right? What's happened?'

Clare slumped on to the bed and Bridget came to sit beside her. 'Clare?'

'I was talking to one of the prisoners,' she said. 'Eric saw me.'

'Why were you talking to one of the prisoners? It's against the law – you know that. You'll get in all sorts of trouble.'

Clare gave a bitter laugh – she was already in all sorts of trouble.

'Why, Clare?' Her sister-in-law persisted.

Clare turned to look at the woman beside her: dutiful daughter, long-suffering wife, adoring sister. Bridget was observing her now with worried, curious eyes. Would she understand?

'I like him,' she said in the end. 'I like the way I feel when I'm with him. Like there might be a life for me without Walter after all.'

Bridget stared. 'Oh God.'

'Yes,' Clare agreed. 'Oh God.'

They sat in silence then for a while. Downstairs they could hear Walter's mother moving around the kitchen, the clatter of pans, the scrape of a chair leg on the flagstones. Mrs Chapman would have heard everything, Clare knew. She turned again to Bridget.

'Do you hate me?'

'I've always hated you,' Bridget said, without emotion, and it was Clare's turn to stare. 'You had everything: a life in the city, a good job, the perfect marriage ...' She trailed off with a shrug.

'I don't have any of those things any more.'

'No. I suppose you don't. But you're carrying on with a German, so there's that.'

'They're not our enemy any more.'

'They killed Walter. Your husband. My brother. How can you even think about them that way? They all but destroyed the whole world.'

Clare drew in a deep breath to quell the rising tide of tears she could feel behind her eyes, but it did no good. She thought of Max, cheek burning where his fingers had touched it, and a flood of shame washed through her. What was wrong with her that she could fall so hard for a German? She wiped at her eyes.

'Walter would be so disappointed in you,' Bridget said, then got up from the bed and walked out.

Clare watched the door slam shut behind her then lay back on the bed, curled up in a ball, and let the tears come unchecked.

It took all Clare's strength of will to go downstairs again to the kitchen. Dinner had been and gone, the table cleared and the plates washed and put away, but it made no difference – she had lost all appetite for food. Bridget was at the stove making tea and turned automatically at the sound of Clare's footstep before she remembered, and slid her eyes away. On the dresser the radio was playing: a man's voice was reporting on the Potsdam Conference, where Churchill and Truman and Stalin were mapping out the future of Europe. On any other day she would have listened intently but tonight the words washed over her, barely heard, and outside the window the last moments of the day flared yellow across the horizon.

'Hello, Clare.' Simon looked up from a piece of leather harness he was cleaning. 'Are you all right?'

She gave him a grateful smile. 'Yes, thank you.' Then, 'Where's Eric?'

'He went back to his room after his dinner.'

In spite of the warmth in the kitchen, Clare pulled her cardigan more tightly around her. The back door opened and closed and Mrs Chapman appeared then stopped, pulled up short by the sight of her daughter-in-law, wiping her hands on the threadbare apron she always wore.

Clare said nothing and waited, still standing near the bottom of the stairs. She assumed the older woman knew by now what had happened. She would have heard the argument, and either Eric or Bridget would have explained. She braced herself, conscious of the accusation in Mrs Chapman's eyes, and her own sense of shame flushed over her skin once more. Walter's mother finished wiping her hands and turned her head away from Clare with a slow and deliberate movement. She walked to the table and sat down and Clare hesitated, unsure what to do next. Bridget poured tea for everyone but Clare.

'Give her some tea,' Simon growled.

Bridget shook her head.

'It doesn't matter,' Clare said quickly. 'I don't want any.' She had no wish to give Simon an excuse to berate his wife.

Mrs Chapman blew on her tea, sipped it with a sigh of satisfaction, and replaced the cup in its saucer. Then, finally, when she had apparently decided she had made her daughter-in-law wait long enough, she lifted her head and pinned Clare with a look. She had lost more weight, cheeks gaunt beneath the jutting cheekbones. She should go to a doctor, Clare thought, and her own detachment surprised her.

'I've heard what you did,' Mrs Chapman said, finally. 'And from what you said to Bridget I can only assume it wasn't the first time you've talked to him.'

Clare was silent. It was like an interrogation, she thought. Or being in the dock at court. She wondered why she was standing there and submitting herself to their judgement. A guilty conscience, most likely.

'Is it?'

She shook her head, and gripped on to the edges of her cardigan with her fingers.

'Leave her alone,' Simon interrupted. 'What does it matter? Walter's dead. You can't expect her to be a nun for the rest of her life. Isn't that right, Clare?' He gave her a wink and she slid her eyes away.

Both his wife and mother-in-law drew in breath with an audible gasp.

'With a German!' Mrs Chapman spat. 'Murderers all. Have you no shame? No respect for your husband's memory?'

'Walter never hated the Germans,' she heard herself say, 'and he would have been the first to forgive.'

For a moment there was a silence, filled only with the sound of Simon taking a slurp from his tea.

Then, 'I want you out of my house,' Mrs Chapman said.

'You can't throw her out,' Simon protested. 'Where's she going to go? There's no housing for love nor money.'

'I don't care where she goes. There's no reason for her to be here, or for us to take pity on her any more. She's lost all right to our protection, betraying Walter like that. We owe her nothing. She's lucky I'm not going to report her. She could end up in court and lose her job, like those two nurses.'

Simon pulled a face at Clare as if to say, *I tried.*

'I didn't betray anyone,' she said, anger starting to kindle at last at their casual judgement. How dare they? 'I talked to a prisoner of war, that's all, a prisoner who saved your granddaughter's life, in case you've forgotten.'

'Talked, eh?' Simon rubbed the teacup with the tips of his fingers and smiled. 'That's a new word for it. Well, they're good-looking lads, some of them; can't say I blame you.'

Clare almost smiled. She knew he was only taking her part to infuriate Mrs Chapman, but all the same she was grateful for the deflection of the older woman's hostility and his recognition of her right to be attracted to a man, however crudely expressed.

Bridget raised her head from her examination of the pattern on the teacloth. 'I heard old Jim Hardy's gone to live with his sister in Taunton,' she said, 'so the flat above the saddler's shop might be free.'

'There you are.' Mrs Chapman nodded in vindication. 'That's that sorted. She can be out of here by the weekend.'

'What about Eric? What about your grandson?'

'He can stay,' Mrs Chapman replied without hesitation. 'I've got no issue with Eric. He's my grandson. Walter's boy. He wouldn't want to stay with you anyway – he made it perfectly plain what he thinks of you earlier.'

No one spoke, and Clare fought down the urge to cry again. Then, because she could no longer bear to be in the same room as them all, she turned and walked away, out into the warm summer night.

Chapter Eighteen

The flat was two shabby rooms above the saddler's shop on the village main street. It had a living room, a kitchenette, a bedroom and a bathroom, and the furniture looked as though it had been salvaged from bombed-out houses. None of it matched. Most of it was chipped, scratched, or in need of a coat of paint, and the green velvet sofa bore evidence of a previous owner's cat, though it turned out to be surprisingly comfortable. But there was electricity and running water, and the whole place smelled pleasantly of leather and polish from the saddler's shop downstairs.

She moved in on the first day of the school summer holidays and Simon helped her carry the few belongings that were not still in storage in Bristol. She would have to fetch it all one day, she thought: she would have liked to have some of it now. A clock, perhaps, and a lamp, one or two of the rugs, a couple of pictures, some linen. But she had no way to transport it and so it would have to wait a while longer.

By lunchtime the move was complete and Simon had returned to the farm. He had barely spoken to her all morning, apparently resenting the hours away from the demands of the land, irritated by the extra work. But she had gone across to the pub and bought bottles of beer as a thank you, and he went away happy enough.

Alone, finally, she wandered through the flat, running her fingers across the furnishings, familiarising herself with her new home. It wasn't much but it was hers, and she liked it. She stood at the window that looked out across the street. Outside the post office a couple of women were chatting, one with a baby in a pram. She thought she recognised her as the mother of a child in her class but she couldn't be sure. The Ashenden children mostly made their own way to school and she seldom saw their parents except for sports day or prizegiving, or if there was trouble of some kind. It had been very different at her old school in Bristol where the church and school had formed the hub of the parish community and she had known a lot of the mothers by name. It seemed like a million years ago now.

She opened the window and leaned out. At the end of the high street, beyond the school, the squat church tower stood dark against a sky that had threatened rain all day, the weather sultry and humid.

It was Friday, and she had a decision to make.

In the last few days at the farm she had decided she would not go. Reminded everywhere she looked of Walter, she felt the weight of guilt like a burden she must carry.

The Germans had killed him and left her a widow.

The Germans had brought the world to its knees.

Eric refused even to be in the same room as her, and that was the hardest blow of all. She hardly missed the company of Mrs Chapman and Bridget, but when her son turned his back on her and walked away her heart broke a little more each time: she could only think it was no more than she deserved. She had been a faithless wife. A collaborator. She had betrayed her husband for the enemy and dishonoured his memory. In those exhausted sleepless last nights at the farm, she had determined she would never see Max Peterson again. She would win back Eric's trust and do whatever it took.

But now, in her own flat above the high street with no one close by to judge and accuse, her thoughts wheeled of their own accord to Max, revisiting the memory of his touch, his kiss, his smile; her laughter on the back of the bike as he cycled, a delight in life she had almost forgotten existed. Even just the thought of his company brought a smile to her face. Was it so wrong to want him? In a world that was full of hate, surely to love someone was no bad thing.

She went to the kitchen, put the kettle on the little Baby Belling stove and turned it on. She would eat less well from now on, she knew. There would be limited meat and cheese, and eggs would become a luxury, but she had already stocked up on a few essentials at the village shop – tea, bread, milk, cheese, jam. There was also the bottle of brandy that Fred Wakeman had given her, saved for a special occasion. Waiting for the water to boil, she turned the possibilities in her mind, deciding first one thing then the other, caught in an endless loop of indecision.

What are the pros and cons? her father used to counsel whenever she faced a difficult choice. *Make a list.*

She found a piece of paper and a pencil and made two columns.

Pros: *I like him*, she wrote. *He makes me laugh. I have a sense of joy when I'm with him. He gives me hope for the future – the possibility of a life beyond widowhood, a new beginning. The laws will change in time. Attitudes will alter.*

Cons: *It's against the law even to talk to him. I could be fined. I could lose my job. I could lose my son. The Germans killed Walter. Max is a German, and I should hate him.*

She stopped, pencil poised above the paper. From somewhere far away she heard the first low rumble of the coming storm, and wondered if approaching gunfire sounded the same. The air beyond the open window was still heavy and oppressive, and she was aware of the sheen of sweat across her skin, the pencil slippery in her fingers. Thunder rumbled faintly again in the distance and a slight breeze began at last to disturb the close humidity. The edges of the curtain lifted in its breath.

Leaving the window open, she picked up the sheet of paper and studied it. The reasons against were compelling – she had never broken the law in her life until now. But how much should a mother be willing to give up for the love of her son? To keep him safe she would have willingly given her life, but he was in no danger – his life was going on unchanged. Would her loneliness suffice to win him back?

She slid her gaze across the page to the other side of the line.

Joy, she read. *Hope, a new beginning.*

She let the paper fall back to the table and got up to make the tea, and when she had drunk it she was still no nearer a decision.

It was dark at the churchyard when Max arrived, the moon and stars cloaked by the blanket of cloud, and the little torch with its fading battery had given off just enough light for him to find his way from the camp. He picked a path between the graves and sat on the bench by the wall to wait, wondering if she would come. He had seen the look of horror in her eyes that her son had caught them and he had spent the days since then imagining the worst, blaming himself for her trouble.

He should leave her alone, he thought again. He had no business falling in love with an English woman, with any woman. An image of his wife tugged at the edges of his mind, blurred and indistinct as it mostly was these days. How could he have forgotten the details of her face so utterly when they had been together for so long? He shook his head as if to pull the image into focus but it made no difference.

It was almost two years since he had heard from her. Two long years of silence. He had lost count of the letters he had written in search of her, but it seemed as though she had simply disappeared off the face of the earth. She, and his daughter. He smiled at the thought of Hanna – he had never quite got used to the fact that he was a father, still lit by a sense of wonder that he had brought such a perfect being into the world. Would he ever discover what happened to them? He doubted it. Berlin seemed to him now like a lost and distant land, a place he had dreamed of long ago.

Absorbed in his thoughts he lost all track of time, but the slight breath in the air had already risen to a breeze and the thunder had shifted closer when he saw at last the movement of a pinprick of light in the distance. Clare. He waited, pulse quickening as the light grew brighter. Then the beam swung crazily through the night as she used both hands to shove open the gate, and he stood up, relief and excitement brushing all doubts about the rightness of it clean out of his mind. All he knew was that she had come, and every fibre of his being was glad.

'Over here,' he said softly, as the torchlight approached. He could not yet make out her form but he knew it was her. It had to be.

'Max.' He heard the echo of his own relief in her voice.

Another few paces and she was next to him and he could just make out the pallor of her face in the gloom.

'Shall we walk a little bit this time?' he asked. 'I don't much like churches.' He raised his eyes briefly to the squat tower beside them.

'Neither do I,' she replied.

'Even though you were a vicar's wife?'

She slid her hand under his arm and they followed the path around the church to where another gate opened on a footpath. He was conscious of her body beside him, the movement of her hip against his leg with each step.

'Walter was the one with faith,' she said. 'I always envied him his certainty.'

'You don't believe?' He was surprised. He had assumed a vicar's wife must share her husband's convictions.

She shrugged. 'I don't really know what I think.' She turned her face up towards him. 'What about you?'

'I think that when you're dead you're dead,' he replied, 'and that heaven and hell only exist here on earth.'

For a moment she was silent and he wished he had said something else. Then she turned to him again. 'You sound as if you're speaking from experience.'

He gave her a bleak smile that he doubted she would see in the dark. 'I've been to hell.'

'Caen?'

'Russia.'

He felt her stiffen beside him and wondered what she was thinking. 'Caen was bad,' he said. 'But Russia was worse. Russia was hell on earth.'

And no one returns from hell unscathed, he thought; such horrors are not meant to be seen by the living. Thunder growled, creeping closer, and the breeze was cool and welcome against his face. 'What happened with your son?'

She let out a sound that was somewhere between a laugh and a sigh, and he felt the hesitation before she answered.

'I've had to leave the farm,' she said. 'I moved today into a flat in the high street. It was lucky really – Mr Hardy had just moved out or else I don't know where I would have gone. Back to Bristol probably to stay with friends.'

The name of the city meant nothing to him. 'And your son?' he asked.

'He … isn't speaking to me. He'll stay at the farm until he goes back to school.'

Her voice was brave and matter-of-fact but he heard the heartbreak underneath the words. His fault, he thought: she had lost her son because of him.

'I'm sorry.'

They came to a stop. The valley sloped down before them towards the river and in the dark he could sense the open space, the sky vast and full of the coming rain overhead. They turned towards each other, bodies close, fingers entwined hand to hand.

'Do you want to stop this?' he asked, and prayed to a god he didn't believe in that she would say no. 'I don't want to cost you your son.'

She swallowed and turned her head away to gaze out across the darkness of the valley. He waited, barely daring to breathe, until at last she brought her gaze back to his face.

'I don't know,' she said. 'I just don't know.'

He wound his fingers more tightly in hers. He understood perfectly – he had the same doubts himself. They stood for a moment of hesitation until he lowered his mouth to hers for a kiss. Afterwards, she put her head against his shoulder and he held her, his lips against her hair, her body small and precious in his arms. He never wanted to let her go.

It was the early hours by the time he walked her back to the flat, still hand in hand through the empty village. A single lamp that hung from above the pub doorway shed a ghostly light across the high street. The storm had kept its distance, the thunder rolling far away and the breath of air just a tease of the cool change still to come.

'Does it remind you of the guns?'

'Yes,' he answered. 'I still can't quite believe it's only weather.'

They arrived at the saddler's and she took him along the lane beside the building to a ramshackle yard and the steps that led up to the flat. They stopped at the base of the stairs and Clare rested one hand on the worn wood of the rail.

'When can I see you again?' He was standing very close so that all her senses were filled with the nearness of his presence. It was hard to think. She hesitated. 'You do want to see me again?'

She heard the uncertainty in his voice. He laid his hand over hers on the rail, massaging her fingers with his thumb.

'Yes,' she breathed. 'I want to see you again.'

He smiled. Then, lifting his hand to her face, he tilted her chin towards him and kissed her.

Chapter Nineteen

Max stood at the gate with Theo and a couple of others, waiting to start work on the barley harvest. Theo handed him a cigarette.

'So you really like this woman?'

Max lit the cigarette and drew back hard. He had barely slept. In the few brief hours he had spent in his bed, he had relived over and over the evening with Clare in his mind, recalling every word she had said and every look she had given him, terrified the loss of her son might yet frighten her away. He nodded, struggling to fight off the weariness.

'*Und ...?*'

'We like each other.' He gave his friend a smile – it was impossible to hide his pleasure altogether, in spite of the doubts.

Theo lifted an eyebrow and Max looked away, suddenly bashful under the teasing of his friend. He took another pull on the cigarette, irritated with himself.

'Are you seeing her again?'

He tilted his head, evasive, and Theo let out a laugh that made the other men turn towards them. Max gave him a warning frown and Theo dropped his voice.

'You lucky dog.'

'Don't tell the others,' he said.

'*Natürlich nicht*,' Theo answered, his tone serious. Of course not. 'I'm pleased for you.'

Neither of them mentioned Lotte. There was still no news, and at times it felt as though his whole life with her had been no more than a dream.

The rumble of the tractor in the lane beyond the gate drew their attention towards it and Max bent to stub out the cigarette in the dirt at his feet before tucking the butt in his pocket for later. The gate swung open and the tractor trundled into view, taking its time to ease the binder behind it through the gap. The men stood and watched, waiting.

Clare's son appeared and stood beside the tractor, running his gaze across the assembled prisoners, and Max observed him. He must take after his father, he thought – he could see little of Clare in the boy's dark hair and pale eyes, and the lankiness that suggested he would grow up tall and thin. The pale eyes came to rest on Max and the boy's fists curled into balls at his side. Max met the look with studied indifference – he still bore the scar from the stone the boy had hurled that first day in the village, and he glimpsed now the same shades of hatred; impotent rage lined the young face and made it ugly. He lowered his head away, not wanting to goad the boy any further. He was Clare's son, he reminded himself, and he had lost his father to the war. In the boy's place he would have felt the same.

A warning nudge at his arm from Theo made Max raise his head again, senses abruptly alert. The farmer had stepped down from the tractor and was striding towards them with the boy trailing at his shoulder, fists still clenched. An unexpected tension stretched taut across the narrowing gap between them, and instinctively Max shifted his feet ever so slightly, straightening, getting ready. He was aware of the surge of adrenalin through his veins, the quickening of his heartbeat. He flexed his fingers and waited. The other men watched, instincts honed for trouble.

Woodman came to a halt less than two feet away, his face close enough that Max could see every pockmark and bristle on the stubbled cheeks. Like the sergeants back in training so long ago, he thought, shouting abuse from an inch away, hoping to intimidate. He waited, gaze locked on the other man's, assessing. He was not afraid.

'You see this boy here?' Woodman gestured to Eric, who stepped to the side to show himself more clearly. 'His father died a hero, fighting you bastards. I don't care what you did for Lizzie - you lay another hand on this boy's mother and I swear I'll kill you myself.'

Max said nothing. What was there to say?

The boy spat but the gob of spittle fell short, just brushing the edge of Max's boot. Woodman leaned in closer and Max braced, ready, so that the punch to his guts barely even winded him. Without missing a beat he hit back – he knew it was unwise but it was instinct to retaliate, a reflex instilled in him long ago in the rough streets of Berlin. Woodman crumpled as Max's fist found its mark. The other prisoners stepped forward, ready, but with a shake of his head Max warned them off. This was his fight and he wanted no one else in trouble on his account.

For a long moment he waited, ready for another go and uncertain what the other man would do. The boy lunged forward but Theo caught his arm and swung him away, and though Eric struggled he was just a boy and no match for Theo, who held him easily. Woodman straightened up, one hand nursing his gut.

'You'll pay for that,' he hissed, through lips drawn tight with fury and humiliation. 'You'll pay, Peterson.'

Max was silent, fists still lightly balled, still wary, but he held the farmer's gaze until Woodman, defeated, turned away and returned to the tractor. Eric followed him, looking back over his

shoulder towards the prisoners in confusion, not quite understanding what had taken place.

'You need to watch your back,' Theo murmured. '*Sei vorsichtig.*'
Be careful.

Max nodded his agreement. One of the other prisoners
offered him a cigarette and he took it with a smile of thanks,
sucking the smoke back hard into his lungs. Then the tractor
Max had repaired throbbed into life and the work of the harvest
began.

Clare wrote to James with the brief details of her change of
address and thought no more about it, so when there was a
knock at the door of her flat a few days later he was the last
person she expected to see.

'James!' She stared in surprise.

He stood on the landing outside the door and twisted his hat
between his fingers, cheeks flushed from the heat.

'What on earth are you doing here?'

'May I come in?'

Clare opened the door wider and stepped back to let him in.
She saw him run his gaze across the shabby flat, the look of
disappointment.

'Tea?'

'Yes, please.'

She gestured for him to take a seat at the little table, and
turned on the stove. 'It takes a while, I'm afraid. But it's nice to
have electricity again. Quite the luxury.'

He smiled, and she set about preparing the pot and putting
out biscuits on a plate. Custard creams, Eric's favourite. She was
aware of James watching her. When there was nothing left to do
except wait for the kettle to boil, she leaned against the counter
and turned to face him. 'What brings you to Ashenden?'

'Surely you don't have to ask? I got your letter and I came as soon as I could.'

'There was no need for you to come. I'm perfectly fine.'

He made a sweeping gesture with one hand to indicate the flat. 'Forgive me for saying so, but that is evidently not the case.'

She followed the arc of his hand and tried to see the place as he saw it. She was already used to its shabbiness, and it was her home. She had never had her own place before, never lived alone, and she was discovering that she rather liked it.

'What happened?'

She sighed. 'It was getting hard at the farm. Walter's mother and I have never seen eye to eye, and she was more than happy to see the back of me.'

'But here?' The derision in his tone was unmistakable.

'It was available. I know it's not much but it's mine and I like it.'

'What about Eric?'

'He wanted to stay at the farm. He's happy there and it's only for the summer. He'll be back at school soon enough.' She tried to sound nonchalant and wondered if he knew her well enough to hear the emotion underneath. Walter would have noticed in a heartbeat.

'He should be with his mother.'

'Why? He's away from me at school most of the time and that's perfectly acceptable.'

Beside her the water huffed to the boil and she poured some of it into the pot to warm it, relieved to have something to do.

'But the summer holidays …'

'He's just down the road. And he's with family. It's not as if I've left him with strangers.' She put the pot on the table between them and sat down.

James leaned forward and rested his arms on the table, lessening the distance between them. Beneath the flush from the heat

Clare noticed that his complexion was rather sallow and his eyes had lost the brightness of his youth.

'What really happened, Clare? Why did you have to move out?'

'What does it matter?' she replied.

He sat back with a sigh and folded his arms. Briefly, he shifted his gaze away from her to look out over the street below. A horse and cart had drawn up outside the pub. The carthorse was pawing the ground with a foreleg, its dark coat shining in the sun, and the drayman was resting a hand on its neck while he waited for the landlord to open up the cellar doors. Eventually, James turned back towards her.

'Before Walter left he made me promise that if anything happened to him I would look after you. I was to take care of you and Eric both.'

'He had no right to ask you that.'

'I was his closest friend. He had every right.'

Clare poured out the tea, then took a sip. James paid no attention to his.

'If you're in trouble,' he said, 'I want to know.'

'I'm not in trouble,' she assured him.

James rubbed at the handle of his teacup between his thumb and forefinger as if scrubbing off a stain. 'I don't know what you're hiding but I'm hurt that you won't trust me. After all I've …' He stopped.

'You're paying for Eric to go to school and so I owe you? Is that what you mean?'

'No, no, of course not.' He gave a vigorous shake of his head. 'That's not what I meant. Not at all.' He looked up at her with an expression in his eyes that she could not quite read. 'I only meant that after all we've meant to each other over the years – you, me and Walter. All the good times we had together. I want to be a good friend to you, Clare – Walter was like a brother to me.'

She said nothing, not quite convinced. Why had he come? What did he think might have happened that she wasn't telling him? Surely, there was no way he could suspect the truth of things, though he might find out in time. She wondered if Eric would spill the beans or if he would guard the truth with care. She suspected the latter – what boy would want the world to know his mother was … what was the phrase he had used? *A collaborating slut.*

'I'm not in trouble,' she repeated.

He regarded her carefully, apparently unconvinced.

'Did you get the bus?' she asked, changing the subject.

'I drove. The school is allocated a petrol ration.'

'And you spent it to come and visit me. I suppose I should be flattered.'

'Clare! For goodness' sake! I'm being serious. I'm worried about you – Walter would be heartbroken to see you in a place like this, without your son.'

'Then he shouldn't have gone off to war and got himself killed. He didn't have to go. He chose to.'

'That's unfair.'

'You said more or less the same yourself, didn't you?' She had not forgotten their conversation after the memorial – there had been times since then that the knowledge that someone else recognised the price of Walter's faith had been like a life raft. 'You said he was selfish.'

'I was angry and grieving.'

She turned to the window and watched the men rolling the barrels into the cellar – the clank and clatter reverberated through the quiet morning. The horse's head drooped, one leg resting.

'You can't stay here.' He leaned across the table towards her again and for a moment she thought he might put his hand on hers, but his fingers stopped just short as though he had changed his mind. 'I insist you come back to Wellington with me.'

'And stay where exactly?' she asked.

'With my sister and me. We've got a house near the school and there's a small room you could have ... you'd be near Eric in term time.'

She shook her head, but said nothing – the argument was pointless, back and forth, going nowhere. He would never let it go. He waited, hoping, she assumed, that she would surrender. The silence lingered.

'I'm not leaving,' she told him in the end. 'I'm not.'

He stood up with a scrape of the chair on the lino, thwarted and angry. 'It's not what Walter would have wanted. I promised him I would take care of you.'

'You did your best,' she consoled, as though he were one of the children in her class. 'That's all you can ever do.'

A muscle began to twitch in his cheek, his mouth set tight against the simmering fury. She had never seen him so full of rage, and instinctively she got up too to move back from the table into the kitchen, putting distance between them.

'Then I'll leave you to it. Perhaps Eric will be more forthcoming.'

'You're going to see Eric?' An absurd sense of dread passed through her, mouth turning dry.

'I'm his godfather, Clare. I have a right to see him.'

'Of course,' she managed to say. 'He'll be delighted to see you. Give him my love.'

'You should be giving him that yourself,' he snapped. Then, snatching up his coat and hat from where he had tossed them on the sofa, he strode the few steps to the door and with a slam he was gone. She heard the patter of his boots on the staircase and the diminishing click of his heels along the lane.

Her heart was still hammering from the confrontation and the worry he would learn the truth from Eric. Or more likely from Mrs Chapman. And however much she told herself it didn't matter what he knew, she could not help but fret. Too restless to stay in the flat a moment longer, she followed James out of the door and started walking, cutting through the churchyard and following the same path to the river she had taken with Max.

By the time she reached the water's edge she had regained her calm. Sitting on the bank in the shade of a vast horse chestnut tree she watched a pair of swans glide by, serene and elegant. They mate for life, Walter had told her once, but she didn't know what happened if one of them died. Did they find another mate or did they pine away, alone, until death came for them too? When the swans had rounded the bend in the river and drifted out of sight, Clare lay back on the grass and watched the clouds begin to gather overhead. After a while they covered the sun and the day turned cool. With a shiver, she got up and wandered slowly home.

Chapter Twenty

The summer days passed in a blur. To make herself useful through the long weeks of the summer holidays, Clare volunteered as a nursing assistant at the local cottage hospital, making beds and cups of tea, fetching and carrying, helping in whatever way she could. The work was menial and exhausting but it was a distraction from thoughts of Eric and Walter and Max, and she liked the people she met there: the women she worked with and the patients she helped to care for, the elderly doctor with twinkly eyes who called everyone '*my dear*', and the young one who was terrified of the matron and teased by the nurses.

In the middle of August the news came that Japan had finally surrendered and the war was over at last. Clare heard the reports of the atomic bombs with horror but even so, she felt the great sigh of relief that vibrated across the world – peace, and new hope for the future. They had a little party at the hospital to celebrate, and from outside they could hear the whistles and cheers of revellers late into the night, the windows lighting up now and then with fireworks. But when one of the patients started up a chorus of *'We'll Meet Again'*, Clare had to walk away to hide her tears.

Each evening all through the summer Clare waited for Max, greeting the darkness every night with the hope of seeing him again, waiting for him to come to the flat. He had asked if he could and she had told him yes, but he did not come and as the days began to turn into weeks without him she started to doubt her judgement. Trawling her memories for every moment they had spent together, she relived every look and every touch, every word they had said to each other, searching for something she had missed, some clue she had been mistaken about him and he was something other than he seemed. But there was nothing. She found only the truth of their connection, and the spark of under-standing that ran between them.

Through the sultry sleepless nights, the endless possibilities rolled through her mind.

He had been moved to another camp.

He was ill or injured.

He was dead.

He no longer liked her.

He was keeping away because of Eric.

The not-knowing slid into her dreams and the repeated nightmare of Walter and Max in battle, one of them finishing the other, so that she woke up frantic and sweating, alone in the dark.

Near the end of August, she came home late one evening from the hospital. When she turned off the village high street, the last light had already left the sky and the little yard behind the saddler's was in darkness. She had gone to the pub after her shift to celebrate with one of the nurses who was getting married, and she was still in high spirits from the conviviality of the evening. It had been far too long since she had gone out with friends and let her hair down – they had drunk beer and danced and laughed together, and she had been invited, last minute, to the wedding the following week. For the first time in as long as she could remember no shadows fell over her thoughts – no images of Walter or Max. No thoughts that she had failed as a mother. No doubts, no regrets, no apprehension for the future.

She leaned her bike against the wall of the yard and walked towards the steps that led up to the flat. In her head, her thoughts were still tapping to one of the songs they had danced to, so when a man's form emerged abruptly out of the dark at the top of the stairs above her she cried out in fright, instinctively backing away.

'It's Max.' Max's voice, a whisper from the shadows. 'I'm sorry. I didn't mean to scare you.'

She peered up through the gloom, eyes straining to make out his face. Her breath was still ragged from the shock, heart knocking hard in her chest. In the pause she breathed deeply to compose herself. She had almost given up on him, reluctantly resigning herself to his absence, although a small and stubborn part of her had refused to give up completely, still clutching to the belief he would come back to her in time. And now, here he was. The small stubborn part of her gave a silent whoop of joy and said, *I told you so*.

He descended the staircase slowly as though he were uncertain, and when he reached the ground and they were level their hands brushed together for a point of connection that seemed to light up every part of her.

'I'm sorry,' he said again.

She took a step towards him. Their faces were close, their bodies almost touching.

'Come in,' she replied, moving past him to climb the stairs. He waited while she fumbled with the key. Then, blinking in the sudden brightness when she switched on the lamp inside, she turned to look at him. He was still standing by the door, watching her. His face was pale, his cheeks rough with stubble, and his eyes were dark with weariness: there was no glint of mischief in them now.

'What happened?' she asked, crossing back towards him and taking his hand in hers once again. The palms and fingertips were callused from work. Walter's hands had been delicate and soft.

'I couldn't come,' he answered with a tilt of his head. 'I got thirty days detention.'

'Prison?' She was horrified. 'Because of me?'

He smiled then and the tiredness left his face, the lovely lines returning to his cheeks and the corners of his eyes.

'Not really.' His eyes grazed the flat and she braced for his judgement, but he said, 'It's nice.'

'You're being kind.'

'No, not at all. I like it. It feels like a home.'

'Thank you,' she answered, and wondered how long it had been since he had known any other home but prison camps and army barracks. But she was pleased that he liked it.

'Sit down, make yourself at home.' She gestured to the kitchen table. 'Tea?'

'Please.'

He sat at the table and she felt his gaze watching her every movement as she fussed with the kettle and the stove and teapot. In the lamp-lit intimacy of the flat his nearness disconcerted her, her feelings unfamiliar, frightening, delicious. Her hands were almost shaking.

'How do you have your tea?' She remembered hearing some-where that Germans liked lemon instead of milk. 'I don't have any lemon.'

'Milk is fine – the English way.' He smiled and she turned her head away, embarrassed by her sudden awkwardness in front of him. 'You're enjoying your independence?'

'I am,' she replied. 'I can drink tea at two in the morning if I choose. Or entertain gentleman callers without judgement.'

'Gentleman callers?' He laughed. 'Have you had many?'

'You're the second.'

The laughter died on his lips. 'Who else came?'

The kettle began to hiss and she made the tea as she spoke, grateful to have something to occupy her hands. She thought back to James's visit – it seemed a long time ago now, half forgotten.

'Eric's godfather. He was Walter's closest friend.' She turned briefly from the tea to look at Max. He was watching her intently as though he would read every thought in her head. 'He arrived unannounced when I wrote to tell him I'd moved. Apparently he promised Walter he'd look after me if anything happened and now he thinks I need to be rescued.'

'Do you?'

'No, not at all. But he wants to marry me, for Walter's sake.'

Max laughed and she looked up abruptly. 'No man gets married for another man's sake,' he said. 'If he's asked you to marry him it's because he wants you. It's nothing to do with Walter.'

She carried the tea to the table. She knew he was right – she remembered James's reaction when she said no, and how sorry for him she had felt.

She said, 'Are you hungry?'

'Always,' he replied. 'They don't give us much to eat at the camp.'

She made cheese on toast and watched him eat it, enjoying his pleasure in the food. Next time, she thought, she would make stew or some soup, something more substantial. He finished eating and when she took his plate away to wash it up, he got up too and came to stand behind her. Her heartbeat quickened with his nearness.

'Leave it,' he said, then rested his hands on her shoulders. His body was close to hers, just brushing against her back. She let the plate slide into the sink and held her breath.

'You aren't going to marry him, are you?' he asked.

She shook her head, then turned it towards him and the moment hung suspended between them, their faces close enough that she could feel the warmth of his breath against her hair. His lips touched the back of her neck and she shuddered as he lifted her hair away with a gentle movement to expose more of her skin to his kiss. His mouth was warm and soft against her nape and she braced her hands against the counter in front of her to steady herself.

Gently, he trailed his fingers down from her shoulder across her breastbone until they slid beneath the loose-buttoned collar of her blouse to graze across the top of her breast. She felt her breath lift and catch as he undid the other buttons and lowered the blouse away from her shoulders. His fingertips were rough, but the sensation was exquisite and she pressed back against him, aware of his mouth close to her ear, his cheek against her hair. Her every sense was filled with his presence, his body hard and warm behind her. The moment hung as if suspended in time – pleasure in the hesitation, a promise not yet made.

Slowly, slowly, she turned to face him, feeling his weight pressing into her, the bench hard and smooth against her lower back. His fingers whispered over her skin and under the brassiere she had not noticed him unfasten. Desire flared through every part of her and she raised her head to search for his mouth with an urgency that surprised them both. They kissed, bodies pressed close together.

Too soon he drew back, breathing hard. 'Are you sure?' he murmured. 'Are you sure you want to do this?'

'I'm sure,' she replied. She had never wanted anything so much in her life before.

He smiled and brushed her cheek with the backs of his fingers, savouring the last moments of anticipation before he pressed his mouth hard to hers. One hand reached beneath the hem of her skirt to search out the soft flesh underneath. Then he lifted her onto the counter in one quick motion and she wrapped her legs around his hips, her arms resting on his shoulders.

He unfastened his belt, and there was no hesitation for either of them now as he entered her. Clare arched her back in response, and nothing else existed but the two of them moving together and the pleasure of his nearness. She wanted the moment to go on forever.

Afterwards, they stayed wrapped in each other, and she rested her head on his shoulder as he stood against her, still holding him tight with her arms and her legs, reluctant to let him go. Neither spoke – there seemed to be no need for words, talking instead with the touch of their bodies. Finally, he stepped away and lifted her down from the counter to set her once more on the ground. She stumbled slightly – her legs weak and unstable – and Max held her arm to steady her before he took her hand and they went together to the sofa, where he put his arm around her as she nestled into his shoulder, feet tucked up beneath her. Her blouse was still hanging half off her arms but she let it be – she wanted to linger in the aftermath forever, her skin still slick with sweat in the balmy night. In all the years of her marriage Walter had never loved her with such urgent passion – they had made love gently and politely, and she had never thought to question it.

Max's fingers lightly rubbed her arm, his body strong and warm against her. Clare settled herself deeper into the arc of his shoulder, and let her hand rest on the rise of his chest. He was more powerfully built than Walter, the muscles taut and strong, but she knew his strength went deeper than mere animal sinew – he possessed an inner toughness, a hard core that still unsettled her. It was an edge to him she did not yet understand.

Brushing her fingertips across the line of his chest, she came to the raised welt of the scar across his shoulder. She traced along the line of it and he shivered.

'Sorry.' She lifted her hand quickly away and brought it to rest instead on his belly, where the slight dusting of fair hair caught the faint light, shining golden. 'Does it still hurt?'

'No,' he said, turning his head on the cushion to look at her. 'It's just the nerves around it are sensitive sometimes.'

'What happened?'

'Belgorod.' He murmured the unfamiliar word so quietly she was not sure she had even heard it correctly.

'What happened at Belgorod?' she asked again.

'I took some shrapnel.' He shrugged. 'It wasn't so bad.'

She knew that he was lying – the scar was proof of it, and she knew from her work at the hospital the scale of the wound that produced such a scar. For a moment she hesitated, wanting to persist and ask him again. But instead she said, 'Why did they send you to prison?'

He turned his head abruptly towards her again, brow furrowed. 'What?'

'The thirty days detention.' She shifted back from him a little, unsure of him. His mood seemed to change on the breeze.

'Oh, that.' He smiled. 'I punched Woodman in the gut.'

She stared. 'You hit Simon? Why?'

'He hit me first.'

'Because of me,' she murmured. 'He must have realised it was you I talked to. I'm so sorry.'

'Your son pointed me out to him.'

Briefly she closed her eyes and let out a long breath of disappointment. She had tried to talk to Eric countless times through the summer, cycling out to the farm where both Mrs Chapman and Bridget refused to acknowledge her, and she was unable to catch so much as the smallest glimpse of her son. She had written letters but received no replies: she doubted he even opened them.

'My son hates me,' she said, and swung herself up and away from the man beside her, the man who had cost her her son. 'He hates us both.' She sat on the sofa's edge with her back to him and, despite the warmth of the night, she shivered at the kiss of the air on her naked skin. Max slid forward to sit close beside her, their thighs touching as he took her hand.

'It's my fault. You can tell me to go to hell if you like. I won't bother you again.'

'It's too late,' she said, resting her head on his shoulder.

'He might forgive you in time, if you ...' he searched for the word but could not find it.

'Repent?' she supplied. 'As if you were some mortal sin I needed to atone for?'

He gave a wry smile and she shook her head. 'I love my son and it hurts like hell that he hates me. But even if I never saw you again I'm not sure it would change anything.' She raised her head to look at him, sitting close beside her. 'Besides, I rather like you.' She smiled. 'I missed you horribly when you didn't come. I was all but dead inside until I met you.'

He said nothing, but cradled her head in his palm and leaned across to kiss her. Then he tipped her back onto the sofa and made love to her again.

Max left the flat in the early hours, tearing himself away from her warmth and softness to head out into the summer damp of the night. She watched him go from the door, her silhouette outlined against the light behind her when he turned back to wave before he cut through the buildings towards the fields behind them. A narrow moon filtered through the cloud and cast a dull gleam across the countryside. He had found his way on darker nights in other more dangerous fields, in other less welcoming countries, and the path was easy to find.

Now and then the rustle of some small creature in the hedgerow disturbed the night as he passed and once he saw the white-tipped brush of a fox, but he paid them no attention, running his thoughts instead across the evening with Clare – the tea, the unexpected sex, and the easiness of her company afterwards. It was not at all what he had planned – he was as surprised as she was by the force of the passion, their desire for each other. Afterwards he could only wonder if she would regret it: they had crossed a line tonight and made a commitment to each other he had not quite yet intended.

But in spite of it, he realised he was smiling to himself in the dark and there was a lightness in his step he had thought he would never find again. Too many years of war had left him detached from the world so that for a while he had forgotten the taste of peace – love, beauty, kindness, the softness of a woman's caress.

With Clare he remembered it all.

Chapter Twenty-One

Late in the summer Susan came to visit, having heard the news on her return from London that Clare had moved out of Rowan Farm. She turned up one Sunday morning after the early church service when Clare was still in her pyjamas, eating bread and jam in the kitchen.

'Good heavens, girl.' Susan's clipped tone was loud in the quiet flat. 'It's after nine. Why aren't you dressed?'

'Hello, Susan,' Clare laughed before the two women embraced. She had missed her friend's no-nonsense tone. 'It's lovely to see you too. Tea?'

'I'll make it. You get dressed and afterwards we can go for a walk. It's going to rain later.'

Clare padded barefoot into the bedroom, scanning the flat for any tell-tale signs of Max. There were none that she could see – the ashtrays were empty, the bed was made. She smiled at the sight of it, remembering the night he had spent there. Max excited her in ways she had never even imagined with Walter, possibilities for pleasure she had not dreamed of, and she had quickly lost her self-consciousness in front of him. She slipped out of her pyjamas and dressed in a blouse and slacks, a sweater looped over her shoulders in case it got cooler later on.

By the time she went back to the kitchen the tea was brewing in the pot.

'You took your time.'

'I couldn't decide what to wear,' she said, and the falsehood fell easily from her lips. She had never been good at lying before but she was learning to become more adept with secrets now: she had little choice. *'Needs must when the devil drives,'* her father used to say. Susan opened up the packet of chocolate biscuits she had brought from London, and Clare thought how she would give the remainder to Max, who was still always hungry. In spite of the end of the war, rationing had tightened again and the prisoners felt the pinch the same as everyone.

'So,' Susan began. 'Tell me everything.'

'About what?'

'About how you came to be living in this god-awful flat.'

'I'm very happy here,' she snapped, irritated by the casual insult. 'It might not be as posh as you're used to, but it's mine and I like it.' She meant it. She loved living in the centre of the village and being able to pop across to the shop for a pint of milk and the paper and a catch-up on the local news with Mrs Bartlett behind the counter. Every Saturday she headed down to the saddler's to pay the rent to Mr Brimble, who liked horses more than people but still thought it was a national disgrace the German prisoners had not yet been sent home.

Outside the window the bus pulled in at the stop across the street. The whine of its engine was loud in the quiet of the morning. Nine thirty-five, Clare thought, and turned her attention back to Susan, who was hesitating, apparently realising she had overstepped.

'I'm sorry,' she said. 'That was unkind. I only meant ...'

'I know what you meant,' Clare interrupted. 'But it's wonderful to be out of Mrs Chapman's hair. And I have electricity and running water, and I never want to live without them again.'

Susan smiled. 'But really, what happened that you had to move out? It can't be easy with Eric still at the farm.'

Clare sighed and swallowed down the temptation to confide the truth. No one could know, she had decided. It was the safest way.

'What did you hear?' she asked, deflecting the question. Besides, it would be good to know the rumours.

'I heard,' Susan said, arching an eyebrow, 'there was a German prisoner involved.'

Clare almost choked on her tea and for a moment she was afraid she had given herself away. But Susan read a different meaning.

'Yes. I thought it was absurd too. Clare? With a German? After what they did to Walter? I thought as much.'

Clare got up to fetch herself a glass of water and sipped it at the sink, giving herself time to order her emotions.

'So what did happen?' Susan persisted.

Clare turned from the sink and leaned her hips against it. It was easier with a little distance between them.

'We just fell out, Walter's mother and I. It had been building up for a long time. I think she thought that with Walter ... gone, she had no more obligation towards me.' She gave a little shrug. 'I always felt like an intruder there. Honestly, I was happy to leave. It was just lucky this place came up when it did. I don't know what I would have done otherwise.'

'Move to Wellington, perhaps?'

'Perhaps.'

'And Eric?'

'He likes being on the farm,' she said smoothly. 'He'll be back at school soon anyway so it's just for the holidays. It's only down the road.'

'I heard you hadn't seen him.'

'Where *are* you getting all your information from?'

Susan tapped her nose. 'Loose lips sink ships,' she laughed, and Clare said nothing. But her fingers twitched in irritation, thoughts scrambling to understand. Who had she been talking to?

'So have you seen him?' Susan persisted.

'He's taken his grandmother's side in things. You know how boys can be.'

'Oh dear. I know how much you dote on him.' She finished her tea. 'Shall we go for a walk?'

Clare hesitated but no excuse sprang to mind – she had been hoping that Susan would leave.

'If you like.'

She cleared the table and set aside the rest of the biscuits for Max. When it was done, she put on her walking shoes and the two women headed out into the morning.

Just at the very end of the summer holidays, Clare went to the farm one more time in the hope of finding Eric before he went back to school, but found Bridget instead, in the kitchen, alone. Her sister-in-law was making bread and her hands were white with flour and dough so she could not easily walk away as she had done the other times. She paused in her kneading and stared into the mixing bowl.

'What do you want?' she said, without looking up.

Clare shook the drizzle from her hair and moved closer.

'Bridget, please. This is absurd.'

Bridget raised her head at last, and Clare couldn't quite read what she saw in the other woman's eyes – hostility, distrust, disappointment, regret? It was hard to say.

'Have you seen him again?' she said, and flicked a glance towards the back door as though to check they would not be disturbed.

'Does it matter?' Clare evaded.

'Yes,' Bridget nodded, 'it does.' She began to knead the dough again with deft and automatic movements. Clare had never been able to master the knack of it. 'To me, anyway.'

She hesitated, uncertain what answer Bridget was hoping for. Would she report them if she knew the truth?

'I'm not going to tell anyone,' Bridget said then, as though she had read Clare's thoughts.

'Yes,' Clare answered. 'I've seen him again.'

Her sister-in-law's hands stopped their rhythmic movements and she looked up. 'Are you in love with him?'

She shrugged, hesitant to admit it even to herself.

Bridget's lips twitched into the beginnings of a smile as she lowered her eyes to the dough and resumed her kneading. 'Then I'm glad for you. I've thought about it a lot since you moved out and I realised that if it had been only a meaningless flirtation Eric saw, that would be worse. But if you love him you can't help where he came from. Walter would be happy for you.'

Clare blinked to clear her eyes of tears. Bridget's under-standing astonished her – she had never even allowed herself to hope for it, resigned to their enmity.

'Thank you,' she whispered, and stopped, wiping at her eyes. If she said any more she would break down.

'Mum won't see it like that, of course.'

Clare managed a smile. 'Please don't tell her.'

'Of course I won't.' She looked up. 'But be careful. It's still against the law and it's not just Mum who'd turn you in. People talk.'

'They should let them all go,' Clare said. 'It's not fair to keep them locked up now the war is finished.' The papers had reported discussions in Parliament, a few brave MPs accusing the govern-ment of using slave labour. But there were no signs yet of the prisoners' release, and public opinion was still hostile, baying for retribution.

'But then he'd have to go home.'

They stood in silence for a moment and Clare admired again Bridget's skill with the dough. Then she said, 'Is Eric here?'

'He's out with the others – I think they're fishing at the river. You could go and look for him but I wouldn't. He's still furious with you – there'd only be a fight. Mum encourages it, of course, or he probably would have come round by now.'

'How's he getting back to school?'

'The same boy who brought him home. They've been writing to each other over the summer.'

She nodded, relieved. She had wondered how he'd manage otherwise.

Bridget cast another glance towards the back door. 'You should probably go,' she said. 'Mum will be back in a minute.'

'Thank you,' Clare replied. 'Come and see me. You know where I am.'

Bridget gave her a quick tight smile before lowering her eyes again to the bowl on the table, and when they heard footsteps on the path outside the door, Clare ducked out through the front with a hurried, whispered farewell.

Chapter Twenty-Two

Summer slid into autumn and as the days began to grow cooler the new school term began. Clare gave up her position at the hospital and returned to school, and though a part of her was sorry to leave it was wonderful to simply walk across the road to work, instead of the half-hour cycle she was used to. Eric left for Wellington without a word, and Clare fretted that she should have tried harder to see him over the summer, that she had been a bad mother. He was still her son even if he hated her, and she struggled to shake off the sense she had let him down. Now and again she toyed with the idea of moving to Wellington to be near him after all, and she wrote to him often all through the school term, offering to visit, but she received not a single reply: she supposed he never even opened them. So there was nothing else she could do except wait and hope that time would bring him round.

With the change in the seasons and the early-falling dark, it was easier for Max to slip out of the camp. He was not the only one, he told her. Other men had secret lovers too and their comrades covered for them all by fudging the roll call, which had become a rather perfunctory affair in the months since the end of the war. The camp commander was an old soldier from the Great War who was sympathetic to their plight, often choosing to turn a blind eye to small misdemeanours. The prisoners were lucky to have him, Max said – he had heard of other camps where the regime was far more strict.

In the longer nights they took more risks. Each time Max arrived was a surprise, and all the more delightful because of it. Some evenings they went for a walk, arm-in-arm against the cold with their bodies pressed close, and it was wonderful to pretend they were just a normal couple walking out together. There was still no news about the prisoners' release and they never talked of it, maintaining the bubble of make-believe that this secret might go on forever, perfect and unchanging.

With the onset of winter the weather turned bitter-cold, the ground hard and frosty underfoot and ice on the windows of the flat in the mornings. The little electric heater barely touched the chill. Clare was clearing up after dinner, enjoying the warmth of the washing-up water and thinking more or less of nothing when she heard Max's step on the stairs. Turning from the counter with a smile as he stood in the doorway in the dark wool coat of Walter's she had given him, she thought again how handsome he looked in it.

She went across to welcome him, breathing in his scent, his skin chilly from the winter night when she kissed him. He held her tightly and gave a little shiver. Laughing, she led him to the kitchen and she was conscious of him watching her as he leaned against the counter and she moved around him to make the tea.

After a while he let his gaze fall away from her and it landed on the unopened letter that was on the counter beside him. He picked it up. She had tossed it there that morning, she remem-bered, meaning to read it later, and she had forgotten it until now.

Max read the return address. 'James Clough.' He looked up. 'Eric's godfather?'

'We still write,' she replied, though their letters were less frequent than they once had been and had become rather stiff and perfunctory.

'Does he still want to marry you?'

'I think so. He keeps asking me to move to Wellington to live with him and his sister. Apparently there's a spare room that could be redecorated to suit.'

Max laughed. 'Is he attractive?'

Clare tilted her head to one side to consider. She had never really thought of it before. He was just James, Walter's friend. 'He's not bad-looking, I suppose. Tall and fair, thin, freckles.'

'Do I need to be worried?'

It was Clare's turn to laugh. The thought of James as a lover made her shudder – she couldn't even begin to imagine it. 'No, silly. You do not. You are the perfect man and you have no rivals.'

He smiled and took a mouthful of tea. 'Well, are you going to open it?'

She picked up a butter-knife and sliced the envelope free and as soon she started to unfold the single sheet she knew it was different from his usual letters. It was written on the school letterhead and she scanned the few lines hurriedly.

'What's the matter?' Max asked.

She lowered the letter to the table and sighed, guts heavy with a sense of dread. 'Eric's in trouble at school,' she said. 'He's been fighting. And stealing, apparently. James wants me to go for a meeting to discuss it.'

'Boys fight,' Max said. 'It's normal.'

'But stealing?'

'I guess it depends on what he stole.' He shrugged.

Clare said nothing for a moment. She had never stolen in her life, and though she liked to think it was an innate sense of honesty she knew there was an element of fear at work – she had always been the kind of girl that got caught doing wrong.

'Did you use to steal as a boy?' she asked.

'All the time.'

She stared.

He gave her a rueful smile. 'After my father died and the money ran out we moved to a poor neighbourhood. We had nothing. Everything got sold to pay off the debts,' he explained. 'My mother was broken by my father's death, and I had a little sister. Times were hard. There was no work, and if I hadn't stolen we would have starved. Then later I got work in the garage and it was better, but still ...' He trailed off, and she understood he had continued to steal even then.

'That's different. Eric doesn't need to steal to eat.'

'Then why does he? That's what you have to ask yourself. Why does he do it?'

'To get back at me,' she said without even thinking. 'To hurt me.'

Max tilted his head in acknowledgement. 'Then what can you do?'

'I don't know,' she replied. 'I just don't know.'

He got up then and came to stand behind her, hands on her shoulders, his lips against her hair. She leaned back against him, his warm, strong body supporting her.

'It will be all right,' he said.

She turned to face him and when he bent to kiss her, she let all thoughts of Eric slide away for a while. But later, lying wakeful in the dark next to Max's sleeping form, her mind turned once more towards her son, and she could not shed the sense of guilt that wrapped itself around her.

She needed to take time off work to go to Wellington and Miss Finch's lips hardened into a thin tight line of displeasure when Clare finally summoned the courage to ask.

'This is a place of work, Mrs Chapman,' she scolded, as Clare stood before the headmistress's desk with her head lowered and her hands clasped in front of her as if she were a disobedient child instead of a teacher herself. 'You can't just come and go as you please. This is why in my day married women weren't allowed to work.'

Clare said nothing, biting back all the possible replies that hovered on the tip of her tongue. She hated the automatic sense of guilt that Miss Finch provoked, furious with herself for the feeling. Of all the things she had to feel guilty about, this was not one of them.

'But I suppose you're his mother and I can't stop you going. Though,' she lifted her eyes to pin Clare in their watery gaze, 'I understand his grandmother has taken over his care. Perhaps she could go instead?'

Clare swallowed down the rising rage with an effort of will. She needed this job, she reminded herself: she had rent to pay. Then she thought of Max, and wondered what he would have said or done in her place. In her mind's eye he gave her a wry and encouraging smile, and the image gave her courage.

'Eric stayed at the farm for the summer.' She kept her tone even, belying the anger that simmered underneath. 'But I'm still responsible for his care. As you said, I am his mother.'

'Very well. Then I suppose you'll have to go. You'll be docked the day's pay, of course.'

'Of course,' Clare answered. She had expected nothing else. She stood for a moment, awaiting her dismissal before she realised she could simply turn and go without it. She let the door swing shut behind her and heard it slam as she walked away.

The trip to Wellington seemed to take forever and she gazed out of the grimy window without interest at the passing winter countryside – grey, bleak, damp. She had left early, waiting at the bus stop in the cold and sleepy dark for the first bus of the day: the meeting was scheduled for that afternoon and she wanted to get it over with, but the bus stopped at every village it passed through and each passenger took an age getting on or off, chatting to the driver or the other passengers. It was hard to quell her sense of impatience, fingers twitching, shoulders tight with tension. For the first time in ages, she wished Walter were here. He would have known what to do, how to handle his son. But then, she reminded herself, if Walter were here, the situation would be altogether different. Eric would be at home with them at the vicarage as a day boy at the grammar school, and he would have no cause to hate her, because she would still be a faithful wife and mother.

Would that be better? she wondered, and immediately rebuked herself for even thinking it. Of course it would. Of course. It was how things were meant to have been. What sort of person could think otherwise? It was a tragedy. Eric had lost his father and she was a widow.

Max's smile caught at the edges of her thoughts and she had to admit she did not altogether regret what had happened. From all the suffering and heartache something unexpected and good had arisen. She was living her own life and she was loved by a man who had shown her sides of herself she never even suspected. In return she loved him unconditionally, and there was nothing in the world for them but the time they spent together, every single moment precious and treasured by them both. Would she trade it in to have Walter back? If such a thing were to be offered to her now she wasn't certain she would take it, and the realisation sent a hot flush of shame across her skin. Perhaps Eric was right to despise her.

The bus lurched to a standstill with a graunch of gears. A sudden stench of petrol roused a feeling of nausea, and when she opened the window to let in the damp, cold air, she realised they had arrived in Wellington at last. Picking up her bag from the seat beside her, she hurried along the centre of the bus, down the steps, and into the fresh air of Wellington high street.

She had booked her own hotel this time – James had not offered and she had been glad in spite of the cost. She had remembered the last time she came that she had seen a small bed-and-breakfast off the high street, and she had called them from the phone box in the village to book herself a room. She went there now to leave her bag and freshen up before her meeting.

When she got to the school a short while later she was asked to wait in an office that was just as she had imagined it. It was easy to picture James in his teacher's robes at the large oak desk that stood in the centre. Tall Georgian windows looked out across a playing field and the walls were lined with bookshelves crammed full of all sorts of books in no discernible order. She cast her gaze across the spines and made out various bibles and religious treatises she recognised from Walter's collection at the vicarage. It was a beautiful room and she wondered if the rest of the school was as lovely.

She did not have to wait long before James hurried in, robes flapping behind him. He shook her hand and invited her to sit, then settled himself on the other side of the desk.

'Thank you for coming, Clare. I understand it can't have been easy.'

'Miss Finch wasn't very happy but there was nothing else for it.'

'Of course.' He gave her a smile, then looked down at his desk, hesitating.

She waited. Now that she was actually here it was easy to be patient.

Finally, he raised his head to look at her. 'This is difficult for me to say, and I'm sure it will be difficult to hear, but the situation at home seems to have unsettled Eric more than you can know. He's like a different boy from the one who came here in January. He picks fights with the other boys, he steals their things, he answers back to teachers. He has been spoken to, punished, threatened with expulsion, and nothing seems to make a difference. I'm at my wits' end to know what else I can do. I don't want him to be expelled, and I have interceded more than once on his behalf with the headmaster, but he can't go on like this – he's disrupting the other boys and it's bad for the school.'

A sense of failure darkened her thoughts, the familiar fog of guilt. This was her fault. Hers and Max's.

'What can I do?' she said.

'First of all, you need to talk to him. See if you can get through to him how serious this is for his future, for his life. If he leaves here, where will he go? I can't afford to send him anywhere else – he's here solely because of my position.'

'He'd go to the local secondary school like all the other boys from the village.'

'And then what? How many of those children go on to university? How many of them ever leave the land?'

'I'll talk to him,' she said, 'but I'm not sure he'll listen.'

'No, he probably won't,' James agreed.

Clare looked up in surprise.

'He thinks you don't care about him. And he thinks you didn't love his father.' He sat forward and leaned his forearms on the desk, decreasing the distance between them. Instinctively she shifted back in her chair. 'Move to Wellington to be near him,' James urged again. 'He feels abandoned – first by Walter and then by you. I really don't understand why you're being so stubborn about it.'

Because of Max, she thought. Because if she moved to Wellington she would never see him again. She was conscious of the rapid knocking of her heart, her breath quick and shallow. Was it true, what James was saying? How could Eric think she'd abandoned him when she had tried so hard to see him?

She said, 'Let me talk to him.'

James got up from behind his desk and went to open the door. A moment later Eric appeared, smart in his uniform, his head lowered, eyes on the floor. He had grown in the months since she had seen him last and her heart turned in sorrow for the time she had lost with him – this little person who had once been her whole world.

'Hello, Eric.'

Silence.

'Say hello to your mother, Chapman,' James ordered.

'Hello, Mum.'

Clare gestured to the chair beside her and he shuffled into place, but he wouldn't lift his head to look at her. She reached into her bag.

'I made you some biscuits,' she said. 'The oat ones you like so much. I wasn't sure how well they feed you here.' She smiled and held out the little parcel and after a moment's hesitation he reached out his hand to take them.

'Thank you.'

'Do you know why I'm here?' she said.

'Because I've been naughty. Mr Clough's been threatening it all term.'

'I don't think I'm much of a threat to hold over anyone, do you?'

He lifted his head then and for the first time since he had seen her with Max at the gate he looked her full in the face. He said, 'Why did you let that man touch you?'

James started. She heard the creak of his chair.

'I was lonely,' she said, 'and he was kind. That's all.'

'He's a German.' Eric all but spat the word.

'He's a human being. And he did save Lizzie's life, remember?'

There was a pause. Outside the window she could hear the shouts of boys cheering each other on at some game or other and the thud of a ball.

'We're not here to talk about your mother,' James said. 'We're here to discuss your behaviour.'

'Mr Clough says you've been fighting and stealing. Is that true?'

Eric nodded.

'Why?'

He shrugged.

'Is it because you know I won't like it? Is it a way of getting back at me for smiling at the prisoner? Because you know that your father would be very disappointed too.'

'He'd be more disappointed with you than me. Having it off with a German ...'

'Chapman!' James's voice cut through the quiet afternoon. 'Apologise to your mother at once!'

'What makes you say that?' She kept her voice even, no trace of the emotion behind it.

'That's what Grandma said.'

Clare closed her eyes and rubbed her hands across her face. Bloody Grandma, she thought, spreading her poison. Except this time Grandma was actually right. She took a deep breath, and tried again.

'Look, Eric,' she said, taking a different tack. 'What I do or don't do with other men is not the topic under discussion. I'm here to talk about *your* behaviour, not mine. I'm not the one being threatened with expulsion. It's not my future that's on the line. If you keep this up, Eric, you'll end up at the local school with all the other children from the villages around. You'll prob-ably never go to university and chances are you'll spend the rest of your life on the farm. If you want to make your father proud of you then you'll stop all this nonsense. Grandma is not a bad person, but she's bitter that your dad left the farm to join the church, and for some reason she thinks I'm to blame. She doesn't like me, and you can't believe everything she says about me. She would very much like you to stay on the farm forever and take Dad's place. Is that what you want? To be a farmer and spend your whole life at Rowan Farm? Is it?'

Eric was staring at her. She had never spoken to him like this, ever.

'Well, is it?'

'I want to be an engineer,' he said, startled into the truth.

Her heart fluttered in her chest – the same dream as Max. 'Well then,' she managed to say, 'you need to knuckle down and do some work. You have to be clever to be an engineer, you know, and go to university. I'm not expecting that you'll never get in trouble again, Eric. I expect even Dad got in trouble at school sometimes. Just don't get expelled, all right?'

He nodded, mutely.

'Now, I think I should take you into town for some afternoon tea. I bet you know the best places to go. What do you say?'

From the corner of her eye she saw James open his mouth to say something, but she turned away abruptly, and took Eric's hand in hers. He gave her a small uncertain smile as though he was unsure what had just happened, and she had to press her lips hard together to stop herself from crying. She knew it was not yet over, but it was a start and she was grateful for that. Then together they went out of the office, along the corridor and into the cold afternoon drizzle outside.

Chapter Twenty-Three

'How did it go?'

'Better than I expected.'

They were standing in the kitchen of the flat making toast on the evening Clare came back from Wellington, and Max was watching her. She could feel the heat of his gaze against her cheek and she flushed with the pleasure of his attention. Walter had never watched her that way, never kindled the same thrill just by his presence. She turned to him with a smile.

'That's good. So you made up with him?'

'I think so – I took him out for tea and for a while he was just my little boy again. We talked about school and the other boys, the books he's read. He's such a serious little fellow. I don't think he wants to hate me but he thinks he should, that he owes it to his dad in some way. And his grandmother eggs him on.'

'Did you talk about it?'

'No, thankfully. I would have had to lie to him and I'm not very good at lying.'

Max laughed. 'It's one of my best talents – the product of a rough childhood.'

She turned to face him, standing close in the tiny kitchen. 'Have you ever lied to me?'

He gave her a smile she could not read, and wet his bottom lip with the tip of his tongue before he answered. 'Of course not.'

'But then, if you had that's exactly what you'd say.'

'Then I suppose it depends on whether or not you trust me. Do you trust me?'

She tilted her head, considering. She wasn't sure that she did, entirely. She knew that she loved him, wanted him; she wasn't even sure if she could live without him, but she knew too there was a dark core inside of him, facets of himself he had never shown her.

'Hmm.' She put a finger to her mouth, making a game of it. 'I don't know that you're entirely trustworthy. I think there are secrets behind those beautiful eyes you haven't told me yet.'

'Is that what you think?'

He laughed and reached a hand to her face, and when he kissed her she didn't care any more about his secrets.

Later, they lounged together on the sofa and listened to the radio. The broadcaster was reporting on the submissions at the trials of the Nazi high command at Nuremberg.

... The concentration camp was one of the fundamental institutions of the Nazi regime in the battle against the Jews, the Christian Church, labour, those who wanted peace and opposition and nonconformity of any kind ...

Clare got up to turn it off.

'Did you know?' she asked him, returning to her place on the sofa. She was half sitting, half lying against him, his arm around her and her hand on his chest. She tilted back her head to look at him but he did not meet her eyes.

'Did I know what?'

'About the crimes? About the death camps?'

He drew in a long, deep breath and she felt the rise of his chest against her.

'I knew there were camps,' he said after a pause, 'for Jews and gypsies and communists. But I didn't know what happened to them there. Most people didn't. We just assumed they were labour camps of some kind. Although that was bad enough. There were a lot of Germans who didn't support Hitler, who didn't want to fight. But I hardly saw Germany for the whole of the war. I was in Poland, Russia, France, and we soldiers only knew what we were told. We knew a lot of it was lies, of course. We could see for ourselves the truth of what the papers called *heroic defence*.' He shrugged. 'Perhaps the people back home knew what was going on, the women and the old folks. Perhaps. But what could they do?'

'When did you find out the truth?'

'At the camp. Here.'

She started in surprise and shifted back from him, curling against the arm of the sofa, arms around her knees – it was hard to believe that was the first he knew of it.

He went on. 'Just before the war ended, they showed us a film of the liberation of the camp at Belsen. None of us believed it at first. We thought it was some kind of horrible propaganda. Then gradually, as we realised it was true, men began to weep with shame. A couple vomited. We couldn't believe that was what we were fighting for. We all of us thought we had seen the very worst of humanity, in Russia, in France – cruelties and horrors you can't even begin to imagine, from both sides. But none of us had ever seen anything like that.'

'But you knew the Nazis hated Jews.'

'Of course I knew, and I did what I could. The garage where I worked before the war was owned by a family of Jews – Anton was my greatest friend. In '38 I gave him every last penny I had and told him to get out. The last I heard he was trying to get to London. I hope he made it.'

'You don't often talk about Berlin,' she murmured, 'or about your life before the war. Sometimes I feel like I hardly know you.' She remembered his talent for lying and wondered what else he had not told her.

He turned on the sofa to face her. 'You know who I am now, Clare. Berlin was a lifetime ago. I was a different man before the war, so young and innocent I hardly recognise myself. I thought I was so tough and that I'd had it hard. But I knew nothing. Nothing at all.'

'You had to steal to eat,' she said. 'That's harder than most.'

'Getting caught was the hardest part, going to prison.'

She sat up abruptly. 'You went to prison?'

'Six months. I was very young, not much more than a boy. That's where I met Anton.'

She was silent, understanding that he was giving her a gift of sorts, a glimpse inside the hidden core.

'Do you like me less now?' he asked. He was barely breathing.

She shook her head, shifted once more along the sofa and nuzzled into his shoulder again. 'From vicar's wife to ex-criminal's mistress – that's quite a fall.'

'Does it bother you?'

She lifted her head so she could look at his face. The familiar deep furrow creased his brow and he was watching her with a light in his eyes it took her a moment to recognise as fear.

'No,' she said, surprising herself because it was true. 'It doesn't. I don't care about your past. I've never felt so alive as I do with you. Never felt so loved or wanted.'

'Not even by Walter?'

'It was different with Walter,' she said. 'It was …' She stopped, searching for the words to explain. 'We loved each other but it was quieter somehow, more gentle. No fireworks, no burning need. Sometimes I feel as though I might explode with everything I feel for you.'

He nodded as though he understood completely. Then she settled herself back into his embrace and shivered at the touch of his lips against her hair. She never wanted to be anywhere but in his company again.

'What are you doing for Christmas?' Susan asked in the staffroom at lunchtime in the last week of the term. They had hung little silver stars the children had made from the ceiling and they twisted in the warmth from the radiator, catching the light. 'You can't spend it on your own in that awful flat.'

Clare had given up being offended by Susan's insensitivity – she was never going to change and it really didn't matter what Susan thought. Clare loved her flat – it was the home she had made with Max and she would rather be there than anywhere else in the world without him.

'I don't know exactly,' she answered. 'Eric's spending Christmas Day at the farm and, obviously, I'm not invited.' She shrugged, resigned.

'Then come to the Poplars,' Susan said. 'My parents won't be back from London till the evening – some do they can't get out of – so we could have Christmas lunch together. What do you say?' Her red lips parted in a bright and eager smile that was hard to resist.

'Why not?' Clare replied, with a smile of her own.

'No presents necessary,' her friend said. 'Just bring yourself. Mrs Bryant always outdoes herself at Christmas – I think we might even have wild boar.'

'Gosh!' Clare laughed. 'I've never eaten boar. Thank you.' She was touched by the invitation, sure that Susan had far more lively and important friends to spend her time with. But perhaps they were all with their own families for Christmas, and there was no one else to invite. She gave a little shake of her head to chase the thought away, cross with herself for the unkindness of it – she mustn't succumb to cynicism. Not now, when the future was so bright with hope.

'Come over after church,' she said. 'I assume you will be going to church?'

Clare inclined her head, evasive. She had avoided church for months, reluctant to meet Mrs Chapman and face the gossip she was sure had done the rounds. She knew what villages were like: every man and his dog would have an opinion about her leaving Rowan Farm, however far from the truth, and she preferred to avoid it if she could.

'It *is* Christmas,' Susan persisted. 'Don't you have any faith at all? Walter would be ashamed of you.' Her tone was light as though she were saying it in jest, but Clare heard the reproach in the words.

'Walter's faith burned quite brightly enough for two of us,' she answered tartly, and Susan for once was speechless.

In the silence, Clare turned away to rinse out her cup in the sink before she picked up the bell and went outside to ring the end of lunchtime.

Christmas morning, and she did not go to church, though the bells from the early service woke her from her dreams. She lay in the warmth of the bed and listened to the regular toll, her mind wandering back across all the Christmas mornings she had spent with Walter, wrapped against the chill in the old Victorian church where he had led the service, before tea and mince pies in the hall. Then home for a big roast dinner in front of the roaring fire. In the early days of their marriage her father had joined them and she had thought her life was utterly complete. They were happy memories of more innocent days before the war, and she realised she was smiling to herself.

The bells stopped at last and she listened to the silence in their wake. She should have gone, she thought. The early service was quieter, fewer people, and she could have slipped away afterwards unnoticed. Well, it was too late now. She rolled out of bed and shivered with the sudden kiss of cold air against her skin, then put on her dressing gown and slippers, and scuffed out to the kitchen to boil some water for tea. As she waited for the kettle, she turned to admire again the little Christmas tree that Max had dragged home as a surprise from somewhere she didn't dare to ask about. When he had brought it, she had wished with a pang for the old decorations that were still packed away in storage. But without them they had fashioned their own ornaments instead and it had been fun twisting the foil into stars to hang on the branches, and painting the fir cones white to give them snow-covered tips. She had borrowed some lights from the school and when it was finished she thought that it was the most beautiful Christmas tree she had ever seen. Then they had gone out that night to find mistletoe and Max had kissed her beneath it.

Later in the morning, when the congregation from matins had finally dispersed to wander home and the high street was empty once again, Clare made her way through the bitter morning towards the big house. Susan's family had owned it for three generations, and Clare supposed that long ago it had belonged to the lord of the manor.

The great iron gates were open and Clare's shoes crunched on the gravel of the drive. A sharp wind gusted, snatching at her scarf, and she huddled down inside her coat, head bent: she could feel her lips going numb with the chill. At the door, she pulled the bell and heard the dog begin to bark, paws scrabbling on the floor behind it as footsteps approached. Then Susan appeared, looking fabulous as always – hair perfect, lips a brilliant red, and a smart blue sweater that accentuated her figure. Clare felt very dowdy in comparison – it had been a long time since she had bought new clothes, and she began to wish she had not come.

But her friend embraced her warmly and drew her into the warmth of the living room, where a great fire roared in the hearth and an enormous Christmas tree that sparkled with decorations seemed to take up half the room. The walls were hung with red-berried holly, and the air was sweet with a scent of greenery and spices. Mulled wine, Clare suspected, and her mouth watered. Then she turned and saw that James was getting to his feet from the sofa to greet her. She stared in surprise.

'James!' she said. 'I didn't know you would be here too.'

'Surprise,' he replied, and stepped forward to kiss her cheek. Then he said, 'You're freezing,' and, taking her hand, he led her to the hearth, where he helped her out of her coat and scarf and hat. She let him take them and turned puzzled eyes towards Susan, who simply lifted her eyebrows in answer and left the room.

Warming quickly before the fire, Clare shifted to one of the armchairs at the side of it. James, after a moment's hesitation, took one of the others. They sat in silence and after a while Susan returned with a glass for Clare. As she had guessed, it contained mulled wine. She lifted it up towards them both. 'Merry Christmas!'

'Merry Christmas,' they replied in exact unison, and they all laughed.

'You weren't at church,' Susan said.

'No, I decided I just couldn't face it. I was afraid that Walter's mother would be there ...' She trailed off with a shrug.

'She's not so bad,' her friend said. 'You make her sound like an ogre.'

'I'm sure she's lovely if she likes you,' Clare replied. 'But I wouldn't know. She's always been somewhat less than kind to me.'

'Well, you didn't see her, and you're not going to see her.' James tried to make peace, 'And it's Christmas, so let's talk of something else. How's Eric?'

'He's fine,' she said. 'I saw him yesterday. He came to the flat for a couple of hours and I gave him his present. We had mince pies with brandy butter, and talked about the future of Europe. I think he was quite happy.'

'I'm very glad – fingers crossed he keeps it up next term.' He gave Clare an ingratiating smile, and she turned away to look at Susan, who was sitting straight-backed and elegant on the sofa, nursing her own glass of wine.

'So, are we having boar?' she asked.

Susan laughed. 'No. I was only teasing. But we are having turkey with all the trimmings, so I don't think you'll be disappointed.'

They sat in silence for a little while, conversation hard to find, and Clare watched the flames dancing in the fireplace while she wondered why James was there. She had thought he only knew Susan slightly, as an old friend of his friend. Susan had never mentioned that she knew him at all. The mulled wine slid down easily and Clare felt her head begin to go light.

'What spice is in the wine?' she asked, more from something to say than any real interest. 'It's lovely.'

'I couldn't tell you,' Susan replied with a laugh. 'You'd have to ask Mrs Bryant. She's a genius, really.'

Clare tried to put a face to the name but failed. Then, trying again, 'How's your sister, James? Where is she spending Christmas?'

'She's very well, thanks. And she's having Christmas with her new beau's family in Taunton. I think it's rather serious.'

'That's wonderful.'

'It's about time,' Susan said.

'As if you can talk, Sue,' James laughed.

Clare watched, fascinated by the easy banter between them. It was obvious they knew each other well and she was baffled. James drained his glass and held it out for another and Susan gestured to the jug she had left on the hearthstone. He picked it up and poured, then offered it to Clare, who shook her head. She had not yet finished her first and she was already feeling woozy.

The terrier snuffled in and pushed at Clare's hand with a wet nose. She rubbed his ears and he sat on her feet, happy. 'He's very sweet,' she said.

'He's a ridiculous dog,' Susan said. 'But yes, he is rather sweet.' She held out her hand and the dog went to her in the hope of food. When there was none forthcoming he wandered off, back out through the door.

James poured himself more wine. He was drinking rather quickly, Clare thought, and exchanged a look with Susan.

'Slow down, James – it's Christmas all day.'

'Let us eat and drink!' he replied, lifting his glass, 'for tomorrow we die! It's a biblical instruction. And isn't that what Christmas is for?' He took another mouthful. Then, 'Any more thoughts about moving to Wellington, Clare?'

'Not really. I'm still thinking about it.'

'Surely you don't want to stay here in that awful flat?'

'I happen to like that awful flat. I'm much happier there than I was at the farm.'

'Well, yes, that's only to be expected,' he admitted. 'But there's a whole house in Wellington you could make more or less your own. Especially if Louise ties the knot with her young man.'

'Surely you're not suggesting I come and live with you once she leaves?' Clare feigned outrage – she was a vicar's widow after all. And an ex-convict's mistress, she thought, with a secret smile to herself. She was learning to enjoy deception.

'Well, of course, we'd have to do things properly.'

Oh God, she thought. He was still hoping to marry her.

'She enjoys working with me, don't you, Clare?' Susan said.

'That's right,' Clare agreed.

'And with the ever-lovely Miss Finch?'

'Ah well, you can't have everything,' Susan laughed. 'Poor old dear – she's had a very disappointing life, I'm sure. I'd be crotchety as hell too if I'd spent my whole life teaching farmers' kids in Ashenden.'

James gave Clare a meaningful look, as if to say that could be her if she wasn't careful. His eyes were slightly glassy, she noticed, not quite focused. He must have started drinking before she got there.

There was a tap at the door and a middle-aged woman Clare assumed was Mrs Bryant put her head through the gap.

'Lunch is ready whenever you want it, Miss Minter.'

'Thank you, Mrs Bryant. We'll come straight away.'

They followed her along a corridor to the dining room and Clare thought how easy it would be to get lost in such a house. The dining room was hung with holly and ivy too, and the table was set for a feast. It seemed far too extravagant for just the three of them, and she wondered what would happen to the leftovers. She was thinking of the prisoners, always hungry.

They sat at one end of a table that could have sat twenty or more, and James poured more wine for himself. Clare and Susan both stuck to water, and Clare's head began to clear with the food, which was richer than anything she'd eaten since before the war.

'I didn't know you knew each other so well,' she said, when Mrs Bryant came to take away the plates.

'Oh, yes,' James said. 'We've known each other for years. Sue used to come up to Oxford to see Walter.'

Clare caught the warning glance that Susan meant for James but he went on, apparently oblivious.

'We used to smuggle her into college.' He laughed as though he were remembering.

'James,' Susan said sharply. 'Clare doesn't want to hear about that.'

'Yes, she does,' Clare snapped back. 'She really does.'

James seemed to sober briefly, eyes coming to focus first on Susan then on Clare. He said, 'What does it matter any more? Walter's dead, isn't he? Dead, dead, dead.'

The two women stared at him as he drained off another glass.

'She may as well know the truth.'

'What truth?' Clare asked in a small voice, although she was already beginning to piece the story together. 'Tell me.'

'Tell her, Sue,' James said. 'You're supposed to be her friend, aren't you? Some friend, I'd say.'

Clare waited, heartbeat quick in the silent room where the only sound was the hollow roar of the fire as the wind caught in the chimney.

Finally, Susan spoke. Her voice was low and devoid of emotion, but it still carried crystal clear in the quiet. 'It's really very simple. Walter and I were in love. Walter wanted to marry me but my father wouldn't hear of it. Sir Arthur Minter's daughter married to a humble vicar? It was preposterous. Daddy had a list of minor royalty and rich men for me to choose from – all of them awful.'

'Why didn't you marry him anyway, if you were so much in love?'

'Walter wouldn't hear of me going against my family. You know how he could be.'

She was silent, waiting for the rest of the story, but Susan simply turned her head away and gazed at something unseen in the distance.

'When did it stop?' she asked finally, when it was clear Susan wasn't going to say any more.

Her friend turned her head slowly back. 'When he married you.'

Clare drew in a breath, memory scrabbling to piece the dates together. All the time she had spent with Walter before they married, when she had thought they were happy and in love, and all the time he was in love with Susan. Sleeping with her, she assumed.

'He never should have married you,' James said then. 'Bastard. He knew that I liked you, knew I could have made you happy. But he thought you'd be a good vicar's wife and that was all that mattered. He was a selfish bastard till the end.'

Clare felt the tears gathering behind her eyes, lips beginning to tremble.

'I'm so sorry,' Susan said. 'You were never meant to find out.'

'Who else knows?' she asked. 'Bridget? Mrs Chapman?' The thought of it lit a flare of humiliation. So many years of being deceived – she felt like such a fool. No wonder Mrs Chapman resented her. No wonder.

Susan nodded, and though Clare saw that her eyes had filled with tears too, she didn't care. She hated them all. With one swift movement she got up from the table and hurried to the door, almost tripping on the thick carpet in her haste. In the passage she hesitated, unsure which way to go or where she would find her coat and scarf and hat. She heard Susan call out after her but she paid no attention. James appeared beside her.

'Let me walk you back.'

'Leave me alone,' she answered, and started walking away from him, blindly.

'It's this way,' James said gently. 'I'll get your coat.'

She waited, pulses tapping, fingers curling and uncurling with impatience, and when he returned she snatched her things away from him, not stopping to put them on until she reached the door. He held it open for her.

'Are you sure you won't let me walk you home?'

'I can find my own way.'

Outside, the bitter wind grabbed at the flaps of her unbuttoned coat and sliced through the clothes underneath, forcing a shiver. But the hard chill in her lungs was welcome, fresh and clean after the sour taste of what she had heard inside. She fastened her coat with fingers that were trembling with cold and emotion, then leaned into the wind and half walked, half ran along the drive and away from the house.

Chapter Twenty-Four

Max trudged from the camp along the well-known path. A faint gleam of moonlight backlit the clouds, but he could have found his way in utter darkness – he had done it so many times. A frigid wind whipped at his clothes and he huddled deeper inside the coat that once belonged to Walter.

He was glad to get out of the camp, where Christmas had wrought a depressing sense of longing for home among the men. They had celebrated Christmas Eve with songs and carols around the tree in the central square, and afterwards a candlelit feast of sorts of hoarded rations and small illegal gifts of food from the various farms where they worked. They had shared stories and happy memories of other times, other Christmases they had spent with their families, and for that night it had been quite beautiful. But the aftermath in the morning had left them all too aware of their imprisonment a long way from home with no end in sight.

Heimat. Home.

Max tried to imagine it and the strains of the song echoed through his head. What was left of his home any more to miss? The remains of Berlin belonged to the Allies now and the future was unsure. He thought of Lotte and Hanna, their faces bright with joy at the last Christmas they spent together, a hundred years ago. Were they still there, getting by somehow? Had they found somewhere else to settle in a new life without him? Or was there nothing left of them any more to find, their ashes lost somewhere among the ruins of the city that had been their home? There was still not a single word of news about them and he had all but given up hope there ever would be.

When he climbed the stairs to the flat above the saddler's shop the place seemed to be in darkness and he wondered if perhaps Clare was not yet back from her lunch at the big house. He knocked as he always did, and tried the door just in case. It swung open at his touch. He hesitated for a moment in the doorway, senses alert, then noticed the faint orange glow from the electric fire pulled close to the sofa, and Clare's form lying huddled in front of it.

'Clare?'

'*Frohe Weihnachten,*' she said softly.

'Merry Christmas,' he replied, closing the door. Then he was next to her on his knees beside the sofa, reaching a hand to her hair. 'What's happened? Why are you here in the dark?'

She pushed herself into a sitting position and Max looked up at her, her pale skin tinted orange in the light of the heater. He wrapped his cold fingers around her hand and she shivered.

'You're frozen,' she said. 'Let me make you some tea.'

He sat back to let her get up then followed her into the kitchen, switching on the lamp on his way and bathing the flat in a soft yellow glow. The sudden light made him blink. Clare filled the kettle and switched on the stove before she turned to him beside her and he saw she had been crying. Her lashes were still wet, her eyes filmed with tears.

'What's wrong?' he asked again.

'Walter never loved me.' Her voice was soft and hard to hear. She sniffed and rubbed the back of her hand across her nose. 'He married me because he couldn't marry Susan. They were lovers.' She spoke in a flat monotone as though the discovery had leached all sense of feeling out of her.

'Does it still matter?' he replied, tamping down a flicker of jealousy. 'It's in the past.'

'My whole marriage was a lie.' This time he heard the emotion in her voice, anger vying with hurt. 'I trusted him and he deceived me.'

He was silent, aware that she trusted him too. His wife and daughter trod across the edges of his thoughts. He would have to tell her in the end, he thought. He would have no choice.

'What did you see in him anyway?' he asked. 'He sounds like he was a ...' He stopped, searching for an English word that might be acceptable. '... like an awful man. He didn't even know how to make love to you properly.' Max had instinctively disliked Walter from the start, and now that his judgement had proved to be right he hated him anew.

'That isn't fair!' she replied. 'You didn't know him. He was a gentleman. He was clever and funny and kind ...' She trailed off, perhaps with the realisation that he was less kind than she had thought.

'But he didn't deserve you,' Max said. 'He lied to you and let you think he loved you.' He paused. 'Did he ever say the words? Did he tell you he loved you?'

She nodded. 'Yes,' she whispered, 'he told me.'

He took her fingers in his again, shifting closer. How many times had they stood like this before the small stove, their bodies touching lightly as they waited for the kettle to boil? He remembered the first time they made love, right here in the kitchen. A flush of heat flared through him.

The water began to hiss, heating slowly.

'Everyone knew,' she said then. 'Everyone except me. I feel like such an idiot. How could I have not noticed? I thought he loved me. I really did, but ...'

'Do you still love him?'

Her eyes flicked to his in surprise at the question. 'I don't know,' she answered after a moment. 'I was happy with him and I thought he was happy with me, but it seems I was mistaken. All that time he was in love with somebody else. I was his second choice.'

'It was a long time ago – does it matter any more?'

'Of course it matters! It changes everything.'

'What does it change?'

She said nothing and lifted the kettle to warm the pot. He watched every movement she made – the pale, delicate line of her wrist, her small and dainty hands as she turned the hot water in the pot. She emptied it and spooned in the tea, filled it again, then set it down to brew.

'What does it change?' he repeated. 'Does it change how you feel about me? About us? Does it change this?'

He moved to stand behind her and put his arms around her waist, inhaling the familiar scent of her, her body warm against him. He felt the halt in her breathing at his touch and let his lips caress the soft skin at the nape of her neck. She let them linger there a moment before she turned inside his embrace and put her arms around his neck with a sigh.

'I suppose you're right,' she murmured. Her head was angled away from him, and he couldn't read her expression. 'It makes no difference to this. To us. And it was a long time ago.'

'It was a different world – we're all of us different people now. The war has seen to that.'

She turned her head towards him, their faces close. 'All those guilty, sleepless nights,' she breathed. 'All that self-reproach. What a waste.'

He smiled. 'It's in the past. It's not important any more.'

She gave him a half-smile in reply that didn't reach her eyes. 'Perhaps,' she said. 'But still, it hurts. He wasn't the man I thought

I loved, not the man I grieved for. I would never have believed him capable of living such a lie.'

Max said nothing, thinking again of his own lie, and they stood in silence for a moment.

'I thought we were happy,' she whispered then.

He lifted his hand to tuck back a stray hair from her cheek and she shivered as the backs of his fingers brushed against her skin.

'It's over, Clare. Are you happy now? Here, with me?'

She nodded. *'Carpe diem,'* she breathed. 'Right?'

'Right.'

She drew in a deep breath, her small frame lifting in his arms, then let it out with a sigh, as though she were letting go of the hurt and humiliation. Setting back her shoulders, she nodded towards the tree.

'Look underneath it,' she told him. 'There's something there for you.'

'A present?'

He had not expected anything and he felt a sudden wash of excitement like a child. It had been a long time since anyone had given him a gift. Clare took his hand and led him through to the living room where the little tree stood in the corner. The foil stars they had made winked in the reflected light of the table lamp and there were two parcels on the floor beneath it, both wrapped in brown paper with ribbon.

'Both for me? Which should I open first?'

She pointed to the largest, and he knelt on the floor between the tree and the sofa as he untied the ribbon and unfolded the paper. 'Socks!'

'I knitted them myself.' She pulled a face. 'Three pairs. They got better as I went along.'

He laughed, pleased and touched, enjoying the texture of the new wool against his hand. They seemed fine to him: if she had made mistakes in the knitting he couldn't see them, and new socks were a luxury after the much-darned and threadbare army issue he usually wore.

'Open the other one,' she said.

He picked it up and shook it gently but it made no sound, and when he peeled away the wrapping his fingers discovered a harmonica.

'I came across it in a junk shop,' she said, 'so I don't know how well it works.'

He handled it reverently, silenced by the gift – he couldn't remember telling her he used to play. He had lost the harmonica his father gave him as a boy somewhere outside of Kiev, one more piece of debris among the shattered ruins, but he could still recall that Christmas with perfect clarity, the last before his father died.

'Play something,' she said, and he lifted it to his lips, blowing gently to test it.

'What should I play?' He was self-conscious suddenly and could think of no music at all.

'Silent Night?'

Of course. He touched his mouth to the instrument again and the room filled with the tentative mournful notes of the carol that had failed to move him at all when they had sung it at the camp before the Christmas tree. But now, here with the woman he loved, all the sadness of the war, all the senseless loss and destruction seemed to swell inside him, and though he blinked to stop the tears from coming it made no difference. Memories of other Christmases played across his thoughts – decorating the tree at the little flat in Berlin; Lotte's voice deep and sweet as they sang carols around it; and Hanna's face bright with excitement and delight. The year before the war began they had given her a record of her favourite ballet music and she played it again and again on the gramophone, pirouetting around the living room until they simply couldn't bear to hear it one more time. Then they had put on a Fred Astaire record instead, but quietly, because Astaire was banned by the Nazis, and it was their turn to dance.

Max let the harmonica fall away from his lips and tried to breathe more deeply to quell the onslaught of feeling he had kept locked inside for so long. Clare moved to sit beside him on the floor and put her arms around him. Lowering his head against her shoulder and letting her hold him as if he were a child, he gave into the tears he could no longer keep at bay, and wept.

His strong frame shuddered against her as she held him but he didn't weep for long. Sitting back away from her he leaned against the sofa, wiping hard at his eyes with his fingers, and she could see from the determined set of his jaw and the way he kept his gaze away from her that he was angry with himself and ashamed.

'I'm sorry,' he said. 'I'm sorry.'

'It's all right,' she answered. 'Truly.'

He drew in a deep breath and got to his feet in one swift movement. She loved that about him – the energy he brought to everything he did, the intensity, and when he turned the light of his attention to her it was as if she was the only thing in the world that existed. He went to the kitchen and returned with a small package she hadn't noticed when he arrived. He sat down beside her again and held it out.

'It's not much.'

'I didn't expect anything.' The prisoners had no money, no access to tools or materials. She looked up at him, smiling. 'Thank you.'

'Open it.' He shook his head to clear it of the last of the tears, and wiped his cheeks with the back of one hand.

'Are you all right?'

He nodded, once, briefly, closing the subject, and Clare unfolded the paper with care so that it could be used again. Inside the paper she found a tiny toy bicycle, cleverly fashioned from scraps of wood and wire. Miniature pedals turned the wheels, and there was a basket on the front and a rack on the back exactly the same as her own bike.

'It's perfect.' She held it in her hands for a moment, remembering the ride back to the farm after the first time they met at the church, when he had cycled her home. She could still recall the movement of his hips beneath her hands as he pedalled, the closeness of his back, and the way she had laughed with delight for the first time in far too long. She had already been half in love with him then, she thought, and she was wholly in love with him now. He had been right – it made no difference whether Walter had loved her or not. Walter belonged to an old life in a world that had passed out of existence. She was a different person now.

Later, they ate leftover chicken with fried potato and sprouts and the rest of the mince pies she had made for Eric. She opened the brandy she had got from Fred Wakeman and as they drank Max was cheerful again, as if the tears had never been. Afterwards, they found some American jazz on the radio and danced for a while, shifting back the furniture to make more room, and when they were tired of dancing he played some more on the harmonica – unfamiliar and haunting German tunes that spoke to her of love and regret, and of times that would never come again.

And as she lay on the sofa with her head in his lap, watching the man she loved while he played, she thought it was the loveliest Christmas she had ever had.

Chapter Twenty-Five

C lare liked the long winter nights and the early drawing in of the dark that made it easier for Max to steal out of the camp. He came most nights now and they played cards or danced to the radio or read or simply talked, and he taught her some German, which she practised in shy, halting phrases, self-conscious. It seemed ridiculous for her to stutter and falter in German when his English was so perfect, but slowly she began to gain more confidence, and she loved to hear his voice in his own language, a facet of him she had not seen before.

The school Christmas holidays passed too quickly. Eric returned to Wellington with a promise not to get himself expelled, and she saw him off with a hopeful wave. It seemed that for now at least he had forgiven her, but of course he did not yet know the truth.

'Should I tell him next holiday?' she asked Max. She was losing the game of rummy they were playing, her thoughts else-where. 'I hate lying to him.'

'Will he throw stones at me?' He collected up the cards from the unfinished game and she did not even notice.

'I'm serious. I just worry that the longer I keep the lie going the harder it will be for him when he finds out in the end.'

'*If* he finds out.'

She opened her mouth to reply then closed it again, suddenly unsure what she wanted to say. By tacit consent they never talked about the future – there were too many uncertainties, too many unknowns – but she assumed that in the end the government would lift the restrictions and the prisoners would be free to go and love where they pleased. Now and then she allowed herself to dream of a life ahead with Max: a garage business somewhere for him, a teacher's job for her, and they could be together always.

'Well,' she said at last. 'I'm hoping we don't have to be a secret forever.'

He looked up from the pack of cards he was shuffling and gave her a small smile she could not read: there were still times when she felt as though she hardly knew him at all.

'Is there any news?' she asked, half changing the subject, 'about you going home?'

He shook his head. 'There's never any news. The government needs us; they need the manpower to rebuild.' He had begun working in construction, building roads and houses, and he liked it better than the farm work. 'But we should be rebuilding Germany, not England.'

'It's slave labour,' she agreed. 'There's an MP fighting your corner in Parliament though. I read it in the paper yesterday. He's trying to ensure you at least get properly paid.'

'Richard Stokes.' Max supplied the name. 'But he's the only one. The rest of them want us to stay.'

For something to do she got up and went to look out of the window. The high street was empty and the lamp above the pub door glowed with a halo in the damp.

'Do you hate it here?' she asked, turning back to face him.

He shook his head and kept on shuffling the cards with slow

and deliberate movements. She watched the regular motion of his hands, mesmerising.

'Max?'

He put down the cards in a careful pile and shrugged, but he didn't look at her.

'I don't hate it here, Clare. I like England. But I'm a prisoner. I want my freedom. I don't want to have to sneak out through the wire to see the woman I love, and I want to earn more than a shilling a day for shovelling sand. The war's been over for a long time and I want to get on with my life. We all do.'

She turned away to look out of the window again. She could not imagine her life without him – perhaps she would end up like Miss Finch after all, a bitter old woman scraping by with no hope for anything better.

Max came to stand behind her and she flinched, startled by his sudden presence. Absorbed in her thoughts, she hadn't noticed him move. He placed his hands on her shoulders and she could feel his cheek against her head, her hair catching on the roughness of his stubble.

'But I'm not going anywhere any time soon. Nothing is going to change for a while yet, so there's no point in worrying about a future we can't predict.'

She drew in a deep breath and turned towards him. He touched his fingers to her cheek in the way she loved so well.

He smiled.

Then he kissed her, and with the touch of his lips on hers all thoughts of the future were forgotten.

'Happy New Year!' Susan greeted her as soon as she walked through the staffroom door on the day before the new school term. In the past it had always been a day of chatter about the holidays as they prepared for the weeks ahead. Susan always had interesting tales to tell, juicy details of a busy social life in

London. But Clare had no interest in Susan's stories any more: she could barely even bring herself to look at her.

'Morning,' she replied noncommittally, slipping off her coat and going to her desk.

She saw Susan hesitate, moistening her red lips with the tip of her tongue. Lips that Walter had kissed, Clare couldn't help thinking, and an unwelcome image of the two of them together passed across her mind. She rested her fingertips on the top of the empty desk and waited until the thought had shifted to the back of her mind. But its residue still remained as a bitter taste in her mouth.

'Ready for another term?' Susan's usual cheeriness was brittle and forced.

Briefly, Clare paused. Then, with a deep breath, she raised her eyes from their perusal of the desk and looked at her friend. Susan waited, her gaze darting here and there in quick anxious movements before she suddenly blurted, 'I'm so sorry. Walter swore me to secrecy. I wanted to tell you so many times but he made me promise I never would, whatever happened.'

Clare nodded. She could imagine it – Walter earnest and emotional, wracked with guilt, and Susan, loving him and eager to please.

'Did you love him very much?' she said.

'Yes. I would have married him in spite of my family without a moment's hesitation, but he just flat out refused. That stubborn righteous streak that was so infuriating. I begged, I pleaded, but he wouldn't even consider it as a possibility and my father was equally intransigent.' She looked up, and some of the nervousness had left her eyes now that they were talking to each other. 'So here we are. Can you ever forgive me?'

All that time Clare had thought her marriage was happy, and though it was long in the past now, the humiliation of the truth still stung – she had never suspected Walter could lie so well. You can never truly know anyone, she supposed: we all have our secrets. Then she wondered what secrets Max might be keeping and a shiver ran through her at the thought of it.

Susan was watching her now with anxious eyes, hoping for forgiveness. Much as Clare wanted to hate her, she knew it was not really Susan's fault. Her only crime, after all, had been in loving Walter and – as James had so emphatically pointed out – Walter was dead, dead, dead. That morning Clare had woken up next to Max, loved and happy. They had kissed before he left to hurry back to the camp and her heart had begun to race, every fibre in her body alive to his touch. Walter had never once made her feel that way, so what did it matter any more what he had done before he married her or what lies he had made others vow to keep?

The staffroom door swung open with a creak of hinges, and the squat form of Miss Finch appeared in the doorway, interrupting the conversation.

'Happy New Year, ladies,' she said, without much enthusiasm.

Clare and Susan exchanged an instinctive glance and smiled.

'All ready for the new term?'

'Just preparing now, Miss Finch,' Susan answered, lifting an eyebrow at Clare.

'Meeting in my office at eleven, don't forget.' The headmistress backed out of the door and closed it firmly behind her. They heard her boots on the floorboards as she crossed the hall and the click of her office door as it opened and shut.

'Better get to it then,' Susan said. 'Officer on deck, and all that.' She waited, turning a pencil over and over between her fingers.

Clare sighed. They had to work together and it would be hard if they were enemies. But she still struggled to set aside the vivid images of her friend and her husband that flashed across her thoughts at unexpected moments: Susan's bright lips and Walter's pale, lean body, his elegant fingers caressing Susan's curves. She felt again the sense of her own dowdiness against Susan's pert, bright prettiness – how could she compete? Would Max prefer Susan too if he met her?

'I'm truly sorry.'

'I know,' Clare answered. 'You must have hated me.'

'A little,' Susan admitted, with a half-shrug and a rueful smile.

Clare returned the smile with a half-smile of her own. 'And now?'

'I think Walter treated both of us badly, and I hope and pray you can forgive me for my part in it.'

She nodded. There was no point in nurturing hatred. As Max had said, it was all in the past now, a long time ago, and it made no difference any more. So, with a little lift of her shoulders and a deep breath to set her thoughts firmly to the future, she said, 'I suppose we'd better get to it then, or Miss Finch will have our guts for garters.'

'And we don't want that.' Susan stepped behind her desk to cross to the little hob and set the kettle on it. 'Tea?'

'Yes, please,' Clare answered, and a few minutes later they settled down to work.

Chapter Twenty-Six

Winter slowly gave way to spring and the trees and hedgerows erupted into new and verdant life so that it was hard to recall the spare grey lines of the winter branches amid so much vitality. Primroses and hawthorn blossom lined the lanes, and the woodlands were filled with bluebells. It was Clare's favourite time of year, offering the hope of new possibilities, new beginnings.

'Do you have the same flowers and trees in Germany?' She was walking with Max after supper, taking more risks in the dying twilight just to share the wonder of it all.

'Mostly, I think. I grew up in the city.' He shrugged, and she squeezed in tighter against him, sliding her hand inside his coat, feeling his familiar warmth and the well-known curve of his chest and belly. 'But Russia was very different. Miles upon miles of nothingness. You can't even begin to imagine the scale of it.'

He rarely spoke of his experiences in Russia and she waited, barely breathing. 'Where in Russia did you go?'

He shook his head and gave her a wry smile. 'All over the place. Most of the time we didn't know where we were exactly.

Somewhere near Kiev. Somewhere on the banks of the Dnieper. An unknown village not far from Kursk. But mostly in Ukraine.'

'It must have been cold.'

He laughed then. 'I have never been so cold. I mean, Berlin gets pretty cold. But not like that. Russian cold steals the life right off you – you can almost feel the blood beginning to freeze in your veins. I don't know how people live there, how they survive. It's brutal.'

They stopped at the edge of the trees to watch the last light leave the sky across the valley. There was no moon and the stars burst out of the darkness in clusters, sparkling and brilliant.

'I wish I knew more about the stars,' she said. 'I think that every time I look at them. I only know Orion and the Plough.'

He said nothing but took her hand and they turned to walk along the line of the trees back towards the village, cutting across the fields to keep off the roads and lanes. When they reached the village they went into the saddler's yard from the back as they always did, but halfway across it Max pulled up short. It took Clare a moment to see what he had seen as a woman's form emerged from the dark at the base of the staircase.

'*Scheisse!*' Max breathed, and his fingers tightened on Clare's so hard she flinched.

'Clare?'

It was Bridget, Clare realised, recognising the voice, and there was nothing to do but hope. She let go of Max's hand and went forward.

'Can I come in?' Bridget's voice was slurred and weak. Clare cast a look over her shoulder to Max, who stepped to her side just in time to support Bridget as she swayed and began to fall. He held her against him, supporting her, then lifted her to carry her up the stairs and inside. Clare locked the door behind them and turned on the lamps as Max laid Bridget gently on to the sofa. He flicked Clare a look.

'I should go.'

'No,' Clare said, 'please stay.'

He glanced at the door, hesitating, and though she understood his eagerness to go, her instinct warned her against it.

'She's already seen you,' she said. 'The damage is done.'

He said nothing more and Clare dropped to her knees beside her sister-in-law, who was beginning to revive. She peered out through her tangled hair, and as Clare reached gentle fingers to brush it back from Bridget's face she saw the damage underneath. The split fat lip, the half-closed eye that was already swollen and bruised. She looked at Max, whose face had hardened with anger, fist balling at his side.

Clare fetched a cloth and some water and began to wipe away the worst of the blood. Bridget winced with each touch.

'What happened?'

'You know what happened,' Bridget said.

Clare sat back on her heels. It had been months since she had seen her sister-in-law: the beatings must have worsened since she left.

'He doesn't care now about the bruises. He doesn't bother to hurt me only in places no one will see any more. He just hurts me.'

'*Ich bringe ihn um,*' Max said.

Clare didn't know the words but the meaning was clear enough – *I'll kill him.*

'I didn't know where else to go.' Bridget looked up at Max with a small smile that made her wince as the damaged skin around her mouth drew tight. 'I'm sorry.'

'Don't be sorry,' Clare told her. 'He's an animal. You can stay here. Of course you can stay.'

Bridget began to tremble, as though the shock was setting in now that she had found somewhere safe to be. Clare got a blanket and wrapped it around her shoulders, and Max went to the kitchen to make tea for them all.

'What about your mother?' Clare asked.

'She's always turned a blind eye. She needs him for the farm. She hates him, of course, she always has, but without him the farm would go under. He'd never lay a finger on her – he knows which side his bread is buttered.'

A crash at the front door made them all jump, and with a second smash the door was thrown open. Simon appeared, glassy-eyed and swaying. It took him a moment to take in the scene before him, but he did not notice Max, who was still in the kitchen. He staggered towards the two women on the sofa and Bridget cried out.

'You touch her again and I'll do the same to you.' Max's voice cut through the end of the cry, and Simon wheeled in surprise.

'You? You wouldn't dare!'

'Try me.' Max had moved into the living room and Clare stepped back, taking shelter behind the sofa, holding Bridget's hand across the back of it.

'I'm not afraid of you,' Simon snarled.

'You should be,' Max replied. 'I've killed more men than I can count, some of them with my bare hands, and all of them tougher than you.'

But Simon had stopped listening. Fuelled by rage and alcohol he lunged at his wife, fist raised, as she cowered in terror.

Clare barely saw what happened next. But she heard Simon scream as Max hurled the water from the kettle at his face, and she heard the impact of a fist against soft flesh, the wheeze of expelled air. Then she saw Simon lift his hands to protect himself as Max moved in close, but she couldn't make out how the other man ended up curled and whimpering on the rug, shuddering and crying out each time Max's boot connected.

For a moment she could only watch, transfixed by the brutality. Then, realising that Max might actually kill him, she ran and grabbed his arm.

'Stop!'

He shrugged her off with a thrust of his arm.

'Max! Please! Enough. You don't want to kill him.'

He stopped mid-kick, the toe of his boot just touching the prostrate form without landing the blow it had planned. Then he turned away, breathing hard, sweating. Clare picked up the kettle from the floor where he had thrown it and stood over Simon.

'Get out,' she said.

The farmer uncurled himself reluctantly, tentatively, and sat up with one arm cradling his battered abdomen. He glanced at the faces standing over him and his gaze came to rest on Max, who was watching him with rage in his eyes.

'*Raus!*' Max said. 'Get out!

Simon scrambled to his feet and staggered. Blood poured from his nose and one cheek had begun to redden where Max had thrown the hot water. He was lucky, Clare thought, that it had not yet boiled. For a moment he hesitated, still unsteady on his feet, but when Max took a step towards him he gathered himself and made for the door. They heard him stumble down the stairs, and listened to the tramp of his boots fade along the lane into the high street. Max closed the door, which would no longer lock. He picked up a kitchen chair and propped it under the handle.

'You need to get that fixed,' he said.

Clare sat on the sofa beside Bridget, who was trembling.

'Thank you,' Bridget said.

'My pleasure,' Max replied, and in spite of everything Clare smiled.

'I'll make some more tea,' she said, and got up and went out to the kitchen.

Later, when Bridget was settled in bed and they were clearing up in the kitchen, Clare said, 'Is it true what you said, about killing men with your bare hands?'

He gave her a half-shrug. 'In war you do what you have to do to stay alive,' he said, although the truth was that he had learned to fight long before he ever went to war. 'I'm not proud of it.'

'I can't even bring myself to kill a spider.'

He smiled. 'That's why I love you. You're everything I'm not – sweet, kind, innocent.' She settled closer against him, her body warm and soft, and he rubbed at her arm with the tips of his fingers. 'When I'm with you I remember all the good things in the world and I can forget all the things I've seen and done ...' He trailed off, reluctant to say the rest of the words out loud. How was it he could remember the face of every man he had killed with vivid haunting clarity and yet be unable to summon to mind the image of his wife and child?

'I'm glad I help,' she said. She set down the tea towel and touched her hand to his arm. 'I know you don't want to talk about it and I have no right to ask, but sometimes I want to know everything that's ever happened to you so badly it makes my whole body ache. There's so much about you I don't know.'

Lotte trod again across the edges of his thoughts.

'I'll never tell you about the war, Clare,' he replied. 'It was a place no man should ever go to, and I'm not going to show you even the smallest glimpse of it. Believe me, it's better that you never know.'

How could he begin to explain it to her when he could barely make sense of it himself? How could anyone who wasn't there even start to understand?

She reached to touch his shoulder where the scar was hidden by his shirt. 'Was it very painful?'

He shrugged, and the wound began to throb as if to remind him of just how much it had hurt. Images flickered unwelcome through his thoughts – it had been a long time since he had allowed himself to remember it. Clare rested her head against his shoulder and nestled closer into him.

Only later, when she had gone to bed and Max lay sleepless

and uncomfortable on the sofa, did he close his eyes and allow the memory to come.

Not far from the Dnieper river they had formed an isolated bridgehead to stop the Russians taking the railway and the bridge. Rumours were rife that help was on its way to break the encirclement but Max had been a soldier for far too long to put his faith in rumours. It was mostly wishful thinking. He knew there would be no rescue – either they had been sacrificed on the altar of some strategic purpose they would never know, or it was simple incompetence at the top. It was hard to decide which was worse. But what was sure was the growing strength of the Russian forces arrayed against them as their own supplies of food and ammunition slowly dwindled.

For two weeks they fought off the attacks as best they could and listened through the sleepless nights to the wounded Russians crying on the frozen ground in the dark with no one to help them. Even as a raw recruit Max had never much believed in the glory of death for *Führer, Volk und Vaterland,* but now he fully understood that death has many forms. He heard those screams even in the deepest sleep – a living, waking nightmare.

That night he had woken abruptly in the dark from a doze to a murmur of unease across the sector. Instinct hurled him from his makeshift bed to emerge from his trench and stand with the others as they stared out into the blackness beyond their position. The rumble of engines carried towards them on the wind, and now and then a searchlight pierced what was left of the night.

'What do you think they're doing?' Theo stood beside him, arms folded around himself, stamping his feet on the snow to warm them.

'Something big by the sound of it,' Max replied. 'I guess we'll find out come morning.'

They watched, unable to draw themselves away, held by a dread fascination in spite of the cold. He could feel the fear balling in his gut. In the east the night began to give way to the day at last, grey bands starting to creep across the sky, and the echo of his dreams sounded through his thoughts. As one man he and Theo turned and dropped back into the bunker behind them. A moment more and the Soviet barrage began.

It was like nothing he had ever lived through before in its ferocity. Peering over the edge of the trench, he saw that every square inch of the earth was churning. Snow and soil and fragments of metal leaped together in some kind of macabre dance to a music that was deafening – the roar of rockets and mortars and infantry weapons. Men who had been caught outside the shelter of their trenches as the onslaught began fell to the cratered ground – whether they were living or dead he could not tell, but surely no one could survive such concentrated fire. Inside the bunker again he met Theo's silent question with a small shake of his head. There was no point in talking – the bombardment was deafening. They sat huddled as they waited and when, finally, the maelstrom began to ebb he was half-deaf, ears ringing. But even so he could still hear a man screaming and frantic shouts for a medic.

For three more breaths they waited, reluctant to face whatever would come next.

Then another voice cut through the racket.

'*Panzer!* Dozens of them!'

Max slid a glance to Theo and they stood up and looked over the lip of the trench once more. In front of them where the ground had been churned and cratered by the shelling, the snow had melted entirely away. Plumes of smoke hung in the air and, here and there, body parts and trails of gore were strewn across the mud. The stench stung in his nostrils, his lungs on fire, and he felt his stomach threaten to heave. He breathed out, forcing down the nausea – there was no time to be sick. The swarm of T-

34 tanks were heading for the village, engines roaring, pitching fire.

He tracked their progress – they did not have long. In a few more minutes it would be over: the escape to the village would be cut off, their route to the river blocked. Other men were already fleeing the safety of their bunkers to take their chances with shellfire rather than be caught by the Russians.

'I'm not staying here,' Max said, and with one swift movement he was up and out of the bunker. Theo followed a moment behind him, and then they were running for their lives with the others, up towards the village and the frozen river that lay beyond it.

They stripped off their belts and coats to lighten their loads as they sprinted through the hail of shells that were exploding all around them. Just ahead of them two men were caught, blown apart by the blast. Max did not falter in his stride but only slid a quick glance to his side to check that Theo was still with him. His lungs were bursting, and just as he crested the rise a great weight seemed to slam full force into him, knocking him to the ground. He lay in the snow, confused and shocked, until Theo grabbed his arm and pulled him up. Pain seared through his body, blinding, knocking the last of the breath out of him.

'Don't stop now,' Theo said. He paused briefly and looked into his friend's face, and Max struggled to focus, Theo's face swimming before him. 'Keep running.'

His friend turned and bounded down the slope towards the village and Max followed him, instinct taking over, anything to flee from the killing field behind him. They came to a hut of some kind on the outskirts of the village and threw themselves inside it. It felt good to be inside the shelter of a building, however flimsy – a brief illusion of safety. Max crumpled to the floor and Theo peered out through a gap in the broken wall.

'We can't stay here. We've got to go,' he said and turned to Max. '*Steh auf. Komm jetzt.*' Get up. Come on.

He dragged his friend to his feet and they pitched out into the street and set off running again, heading for the river. The tanks had reached the village, and the fleeing men were falling under their fire. In his haze of pain and shock and blood loss, Max was only vaguely aware of them, conscious only of the need to follow Theo – instinct forcing one foot in front of the other as they headed for the river, where a few of the soldiers who had made it this far were sheltering in a clump of trees. They stopped briefly to catch their breath, then hurled themselves after the others in a mad dash out onto the ice where the T34s could not go. But even if the tanks could not follow they could still lob their shells from their positions on the bank, and the bloodstained ice cracked and broke underfoot with the fire. Bodies all around them slid into the churning water, and Max almost stumbled over the form of a man he had talked to only yesterday as it disappeared out of sight beneath the ice.

Finally, impossibly, they reached the far bank of the river and the shelter of the forest beyond. Max sank into the snow, and though the racket of the shells and the screams of dying men still echoed in his head, it all seemed to be very far away. Pain pulsed through every part of his body, and in spite of the sweat that dripped across his face, he could not stop himself from shivering. Vaguely, he was aware of Theo somewhere close, an indistinct form murmuring words he could make no sense of.

Then he had slid into darkness and could remember nothing more.

Saturday morning, and when Clare woke up Max had already gone – she had not heard him leave. Beside her in the bed Bridget was still huddled under the blankets. It was not yet light outside, though when she looked out of the window the first bands of grey were just beginning to lighten across the sky. She dressed hurriedly, the mornings still cold in spite of the changing season.

She would need to find a locksmith, she thought. Perhaps they might know of one at the pub.

Clare made tea and Bridget sat up gingerly, testing the soreness of her body as she moved. She took the cup Clare gave her with a smile of thanks that made her wince.

'How long has it been this bad?' Clare asked.

'It got worse when you left.' She sipped at the tea, then raised her head to look at Clare, who was sitting on the end of the bed. She looked awful, Clare thought, bruised and battered and sore.

Bridget said, 'Does the German make you happy?'

'Max,' Clare replied. 'His name is Max. And yes, he does. He loves me better than Walter ever did.'

A brief flicker of anxiety passed over Bridget's face.

'James let the cat out of the bag at Christmas,' Clare said. 'I know all about Susan and the vow of secrecy.' She raised her eyebrows with a wry smile.

'He did come to love you,' Bridget said quickly, instinctively defending her brother even now. 'He was happy with you.'

Clare was silent for a while, unsure whether or not to believe it, and there seemed to be nothing else to say. Outside, the day had begun. They could hear the traffic in the high street and the call of voices. Downstairs, the bell on the door of the saddler's rang, a distant tinkle.

Clare had just finished clearing up breakfast when there was a knock at the door. She turned abruptly, her breath catching in her throat, chest tight.

'Lock yourself in the bathroom,' Clare said. It wasn't much of a lock but it was better than nothing. Bridget fled.

She went to the door, and jumped when the knock came again, her nerves on edge. 'Who is it?'

'Is Bridget there?' It was Mrs Chapman, and Clare let out the breath she had been holding.

She looked over her shoulder to where Bridget was still hesitating at the bathroom door, and waited. When the other woman nodded her assent, Clare shifted the chair away from the door. Max must have climbed through the window when he left.

She opened the door and Mrs Chapman stepped inside. Briefly she looked the flat over, expressionless. Clare moved back and offered her a chair at the table but Bridget stayed by the bathroom, keeping a distance, as if she were as afraid of her mother as she was of her husband. Perhaps she was.

'Simon said you were here,' Mrs Chapman said. She showed no emotion at the state of her daughter's face. 'Now you need to come home.'

Bridget shook her head.

'Don't be ridiculous. You can't stay here.'

'Yes she can,' Clare heard herself say. 'She can stay as long as she wants.'

Bridget's one good eye met Clare's, and it was bright with gratitude.

'Come home,' her mother persisted, 'where you belong.'

'I'm not going back as long as Simon is there,' Bridget said. 'It's either him or me. Your choice.'

Clare heard Mrs Chapman take in a sharp gasp of air, astonished by her daughter's rebellion. Bridget had never once defied her before. She said, 'You're being absurd. We need him.'

'The farm needs him,' Bridget corrected.

Mrs Chapman wheeled towards Clare. 'Did you put her up to this?'

'Look at her!' Clare replied. 'Look at what he did to her. Your daughter. And you want her to come back for more?! What's wrong with you?'

'You've always been trouble,' Mrs Chapman went on, as though Clare had not even spoken. 'I knew from the first moment I met you Walter had made a mistake.'

The two younger women exchanged another glance.

'I think you should go,' Clare said. 'And if you come to decide that your daughter is more important than the farm let us know. You know where we are.'

Mrs Chapman looked from one to the other in surprise, as if she couldn't quite understand how the conversation had got to this point. It was clearly not how she had planned it.

'You're not coming?' she asked finally.

'No,' Bridget replied. 'I'm not coming.'

In the pause her mother lifted a glance to the window before she turned back to face her daughter.

'If you don't come back, I shall be forced to tell the police exactly how your husband got his injuries.' She lifted her chin defiantly, playing her trump card.

Bridget let out a moan. 'You can't do that. Simon would have killed me.' She looked to Clare in desperation, caught in her mother's trap.

Dread seeped through Clare's veins as a heaviness in her guts and in her limbs. She would have to go to court and the whole world would know. Max would get detention again. She had read only last week of a woman who was fined five pounds for nothing more than passing a piece of cake through a fence to a German prisoner. Her innards churned.

'Then you do that,' she said, drawing herself up, shoulders straight. *You do what you have to do to survive*, Max had said. She knew what he would do if he were here, and it would be without a second thought. 'Bridget is staying here.'

'I'll go,' Bridget murmured. 'I can't ask you to do that. I can't.'

'You're staying,' Clare said, and though her heart beat fast she was surprised at how calm she felt now she had made the decision.

She turned to Mrs Chapman. 'Walter's widow fraternising with a German. How everyone will pity you.'

A muscle began to twitch in her mother-in-law's cheek, and her lips were pressed tight with fury, knowing Clare was right.

Clare watched the conflict with detached curiosity, wondering if the old woman would actually carry out her threat or if it was merely a bluff. She assumed she would not have to wait long to find out.

'And the children?' Mrs Chapman still had one card left. 'What about your children?'

Clare watched the fight slide out of Bridget as if someone had turned on a tap: she would never abandon her children.

'Are you going to bring them here too? Or are you going to leave them for their father to look after? Who can say who'll bear the brunt of his temper if you're not there to protect them?'

'Send *him* packing!' Clare shouted. 'He's the one who should be going.'

'Who will look after the farm in his place?' Mrs Chapman turned an icy glare towards her. 'You? Will you come and get your pretty hands dirty on the farm?'

'I'd help in any way I can,' Clare said. 'But it's inhuman to put the farm before your daughter.'

'It should have been Walter,' Mrs Chapman murmured, more to herself than to the others. 'He should have been here, working the farm as his father wanted.

'That was what *you* wanted,' Bridget returned. 'Not Dad. Dad just wanted Walter to be happy.'

'If he'd stayed on the farm he'd still be alive.'

No one spoke for a moment. Clare slid a glance towards the door and wondered where Max was now, if he was all right.

Bridget said, 'Tell the children I'll be home later.'

Mrs Chapman got to her feet and walked to the door, and disappeared without another word. The two younger women heard her footsteps dwindle in the lane, and Clare propped the chair back against the door.

'What else could I do?' Bridget said. 'She's right. I can't bring the children here.'

Clare took her coat from the hook. 'I'm going out to see about getting a locksmith,' she said. 'I shouldn't be long. Prop the chair against the door while I'm out and don't let anyone in.'

Then she went out into the morning and across the road to the pub to see if anyone there could help.

Chapter Twenty-Seven

The locksmith had not long left when there was another knock at the door of the flat, a confident rap-rap-rap that Clare did not recognise. She looked at Bridget, who shrugged. Then she went to the door, fastened the brand-new chain, and peered out through the narrow gap to see a policeman standing on the step. Cold dread flared inside her – it appeared Mrs Chapman had made good on her threat even though Bridget had said she would return. Clare let the chain off its hook and opened the door.

'Mrs Chapman?' the officer asked. 'Mrs Clare Chapman?'

She nodded. Policemen were a rare sight in Ashenden – she imagined his arrival had not gone unnoticed. This man was in his forties, with fleshy jowls and a drinker's red nose. There was no malice in his eyes as he looked her over but she shivered just the same, unable to find again the reckless courage of before.

'Can I come in?'

Clare hesitated, conscious of the rapid patter of her pulse, her mouth dry. Then she let the chain off the latch and opened up the door. 'Please.' She gestured to the kitchen table, and the officer took off his helmet and slid his bulk onto one of the chairs.

The two women exchanged a glance. Bridget moved to the kitchen to make tea.

'What can I do for you, Constable?' Clare stayed standing, fingers resting lightly on the back of the other chair.

The policeman laid his helmet carefully on the table in front of him before he spoke. 'I believe you are a war widow, Mrs Chapman. Am I right?'

She nodded.

'And your mother-in-law would be Mrs Vera Chapman of ...' He pulled his notebook from his pocket and consulted it. 'Rowan Farm?'

Clare swallowed and nodded, still barely daring to breathe.

'Mrs Chapman has made a serious allegation against you. Were you aware of that?'

'No, I wasn't,' she lied, and the steadiness of her voice surprised her. 'What has she alleged?'

'She claims you have been fraternising with a German prisoner-of-war.' He raised his eyes and looked directly at her for the first time, and she saw the judgement in his gaze. Panic threatened, a wave that pulsed right through her. She did not know what to say.

The constable waited, watching her for a moment before he spoke again. 'Is it true? Have you been fraternising with a prisoner-of-war?'

She swallowed, unsure. Instinct warned her to lie, to deny it completely, but reason advised it would be worse for her in the end if she did. She flicked a glance to Bridget who simply stared, caught in the same uncertainty.

'Fraternising how?' she stalled. 'What exactly is she accusing me of?'

The constable hesitated, as if wondering himself how best to play the situation. 'She said you've been seen with him more than once, and that he comes here to your home. What do you say to that?'

Again, the instinctive lie lay on her lips and for the length of a heartbeat she paused, wondering if she could get away with it, if it was simply Mrs Chapman's word against hers. But too many people knew – Simon, Bridget, Eric. Oh God, she thought. Eric.

'I've talked to him a few times,' she said. 'That's all.'

'You're aware that even talking to a prisoner is against the law?'

She tilted her head in assent.

'Then I have no choice but arrest you for fraternisation.'

'He saved my daughter's life,' Bridget said then, stepping forward. 'She would have drowned.'

The constable swivelled awkwardly in his seat to look at her. 'You can tell the magistrate that. He might look more kindly on you for it, but I'm afraid it makes no difference to me. The law is the law.' He stood up. 'You need to accompany me to the station, Mrs Chapman.'

Tears burned behind her eyes and it took all her force of will to stop them spilling. She turned to Bridget. 'Will you be all right?' she asked.

The other woman nodded.

'May I just fetch my coat?' Clare managed to ask. The spring afternoon was still cool.

'Of course.' He moved towards the door to wait and Clare picked up her coat and hat and handbag. Then she turned to Bridget, who was watching in horror from the kitchen.

'Keep the door locked,' she said, in a voice that belied the fear running through her. Her mouth was dry and her heart raced, quivering, as she followed the policeman along the lane to the car that was parked outside the saddler's.

A couple of farmworkers stopped on their way into the pub to watch, and she saw the curtains twitch in the flat above the post office. The news would be all around the village by the morning, and the rumours would be rife. Far worse than the truth, she supposed, though the truth was bad enough. It would be reported in the papers and she would be shamed and abused. Though public opinion was beginning to turn, sympathy starting to grow for the prisoners' plight, enough hostility remained that she knew there would be little mercy for a woman like her. Eric's words echoed in her head – *collaborating slut, having it off with a German* – and she flinched at the sound of them. It was hard to think of herself that way – they were just two souls in love, caught on opposing sides of history.

Max.

From the back of the car she stared out of the window at the spring afternoon as they pulled away from the kerb. The window box at the post office was bright with daffodils, and next to the pub the Reverend Keane was chatting to Fred Wakeman in the afternoon sun. They stopped their conversation to watch as the car drove away. Would the vicar denounce her from the pulpit tomorrow? His brand of Christianity was very different from Walter's and he had no reason to defend her, absent as she mostly was from his congregation.

She wondered what would happen to her now. She would have to go to court, she supposed, and face the magistrate. Prison loomed as a possibility and her limbs turned heavy with dread. Max, she thought then. What would happen to Max? Recalling his face after his last detention, pallid and drawn, her dread slid into anger at the injustice of it. The world had been at peace for a long time now – they should be free to love as they wished.

The questioning at the station was brief and to the point. Two men who did not trouble to introduce themselves took turns.

'How many times have you seen him?'

'We've met by chance a few times ...'

'How many times?'

'I couldn't say.'

'When did you first speak to him?'

'When he saved my niece's life. She fell in the river by the farm where he was working. I was living there at the time.'

'That was at your mother-in-law's farm? That you've since left?'

'Yes. My husband was killed in the war. I went to live there when he joined up. He was a chaplain.'

'A war widow, eh? Fraternising with a German. What would your husband say to that?'

'My husband would have said that German prisoners are human beings and deserve the same kindness and respect as anyone else.'

The two men exchanged a glance she couldn't read.

'And how many times has the prisoner been to your home?'

'Last night was the first,' she said, and she was surprised at how easily the lie tripped off her tongue. Max would be proud of her.

'And how did that occur?'

'I bumped into him on my evening walk,' she said, 'and he walked back with me to the flat. That was when we saw Bridget – my sister-in-law – and he stayed with us in case Woodman came after her again. It was lucky he did.'

'What was the prisoner doing outside at that hour?'

'I didn't ask,' she replied.

'You were aware you were acting against the law?'

She hesitated. 'The war ended such a long time ago I didn't think I was doing anything wrong. There are prisoners billeted with families now out on the farms, and we were only talking …' She trailed off, uncertain how well the act was going.

'Any contact with a prisoner of war, however minor, is still against the law, Mrs Chapman.'

'I see.' She folded her hands in her lap and lowered her eyes, every bit the picture of contrition. 'I didn't realise. I thought we were at peace.'

'And therefore we have no choice but to charge you with

fraternisation. You'll appear before the magistrate in due course and he will decide your punishment. Do you understand?'

She nodded, weary suddenly, and signed the charge sheet he put in front of her with an indifferent scrawl. Then the same policeman who had arrested her drove her home again.

Max was ordered to the commandant's office as soon as he stepped off the lorry that had brought him back to the camp. He exchanged a glance with Theo, then examined his knuckles where the broken skin and swelling were impossible to hide.

'See you in thirty days,' Theo said, and Max answered with a wry laugh.

'*Vielleicht.*' Maybe.

He followed the guard along the centre road and towards the administration office at the end. Just beyond the building was the hidden gap in the fence that led out to freedom and to Clare. He kept his eyes on the back of the man he was following.

The guard showed him into the office. Lt Col Quinn was at the window admiring the beginnings of the sunset outside. He turned at the sound of the door and greeted Max with a smile.

'Lovely time of year. Whenever I've been overseas, it was the English spring I missed the most.'

'Yes, sir,' Max answered, and stood at attention. Quinn was a fair man and he commanded the prisoners' respect, but in the end he still had a job to do, rules to enforce, and Max knew there was a line he could not cross.

'Although of course, German spring has its own beauty. At ease.'

Max stepped neatly into position and waited, thinking of Clare. Quinn moved from the window to stand behind his desk but he remained on his feet, fingertips resting lightly on a sheet of paper with writing on it that was too small for Max to read. He assumed it was some kind of charge sheet.

'I had a visit from the local police today,' Quinn began, looking up from his desk. 'Apparently you have been fraternising with a certain Mrs Chapman?'

Max lowered his head. There had been two possibilities – fighting and fraternisation. If it was the latter then Clare was in for it too, and she would pay a far higher price.

'According to her mother-in-law, you were seen at her flat in the village last night. Is that correct?'

He hesitated, unsure how much to give away. How much had Clare admitted?

Quinn must have understood the hesitation because then he said, 'Apparently, she confessed to meeting you.'

'Yes, sir,' he answered softly. There was nothing to be gained from denying it.

Quinn sighed and raised his head to look once more out of the window. The sky was turning pink, and the clouds were edged with gold. The two men observed the beauty of it together for a moment before the older one spoke again.

'I'm sorry, Peterson. It's an idiotic restriction. The war's been over a long time but, unfortunately for you, the law is the law and my hands are tied; I've got no choice but to give you twenty eight days. It's the minimum punishment, you understand. If I could give you less I would.'

'I understand, sir.' He hesitated, and Quinn nodded his encouragement.

'What will happen to Clare ... Mrs Chapman, sir?'

'She's been charged and will have to face a magistrate. Then who knows? Public opinion is divided – I suppose it depends on which side of the fence the magistrate falls. I expect she'll be fined.'

'Thank you, sir.'

Clare, he thought, in court because of him. He could imagine the public shame, the fallout. And she would be alone to face it. His fists balled in impotent frustration – he didn't give a damn about his own punishment, but that Clare should suffer because of him lit a rush of fury in his guts.

Quinn looked him up and down, and Max was conscious of the dust and dirt from the building site in every crease of his skin and clothes, his hair full of grit.

'Go and wash up, and report to the detention block at 18:30 hours.'

'Thank you, sir,' Max answered, but he was thinking only of Clare.

'Dismissed.'

Outside, Theo was waiting for him.

'Thirty days?'

'Twenty-eight,' he answered, and half walked, half jogged back to the hut they shared with a dozen other men to clean up and grab what he could take with him into the solitary cell.

Chapter Twenty-Eight

ASHENDEN SCHOOL TEACHER CHARGED WITH FRATERNISATION AND FINED £10.

The headline was the first thing Clare saw on the board outside the post office when she crossed the high street to go to work the day after the hearing, and she turned her eyes away from it. The rumours had started before she ever went to court, fuelled by the visit from the police. She had heard the children whispering at school in the weeks since then, repeating half-heard overheard conversations from their parents.

She was a spy ...

She was a fugitive on the run ...

She had committed treason ...

She was a witch ...

Miss Finch had called her in to the office for an awkward conversation in which it was decided Clare would continue work until the hearing. It was almost a relief to have the record set straight at last and have it over with.

In court the magistrate had done his best to frighten her, threatening her with prison. 'People have been interned for less,' he had said, and for a while she had expected the worst, her limbs growing heavy with dread, fear a hard ball in the base of her gut. In the end, though, he let her off with a fine and the promise that next time she would not be so lucky. She had almost cried with relief in spite of the fine she could not afford, but even so, she knew she would see Max again whatever the risk – he was the anchor in her life and without him she would be adrift.

Now, as she approached the school gate, she saw a small crowd had gathered. Both parents and children fell silent at the sight of her and she could see the coldness of their eyes, hostility etched into the set of their mouths. One or two of them turned their backs towards her as she passed. Wishing them a good morning as she always did, her voice sounded like someone else's. She hurried on into the staffroom, shaken by their reactions: she had not thought so many would be against her.

'How could you?' Susan hissed at her as soon as she opened the door. 'After what they did to Walter? How could you?'

Clare felt the tears she had controlled until now begin to prick behind her eyes. She squeezed her eyelids tight shut for a moment and took a deep breath. She refused to cry in front of this woman.

'How dare you judge me!' she snapped, when she thought she could trust herself to speak. 'Walter would have been the first to forgive them.'

'He would be so hurt.'

'Why? Why would he be hurt when he never even loved me in the first place?'

'He trusted you. You were his wife!'

'I trusted him too and he lied to me our whole marriage. I don't owe Walter anything.' She slammed her bag on to the desk and a pile of papers scattered and drifted to the ground with the disturbance in the air. She left them where they fell.

Susan stared.

'Walter is dead,' Clare went on, unable to stop herself. 'And I don't plan to spend the rest of my life mourning a man who didn't love me.'

The door opened and Miss Finch appeared.

'Mrs Chapman. A word in my office, if you please.'

For a moment she paused, trying to steady her ragged breath, but her heart was still knocking in her chest with rage and apprehension as she trudged across the hall to the headmistress's office. Was she about to lose her job? It seemed likely.

'Close the door,' Miss Finch ordered, settling into the chair behind her desk. She did not offer a seat to Clare but peered over the tops of her glasses with rheumy and hostile eyes.

'I've had complaints from parents this morning,' she said, 'and I expect to get more.'

Clare was silent – what could she possibly say? She stared at the threadbare rug at her feet like a child being scolded. In places the weave had almost been worn away by the feet of those standing as she stood now, waiting for their punishment.

'As you well know,' Miss Finch continued, 'some of the children at this school lost fathers during the war.' She paused for effect. '*Your own son* was one of them. *You* might have forgiven the Germans but in Ashenden you are in the minority. It makes no difference how long they've lived amongst us, nor how long we've been at peace. The wounds the Germans inflicted are too deep to be so easily forgotten. I would have expected you of all people to understand that.' She slid her eyes away from Clare and sat back in her chair. 'Of course, it's none of my business what you do in your own time, Mrs Chapman, but you've been convicted of a crime, so I have no choice but to write to the school board today to ask for their advice.'

'And in the meantime?'

'I suggest you take some time off.'

'But my class ...'

'I can fill the gap on a temporary basis, as I have in the past. I don't want to lose you but I'm afraid that's the most likely outcome of all of this so I would advise you to start looking for another post. I will be more than happy to write you a reference. Perhaps it's time you moved on from Ashenden altogether, and started afresh.'

Clare nodded, mutely.

'I'll let you know the board's decision as soon as I hear anything.'

'Thank you,' she managed to murmur. Then she turned and went across the hall to the staffroom to pick up her coat and bag.

'What happened?' Susan asked, turning from the hob where she was making tea. There was no trace now of her earlier anger. Perhaps Clare's words had hit home. 'What did she say?'

Clare hesitated. 'I'm going to be fired.'

'Oh,' Susan replied. She seemed surprised. 'What will you do?'

She shrugged. 'Find another job, I suppose.'

'Yes, but still …' Out of habit she poured out a cup for Clare and brought it over. Then they stood together for a moment sipping their tea as they had done a hundred times or more across the time they had worked together. Beyond the window they could hear the shouts and clatter of the children playing. Susan ran her tongue across her red lower lip, took a breath as if she were about to say something, changed her mind and took a mouthful of tea. Clare watched her and waited patiently – she was in no hurry to face the mob outside.

There was a pause. Then Susan swallowed her tea and lifted her eyes to meet Clare's. 'I'm sorry about before.'

'It's all right.'

'It's just hard to accept that he's never coming back.'

Clare said nothing. What was there to say?

The other woman took a deep breath and lifted her shoulders, visibly subduing her emotions. Clare remembered seeing Walter do the same now and then.

'Are you all right for money?' Susan asked then. She had resumed her usual chirpy, matter-of-fact tone, and for the first time Clare understood the effort behind it. 'It was rather a steep fine.'

Her first impulse was to say that of course she was all right, out of pride and the fierce desire to be independent. But the truth was anything but. She had lain awake half the night wondering how she could raise the money to pay it. And now she had lost her job on top of everything – the board's decision was no more than a formality. She could end up in prison after all. She shook her head.

'Would you like to borrow the money? The ten pounds, I mean. I could lend it to you and you could pay me back when you can. There would be no hurry, of course.'

'Why?' Clare asked. 'Why would you lend me the money after everything you said? Don't you want to see me suffer for my sins?'

Susan let out a long breath between pursed lips. 'No,' she said. 'Not really. Besides, you were right about Walter – he would have forgiven them for everything. The war is over, after all, and we'll never have peace unless we forgive each other.'

'I can understand why Walter loved you,' Clare said, and meant it.

Susan sniffed and turned away to hide the rush of emotion but Clare saw it anyway.

'Yes,' she said, 'I'd very much like to borrow the money if you're sure you don't mind.'

The door of the staffroom opened and the headmistress stood in the doorway. 'You're still here?'

'Just leaving, Miss Finch,' Clare said with a glance towards Susan, who mouthed something about bringing a cheque over later. Then she picked up her bag and left.

Walking away from the school, Clare could feel the eyes of the parents who had lingered at the gate following her, and when a woman spat at her and the spittle just grazed her shoulder, she had to blink to see through the sudden blur of tears. So she didn't notice the squat form of the saddler at the door of his shop until she was quite close and he spoke to her.

'Mrs Chapman?'

She halted and stifled a sigh. Was she about to lose the flat as well? She rubbed a hand across her eyes to clear them. 'Are you going to evict me?' she said.

Mr Brimble smiled and shook his head. 'Come inside,' he said.

Clare hesitated. She wanted only to be alone to lick her wounds, to curl up on the sofa and give in to the tears, but she had no heart to say no to the kindness in his voice.

'Thank you,' she said, and followed him into the shop where the soft scent of leather and saddle soap felt like a balm.

She lowered herself onto the stool at the counter. When she cast her eyes across the racks of saddles and bridles and riding boots, she saw he had turned the shop sign to *Closed*. He rested his arms on the counter and looked at her. Though she knew him only slightly from their brief weekly conversations, he had kind eyes and she liked him.

'Now why would I evict you?' he asked. He ran a hand over the thinning hair that was combed across his pate.

'I lost my job.' She shrugged. Although Susan's offer would cover the fine, her widow's pension would not meet the rent and she had no savings to speak of.

'You'll find another,' he reassured her. 'How about the hospital where you volunteered last summer? I'm sure they'd take you on. It might not pay as much as teaching but it would tide you over for a bit. I think it's a shame the way you've been treated. People are too quick to judge. It's far easier to point fingers than look at their own lives.' He gave her a conspiratorial lift of his eyebrows and she smiled. 'The Germans are people just like us, and only a fool would believe the English are immune to atrocity. We've our own dark history too, though no one likes to talk about it.'

'You like history, Mr Brimble?'

'I do. But the more of it I read, the more I prefer horses to people.'

She laughed.

'Present company excepted, of course.'

'Of course.'

He picked up a rag to start rubbing at a piece of harness on the counter. 'You need to be very careful with your young man now,' he said in an undertone, although they were quite alone. 'People will be watching, trying to catch you out.'

'Yes, I know.' Then, sensing the conversation was at an end, she slid from the stool and stood up. 'Thank you. You've been very kind.'

'You're welcome, Mrs Chapman. And if there's anything I can do to help, just let me know.'

She smiled and as she took a step towards the door he added, 'You can go out the back if you like – save having to face the village again.'

'I'd like that very much,' she replied, and a minute later she was in the yard behind the shop.

Dredging deep for courage, Clare got on the next bus to Wellington in the hope she could be the one to deliver the news of her disgrace to Eric before he heard it on the rumour mill. The journey seemed to take forever – she had forgotten the way the bus threaded through the countryside to stop at every village and countless other places on the roads in between. She wondered where the people lived that got on and off at these lonely spots where no houses could be seen from the road, and she almost envied them, living as they did far away from the prying eyes of others. But in fact it was the anonymity of the city that she pined for, where you could hide in plain sight among strangers.

For most of the tortuous journey she felt sick, a hard ball of nauseous dread forming in the base of her gut, and by the time she stepped onto Wellington high street late in the afternoon, she was still no nearer to deciding what she could say to her son. But the freshness of the soft spring damp as she made her way to the hotel to freshen up helped to ease the nausea a little.

Washing her face in the hotel bathroom, the reflection that looked back at her from the mirror seemed to be an older version of herself she hadn't met before. Dark circles ringed her eyes and her cheeks were pale and drawn. She wondered if Max would still want her when he saw her again – she was no longer the laughing girl who had ridden with him on the back of the bike a few short months ago. Then she scolded herself for being maudlin, and put on some powder and lipstick (her warpaint, as Walter used to call it). The makeup helped. She took a deep breath for courage and went downstairs, out of the hotel front door, and along the road towards the school.

At the main entrance she paused again to compose herself - she could feel the anxiety tingling in her fingers. Just get on with it, she told herself, and stepped inside. On one side of the spacious hallway there was a man at a reception desk and, gripping her resolve tightly in both hands, she approached him with a smile.

'Good afternoon. My name is Mrs Chapman and my son Eric is a pupil here. I'm sorry to come unannounced so late in the day but it's rather important I speak to him as soon as possible.'

'A family matter, Mrs Chapman?'

'Quite.'

'Let me see if I can find him for you. Should I fetch Mr Clough too?

'No, that won't be necessary, thank you.' The last person she wanted to see was James.

'Very good. Please, take a seat.' He gestured to a row of chairs against the opposite wall and Clare wandered towards them, looking around the entrance hall, trying to imagine her son's life within these walls. A faint scent of wood polish mingled with the headier and unmistakable smell of refectory food, and two boys about Eric's age clattered past her to disappear along the corridor.

It wasn't long before Eric himself appeared, his young face serious with concern. He was so like his father, she thought again, and getting more so each time she saw him, although his body had yet to grow into the length of his arms and legs. He was almost a young man already, and would be an adult soon – she must remember not to treat him like a child.

'Mum!' He seemed pleased to see her at least. 'Is everything all right?'

'Let's go for a walk,' she said with a smile, reaching out a hand to touch his shoulder lightly. She would have liked to embrace him but knew better than to embarrass him at school.

In the grounds they fell into step beside each other. 'Are you allowed to go into town?'

He nodded. Then, turning his head towards her, he said, 'What's happened? Why are you here?'

She took a deep breath, and felt the rush of something close to panic through her blood. She slowed her steps.

'This is rather difficult to explain,' she began, 'so please just hear me out before you say anything.' She hesitated. All the possibilities she had run through her head on the bus had deserted her, and she could find no words to help her. 'Do you remember the German prisoner of war?' she asked. 'The one who rescued Lizzie?'

'Of course I do. Grandma kicked you off the farm because of him.'

They turned out of the gate and began to wander slowly towards the town. There were few people about. Gunmetal clouds hung low overhead and were full of rain – she raised her head to them briefly, searching for inspiration.

'I've seen him again a few times,' she said.

Eric halted and looked down at the pavement.

'I'm telling you the truth,' she said, 'because you're not a child any more. You're a young man and you have a right to know what happened. But the thing is ... Grandma reported us to the police, so they arrested me and I had to pay a fine. It was in the local newspaper, but I wanted you to hear it from me first.'

He was silent, gazing into the distance ahead, and she waited, barely breathing. Finally, he turned to look at her.

'Grandma reported you to the police?' She could hear the disbelief in his voice.

She nodded.

'And what happened to him? The German?'

'I expect he would have been disciplined. I don't know. I haven't seen him since.'

Eric seemed to think about this for a moment, still staring along the road towards town.

'Why did you see him again, after what happened before? Surely you must have known where it would lead?'

She almost laughed. 'It just happened,' she said. 'I didn't plan it. Neither of us did.'

'And when he's free again?'

Clare shook her head. 'I don't know.'

'Promise me you won't see him again.' He lifted his eyes to her, Walter's eyes, pale and blue and sad, and she had to look away.

'I can't promise you that.'

'He's a *German*, Mum. They killed Dad. How could you?'

'I know.' She sniffed back tears, eyes burning. 'But the war is over, and he was just a soldier on the wrong side – that doesn't make him an evil man.'

Eric shook his head. Then abruptly he drew himself up, pulling himself together as she supposed boys were taught to do at schools like his.

'Well, thank you for coming to tell me,' he said, and the coldness in his tone almost felled her. 'I appreciate it. But I have study to do. Have a safe trip home.' He gave her a polite little nod of farewell before he turned and began to walk away. He had only gone a few steps when he turned back, and her heart skipped with hope for kind words, a change of mind. But he said, 'Peter has asked me to spend this summer with his family at their house in Cornwall. Uncle James said that would be fine, so I've accepted.'

'It's not Uncle James's decision to make!' Disappointment fuelled her outrage. 'Next time you ask me.'

He looked at her, expressionless. 'So can I still go or not?'

She nodded, words too hard to form, then watched him turn again and walk away from her, the long straight back rigid with tension, until he went through the school gate and was lost to her sight.

She had almost reached the turning to the hotel when she heard her name being called behind her.

'Clare! Clare!'

James, she thought. Dammit. She had hoped to get away without seeing him. Reluctantly, she slowed, stopped, and turned to face him. He was half walking, half running along the road from the school towards her, and when he stood in front of her at last he was breathing hard, one hand against his chest as if feeling for the wheeze. She remembered about his asthma and, mostly for selfish reasons, she hoped he would recover quickly. They stood in silence while he caught his breath, and she cast a wistful glance towards the hotel just along the road.

'What on earth are you doing here?' he asked when he found his voice again.

'I came to tell Eric something,' she replied. She didn't feel like explaining herself.

'Couldn't you have written?'

'I wanted to tell him in person.'

He hesitated. Then, with a lift of his arm back towards the school, he said, 'Come back to the school and have some tea. You look done in.'

Should she accept? She didn't want to, but she supposed she ought to tell him – he would find out soon enough and it might help Eric to have his godfather's support. She imagined the teasing would be merciless. She gave him a small smile.

'If you like,' she said, and they walked side by side together back to the school.

In his office she sat before his desk, running her eyes once more across the rows of books on the shelves behind him while James settled himself in his chair, tidying the piles of paper between them.

'What's happened?' he asked, and gave her an encouraging smile.

Did he still like her? she wondered. Did he still nurse hopes that one day she might marry him?

'I lost my job,' she said.

His face contracted in shock and briefly he was lost for words. 'What … how …?' he managed to stutter out after a moment.

She sighed, and decided she may as well be blunt.

'I was charged with fraternisation,' she said, 'and fined ten pounds. It was in the paper and that's why I came today. I didn't want Eric to find out like that.'

James stared. 'Fraternisation? With a *German*?'

She heard the disdain in his voice and nodded.

'After what they did to Walter?'

'Yes.' She kept her chin tilted, defiant. She felt no need to justify her decisions to this man.

'How could you?'

'I didn't come here to argue with you, James. I came to see Eric.'

'Yes, of course.' He lowered his gaze to the desk between them, apparently remembering their relationship had changed and he no longer had the same rights to chide her as he used to. 'And how did Eric take the news?'

'Badly,' she said.

'I expect he'll come round in the end.'

Perhaps he would, she thought. His father's death was still fresh in his mind and his grandmother's poison had done its work. He was still young, with a youthful understanding of the world. Black and white, good and bad. She hoped in time he would come to understand that life was more complex, messy as hell in fact, and that we can't always love where we would choose.

'Was it the same man as last time?'

She almost laughed at the question, and the opinion of her it revealed. 'Yes,' she answered. 'The same man – the one who saved Lizzie's life, and who also stopped Simon from bashing Walter's sister to death.'

James raised his head at that and gave her a look she didn't know how to read. 'Well, I hope you'll be very happy together once you're legally allowed to meet.'

She allowed herself to smile at that. 'Thank you,' she replied. 'Now if you'll excuse me, it's time I was going.'

'Yes, yes, of course.' He got up abruptly as if he couldn't wait for her to go, and showed her to the door. 'You can find your way out?'

'Yes,' she replied.

He gave her a tight smile of farewell but did not offer her his hand. She nodded briefly in reply, then turned and walked away.

Chapter Twenty-Nine

The saddler's suggestion was a good one. The cottage hospital offered her a job as a nurse's assistant when she wrote to them, and though it paid less than teaching it would be enough to tide her over and pay the rent, as Mr Brimble had said. Clare handed in her resignation to Miss Finch that afternoon after school, sparing the school board the effort of making a decision. Miss Finch took the proffered envelope without a word.

Later, she went down to the yard to check over her bicycle: it was a while since she had ridden it and she would need it to get to work. The evening was warm with the early promise of summer and a lingering twilight lit the sky, a flare of yellow still at the horizon. A slight breeze breathed at her hair, lifting it gently away from her face and, when a full moon peered above the trees, she realised a full month had passed since the day she was arrested – the weeks had been a blur. She squeezed the tyres on the bike between her fingers and the rubber gave with the pressure, so she attached the little pump and began to work it back and forth, absorbed in the effort and thinking more or less of nothing.

'Do you need a hand with that?'

A voice came out of the shadow of the shed behind her.

'Max!' Throwing down the pump, she ran to him and he swept her up in his arms with one movement, lifting her high off the ground. Wrapping her legs around his hips she lowered her head to meet his mouth as he tilted his face up towards her. They kissed and it was wonderful, and everything she had paid to be with him was worth it.

Gently, he slid her back to the ground, but their arms were still around each other and she pressed her face against his chest, savouring his warmth and the steady beat of his heart. All the words she could think of to say came nowhere close to the feeling behind them and so she was silent, basking in the pleasure of his closeness. Finally, they stepped back from each other.

'Welcome home.' She looked up into his face – thin, drawn, pale – but he was smiling and the green eyes were bright.

'It's good to be here.' He bent to pick up the pump from where she had dropped it.

'Leave it,' she said. 'I can do it tomorrow.'

He dropped it into the basket on the handlebars and followed her up the steps into the flat. She saw him cast an approving eye over the new lock and glance around the flat.

'What happened?'

She hesitated a moment. So much had happened she couldn't think where to start.

'Bridget went back to the farm because of the children,' she said. 'I haven't seen her for a while so I don't know how she is now.'

She stopped and in the pause he came to stand close beside her in the kitchen, leaning against the counter and watching her in profile.

'What happened to you?' His voice was gentle. She flicked a look towards him then dropped her eyes down and away – the words were surprisingly hard to say.

'I ... got arrested,' she began, 'and fined, and I lost my job.'

He said nothing and she risked another glance towards him. He was still watching her. She gave him a small smile and shrugged. 'We both knew the risks.'

'Higher for you than for me.'

'How was prison?'

He gave a wry laugh. 'The harmonica helped to pass the time. But I'm very hungry.'

She smiled. 'Eggs?'

'Sure.' Then, after a moment, he said, 'Are you okay?'

She nodded but didn't look at him, her attention still intent on the eggs. He laid a hand on her wrist and she let her own hand slide away from the pan.

'Clare? Are you all right? Truly?'

She could feel the tears beginning to gather in her throat and behind her eyes, and she knew that if she spoke she would break down altogether. She nodded again, but he slid his arm around her anyway and drew her to him as she let the tears come at last. All these weeks she had held herself together, meeting each day with an effort of will, guard up, mask in place. But now that Max was here she could let the armour slip away and acknowledge the pain and sorrow underneath.

When she had cried herself dry, she stepped back from him, wiping at her eyes with the backs of her hands. Automatically she turned to the kettle, which had begun to boil on the hob.

'I'll do it,' he said, and moved between her and the stove.

She leaned against the sink, arms folded tightly around herself as she watched him work, observing again the energy within him, a latent power that Walter had utterly lacked. He was like one of the lions in the zoo, she thought, pacing out the time in his cage. She remembered his savagery with Simon, and hauled her mind away from the thought of it. *He had killed men with his bare hands*, he had said. Hands that had touched her and brought her pleasure. Hands that were now making tea. It was hard to imagine they could be the same hands.

Max looked at her over his shoulder. 'Sit down,' he said. 'I'll bring it over.'

She did as he told her, and her body felt heavy and weak as she slid into place at the table, as though her strength had been diminished by the tears. He set out the tea things and brought over the eggs – they were perfectly fried and laid neatly on top of the slices of toast, and she smiled up at him.

'Thank you.'

'My pleasure.'

They began to eat.

'How will you manage,' he asked between mouthfuls, 'without a job?'

'I've found another one,' she replied, 'at the hospital where I used to volunteer. I start on Monday. It won't pay as much but it'll cover the rent at least, and I have my widow's pension. It isn't a lot but it's a help.'

'I wish I could do more.'

'With your shilling a day that you don't actually get paid till you go home?'

He smiled. 'They think we might escape if we have money.'

'Would you?'

'Where would I go? Britain is an island. Anyway, everything I want is right here in this room.'

She looked up from her food – he was watching her with his cat-green eyes, and she had to look away from their intensity.

'Still no news about repatriation?' she said.

He shook his head. 'Just rumours it might start at the end of the year. But there's a lot of us and it's going to take time.'

There was a silence. Now the possibility was drawing closer it was harder to pretend it would never happen. In the end, decisions would have to be made and the thought of it terrified her.

Without Max, she would have nothing.

Chapter Thirty

Max woke abruptly from the nightmare. He sat up, breathing hard, his body burning with sweat in the cold room. His mind groped in desperation to remember where he was and recall that he was safe. He had been dreaming of a city that might have been Berlin, but amid the fire and smoke and destruction it was hard to tell. It could just as easily have been Kharkov or Kiev or Caen, or any other of the countless nameless places he had witnessed burn and fall. In the dream he had been searching for his wife among the ruins but found only the bodies of other soldiers, men he had known and fought with – no wife, no child.

'Who's Lotte?'

He turned in surprise at the voice. Clare was lying on her side, propped on an elbow watching him.

'What?' He was confused for a moment, still caught in the tail of the dream.

'You were calling her name. Lotte.'

He rested his arms on his knees and let out a deep breath, gazing down at the bedspread. A faint gleam of moonlight behind the curtains made everything shimmer, and the shadows in the room seemed to shift and alter. He let go of the last remnants of the dream and they faded into memory.

Lotte.

There was no doubt in his mind that she was dead. More than three years without a word from her – surely a letter would have found its way to him by now? In Russia he had blamed the silence on the constant movement and the ever-changing direction of the troops. In France there had been chaos, and he was not the only one who never got mail. But he had been in the same place in England now for almost two years. Her letters would have found their way to him somehow, he was sure of it.

'Max?' Clare's voice brought him back to the here and now, to the woman he loved that he was probably just about to lose. She touched his arm with her fingers. 'Who is Lotte?'

He could hear the rising worry in her voice at his silence, but he struggled to bring the words to his lips. He had thought about this moment so many times, dreading it, putting it off. Even now he could lie about it, he thought, and hold on to her a little while longer. But to lie by omission was one thing. To lie to her in answer to a direct question was something else again, and he could not do it: he owed her the truth.

This is it, he thought. With his next words he would lose her. A flicker of nerves rippled through him. His mouth dry, his heartbeat quickening, he turned his head to look down at the woman lying at his side. The woman he loved.

He said, '*Meine Frau.*' It was instinct to use the German words, unplanned. My wife.

In one swift movement, Clare swung herself away from him and out of bed. Grabbing her robe from the chair she shrugged herself into it as she walked out of the bedroom. He waited a moment, hesitating, before he wrapped a towel around his nakedness and followed her. She was in the kitchen with her back to him, leaning on the counter, head lowered.

'Clare?'

She did not turn. He wet his lips with the tip of his tongue and moved closer, halting at the edge of the kitchen, an arm's length away from her so that he could see her in profile. She was breathing deeply, and her hair had fallen forward across her face. He wanted to reach out and tuck it back behind her ear, then hold her in his arms and tell her that everything would be all right. He waited. The moment seemed to last forever before she finally turned her head towards him, and in the pale dark it was hard to read her expression.

'You're married?' she whispered. 'All of this and you have a wife?'

He swallowed. 'I haven't heard from her in over three years ...'

'But she could still be out there somewhere, waiting for you to come home, hoping.'

'I'm sorry.' The words were so inadequate, useless to express everything he wanted to say to her. 'I didn't mean for any of this to happen. I didn't plan to fall in love with you.'

'No wonder we never talked about you going home.' She shook her head, and he caught the glint of a tear on her cheek. It took every ounce of his willpower not to move towards her to wipe it away.

'I gave up everything for you,' she said, turning her body to face him, her dressing gown gripped tightly in front of her like a shield. 'My home, my son, my job. I was even spat on in the street because of you. And all this time you were lying to me. How could you? How can you live with yourself?'

His eyes closed as his heart turned over in self-reproach. He shrugged. 'I was afraid I'd lose you.'

She nodded, and lowered her head away.

'Clare?'

'Just leave,' she said, without looking up. 'Just go.'

'Please, Clare ...'

'There's nothing else to say.' She wiped at her eyes with a

savage hand but she did not raise her head to look at him. 'Just go. It's over.'

He stood, frozen with disbelief that it could end so abruptly. With just a few words he had lost her, his world collapsing in a moment. When he did not move, she lifted her head at last.

'Get out! I never want to see you again!'

Still he hesitated, and after a moment she lunged towards him, flailing at his chest with her fists. 'Just go!'

He caught her wrists in his hands and held them while she struggled against his grip, still trying to strike him. She was crying in earnest now, her face wet with tears, her breath ragged and uneven with sobs. She stopped struggling and he loosened his hold on her wrists but he didn't let go, and briefly they stood in silent hesitation. Her head was bowed again as though she could not bear to look at him. He let go of one of her arms and lifted his hand to her face, tucking his fingers under her chin to tilt it towards him, half expecting her to pull away, or strike at him again. But she let him do it, and the pain he saw in her eyes when they finally met his hurt far worse than any blow she could have struck with her fists.

Instinctively he drew her towards him and put his arms around her, and as they held each other he made himself remember every detail of the moment so that he would not forget the details of her as he had forgotten the details of Lotte. He observed the scent of her hair and its texture against his cheek, the warm fragility of her body, the line of her shoulder under his arm as he caressed it, the pressure of her arms around his waist. She was sobbing, her whole body shaking in his arms, and he wanted to stay there forever, prolonging this temporary lull before the battle resumed.

Eventually though, she pulled away from him, stepping backwards, putting distance once more between them.

'Get out,' she said. Her chin was tilted in an effort at defiance, but he could see how much it cost her. She shuddered in the aftermath of her weeping.

He nodded. However much he loved her there was nothing more to say. He had lied to her, betrayed her trust. Reluctantly he backed away and went to the bedroom to pick up his clothes from where he had dropped them in the heat of their passion just a few short hours before. When he went back through the living room Clare was still standing exactly as he had left her, but he kept on walking, and even when he had reached the yard he didn't stop to look back.

The walk back to the camp in the growing dawn seemed to be a very long way.

Clare stood in the kitchen for a long time, as though she were rooted to the spot. Her mind groped to make sense of what had happened and when the night began to give way to the morning beyond the window she was still numb with disbelief. A pigeon landed on the kitchen windowsill and she watched it, marvelling at the balance of its fat, grey body on the tiny ledge, its head tilting this way and that as though it were trying to make sense of the world. She wished it luck. She would never understand it, she thought.

With a sudden shiver, she realised she had grown cold standing barefoot on the lino, and she turned at last to fill the kettle for tea. With the movement the pigeon launched itself into flight; Clare wished she could fly away as easily.

Lotte.

She let her mind wander over the thought of Max with a wife, but it was hard to imagine. She pictured a Teutonic princess – blonde and bronzed with strong, clean limbs and a sense of self-assurance Clare could only envy. Had there been children too? She hadn't thought to ask. All this time, she thought, he must have been desperate to know. How had he borne the uncertainty?

And what had he hoped for – her life or her death? What future had he dreamed of? She shook her head, unable to wrap her thoughts around it. All she knew was that she had trusted him and he had lied to her, just as Walter had done.

She made the tea without warming the pot, and berated herself for trusting too easily. But her father had taught her always to see the good in people and even as she hated Max for lying, she understood his reasons. He had lied because he loved her. Walter had lied because he didn't.

Slumping into her chair at the kitchen table, nursing her teacup between her hands, Clare heard the church bell begin to toll for the early service. Sunday, thank God. She could not have faced the world today – her eyes were sore from crying and her head was starting to throb. The insistent strike of the bell seemed to vibrate inside her. Idly, she tried to remember the last time she went to church on a Sunday but she could not recall – she had barely been at all since Walter had left. Perhaps she should go today, she thought; perhaps the ancient words and rhythms would be a comfort. But she did not get up from the table. Her own vague faith in God had dwindled without Walter's encouragement and now there was nothing left of it at all.

Chapter Thirty-One

Through the weeks and months of the summer, Max tried to see her twice. Clare heard his knock at the door and both times she answered it with silence. There was nothing left to say between them, nothing that could help. He had not called out and she was grateful for that – she wasn't sure she could have resisted his voice. He had simply knocked and waited, and when she had made no answer he had gone away.

This was the third time he had come, and she was in the kitchen when he climbed the stairs so that she caught a glimpse of his head through the window as he passed through the light. Ducking away out of sight she found herself with her back to the door, and when he knocked she felt it as a tremor through her body as the wood vibrated against her.

'Clare!'

Did he know she was there, just inches away? He knocked again.

'Clare, I need to see you. I have something I have to tell you. Please.'

She held her breath.

'This is the last time I'll come, the last time I'll bother you. I promise.'

She heard him move back a step on the little landing and the scratch of a match as he lit himself a cigarette. The scent of the smoke crept through the gaps around the door and she inhaled it, liking the smell because it reminded her of him.

'I'll wait,' he said, 'all night if I have to.'

She slid down the door to sit with her back against it. He was so close and she felt all her resolution start to slide away. Why had he come?

'Clare!' He called out to her again. 'I know you can hear me. Open the door.'

Slowly, like an old woman, she got to her feet. She felt as though she had aged a hundred years in the last few weeks. Drowning her grief in extra shifts and hours at the hospital, she had numbed herself with work, giving all her energy to the patients so she slept like the dead when she crawled into bed at the end of each day, too weary even to eat. But every morning she awoke to the same bleak reality: he had a wife, he had lied, and she had lost him.

She turned and rested her forehead against the wood, one hand on the lock of the door. Why had he come? There was nothing he could say to change things. Nothing he could do but stir up the feelings she had struggled so hard to tamp down. She tried to remember if she had hurt this much when Walter died; if she had, no memory of it remained, no memory at all.

'Clare.' His voice was very close to the door, mere inches away on the other side of the wood. 'Please let me in.'

She hesitated, hand still resting on the key. It would be so easy to turn it and open the door, to let him back into her life. Did she dare?

'What do you want, Max?' she asked. 'Why have you come?'

'Please open the door. I need to talk to you.'

Reluctantly, sure she was making a mistake but unable to help herself, she turned the key with a clunk and pressed down the handle. The door swung back and she stepped away, her hand still gripping the edge of it as though it might protect her in some unknown way.

'*Danke.*' He stood in the doorway and she had to look away. He was just as she always pictured him in her thoughts, with his fine blond hair and olive-green eyes that caught hers now for an instant and kindled the familiar, excited self-consciousness. She felt the blush sweep across her face and neck, and knew that he would see it. Furious with herself for betraying her feelings so easily, she moved back into the room and let him in.

He closed the door gently behind him and stayed beside it. Clare went to the kitchen and leaned against the counter, putting distance between them despite the clamour of all her instincts to be close to him, her heartbeat racing, her breath coming short.

'Why have you come?' she asked him again.

'They're sending me home. I'll be in Germany by the end of the year.'

'So soon?' she asked, and the words were out of her mouth before she had time to consider them. His own mouth twitched with the hint of a smile.

'They want men with useful skills – engineers, technicians, miners.'

'Mechanics?'

He nodded.

There was a silence. She wanted him to go. She wanted him to stay. She wanted to throw her arms around him and beg him not to leave. Paralysed by indecision, she finally allowed her gaze to coincide with his. He was watching her, trying to read her expression, trying to understand.

'Can I sit down?' he said.

In spite of herself she gave him a small smile. He had read her correctly – he knew she would not refuse him and she hated herself anew for being so transparent. He smiled in return and went to sit at his old place at the table. He looked so at home, so right: they had shared a hundred meals or more at that table and too many cups of tea to count; she could imagine a whole life spent with him there. She reminded herself that he was married and he had lied to her.

'Tea?'

He nodded, and it felt like old times as he watched her fill the kettle and set out the teapot and cups. When there was nothing more to do but wait for the water to boil she turned towards him. The silence was awkward – there was so much to say but no words to say it, and the pause lingered unwelcome between them, neither of them knowing how to break it. She was grateful when the water finally huffed to a boil and she had something to occupy her attention.

'There aren't any biscuits,' she said, when she took the tea to the table. 'I haven't had any time to shop.'

'I didn't come for biscuits.'

'I know, but you're always hungry ...' She trailed off with a shrug, wondering why she should care any more. She slid into the seat across from him and they sipped their tea in silence. He was watching her and she kept her own eyes resolutely lowered away from the intensity of that gaze.

'You can go back to having tea with lemon,' she said.

He laughed. 'Yes, I suppose I can. But I would rather drink tea with milk, here with you.' Then, 'Will you write to me?'

'What for?' she replied. 'What would be the point?'

He dropped his head away, and she saw from the sudden tension in his jaw that she had hurt him. But really – what could they be to each other once he left? Max stared out of the window into the dark, fingertips rubbing absently at the sides of the teacup. She watched the rhythmic movements and remembered their touch against her skin.

'Where will you go?' she asked, to break a silence that was becoming painful. 'Back to Berlin?'

He turned back to look at her. 'What do you care?'

The question stung like a slap and she flinched. The tears she had held in check until now began to burn behind her eyes and she blinked, angry with her weakness. Max reached across the table and grabbed her hand.

'*Weine nicht,*' he said. Don't cry.

It was the gentleness in those two words that undid her, and she let the tears rise and fall: as she wiped them from her cheeks they were quickly replaced by more. Max wound his fingers in hers and they sat like that for a moment either side of the table until he got up with one quick movement and moved around it to crouch beside her, looking up into her face. She tried to breathe deeply to calm herself but it made no difference. He reached a hand to her face and brushed the tip of his thumb across her cheekbone, wiping the tears away.

Clare caught his hand in hers in an automatic movement, then hesitated for a moment, as though she were unsure what to do with it until she brought back to her cheek and pressed her face against it. She no longer cared about the lies, or his wife. She just wanted to be with him, now, while she still could. She turned to bring his hand to her lips and he knelt up so that their faces were almost level and close enough that she could feel the touch of his breath against her skin.

He cupped her face between his hands.

'*Carpe diem,*' she whispered, and he smiled.

'*Carpe diem,*' he replied, then touched his lips to the wet skin on her cheek. She closed her eyes and felt the warmth swell inside her. He kissed her brow, her eye, her jawbone, and she tilted her head so that his mouth could find the soft skin of her neck. Then he paused, their faces touching, and she was aware of the softness of his hair catching on the tears, the familiar soap smell of it, the gentle strength of his hand behind her head.

She shifted her head to search out his mouth with her own and kissed him.

. . .

Later, they lay together in the bed she still thought of as theirs and she found at last the words that had eluded her before.

'Tell me about your wife, Max. Tell me about your life in Berlin.'

'Why do you want to know? There's nothing left of it now.'

'Because it's part of who you are. And ...' she hesitated, self-conscious again, 'I have this image of her.'

'What image?' He smiled. They were lying face to face, knees touching.

'Tall, blonde, athletic – you know, Germanic, I suppose.'

The smile broadened. 'No, that's not how she was at all. Lotte was shorter than you with dark hair, dark eyes.'

Was, she heard, and realised that in his mind, his wife was already dead. She waited, hoping for more.

'We got married very young. Too young probably, but we were happy enough. Then Hanna came along.' He paused, and dropped his eyes briefly to the sheet between them. 'She would be thirteen now.'

So there had been a child. A daughter.

'And you don't know if they're alive or dead.'

He shook his head.

'How can you bear it?' To lose a wife was one thing but she could hardly imagine the pain of losing your child.

He shrugged. 'What choice do I have?'

She said nothing, but shifted closer.

'And now I'm going to lose you too.' He ran the back of his fingers across her temple and along the line of her jaw until she tilted her face up to meet his and they kissed again.

That night they did not sleep, and it was still the early hours when he left to get back to the camp before the dawn had finished breaking. She walked with him. Each moment they could spend together was too precious to give away. Just out of sight of the camp's back gate they halted.

'Come tonight,' she said.

He nodded, and as he walked away her gaze wandered over the high wire fence that surrounded the camp. Even though the war had been over for more than a year, the men were still prisoners, working for a pittance, their lives restricted and policed. Slave labour, she thought, the same as the Germans had done, though no one seemed to want to talk about that. To the victor the spoils, she supposed, and turned away to walk home through the lightening morning.

She met Bridget. They had seen each other briefly now and then through the summer, catching up on each other's news in snippets when they could steal the time away from work or the farm. But today they had a whole afternoon together and they went to Barnstaple on the bus to have tea and browse the shops, though the windows had remained mostly empty, rationing still in full force. It was a perfect autumn day with a clear blue sky and a warm breeze that ruffled their hair, and it was lovely simply to wander the streets with a friend, chatting.

They found a tea shop that Bridget had been to before and liked, and so they went in. They ordered ham sandwiches and tea, and looked out of the window at the passers-by.

'Mum isn't well,' Bridget said, when their lunch arrived.

'I'm sorry to hear that,' Clare replied, the courtesy automatic. 'What's wrong with her?'

Her friend shook her head and stirred her tea. 'It's hard to say. She won't see a doctor, of course, but she's not eating and she won't get out of bed. I think she's just given up.'

'Will she recover?'

'I'm not sure she will – I don't think she wants to. She's just skin and bone.'

Clare remembered the last time she had seen Mrs Chapman: she had been gaunt and sallow even then.

'What about you? What will you do?'

'If Mum dies?' Bridget let out a long breath and watched a mother scolding a little boy in the street outside the window. 'I don't know.' She paused. 'Is it terrible of me to be thinking about what I'll do once she goes?'

'Not at all,' Clare answered. 'I find myself hoping that Max's wife is dead and I feel awful to be so callous but I can't help it.' She dreamed of it sometimes, waking in the early hours guilt-stricken and utterly ashamed. 'Besides, you'll have to make the decision sooner or later, so you may as well plan for it.'

'I thought about selling up but it's all I know. What else could I do?'

'Well, you could leave Simon for starters.'

'Oh, I plan to.' She smiled.

'How's it been lately?'

'Better, since Max kicked seven bells out of him. I think he's afraid it might happen again. He's a coward really, like most bullies. He's happy to bash me if he can get away with it but he's less willing if there could be consequences.'

Clare smiled, relieved for her friend. Then she remembered that Max would be leaving soon and the smile died on her lips.

Bridget noticed the change. 'What's the matter?'

'Max is going home.'

Bridget said nothing for a moment and reached across the table to take Clare's hand. 'Can't he stay? I read in the paper that some of them have applied to stay here.'

'He had a wife and a daughter in Germany, remember? They're probably dead but he has to go back to look for them, just in case. I don't like it but I do understand.' She looked up and gave her friend a tight little smile.

'Well,' Bridget said, 'hopefully he'll discover that she *is* dead ...'

'Don't,' Clare chided, but she had to stifle a laugh.

'... and he can come back for you.'

'I feel so wicked for hoping it,' she confessed. 'Walter would be mortified.'

'Walter was no saint, as you well know.'

Clare had no answer to that. There was a silence and the waitress brought the sandwiches. They were as good as Bridget had remembered them, and the conversation moved on to other things.

Chapter Thirty-Two

The season had turned from autumn to winter by the time Max left the camp for the long journey home. The last of the leaves had fallen, carpeting the ground underfoot, and in the early mornings the frost had begun to bite. He spent his last night with Clare, lying together in the soft warmth of the bed but not daring to sleep, determined not to waste a single moment of their precious final hours together. But even in their closeness they barely spoke – there seemed to be no words left to say. Instead, they shared their sorrow in silence – a meeting of their eyes, a touch of their fingertips, and he recalled that the final nights with Lotte each time he returned to the front had been the same, each parting filled with the fear it would be the last.

Now Max stood with the others at the rail as the ship drew slowly away from dock and their final sight of England was quickly swallowed in the pouring rain. The last night with Clare already seemed like a long time ago. A man he had never met before turned to him.

'*Gott sei dank,*' the man said. Thank God for that. 'I thought we'd never leave,' and though Max gave him a brief wry smile in reply, his gaze remained shoreward, towards England, towards

Clare. He felt adrift, caught between two worlds, two versions of himself, and a thread of guilt wound through him for the feeling: he should be eager for home after so long away but in fact he was dreading it, afraid of whatever truth the future held, and angry with himself because of it.

Home was hard to imagine – his wife and daughter were as ghosts to him now, phantoms from another life. In the silence of the last three years he had lost all hope of their survival, watching them die in his dreams in a hundred different ways that had shocked him from his sleep breathless and sweating, calling out their names to the dark. In the crucible of the war he had not allowed himself to give up hope, afraid that the sorrow would break him, and by the time he was in England and safe enough to mourn, the feelings were buried so deep he could no longer reach them in his waking hours. So he had let them be, unvisited, starting out anew when meeting Clare stirred the first tentative steps towards connection, a fresh chance at love. But now he was retracing his steps towards the man he used to be before the war ripped everything to shreds, and he took the path with reluctance, uncertain what he might find at the end of it.

The crossing was rough. The ship yawed and shuddered on violent, crashing seas, waves like walls of water rearing overhead to pound the deck with a fury. Most of the men stayed below so that the cabins soon stank of vomit and sweat, and the rank stench of close-packed humanity. Nauseated by the smell, Max remained on deck as much as he could, holding on for dear life as the ship bucked and reared beneath him, allowing himself to be cleansed by the primal forces of the storm.

And by the time the ship hove into the quay at Cuxhaven on a quiet sea he was as ready as he ever would be for whatever lay ahead.

. . .

When he stepped off the gangplank at the port he almost stumbled on the dock, his body confused by the stillness of the ground after the shifting motion of the ship, head spinning as though he were drunk. The man in front of him knelt to kiss the ground and Max had to sidestep smartly to avoid tripping over him.

Germany at last.

He looked around as the men milled on the quayside. One man was weeping with relief to be home, his face wet with tears, but most of them stood quietly with a wary look in their eyes, unsure what to expect and knowing this was a Germany they would barely recognise. When the last man had descended the gangplank and their kitbags had been unloaded, gruff British soldiers directed them towards the train that would take them onward.

'Like old times, eh?' the man next to him said with a laugh. 'How many times did we do this? Wait here, get on the train, get off the train, wait here. But not for much longer. Soon we'll be free men.'

Max smiled. It was true. They were still in the army after all, still soldiers if only in name, and they slid back into the old routines with surprising ease. The train pulled in, and he was lucky to find a seat. Other men crowded in the corridors, jostling and uncomfortable, complaining. Max thought of Theo and wondered what he was doing back in Ashenden now, still a prisoner. He wished his friend was with him for this – they had been through so much together – but Theo had been a storeman before the war and his name was a long way down the list for repatriation.

After a delay that felt like hours, the train began to rattle away from the station with a hiss of steam and a scream of the whistle. Max stared out of the filthy window at a landscape of devastation. He had seen bombed-out cities before in Russia and France, but even so he was not prepared for the scale of the ruin. Mile upon mile of destruction slid past: crater-pocked roads ran between the jagged walls of what remained of factories and houses, and in their midst a pale and weary-looking population dressed in threadbare clothes moved like shadows. Dirty children begged for bread at the stations they passed through but the men had nothing left of their rations to give them. Proud Germany brought low by her own foolish ambition, he thought. For what? The journey seemed to take an age, and after a while he turned away from the window, depressed by what he saw, to fall into fitful dozing and dreams of Clare and Lotte and Hanna in a world he could not recognise.

In the late afternoon they disembarked at an unknown station, and when they stepped onto the ill-lit platform the air was cold and dank. They marched in a column through the winter damp, their breath in clouds in front of them, until they came to a sprawling transit camp with high barbed wire that gleamed in the lamplight. Max shivered at the sight of it, and each man paused almost imperceptibly before stepping through the gate. It was hard to go into captivity again. The journey had given them a brief sense of freedom, a return to normal life, but it had been no more than an illusion and they were not yet free. They waited in a huddle as the gates were closed and fastened behind them, and, after the usual delays and confusion, Max was finally assigned to a bunk in a hut that was already overcrowded, and ripe with the stench of unwashed flesh. He suppressed a shudder, and when he finally drifted off to sleep amid the snores and mumbles and creaking bunks as the men shifted and tried to get comfortable, his last thought was of the soft bed in the flat above the saddler's with Clare's warm body next to his.

At the camp there was a notice board outside the Red Cross Office where desperate men searched for the people they had lost, hoping for a letter or some news, any news that might put an end to the waiting and uncertainty. Max held little hope but he went just the same to jostle with the others in front of the board where a list of names was pinned of those men who had mail to collect. The place festered with simmering frustration, so many men crowded into close captivity awaiting the freedom they could see just beyond the wire.

He made his way to the front of the little crowd at the board, bumping shoulders with a man who swung round with a snarl, baring what was left of his teeth like a dog. Max raised his hands in front of him in apology, and the man hesitated before lowering his head away and spitting on the frozen ground between the mill of boots. Max waited a moment more, braced and ready, but the man moved away, shoving a path back out of the crowd. A boy with sad eyes shouted in protest as he was half knocked off balance, but the other man paid him no attention. Max locked eyes with the boy, who shrugged and turned away.

When he got to the board at last he ran his eyes across the typed list of names. A man beside him reached out as if to rip it from its pin and another man knocked his arm away.

'Hey!'

'My name is on it!'

'Lots of names are on it. It's not yours ...'

Max Peterson. Max saw his own name and the argument beside him shifted to the background of his thoughts. He could hear their voices on the edge of his awareness as his breath caught in his chest in disbelief – it must be another Max Peterson. Surely it couldn't be for him after all this time? Surely not. But there it was. His own name in black and white on a list of the men who had mail to collect. He backed away from the board and other men surged forward to take his place, jostling.

Inside the little office a middle-aged man with one arm was remonstrating with the harassed-looking Red Cross worker behind the desk. She was only a young woman, younger than him, but her face was marred with lines of grief and disappointment and her mouth was set now in a thin hard line as she struggled to keep her patience with the man in front of her.

'There must be a letter!' he was insisting, his one arm raised in emphasis. 'There must, there must!'

'There is no letter for you, Herr Huber. *Es tut mir leid.*' I'm sorry.

The man leaned across the table. 'Give me my letters, you bitch!'

A couple of men in the doorway turned to watch. Max took a step forward and tapped the man on the shoulder. He spun, startled.

'She says there's no letter,' Max said. 'It's not her fault.'

The man's eyes darted over Max's face in confusion. He was unshaven and unkempt, and Max had seen that wildness in men's eyes before – it was the look of a man pushed beyond the limits of his endurance, a man about to break.

'Maybe there'll be a letter tomorrow,' Max said. 'Come back then.'

The man paused and for a moment Max thought he might be about to swing a punch, but then all the tension seemed to leave his body and he slunk away without another word. Max watched him to the door, just in case, then turned to the woman at the desk.

'Thank you,' the woman said.

'My name is on the list,' he told her. 'Max Peterson.'

She nodded and got up to check in one of the boxes on the table behind her, fingers rifling through the stacks of envelopes and cards. He waited as she searched and he was conscious of the beat of his heart but he still refused to allow himself to hope, focusing instead on the back of the woman, observing the slightly stooped and bony shoulders beneath a fraying cardigan, and the greasy hair drawn tight and neat into a bun. Finally she turned with an envelope between her fingers, and his breath caught again.

'You have to sign for it,' the woman said, pointing to a spot on the register that was open on the desk. Picking up the pen, he filled in the details it asked for in an unsteady hand, before straightening to take the precious envelope.

'I hope it's good news,' she said.

'So do I,' he replied, with a raise of his eyebrows, and she smiled. She was pretty when she smiled.

Turning away, tapping the edge of the envelope against his fingers, he went out into the hard, cold morning, past the mill of men at the board, and found a spot where he could lean against the wall of the building next door. Then he lowered his eyes to look at the letter in his hand. He didn't recognise the writing, a hurried scrawl addressed to him care of the unit he had been part of when he first went to Russia. There had been a dozen different units since that one, as remnants of old ones merged and re-formed, and he was surprised the letter had found him at all. He tried to read the date on the postmark but it was blurred and illegible. There was no return address.

When there was nothing more to look at on the outside, he forced his fingers to tease it open and drew out the single slip of paper inside. Instinctively his eyes scanned down to the signature before he read the rest. It was from his sister, Marta, and he had to blink to force back the tears that threatened behind his eyes. The words blurred and shifted until his eyes had cleared, and he could read what she had written.

Dearest Maxi,

She was the only one who ever called him that. He smiled.

I don't know if this will ever find you but I can only hope. That's really all we have left here in Berlin. Hope for an end to the suffering. Hope for food. Hope for warmth. Hope we may one day see again the people we love.

I miss you, Maxi – be safe and well wherever you are.

I'm living at Turiner Strasse. It's not much, but it's a roof at least, which is more than many have got these days. If you make it back to Berlin, perhaps you can find me there.

> *All my love, as always,*
> *Your little sister, Marti.*

He lowered the letter out of sight and gazed out across the camp. On the other side of the road some men were kicking a football around a patch of dirt in the pale morning sun, and the shouts and thud of leather stirred a sudden childhood memory of going to the stadium in Westend to watch Hertha play. He remembered the excitement of the crowd and the wave of noise, the sense of being part of something much greater than himself, and for a time after that he had nursed a dream that one day he would play for them: centre-forward, the crowd roaring as he scored goal after goal. He could remember practising his skills in the garden while Marta sat counting as he bounced the ball from knee to knee, foot to foot. It was a memory he had not thought of in years.

He smiled and tapped the letter once more against his fingers. Marta was alive and in Berlin, and as soon as he was free, he would find her.

Chapter Thirty-Three

At the funeral the mourners shivered in the cold beside Mrs Chapman's grave. December had dawned bright with a hard and bitter chill, so that the ground was treacherous with ice, and in the churchyard the grass shimmered prettily with frost. Clare shifted gently from foot to foot, toes going numb, thoughts drifting.

Man that is born of woman hath but a short time to live, and is full of misery.

The Reverend Keane's voice carried across the churchyard in the clear winter air, and the words sparked a sudden memory of her dream – Walter presiding at his own funeral, his broken, bloody body in the ground at her feet. Taken by surprise, she shuddered; she had not thought of it for months. Beside her, Eric stood tall and straight-backed and serious. He had come home from school for the funeral the day before but he had chosen to stay at the farm and there had been no chance yet to talk to him alone. So far though, he had treated her with courtesy and so she nursed a little flame of hope that she might have been forgiven.

He cometh up, and is cut down, like a flower ...

On her other side was Bridget, dry-eyed and rigid, pale with exhaustion. Simon was nowhere to be seen, but most of the village seemed to have turned out in spite of the weather. A couple of them turned their heads away from Clare, but no one said anything against her and she was grateful for that.

Thou knowest, Lord, the secrets of our hearts ...

She let the vicar's voice drift to the back of her mind, the service becoming a background hum to her thoughts.

Three weeks since Max had gone. Three weeks alone.

Sliding her glance away from the grave, she caught sight of the bench that stood against the wall of the church. *In memory of Charlotte Lewis*, she remembered, and thought of the first time she had met Max there, the excitement of his company. Even now the memory still elicited a smile inside and she had to set her face to stop it showing. Would she do it again, she wondered, knowing all it would lead to? Probably, she thought. *'Tis better to have loved and lost, than never to have loved at all.* The line from Tennyson's poem sounded in her head. She supposed it was a cliché but it still contained a truth: loving Max had kindled a new desire for life in her, hope for the future, and in spite of everything she would not change a moment.

The tone of the vicar's voice changed, interrupting her thoughts. She hauled her mind back to the funeral. Mrs Chapman was dead. Was she finally at peace, with her husband and son? Clare hoped so – despite their differences, she wished the woman no ill.

... we therefore commit her body to the ground: earth to earth, ashes to ashes, dust to dust ...

Beside her Bridget sniffed.

... Lord, have mercy upon us ...

When it was over the mourners filed into the church hall for tea and sandwiches as they had done after Walter's memorial. Clare slipped away from the group and picked her way through the long grass between the graves towards Walter's headstone.

The grass around it was overgrown and there were no flowers. A sense of guilt for neglecting it rippled through her.

'Sorry, Walter,' she murmured, crouching to wipe away the twigs and leaves around it. 'I got distracted.'

'Mum?'

Eric appeared at the corner of her sight and she jumped.

'Sorry. I didn't mean to startle you.' His voice was getting deeper, and she could catch glimpses in his face now of the man he would become. There was little trace left of the boy she had sent away to school.

'That's all right.' She turned back to the grave. 'I don't come here often enough. It's a bit overgrown.'

'It doesn't matter.' Eric shrugged. 'He's not there anyway.'

'No, I suppose not. It's just a custom.' Then she said, 'Are you all right? I mean, about Grandma?'

'I'm fine.' He hesitated, digging his hands deeper into the pockets of his coat and swinging one foot across the tips of the grass, watching the movement for a while before lifting his head again to look at her. 'I've been thinking...' he began.

Clare gave him an encouraging smile.

'I've been thinking about going into the church. Like Dad.'

She suppressed a gasp of surprise. 'You don't want to be an engineer any more?'

He shook his head. 'I...' He paused, and she waited patiently, curious. 'Well, it's just...' He stopped and gathered his thoughts together with a visible effort, then started again. 'We've been studying about the war at school, how it began, how Hitler came to power ... all of that,' he said, dragging one hand from his pocket to make a sweeping gesture, to encompass it all. 'And I know now that this war happened because of how we treated Germany after the last one. If we had been less punitive, if we had forgiven them and shown them more mercy, this war ...' He nodded towards his father's headstone, 'might never have happened. That's what Uncle James says, anyway. And I agree with him.'

Clare swallowed. God bless Uncle James. She said, 'Your father said the same thing, many times.'

'Did he?' Eric looked up at her, earnest and pleased. 'I'm glad. Because without forgiveness we're lost. Jesus forgave the very men who crucified him.'

She said nothing, only watching as her son squatted down and yanked at the grass stalks beside his father's headstone. They did not shift, caught fast in the frozen ground. He lifted his head to his mother with a rueful smile.

'Oh well, I tried.'

'In the end that's all you can do.'

He stood up and wiped his hands on his coat, a boyish gesture. 'Are you still seeing the prisoner of war?' His tone was carefully casual.

'He's gone back to Germany,' she said, her own tone careful in reply.

'Ah,' Eric replied, and she waited, unsure. 'I was only going to say that ... he did save Lizzie's life ...' He trailed off, unable to put his thoughts and feelings into words, but she understood well enough.

'He's a good man,' she said softly, with another glance to the headstone. 'Your father would have liked him.'

'Dad would have forgiven him,' Eric said. 'I know that now. I'm sorry, Mum.' He turned to her, and the tears in his eyes reflected her own.

'It's all right,' she replied, and held out her arms. Eric stepped into them and they held each other until they heard voices in the churchyard and shifted apart. Eric dropped his head, apparently embarrassed, and resumed his kicking of the grass with one foot.

'I think you'd make a fine vicar,' she said. She cast a look towards the church. 'Far better than Reverend Keane, anyway.'

He looked up in surprise and they both laughed.

'Bit different from Dad, isn't he?'

'Chalk and cheddar.'

They stood for a moment then, comfortable with each other once more. From the other side of the churchyard they could hear the sound of the villagers' chatter as people started to drift away.

'Shall we go back,' Clare said, 'and see if there are any sandwiches left?'

He nodded his agreement, and together they threaded their way through the tumble of graves towards the gate and the church hall beyond it.

Chapter Thirty-Four

M ax stood outside the camp gate, a free man at last. He was still wearing the clothes that once belonged to Walter, but his hair was short and neat again and his face was freshly shaved. With the army back-pay and the collected money he had earned for his labours in England, he had bought a new pair of shoes that chafed at his heels (he would have blisters by the end of the day), and in his pocket was a slip of paper with an address in Berlin where he was to register for work. But as he heaved to his shoulder the kitbag that contained everything he owned he felt like an imposter, as though he had no right to wear civilian clothes any more and he was living another man's life.

A truck pulled up beside him and the driver opened the window.

'*Zum Bahnhof?*'

'*Ja.*'

'Hop in.'

At the station he bought a ticket for the first train to Berlin. It felt odd to handle money again after so long, and the coins were strange to him. As he struggled to count out what he owed he felt like a tourist in a foreign land. He bought a newspaper and a hot drink that advertised itself as coffee, then sat at a café near the platform. He read nothing but the headlines – a coal miner's strike in America, tensions in French Indochina – and watched instead the people that came and went. The well-fed, well-dressed Allied occupation personnel contrasted starkly with the thin and ragged local population, who wore wooden clogs on their feet, or had wound cloth around them in place of shoes. Clothes were threadbare and the faces he saw bore marks of desperation – grey and sallow and lined. A small girl with grubby cheeks and matted hair approached him with her hands held out in supplication.

'Bitte?' Her voice was thin, and there was no hope in her eyes. Reaching into his pocket, Max pulled out some change and gave it to her without even counting it. Her thin face lit up with joy. Carefully stuffing the coins inside her clothes, hiding them well, she gave him a small smile then turned and ran away.

The train huffed in at last with a hiss of steam and a squeal of brakes, and though it was only a cattle truck he still had to shove his way through the crowd to get on. He sat on his kitbag with his back against the slatted wall as the truck quickly filled to over-flowing. A few minutes later, and he was on his way back to Berlin.

It was a hazardous journey. Though Berlin itself had been divided between the Allied powers, the city lay in the Soviet zone of what was left of Germany. The Russians had no legal right to impede his travel but he knew he was taking a risk in spite of the papers tucked carefully in the inside pocket of his coat; he could easily be sent east to join the thousands of German soldiers still held as prisoners of war. Rumours of the horrific conditions had filtered to the camp in England – back-breaking labour and star-vation rations, a quick end for the sick. But he remembered too the brutality the Germans had meted out to the Russians they had captured in the war. An eye for an eye: biblical justice. He felt for the men on both sides caught in the crossfire. He had been lucky, if you could call it luck, to be caught by the British instead of the Soviets.

The train stopped and started often as it rattled across a scarred and barren landscape Max barely recognised as Germany. It was almost a relief when darkness fell and he could see no more. Drifting in and out of sleep, he woke with a start now and then as the train lurched and jerked, and he dreamed, but this time not of Lotte and Hanna. In these dreams he was searching for Clare, but she had left the village and he could not find her.

He came to with a jolt as the train pulled in to yet another station. The door slammed open and the passengers spewed out onto the platform as a mass. Max peered out into the dark.

'*Wo sind wir?*' he asked the man next to him.

'*Anhalter-Bahnhof, Berlin,*' the man said. '*Endstation, mein freund.*' End of the line.

Max nodded and got to his feet. Jumping on to the platform, he shivered and turned up the collar of his coat against the winter night. The station was lit by a few meagre lightbulbs and above him he could see the stars. He looked around him, trying to get his bearings, but the place had changed almost beyond recognition – one whole wall was missing and the roof had gone. He had left from this station so many times, his wife and daughter tearful on the platform as the train pulled away. His last ever sight of them had been at Anhalter-Bahnhof, and now that he was here again their faces were vivid once more in his memory. They had waved and blown kisses, he remembered, Lotte's lips pressed together with the effort not to let him see her cry. She was wearing the blue wool coat he had given her the Christmas before the war, and Hanna wore a yellow ribbon in her hair. Yellow was the colour of luck, she had said, and he had hoped that she was right. Because he had known by then that it was blind luck that counted more than anything in war.

He walked along the platform, dislocated in time as other passengers pushed past him, hurrying to get home and out of the bitter cold. Just outside the main entrance, he stopped. The city was all but dark, dotted only here and there with faint lights that seemed to come from underground, but he could see enough to realise that the street he had expected to see across the road was no longer there, replaced by mounds of rubble and odd jagged walls that loomed as blackened shapes in the dark. He shuddered. His city was in ruins and, though he had been warned of it, the scale of the destruction still took his breath away.

Close by, something shifted between the piles of debris across the road, but he could make out nothing more than the flit of a shadow. A beggar, perhaps, who would set up trade with the first travellers in the morning. Guessing it was still some hours away from the dawn and reluctant to venture into a city he no longer knew in the dark, he turned back into the shelter of the station to wait for daylight.

In the morning he walked for hours trying to find the address Marta had given him, and the blisters formed and popped on his heels, the skin rubbing raw. Many of the streets he remembered simply no longer existed, and there were no road signs left to guide him. It was curiously quiet – the busy beating heart of the city, his city, had been all but stilled, even now so long after the end of the war. There were a few signs of rebuilding – work gangs repairing a railway bridge, a surveyor inspecting a row of damaged buildings. A group of women was sorting bricks from a pile of rubble. But the streets no longer bustled as they used to. The only lights were the flickers of candles from underground – a subterranean world where people were living in the cellars of the bomb-damaged buildings. Every so often, he turned into a street to see a whole row of houses that by some miracle had remained almost untouched, as if a divine hand had reached out to shelter them from the hail of bombs and artillery. A jeep pulled up as he was watching and a well-dressed couple trotted down the steps of one of the still-standing houses while the driver held open the door. Not German, he assumed.

The address Marta had given him was in his old neighbour-hood of Wedding, but when he finally managed to find it, it turned out to be no more than a pile of rubble. No one was living there any more – the whole block had collapsed – and all the hope that her letter had kindled spluttered and died inside him, the weariness of the sleepless night and the journey beginning to take its toll. Even so, he clambered over the debris just in case there was an entrance hidden from the street, but there was nothing except rock and dust and patches of weeds. Setting down the heavy kitbag, he sat on it just where the doorway might have been and lit himself a cigarette. He rarely smoked now, saving the ones he had brought from England for trade – tobacco had more value in Germany than money.

He surveyed the scene before him and in his mind he tried to piece back together how it had been before the war, but it was almost impossible to remember – there was so little left to jog the memories. Depressed by the destruction, he finished his cigarette and walked on until he found the street where he used to live. It was hard to gauge exactly where the apartment block had been. Great piles of rubble lined the pockmarked street, and here and there a single wall protruded, fire-blackened and jagged-edged. The place was eerily quiet. It had been a noisy neighbourhood once, vibrant with life, and he tried now to recall it: the tenement building where Frau Schröder lived with her five rowdy boys, and Herr Rosenstein, who collected clocks and kept a songbird in a cage. Max used to take Hanna to see it sometimes after work – she had loved that bird, pleading over and over for one of her own. An image of her laughing face flickered through his memory, clear enough to break his heart again. He imagined Herr Rosenstein had been long gone from the building by the time it was destroyed and absurdly he found himself wondering what had happened to the bird – perhaps Hanna got to care for it in the end. He hoped so. Their loss cut far more keenly here, where they had lived and breathed and loved together. Here, he could feel the ghosts of their presence, lives ripped away and destroyed. They should have been here to welcome him home, and the silence that greeted him instead opened up the wound of his grief.

He lit another cigarette and trudged on, past the remains of the bakery where they used to buy the bread rolls for breakfast, and the little bookshop next door that Hanna loved to browse. There had been a café on the corner where they sometimes went for coffee and cake, but the corner was gone now. It was no longer the world he had known and he was acutely aware of himself as a stranger here. The Berlin he had left had changed beyond all recognition in his absence. Perhaps it would rise again, he thought, out of the ashes, as a better place. He hoped so.

He kept walking despite the rub of his heels. It was too cold to stand still for long, and he was grateful for Walter's coat that now and then still gave off a faint scent of the man who used to own it. He knew he was lucky to have it – there were no clothes to buy in Germany. There was nothing to buy at all, barely even food or fuel. He had seen women stripping the bark from branches in the park, children collecting twigs. He patted his breast pocket to reassure himself he still had the ration card he had been issued at the camp, but he wondered where he was supposed to use it – he hadn't seen a single shop with goods to sell all day.

Heading south towards the address on the slip of paper in his pocket, he found the office in a street that was almost untouched by the war. A few bullet holes pocked the masonry and there were potholes in the road, but the solid stone fronts of the buildings gave a brief glimpse of the old Berlin. Above the door a single Union Jack hung limply from the flagpole and he smiled to see it. He had always hated the endless swastikas draped everywhere you looked in case anyone might forget the Nazis were in power, but even so, the buildings seemed surprisingly bare and grey without them.

In the office he showed his papers, and by the time he walked back out into the morning he had a job as a mechanic for the British occupying force, with a room in a barracks that went with it. The pay wasn't much, but there was nothing to buy anyway, and he knew that just having a room to live in in this city made him a rich man. He would begin the following day.

Chapter Thirty-Five

They had planned for him to work at the Volkswagen plant, but a lack of steel and fuel had forced a temporary shutdown. So he was assigned instead to repair broken vehicles at a garage in the British zone of the city. It felt good to be working at his own trade again, thoughts absorbed each day by the job at hand. The work wasn't hard and it felt like a tentative step towards the start of a normal life.

In his free time, Max searched for his sister. Wandering the streets of Wedding, he asked every person he met, '*Do you know Marta Decker? Lotte Peterson ...?*' But the answer was always the same. No one knew of them. No one knew of anyone. He explored the ruined buildings, scaling the heaps of rubble, squeezing through gaps into underground passages. Here and there he found notes pinned or glued or chalked on what remained of the buildings with messages written in hope they would be discovered by the right person, but there was never anything for him.

Every so often he braved the crowds at the Postal Enquiry Bureau, where desperate souls searched for the people they had lost. The wall outside fluttered with notices:

Ich suche meine Frau. I'm searching for my wife ...

Ich suche meinen Mann, meine Tochter, meinen Sohn. I'm searching for my husband, my daughter, my son ...

Wer kennt Frieda Kuhlmann ...? Who knows Frieda Kuhlmann ...?

Leave a message at ...

But there were too many to do more than glance across them and the clerks inside were simply overwhelmed by the numbers. The place exuded an air of misery – a vibration, a taint – and the voices of women, high-pitched with despair, echoed against the walls to compete with the lower-toned hubbub of conversation. He wondered if any of the hundreds of searchers that went there each day ever found what they were looking for and he left, always, depressed and suffused with the same sense of hopelessness that he sensed in all the others.

Christmas Eve, and after work Max lay on his bunk in the barren room that was his home. With little else to distract him, his thoughts wandered back a year to the Christmas he had spent with Clare, turning over the memory in his mind – her smile, Fred Wakeman's brandy, the way they had danced together in the lights of the Christmas tree. It seemed impossible that a year had passed since then. He had wept in her arms, he recalled, the only time he had allowed himself to cry. Afterwards he had been ashamed, but she had thought no less of him and he loved her all the more for that. He remembered, too, the gift she gave him, and for the first time since leaving England he took the harmonica out of his kitbag and began to play, filling the small room with the mournful strains of *'Silent Night'*.

It was her favourite carol, Clare had told him, ever since she heard the story of the soldiers in the Great War calling a truce one Christmas to sing it together. After that it became for her a hymn to hope and peace, a symbol of reconciliation. What would she do this Christmas without him? he wondered. Where would she go?

One by one the other men in the barracks drifted towards the music, impelled by its call. Like the pied piper, Max thought, wryly. They settled down on the bare wooden floor with their backs against the walls to listen – men he had only ever talked to in passing as they came and went, brought together now as though by instinct.

One of the men who had not been there long and whose name Max did not know, began to sing in a soft, sweet voice. Gradually, the others joined in and it was the strangest thing – singing so beautifully together, though each of them was lost in their own private memories of Christmases long ago. Another man handed round a small bottle of schnapps in a rare spirit of generosity: such a luxury was scarce and seldom shared. Each man took a solemn mouthful, conscious of it as a gift. Max found himself torn between memories of his wife and child, and memories of Clare, and he mourned for them all.

He played for a long time, and when he grew tired and stopped for a while to rest, the others still sang without him – songs of hope and faith, and songs of home, made more poignant now because, though they had returned to the home they had pined for all through the war, there was almost nothing left of what they remembered. Late into the night they fell silent at last, each man lost in his own memories, and slowly they drifted away to the solitude of their own beds to nurse their griefs in private.

Christmas morning dawned bitterly cold, and as Max stepped out from the warmth of the barracks he turned up the collar of Walter's coat and dug his hands deep in the pockets. The chill burned his ears and the air was hard in his lungs, the street icy underfoot. He walked quickly, warming slightly with the movement, heading for the old neighbourhood to search for his sister again, determined he would find her in the end, refusing to give up hope. She had written to him once and though the letter had not been dated, it showed she had survived. He would find her, he told himself again; if he just kept on looking, in the end he would find her. Perhaps Christmas would bring him a gift.

He spent the morning wandering the streets, greeting the ragged passers-by with a *Frohe Weihnachten*. Most of them looked at him askance in his warm winter coat and good shoes, then shook their heads when he asked about his sister and his wife. He was about to give up for the day when an old woman emerged from the mouth of a cellar just up ahead. She was wrapped in the remains of a threadbare shawl, and her shoes were held together with rags tied around them. She was hunched and thin, and instinctively he slid his eyes away from her suffering.

But when she noticed him, she stopped mid-step and lifted her head to look at him more closely. He slowed and turned towards her, surprised by the scrutiny. Most of the people he met avoided his eyes, untrusting, all their attention turned to the harsh business of survival. They looked at each other. There was something familiar about her and he groped through his memory, trying to remember the face.

Then she spoke. 'Maxi?' Her voice was low and harsh, but she spoke his name as if she could not quite believe it. 'Maxi?'

He swallowed. Only his sister had ever called him that.

'Marta?'

The emaciated face cracked into something that resembled a smile, but there was enough of his sister in that look for him to be sure. He stepped towards her and opened his arms.

'Marta!'

They held each other, and when the tears came this time he was not ashamed of them. Her body was tiny and fragile in his embrace and he remembered how he used to hold her as a child, when she had been plump and soft and sweet-smelling. Finally, she stepped back from him, and though her face was wet with weeping, she was smiling. She took his hand in hers and led him back into the ruins she had come from.

Her place was down a set of steps beneath a half-standing house whose empty rooms were on display to the street like a doll's house with an open door, its secrets exposed to the world. Small puddles in the passage were partly frozen and he kept his hand tightly in hers to steady them both as they picked their way between them. After passing a couple of unmarked doors they came to one that was slightly ajar. She pushed it open and they went inside. A stench of decay and sickness flooded out and briefly dragged his thoughts back to Russia. He started to reel back in revulsion but stopped himself – he had found his sister and she was alive.

The room was small and sparse. There was a mattress on the floor and a rough table with a couple of stools. A small electric stove stood in the corner.

'For when the power is on,' she said. 'Which isn't often.'

'It's freezing in here,' Max said, and when she smiled in reply he caught a glimpse of the old Marta.

'*Wilkommen zurück in Berlin*,' she said. 'Welcome. I'd offer you tea but ...' She gestured to the state of the room. 'It's not exactly Dahlem.'

They were silent, and he knew they were both remembering the big, bright house of their early childhood when their father was still alive, and there had been a servant to bring them coffee and pastries and cake on cold afternoons, a roaring fire in the hearth on winter days. It seemed like an impossible fairy tale now.

'Is there anything left of the city at all?'

She shrugged. 'The Allied forces have requisitioned pretty much everything still standing. But at least we're in the British zone.' She sat on one of the stools and he took the other.

'*Oh Gott*, Marti. What the hell happened? I got your letter, but you'd moved on.'

'Hitler happened ...' She hesitated. 'And the camps ...'

'You were in a camp?'

She eased herself on to one of the stools at the table. She moved stiffly, as though her muscles and joints gave her pain. Like an old woman, he thought again. The beautiful hair that had been her pride and joy hung in limp, greasy hanks, and her skin was the colour of dough. She nodded.

'*Wieso? Warum?*' How? Why?

'Does it matter? By the end they didn't need a reason ... a simple word of complaint in the wrong person's hearing ...' She shrugged.

'But you survived.'

'Sort of,' she agreed. 'If you can call this survival.' She gestured to the miserable room, her eyes tracking the damp walls, the mould, the crack across the ceiling. Then with an effort of will she turned her attention back to him.

'Where did you end up?'

He tried to recall the last time he had seen her, the last time they had written. It had been before he went back to Russia, he recalled, after he was wounded. He had lost touch with her after that. He had lost touch with everyone.

'I was captured by the British and ended up in England.' Clare touched at the edges of his thoughts. 'It wasn't so bad. How long have you been living here?'

'I can't remember. A while. The days blur. Every one of them is the same: search for food, search for warmth. Are you staying?'

'I've got a job with the British,' he said, by way of answer. Then, casually, because he could think of no other way to ask, he said, 'Is there any news of Lotte and Hanna?'

She stared, and his heart turned cold inside him.

'*Du weisst es nicht?*' Her voice was barely more than a whisper. 'I thought you would have known. I thought the army passed on news like that.'

He waited, barely breathing, and he was acutely aware of the touch of the cold air against his face.

'They were killed in an air raid, a long time ago.' Her eyes grazed the damp walls of the basement as she tried to remember. 'Nineteen forty-three,' she said. 'November. The whole street was flattened. I was living in Schöneberg then but I still saw them often. They just disappeared. I looked for them, of course, but no one could tell me anything. I guess there was nothing left of them to find. The heat, you know. It was terrifying. The incendiary bombs were the worst.'

He said nothing. It was no more than he had expected, but still the pain of the certain knowledge almost felled him like a blow, and he saw it like a newsreel that played in his head: the two of them huddled in the basement shelter below the flats, cowering as the world above shook and roared as though it were the end of days. For them, he supposed, it had been just that. He hoped it had been quick, a direct hit they never even heard. He swallowed down a rising sense of nausea and the sour taste of bile filled his mouth.

'I did find something in the rubble a few days afterwards, though,' his sister was saying. Her voice seemed to come from far away, and he had to force himself to listen. 'I kept going back, just in case. I found it under a piece of masonry.' She hauled herself to her feet and rummaged in a battered suitcase that appeared to hold everything she still owned. When she turned again she was holding a small picture in a wooden frame that he recognised straight away. She handed it to him and he took it with shaking fingers. The glass was broken and the frame itself was battered and misshapen but the picture inside was still intact. He tilted it towards the faint light that came in through the door. It was a family photograph that had been taken just before the war, when Hanna was still little and they had gone to Wannsee for a weekend to stay in the house of a friend. They were all in their swimsuits, smiling, even though they already knew by then that those days of happiness would soon be coming to an end. Not long after that had been the start of the tearful farewells at Anhalter-Bahnhof, when he had shipped out to Poland for his first taste of war.

He ran his thumb across the faces, caught between a smile and sob.

'It's incredible it survived and that I found it. I took it as a sign you'd be back to claim it one day.'

Max raised his head and tried to speak but the words stopped short of his throat, caught somewhere close to his heart. His beautiful girls, and this was all that was left of them. Lotte, whose smile even now made him want to take her in his arms. He wished he could dive back into the picture and be again the man he was then, before all this madness, all this death.

'I'm so sorry,' his sister said. 'I thought you knew ...' She trailed off and Max put the picture face down on the table, unable to look at those faces smiling out at him any more. But he rested his hand on the back of it and held on to the memory – happier, more innocent times.

The scuff of feet in the passage dragged him back to the present and he turned towards the door. A man with dark hair appeared, cadaverous and pale.

'Josef!' Marta greeted him with a smile, and Max saw at once the relationship between them. She had lost her own husband in the first few months of the war. She gestured to Max. 'Josef, this is my brother. I told you he would come. I told you.'

Max got up to shake Josef's hand, and was surprised by the strength of the grip in the other man's grasp. A steely will glinted in the dark-set eyes, and Max liked him immediately.

'He's Anton's cousin. When he got out of Dachau he came to the garage looking for you. He thought you might have word of Anton. And that's how we met. We were both looking for you.'

'Anton always spoke well of you,' Josef rasped. His voice was hoarse. 'Before he left he told us what you did for him.'

'He was a good friend.'

'You took a risk.'

'He was only ever good to me.' In prison he had taken Max under his wing and kept him safe, and afterwards he had given him a job. No, more than a job; a trade. And a lasting bond of friendship. 'Last I heard he was heading for London. That's all I know.'

Josef nodded, and lowered himself onto one of the stools at the table. He too moved slowly, like a man double his age. He fumbled in his pocket and drew out a small, folded piece of paper.

'I got some tea,' he said, smiling as held out the little pack towards Marta, 'and a little bit of wood.' He tipped a few twigs out of his bag. It would not be much of a fire, but perhaps it would be enough to heat water for tea.

Her eyes widened. 'How?'

'Those of us that are left look after one another.'

Max was silent.

'We're going to get married,' Marta told him, and began arranging the wood in a makeshift fireplace in the corner.

Max watched her kneel on the cold stone ground, struggling to make a fire, and thought of Clare and the bright little kitchen above the saddler's shop, the endless cups of tea.

'Congratulations! That's wonderful news!' He turned to Josef. 'You'd better look after her.'

'Of course. Nothing would please me more.'

'We haven't set a date yet,' Marta said. 'We're waiting till things improve a little.'

'Are you going to stay here?'

She shrugged. 'I've heard most of Germany is the same. Where else would we go? This is our home.' Then she turned to her brother. 'What about you? What are you going to do?'

It was Max's turn to shrug. 'I've got a job with the British, fixing up old cars.'

'You can stay here if you want.'

'Thanks, but they gave me a room.'

'Lucky you.' Josef lifted his eyebrows and Max smiled. Then he shifted the stool a little so that he could lean against the wall behind him, and let his thoughts drift away as his sister and her man talked quietly in the intimate way that lovers do, while they heated water on the little fire for tea.

For the first time he truly understood the sense of guilt that haunted Clare. A new love and hope for the future doing battle with a need to honour those we loved before. Betrayal of the living seemed as nothing compared to betrayal of the dead. He ran his hands across his face but it did nothing to clear the confusion in his mind.

His sister turned from fire. 'Come get warm before it dies.'

He got up and went to squat by the flames, reaching out his hands towards the faint, flickering warmth. Marta put her hand on his shoulder and he turned to her with a smile.

'I may go back to England,' he said.

'Did you like it there? I always wanted to go to London before the war, to have tea with milk and cucumber sandwiches like in the novels.'

He laughed. 'I didn't see much of London. But yes, I liked it there.'

She gave him a shrewd look. 'What did you like?'

He lowered his eyes away from her, watching the embers pulse in the ashes of the fire. The kettle had almost boiled and the water was popping inside it – it would be hot enough for tea. What could he say?

'Tell me about England,' she persisted.

He said nothing and tilted his head, evasive. His sister poured the boiling water into the pot then turned again to look at him: he could almost feel the heat of her gaze on the side of his face.

'You met someone too,' she said, after a moment. 'A girl?'

He gave her a small smile and nodded.

'That's good.' She got up and took the pot to the table, and he followed her. The fire had burned itself out and the scent of the smoky room reminded him of childhood winter days. 'Lotte would want you to be happy,' Marta said. 'She would be pleased.'

'Perhaps.' He leaned his head back against the wall behind him, considering. 'But it still feels like a betrayal. I wasn't even sure before that she was ...' He couldn't bring himself to say the word. Not about Lotte.

'Ach, betrayal is when you inform on someone to the Nazis, or look the other way instead of helping when you can. Falling in love – that's not betrayal. That's a spirit yearning to be free.'

She looked up at Josef beside her, and he touched his fingers to her shoulder.

'When did you become such a philosopher?' Max asked. The sister he remembered liked to read romantic novels and curl her hair.

'At Ravensbrück,' she replied without hesitation. 'When the difference between life and death was no more than the width of a hair, the whim of a guard, the luck of the draw. I used to think about Mutti after Papa died and how she just gave up, complaining that life had treated her unfairly. I promised myself that if I survived I would greet every morning with a prayer of thanks for the day.'

Clare loitered at the edges of his thoughts, waiting. '*Carpe diem*,' he said. 'Seize the day.'

'Exactly.' Josef folded his long limbs to sit on the mattress and Marta poured the tea. As they drank Max remembered it was Christmas.

'*Frohe Weihnachten.*' He lifted his cup in a toast.

His sister laughed. 'You know, I'd completely forgotten. *Frohe Weihnachten.*' She held her cup aloft. 'And to love and a better future.'

The two men echoed the toast. In spite of everything, his sister was as happy as Max had ever seen her. She was in love, and all that had gone before she had consigned to the past. He admired her strength and was almost envious, wishing he could set aside his own dark memories as easily. His fingers reached for the photograph that still lay face down on the table, but he just stopped himself from turning it over. There was no point.

'What's her name?' Marta cupped her tea between her fingers, making the most of its warmth. Dark-ringed fingernails, he noticed, and chapped red skin. He thought of Clare's pale and dainty hands, cold and small in his.

'Clare,' he said.

'That's all you're going to tell me?'

He smiled – it had always been easy to tease her. 'She's a school teacher. Or she was. She lost her job because of me.'

'She must love you very much.'

He said nothing but he knew it was the truth.

'You should go back to her,' Marta said. 'There's nothing here to stay for. Berlin is a ghost town, full of bitter memories that are better off forgotten. Go,' she urged. 'Go back to your girl that loves you. Make a new start.'

'I came back to find you,' he replied, 'and Lotte and Hanna.'

'Then you found what you came for – there's no point in staying around any longer.'

'Are you trying to get rid of me?' he teased.

'Yes,' she laughed. 'Josef and I don't want my big brother tagging along like a third wheel.' She slid a sly look towards Josef, watching from his place on the bed.

Max drained the last of his tea. 'Will you be all right?' he asked her then, becoming serious. 'Things are bad here.'

'It will get better,' she replied, with a noncommittal shrug. 'But for now we have a roof, just enough food, and we have each other. It's not much, I know, but it's enough.'

'Go back to England,' Josef said. 'Find Anton. Then we'll come and visit you.'

'For cucumber sandwiches and tea with milk,' Marta added.

He laughed but he was touched by their love and support when they had been through so much themselves. He let his hand rest on the back of the photograph and though a part of him still ached for his lost wife and child, he needed now to look to the future.

His sister was right: he had found what he was looking for and a kind of peace rippled through him, a decision made.

Chapter Thirty-Six

It was the harshest winter in living memory. Snowfall halted the trains and blocked the roads, and Clare woke each morning to a coat of ice on the inside of the windows and her breath in puffs of cloud before her face. It was impossible to get to work because of the state of the roads and so she stayed in the warmth of the bed until the need for food or the bathroom compelled her to brave the chill outside the covers. Later, she would force herself to leave the flat, picking her way carefully down the snow-covered steps, gripping on to the rail with a gloved hand as her feet threatened to slip out from under her. The cold air hurt in her lungs and her cheeks stung. Like Russia, she thought: Max had spoken of it briefly now and then, and she had shivered just listening to him talk.

Christmas had been lonely without him. Though Eric had stayed and they had gone to the farm for the day, Max's absence burned as a physical ache inside her. It seemed a cruel irony that the government relaxed the restrictions just a few days before-hand to allow the prisoners more freedom. They could go out unescorted and talk to British people. They were allowed to visit private homes. Clare seethed with the unfairness of the timing but she wore a brave face for Eric's sake, and when memories of last year's Christmas flashed across her mind – the haunting unfamiliar music of the harmonica and the warmth of Max's body as they danced together – she dragged her thoughts away from them.

She went to the shop for milk and in hope of a paper.

'Still no luck, Mrs Chapman,' Mrs Bartlett told her with a smile. It was only slightly warmer in the shop than on the street and the woman was rotund in her woollens, a scarf around her head. 'Still barely anything getting through at all, not even the post, though I don't know there's much worth reading about in the news these days, just doom and gloom: power cuts, more rationing. Did you know they've limited the radio broadcasts now too to save on fuel – they didn't even do that during the war ...'

Clare smiled. She was used to Mrs Bartlett's grumbling. 'I don't get the paper for the news,' she lied. 'I like to do the crossword.'

'Ah, yes. Well, you would, being a teacher and all. I suppose you need to keep your mind busy since you ...' She trailed off, and Clare suppressed another smile. Mrs Bartlett changed the subject. 'You keeping all right?'

Clare nodded. 'Except I can't get to work.'

'And no end in sight, so they say.'

Clare paid for the milk and said goodbye, then took the bottle from the counter and went outside. The bell on the door tinkled gaily when she opened it.

On the pavement she stood for a moment looking up and down the street. Reluctant to go home straight away to the lonely cold of the flat, she hesitated, wondering where else she could go. Across the street a delivery van parked carefully on the compacted snow. The driver jumped out, blowing on his hands to warm them as he crossed the road and banged on the closed pub door. The thud of his fist carried in the clear winter air. With nothing else to do, Clare stayed to watch. On the other side of the van, another man got out – she could just make out the movement of his form through the window. The driver returned, opened up the back and pulled out a box that was brimming with vegetables. A bunch of carrots swayed precariously on top. She would go to the pub for dinner later, Clare decided, and hang the expense: they made a good vegetable pasty and there was a log fire to sit beside. It was an appealing thought. The driver handed over the box to the landlord, went back to the van, and pulled away with a crunch and skid of the back wheels on the snowy ground. Clare shivered and prepared to go home – there was really nowhere else to go and it was too cold to stand in the street any longer.

Then she noticed that the man who got out on the passenger side had stayed behind, and he was standing now in the snow on the road with a kitbag at his feet, watching her. Her heart seemed to miss a beat and she held her breath. It couldn't be.

They stared at each other for a moment that seemed to stretch forever.

Max.

She blinked, thinking that perhaps he was a mirage she had conjured up from loneliness and desperation, but he was still there when she opened up her eyes again, and he was looking at her in that way that always lit a flush of self-consciousness across her cheeks. She remembered the first day she had seen him just a little further up the road outside the school when the boys had been throwing stones. He had looked at her the same way then and she had hated him for the way he made her feel.

But now…

He smiled, picked up the kitbag, and crossed the road towards her.

'Hello, Clare.'

'Max.' His name left her lips as a whisper. There was a pause. He looked weary, she thought, and he was thinner than when she had seen him last, new hollows beneath his cheekbones. He lifted a hand to rub at the stubble on his chin as if suddenly aware of his appearance, but his eyes never left her face and she saw the uncertainty in their depths.

'I heard there might be a place to stay in the village.' He tilted his head in question.

'That depends,' Clare replied, and though she dropped her gaze away towards the snow at their feet, she was still aware of him watching her, searching her face for an answer. She could feel the knock of her heart in her chest, and her breath was tight and short. She gripped the milk bottle tightly in her hands.

'On what?'

'On how long you plan to stay.' She lifted her head to look at him then and this time she met his eyes. She waited.

'For however long you'll have me,' he said. He gave her a small hopeful smile. 'There's nothing left in Berlin for me now. Nothing at all.'

She swallowed and slid her eyes away, still reluctant to believe it. He had lied to her before, and though she had forgiven him she had not forgotten. Max lifted his hand and brushed her face with the backs of his fingers, and with his touch all the doubt melted away. She shivered, but this time it was not from the cold, and reached out to take his hand in hers. Two children coming out of the bakery with buns in their hands stopped to stare but they paid them no attention.

'Let's get out of the weather,' she said.

'Sure.'

Max picked up the kitbag from where he had dropped it at his feet and she looped her arm through his. His body was lean and strong next to hers and as they picked their way across the rutted snow towards the saddlers' shop, the bitter cold was utterly forgotten by them both.

Acknowledgments

The story of German prisoners of war in England is generally little known, but in fact over 400,000 soldiers were taken prisoner and the last of them didn't leave England until 1948. Some 25,000 men chose to stay and make their life in Britain after the war, and many of them married the women they had illegally loved.

Although I consulted countless sources, the best books on the subject include *Hitler's Last Army: German prisoners of war in Britain* by Robin Quinn, and *Thresholds of peace: four hundred thousand German prisoners and the people of Britain, 1944-1948* by Matthew Barry Sullivan. *Betty's Wartime Diary* is a perceptive and insightful look at country life in wartime, and the wonderful BBC TV series *Wartime Farm* offered valuable insights into farm life at war.

In addition to the numerous books and history programmes, many people provided personal and professional support and I am grateful to them all: Ian Allen for eagle-eyed editing, Jess Gardner for recommending him, Misha at ArtMishel for another wonderful cover and ongoing support, Martina Speyer for help with German language and culture, Mike Hatton for tractor expertise, Jan Bradbery for early feedback, and last but not least, Steve and Jake for their endless patience, interest, and numerous cups of tea.

Also by Samantha Grosser

THE OFFICER'S AFFAIR

England, 1944. Rachel Lock has waited for more than two years, but when husband Danny comes home from the war at last he has changed beyond all recognition.

Trapped in a loveless marriage with a man she no longer even knows, Rachel begins to lose all hope for the future. Until Captain Andrews comes to visit and changes everything.

Rachel's attraction to Andrews is instant, but the tension between the two men seems to stem from an earlier time. What happened in Italy to make Danny so hostile to an officer he once trusted and admired? And why has Andrews come to visit him in the face of it?

As all three strive to shake off the ghosts of the war, the secrets of the past come slowly to light. Amidst the lies and the regrets, can Rachel find the courage to be true to herself?

Set in the final years of the Second World War, THE OFFICER'S AFFAIR is a heart-wrenching novel of love, loyalty, and sacrifice in a war-torn world.

"Full of true-to-life conflict, passion and guilt – highly recommended." – *Readers' Favorite.*

Available from all good online bookstores

FOR NEWS AND UPDATES GO TO:

www.samgrosserbooks.com

Also by Samantha Grosser

ANOTHER TIME AND PLACE

ENGLAND, 1944. A chance meeting changes two people's lives for ever. Young American pilot Tom Blake isn't looking for love, but seeing Anna Pilgrim in a tearoom on a cold winter afternoon changes everything. So begins a passionate affair.

Their happiness does not last. Shot down over Europe, wounded, in hiding, Tom has no way of telling Anna he is alive. And Anna, left waiting in England, has no way of finding out. How can she know that Tom is struggling to return to her? Or that the thought of her is all that keeps him going on the long journey home?

Interwoven with the danger of Tom's fight to survive is the story of Anna's own struggle to face the uncertainty of waiting. Set vividly against the hardship of the Second World War, *Another Time and Place* is at once a compelling love story, an enthralling adventure and a moving depiction of the resilience of the human spirit.

"Gripping - a good story well told." Historical Novels Review

Available from all good online bookstores